BLOOD TIES

Also by Sophie McKenzie

GIRL, MISSING
Richard and Judy's Children's Books Winner 12+
Winner of the Red House Book Award older category
Winner of the Bolton Book Award

SIX STEPS TO A GIRL
THREE'S A CROWD

www.sophiemckenzie.net

BLOOD TIES
SOPHIE McKENZIE

SIMON &
SCHUSTER

London · New York · Sydney · Toronto

A CBS COMPANY

First published in Great Britain in 2008 by
Simon and Schuster UK Ltd
A CBS COMPANY

Simon & Schuster UK Ltd
1st Floor
222 Gray's Inn Road
London WC1X 8HB

A CIP catalogue record for this book is available from
the British Library.

ISBN: 978-1-84738-275-7

7 9 10 8

Printed and bound in Great Britain by
CPI Cox & Wyman, Reading, RG1 8EX

www.simonandschuster.co.uk

For my father with love.
And for Moira, Gaby, Julie, Melanie and Sharon,
for making the difference.

Part One

London

1

Theo

I could see him waiting for me outside the steel school gates.

Roy.

He was leaning against a lamppost, his arms folded. From the second-floor window behind my desk I couldn't make out the expression on his face. But the way he was slumped against that lamppost suggested he was bored.

Good. Bored was good. If Roy was bored, he wouldn't be suspecting anything.

'Hey, Theo,' Jake hissed.

I turned away from the window. The last lesson of the day was almost over. History. Something to do with the Second World War. I wasn't really paying attention.

'Twenty seconds until Operation "Liberate Theo" commences,' Jake whispered. His eyes were fixed on the stopwatch function on his phone – he'd synchronised it with the school bell earlier.

I rolled my eyes, pretending I was way too cool to be excited. But the truth was my heart was pumping like it might burst. This was my first serious attempt to escape from Roy. I mean, I'd tried – and failed – to run away from him before. But this was the first time I'd planned out an actual escape route.

'Fifteen . . . fourteen . . . thirteen . . .' Jake said under his breath.

I glanced towards the front of the classroom.

'Eleven . . . ten . . .'

The teacher was writing on the white board.

'Eight . . . seven . . . six . . .'

My books were already in my bag. I picked it up off the floor and slid it silently onto my back.

'Three . . . two . . . one.'

The school bell cut through the squeaking of the white-board pen.

I leaped to my feet.

'You are go. Repeat. You are go.' Jake's voice rose above the commotion that filled the room.

I stormed towards the door. Wrenched it open. Sped down the corridor. Other doors were opening. Other classes spilling out. I pounded down the stairs. Down, down to the ground floor. A huge group of Year Sevens and Eights were jostling and shoving their way across the entrance hall.

But I was bigger.

Faster.

Stronger.

The younger boys shrank away as I barged through, my eyes on the fire door at the end of the corridor.

I reached it. Shoved it open. Burst into the tiny courtyard at the back of the school – a patch of concrete surrounded on three sides by the school building and on the fourth by a high brick wall. I raced towards the large tree next to the wall. As I ran, I glanced over my shoulder. No one was following me. I looked up at the windows overlooking the courtyard. No one was watching me.

I reached the tree. Jake and I had dragged a school chair outside at break and stashed it behind the trunk. I hauled it out and climbed up, steadying myself as the chair wobbled on the uneven tarmac. The nearest branch still looked a long way up. I bent my knees. Jumped. *Yes.* My hands gripped the branch. My arm muscles tensed, straining to hold my weight. I swung for a moment, the bark cutting into my palms. *Do it.* Using all the strength in my arms and shoulders I hauled myself up. Up. I gritted my teeth. Hooked one elbow over the branch. Then the other. I was scrabbling up with my legs now. Locking a knee over. Kneeling up. Reaching for the branch above. *Yes.*

I stood up, panting, catching my breath.

The air was cold, despite the sunshine. A gust of wind blew my fringe across my eyes. Mum's always nagging me to get it cut. It *is* sometimes a bit irritating. Still. Her being annoyed about it is worth any amount of irritation.

I took a deep breath and pushed the hair off my face. I gripped the branch above me more tightly. Hauled myself up again. *Jesus.* Even a few months ago, there was no way I could have done this. Back then my escape attempts

5

depended on distraction techniques. But now I was tall enough and strong enough to overcome any physical obstacle. Well, that's how it felt. That's how *I* felt.

Powerful. Unbeatable. Invincible.

I'm Theo Glassman. I need no one.

I scrambled up and up. It got easier as I climbed, the branches closer together. Soon I was level with the top of the wall. I looked down. My stomach tightened. The ground was a long way beneath me – maybe four or five metres. I edged across the branch until I reached the wall.

'Oy! You there! Boy!' The voice was deep and male. One of the teachers. Shouting from a school window.

Crap. I didn't have much time. If whoever that was realised it was me out here, he'd be straight down to tell Roy. I stepped onto the wall, carefully avoiding the spiky shards of glass poking up at intervals along its surface.

'GET DOWN FROM THERE!' the teacher yelled.

My plan exactly.

The wall was three brick widths across – enough room for me to stand on both feet and turn right round. I'm good at balancing, and I don't mind heights. But this was way high. I held tightly onto the branches above my head as I shuffled round. The grassy park on the other side of the wall was littered with heaps of blown leaves – all reds and browns. A long way down. *Don't think about it.*

I jumped. *Whoosh.* Through the air. Through the leaves. *Wham.* The impact jarred all the way up my legs. I fell over onto my side, breathing heavily for a second. Then I pushed

6

myself up. Tested my legs. They were fine. I was fine. *Yes*, I'd done it.

I'd escaped from Roy. I'd escaped from my bodyguard.

I smiled to myself as I started running across the grass. My plan was to head for the nearby high street, meet Jake in Starbucks and go to the cinema.

Maybe that sounds weird to you. That I'd risk getting detention, falling out of a tree, cutting myself open on glass and the rest of it, just to hang out in the high street for a bit and catch a movie.

All I can say is: you'd understand if you lived my life.

2

Rachel

'See you later, then, Rachel.'

'Bye, Dad.' I switched off the call and turned my key in the front door. As I shut it behind me my phone beeped. *No.* School had only ended ten minutes ago and I was getting hate texts already. That was quick, even for Jemima Robertson. I hesitated, then pulled the mobile out of my bag. 1 MESSAGE RECEIVED. I switched it off.

I couldn't bring myself to read the text. Not yet.

'Is that you, Rachel?' Mum's sickly, cloying perfume wafted out into the hall. I sighed. Mum was usually home when I got back from school. She doesn't work, you see. She dabbles. A bit of painting. A few adult education classes. The gym. Tennis lessons. And a lot of manicuring, body-wrapping and spa days out.

I trudged across the hall, hoping I could make it up to my room without her seeing me. I reached the bottom step of the stairs just as she click-clacked out of the kitchen.

'Hiya, Rachel darling.' That's Mum's signature sound.

Cooing and soothing and totally fake. A sweetie wrapper round an arsenic lollipop.

'How was your day, darling? Mine was frightful. Giovanni completely messed up my hair. I swear he'd taken so much charlie last night his hands were shaking too much to hold the scissors straight.'

There. Now you have my mum. Her hairdresser's a junkie from Harlow with a fake Italian name. And she thinks it's cool to use outdated drug slang.

Oh yes. And she's botoxed up to her eyebrows. Above them in fact. I guess it's because she's so much older than other mothers. She was forty-seven when she had me. I'm not kidding.

That was fifteen years ago.

'Hi, Mum.' I carried on stomping up the stairs.

'Darling, don't slouch.' I could hear her trit-trotting back to the kitchen.

I went upstairs and lay on my bed. The day circled round and round in my head. I had a system. A way of grading each day. And today had been bad. It looked something like this:

Fat comments: five. (The worst was Jemima Robertson saying my arse looked like two satellite dishes side by side, when we changed for gym.)

Stupidity comments: three. (Including one from my maths teacher, who told me off for misunderstanding our homework. I still don't get it. I mean, why would two kids, taking half-metre strides every three seconds, across a thirty-four-metre wood in the middle of the night, be doing that? Isn't 'why' more interesting than how long it would take them?)

Ugliness comments: six and a half. (Several mentions of the spot on my nose, at least two references to how I was too ugly for any boy to want to snog me at next month's school disco, and Jemima, again, pointing out very loudly that my hair is skank. Which it is. She's right. Still.

The half was some guy on my way home making a comment about my legs. I didn't understand what he said, but it didn't sound very nice.)

A grand total of fourteen and a half. Any day with a score over ten is a bad day. Still, at least no one hit me or stole money from me today. That happens sometimes. Not that often, I guess. Maybe once or twice a week.

But, hey, I'm used to it. Don't think I'm complaining. That's just my life.

Mum rapped at the door. She stepped inside without waiting for me to say anything.

'Sweetie, don't lie on the bed in your school uni. The skirt pleats will get creased.'

My school uniform is a green tartan pleated skirt and a tan polyester blouse. You've never seen anything more hideous in your life.

Except my body inside it, according to Jemima Robertson.

'Sweetie.' Mum's voice was insistent now.

I sat up and swung my legs over the side of the bed.

'Piano lesson in half an hour. And it's chicken salad for tea.'

'Great.' I tried to smile. It was easier not to resist.

Mum sighed. 'I wish you'd show a bit more interest, sweetie. Especially in the piano. You know how good you could be if you tried.'

I froze. That was another way in which I graded the days. By the number of mentions of Rebecca.

We were building up to today's first.

'What d'you mean, Mum?' I said in this fake cheerful voice. I knew perfectly well what she meant. And I didn't want to hear her say it. But somehow I couldn't stop myself.

'You know, darling,' Mum cooed. 'Rebecca took Grade Six with distinction when *she* was in Year Ten. It's a shame for you not to make the best of your talents too.'

Suddenly I wanted to cry.

'Right.' I stood up. 'I'd better get changed then.'

Mum nodded and backed out of the door.

Tears leaked down my face as I changed into jeans and a loose top. Fat, shapeless, nothing clothes for a fat, shapeless, nothing person.

I didn't want to do *anything* Rebecca did. But how could I avoid it? Rebecca had done *everything*. Worse. Rebecca had done it all brilliantly.

She died before I was born. A road accident when she was sixteen. There were pictures of her all over the house. Pictures of her winning school prizes for everything. Pictures of her horse-riding and swimming and coming first in piano competitions. And pictures of her looking like a model in pretty dresses with slim legs and her hair swept stylishly off her face.

Rebecca. My sister. I used to look just like her when I was younger.

I don't any more.

But Rebecca's still here. Haunting me. Taunting me.

The doorbell rang. My piano teacher – on time as always. I could hear Mum's heels tapping smartly across the hall. The door opening.

'Rachel, sweetie. Miss Vykovski's here.'

I caught sight of my phone, lying innocently on my bed.

Maybe I should look at the message now. Whatever it said, I'd have the piano lesson to distract me.

Heart thumping, I opened the text.

I stared at it, not quite taking it in.

Well, I wasn't expecting *that*.

3

Theo

I reached the high street and slowed to a stroll.

Roy wasn't the first. I'd had a bodyguard ever since I could remember. Always there, following me wherever I went.

The weird thing was, I had no idea *why* I had a bodyguard.

I stopped to look at the latest MP3 phones in Dixons' window. I really wanted one. But there was no chance. You see, we weren't rich. I mean, yes, somehow Mum found the money to pay for Roy. And I went to this private boys' school with a posh uniform and everything. But we lived in a tiny house with all worn-out furniture. I didn't even have a mobile.

'You don't need one,' Mum always said. 'You've got a bodyguard.'

Right.

Still no sign of Roy as I sauntered up to Starbucks. I peered through the glass door. There was Jake. *Oh crap.* He was chatting to a group of girls at the counter. My heart sank. What was the matter with him? I mean, don't get me wrong. Girls are fine. Girls are great, in fact. But recently Jake had got completely obsessed with them. Not girls in magazines or on the internet – everyone's obsessed with *them*. But real girls. Girls our age.

Trouble was, Jake acted all weird when he was around them, like he was trying to impress them or something.

He came across like a complete idiot.

I hesitated, my hand on the door. The last thing I wanted was for Jake to haul me over and start mouthing off about my climbing over the school wall. He'd exaggerate the whole thing. Make out I was some kind of action hero. And then I'd end up looking as much of a prat as he did.

'Gotcha.' A huge fist gripped my shoulder. Spun me round. Slammed me against the door. My heart pounded. I looked up.

Roy's purple, snarling face loomed over me.

He grabbed my arm and dragged me over to the car. It was clearly taking every ounce of self-restraint he had not to punch me.

'Wait till your mother hears about this. You little . . .' He swore loudly, calling me pretty much the worst thing you can call someone.

'She's not going to want to hear *that*.' I grinned.

I was guessing that appearing unbothered about being caught would wind Roy up more than if I got angry. Anyway, after the initial shock, I realised I *wasn't* that bothered. I mean, I was disappointed he'd caught me so quickly. And I *had* been looking forward to seeing a movie. But I was also relieved that I hadn't had to go inside Starbucks and deal with Jake on the pull.

14

And I'd got away. Roy knew it as well as I did. If I'd gone straight to the tube instead of dawdling on the high street, Roy would never have found me.

He called Mum from the car. Told her what had happened. She was waiting by the front door when we got back.

'What the hell is the matter with you?' she shouted. 'You could have been hurt or killed.'

I watched Roy disappear into his room. He had, like, a bedsit in our house – with his own kitchen area and bathroom. I hated that. He took up half the downstairs.

'Theodore?' Mum dragged me into our tiny living room and slammed the door. 'What has got into you?'

I focused on her. Mum's small – the top of her head only comes up to my chest. But don't let that fool you. She's fierce, my mum. Got a hardcore temper.

'Are you listening to me, Theodore?'

I grunted. I hate her calling me Theodore. I mean, okay, it's my name. It's just so poncey. But she refuses to go with Theo. Just like she refuses to let me do anything.

'Theodore.' Mum held up her thumb and forefinger so they were almost touching. 'So help me, I am this close to grounding you for the rest of the year.'

I met her eyes. 'Whatever,' I said.

'Theodore.' Mum shook her head so furiously that her pointy, silver earrings stabbed at her neck. 'Promise you'll never run away from Roy again. He'll resign if you do.'

'Good.' I shoved my hands in my pockets.

'For goodness' sake.' Mum crossed the room to the kitchen

area in the corner and pulled open the fridge. 'Roy is here for your protection. Why won't you grow up and accept that?'

'If you want me to act like a grown-up then treat me like one,' I snapped. 'Tell me what it is I need protecting from?'

Mum groaned. 'Not this again.' She took a bottle of wine out of the fridge and uncorked it. 'I can't tell you. You just have to accept that you—'

'No.' This hot rage filled my head. 'It's not fair,' I shouted. 'I can't do any—'

'Do not raise your voice at me!' Mum shrieked.

We glared at each other. Then Mum took a wine glass out of the cupboard above her head and set it on the counter. 'I'm getting a migraine,' she said. 'I can feel it.'

'Right.' I rolled my eyes. Mum was always getting migraines.

Mum slammed her hand down on the counter next to the wine glass. 'That's enough, Theodore. There's clearly only one punishment that you're going to take seriously. From now on Roy comes into school with you and waits outside the classroom during every lesson.'

'No,' I gasped. No way could I handle Roy following me everywhere I went at school. I'd have even less freedom than I had now.

'You can't do that, Mum.'

Mum's lips narrowed into a line. 'Watch me,' she said. 'I'm going to speak to school tomorrow morning and insist.'

Fury surged up from the depths of my being. Less than an hour ago I'd climbed a huge tree, scaled a glass-strewn wall and risked a massive jump onto the ground. I'd been power-ful. Unbeatable. Invincible.

'No!' I yelled. I strode right up to Mum so my face was centimetres from hers. 'NO.'

Mum started. And for a moment, for one tiny moment, I saw fear in her eyes.

The feeling of power I'd had earlier on, climbing the tree, flooded back. 'I don't need Roy. I can look after myself,' I yelled. 'You're just imagining there's a threat.'

'No,' Mum gasped. 'No, Theodore. I'm not.'

I suddenly saw how badly she needed me to believe what she was saying. I drew myself up. I *was* powerful. I could do whatever I liked, whenever, wherever and however I wanted.

I turned and strode out of the room. I ran up to my room, went straight to my desk and took out the fifty quid I'd saved up. I tore off my school jacket and tie and grabbed a jumper from a pile of clothes on the floor. I headed to the door as Mum appeared in the doorway.

She put her arm out. 'What are you doing?'

'Leaving.' I pushed the arm out of my way, then raced down the stairs, my heart pounding.

'No. Theodore.' I could hear the panic rising in Mum's voice. Then she yelled out: 'ROY.'

He shot out into the hall so quickly that I knew he must have been listening. This made me even more furious. How dare he be here. How dare he interfere in my life.

'Get out of my way,' I yelled.

Roy shook his head.

I barged past him. He blocked me with his shoulder. I ducked, tried to dart round his other side.

He grabbed my arm and pushed me back. 'You sodding little brat.'

Something snapped inside my head, like a firework exploding. Before I could even think, my hand was a fist and my fist was driving forward, hard, into Roy's face.

Contact. My hand stung. My whole arm jarred with the pain of it. Roy staggered backwards, clutching his jaw. His eyes widened. And then he grabbed me round my throat and pinned me against the wall.

Blood pounded in my ears. All I could see was Roy's furious face. All I could hear was my own voice, spitting out swearwords.

And then, dimly, I became aware of Mum shouting beside us. 'Stop it, stop it.'

Roy let go of my throat. He stepped back, panting. Mum moved across and whispered furiously in his ear.

I bent over, my breath all jagged. My hands were shaking. A door slammed. I looked up. Roy had disappeared back into his own room.

Mum stared at me. Again, I could see the fear in her eyes.

I took a step to the front door. The powerful feeling surged through me. Nothing could stop me leaving now. Not Mum. Not Roy.

Nothing.

I reached out for the door handle. Twisted it. Pulled open the door. I looked over my shoulder. 'Bye, Mum.'

'Please, Theodore.' Her eyes filled with tears.

When I was younger this would've really got to me. Back then all I wanted was to look after her. To do what my dad would've done if he'd been alive. But now . . . now I was sick of her trying to manipulate me.

I turned back to the front door. I had a bit of money. Enough to find somewhere to sleep tonight. I'd go into town. Get a job.

I took a step outside.

'Please.'

Something in Mum's voice made me look round again. Tears were streaming down her face. For the first time since I'd got home doubt crept into my mind. And guilt.

I didn't want to hurt her. If I was honest, I didn't want to go away either.

All I wanted was the truth.

I took a deep breath. 'Just tell me why I need a bodyguard.'

There was a long pause. Right up until that moment I thought she was making it up. That me needing a bodyguard was based on some stupid imaginary fear of hers that came out of the same place as her endless migraines.

Then she nodded.

'Okay,' she said. 'Come inside and sit down. I'll tell you everything I can.'

4

Rachel

GODDESS STILL SAFE IN HEAVEN. RICHARD.

I had to read the text twice before I took it in. I'd been so sure it was going to be some toxic message from Jemima that it took a full minute before I realised it wasn't. I checked the caller I.D. – a number I didn't recognise. So, no one on my contact list.

I breathed a sigh of relief. Just some random message. A wrong number. Nothing that made any sense.

I almost skipped down to my piano lesson.

The lesson itself wasn't too bad. My fingers wouldn't move like they're supposed to, and the more they wouldn't move, the more embarrassed I got. Still, Miss Vykovski was really nice and we ended up having a laugh. So I was in a good mood when Mum called me for supper. Mum likes it when we eat together, though Dad doesn't often get home in time. He manages a cosmetic surgery clinic in central London. I reckon that's why Mum married him, to be honest, so he could get her free treatments.

'Richard!' Mum yelled up the stairs as I scurried past her to the dining room. 'Richard. It's on the table!'

I stopped, a spoonful of salad leaves midway between the bowl and my plate. *Richard.* My dad had the same name as on the text. It hadn't occurred to me the message could be from him. *No*, that didn't make sense – we'd been speaking just seconds before I received it. Anyway, why would my dad send me some weird text about goddesses in heaven? The name had to be a coincidence. Plus, surely he'd sign off *Dad.* Which also proved the message couldn't be from him – his number is logged on my mobile under *Dad.* So, if he'd called me, that name would have shown up.

Still.

'Hey, Dad,' I said as he sat down. 'I just got this weird text.'

'Mmmn,' Dad said, helping himself to a slice of chicken breast. 'Nothing X-rated, I hope.'

'Just weird,' I said. 'It—'

'How was piano, sweetie?' Mum bustled in, a bowl of potato salad in her hand.

'Fine.' I reached for the potatoes.

Mum gave a little cough. 'Are you *sure* you want to do that, sweetie?'

I stared up at her blankly.

'Carbs weigh very heavy on the stomach overnight,' she smiled. 'I'm just saying.'

My mind flashed back to Jemima's comment about my double-satellite-dish bum. I swallowed, torn between knowing Mum was right and really, really wanting the food.

'Oh, let her eat a sodding potato.' Dad rolled his eyes at me and grinned.

'I'm not stopping her,' Mum snapped. She set the bowl down on the table. 'I'm just pointing out the consequences.'

The consequences: being fat. Being ugly.

This was about Rebecca too. That was what Mum was really saying. *Rebecca didn't eat too much potato salad. Ever. She had a marvellous figure, sweetie.*

I gritted my teeth and hauled as many potatoes as I could onto my plate.

'So tell me about that text, Ro?' I could hear the kindness in Dad's voice. It just made me feel worse.

I shook my head and stuffed a potato into my mouth.

Dad sighed, then started chatting to Mum about his day. Dad does that a lot – acts like a big cushion protecting me from Mum. I kept my head down, shovelling in one potato after another. After a couple of minutes I stopped. Now I'd made myself even fatter. I felt so miserable that, for a second, I seriously thought about going upstairs and making myself sick. Some of the girls at school have done that. Cassie Jones swears by it. *Eat what you like then just chuck it up before it makes you fat.*

She calls it: *Having your cake and hurling it.*

Cassie Jones is stupid though. I know that making yourself sick over and over is a majorly bad idea. It's bad for your body, bad for your heart, bad for your teeth even.

It's bad for your head, too.

And my head's screwed up enough as it is.

Anyway, I hate how it feels when you vomit. Maybe that's the real truth. I'm just too scared to stick two fingers down my throat and feel that acid burn up into my mouth. *Ugh*.

'Ro?' Dad's voice was insistent. 'Ro, earth to Ro!'

I jerked back into the real world. Mum had vanished into the kitchen. Dad was smiling at me.

I tried to smile back. Dad doesn't realise I know it, but he calls me Ro when he's trying to make me feel better about something. Trouble is, I'm sure that's what he used to call Rebecca, too.

'Hey, Ro,' he said. 'You were saying something before Mum came in?'

'It wasn't anything major,' I said. 'Just a text. A wrong number. It said something about a goddess being in heaven. From some guy with the same name as you.'

'Oh.' Dad paused for just a second too long. 'Well, that *is* weird,' he said.

'Dad?'

'What?' He smiled at me, but his eyes were all wary.

Mum bustled back in. 'Homework, Rachel, sweetie.'

'Yes, I've got loads of paperwork to check over.' Dad stood up so abruptly he knocked his chair and had to steady it to stop it from falling over.

He left. I helped Mum carry the plates and stuff out to the kitchen. She was chattering away about her tennis again, but I wasn't listening.

Why had Dad acted strange like that? Was I being paranoid or had he practically run away from me just then?

23

A few minutes later he was back, holding a bundle of papers, completely normal again. 'Hey, Ro?' He kissed my forehead. 'Give us a shout if you need any help with your homework.'

He wandered through to the living room and switched on the TV.

I trudged upstairs. Back in my room I pulled out my phone.

Dad knew something about the message, I was sure. But if he'd sent it to me by mistake, why not just say so?

My heart beat faster. Was I imagining this whole thing? Before I could think about it any more, I pulled my mobile out of my pocket and scrolled through to the last logged message. I clicked on the number and pressed *call*.

I wandered out to the landing. Dad was downstairs, through two open doors. If his phone rang I was sure I'd hear it from here.

Nothing.

I turned to go back into my room. And then I caught it. A faint, muffled ringtone.

It was coming from across the landing.

From Dad's study.

5

Theo

It took Mum several glasses of wine to get going. But when she did, I felt like asking for a glass myself.

'There are people who . . .' She hesitated. '. . . People who might harm you.'

'Why?' I frowned. I'd heard all this before and it didn't make sense. 'What people? Why would anyone want to harm me?'

Mum took a deep breath. 'People from a long time ago. From when you were born.'

'Is it to do with Dad?' I stared at her. I didn't know much about my dad. Just that he'd been a soldier. Killed abroad before I was born. Before he and Mum had even known each other that long. I knew his name – James Lawson. In fact, I'd often wished I was called Lawson, instead of Mum's name, 'Glassman'. And I had a photograph. Nothing else. Mum said he had no family.

Mum nodded. 'Some of the things I told you about your dad weren't true.' She leaned back against the kitchen counter.

25

'What things?' My heart thudded. I don't know why it mattered so much. It wasn't like I knew a lot about the guy. Just that he'd been a soldier, killed abroad before I was born. Maybe that was it. Maybe I didn't want to have what little I did know taken away from me.

'He *was* a soldier, but not in any conventional army. He was a scientist. A geneticist.' Mum looked down at the floor.

I stared at her. *Not a soldier?* All my life I'd pictured him in some British Army camouflage uniform. With a gun and a determined face.

A hero.

And now the hero was a man in a lab, wearing a white coat.

'A scientist?' My voice sounded hollow and small.

'A geneticist,' Mum repeated. 'He worked for a fertility clinic, researching ways of manipulating genes so that people who wanted children and who couldn't have them were able to. He saw himself as a soldier. Fighting bigots who thought his work was unethical. Immoral.'

'What's so bad about helping people to have kids?'

'Some people just think it's wrong. Especially when it involves messing about with embryos outside the womb and people's genes and stuff.'

'Okay . . . but . . . but you said he was shot abroad, being a soldier.'

Mum touched my arm. 'He was,' she said, softly. 'He knew people were after him and his colleagues, but he didn't take the threats seriously until you came along. Then he got

26

worried. He tried to hide you, tried to organise security . . . but the clinic he worked at was firebombed a couple of weeks after you were born. That changed everything. He was listed as dead, but he got away. Then . . .' She looked away, her voice all shaky. 'Then, later, they found him . . . people from this organisation. It's those people who . . . who would take you . . . hurt you, if they found you.' She poured herself another glass of wine. Her hand was trembling so much some of the wine splashed onto the counter.

'I don't understand,' I stammered. There were so many things I didn't understand it was hard to know where to begin.

Mum picked up her glass and drew me across the kitchen and onto the couch. I sat down, trying to absorb what she was saying. My dad had been a scientist. Some organisation had killed him because they thought his work was immoral.

'But why would the people who hated Dad want to hurt me?'

'Because you're your father's weak point. His only family. The one way people can get to him.'

'Get to him?' I frowned. With a sick feeling I wondered if she was actually mentally ill. You know, suffering from paranoid delusions or something. 'How can anyone "get" to him now? He's dead.'

Mum just sat there, looking into my eyes. And slowly the truth dawned on me.

She nodded. 'That's right, Theodore. Your dad's alive. In hiding still, but very, very much alive.'

6

Rachel

I opened Dad's study door. The muffled ringing grew louder.
I looked round the room. The sound was coming from Dad's
desk in the corner of the room.

I walked over, my heart racing.

The ringing stopped as I reached the filing drawers under
the desk. I reached for my phone and dialled the number again.

Ring, ring. The sound started again.

I sank to the floor in front of the drawers. They were shut.
Locked. The message *had* come from Dad. From a phone he
kept hidden in a filing cabinet.

'Rachel?'

I spun round.

Dad was standing in the doorway, a look of guilty confusion on his face.

We stared at each other for a second. The ringing stopped
again. Silence filled the room.

'That message,' he said. 'The one on your phone. It wasn't
for you.'

'I don't understand.'

Dad sighed. He rubbed his chin. 'I sent a text to you by mistake, that's all. It was a work thing. Nothing mysterious.'

I scrambled to my feet. 'What have goddesses in heaven got to do with your work? And why do you have a separate phone, anyway?'

'I told you, it's work. It's a work phone.' Dad's face was red. 'The message was just code for something. A work thing. Honest, Ro.'

He was lying. I was sure of it.

'Right.' I didn't know what to do. 'Fine.'

I walked out and went to my room. Dad started to follow me, but then must have thought better of it. He went downstairs. I lay on my bed, thinking. Maybe I was wrong. Maybe he wasn't lying. Maybe it *was* just some work project after all, some coded message he'd texted me by mistake – though why, I couldn't imagine. Dad works in the cosmetic surgery business. It's not exactly MI5. But he'd still lied to me before, when he pretended not to recognise the message he'd sent.

I turned over and buried my face in my pillow. Mum was one thing, but I couldn't handle it if Dad was going to start being weird with me too.

I pushed down the sob that rose up from my chest. I wouldn't think about it, that was all. I'd pretend it had never happened.

It was only a stupid text anyway.

Meaningless.

7

Theo

I was tired the next morning. I'd hardly slept, my mind full of what Mum had told me. Trying to take it in.

My dad was still alive.

I couldn't stop thinking about it.

About him.

I got out the picture of him Mum had given me years ago. I'd looked at it so often the edges were curling and the colour faded. I stared at the smiling face, the dark blue eyes, the dimpled chin. Not for the first time I wished I looked more like him. James Lawson – a scientist, not a soldier.

Well, that kind of made sense. I'd always liked science, especially when we did experiments. Maybe I was more like him than I'd thought. And my dad was no ordinary scientist . . . even if he wasn't a proper soldier, he was still brave. A hunted man.

Alive.

Mum had refused to tell me anything else. I tried again while she was getting ready for work.

'But doesn't he – my dad – want to know me now?'

'Of course.' Mum looked up from her handbag and sighed. 'It's just too risky. He'll come for you one day, though. When he's ready. When it's safe. Until then you'll just have to be patient.'

She had no idea. How could I be patient? All I had was a photograph and a name. And a million unanswered questions.

Where was he?

What was this group that was after him?

When was I going to meet him?

Mum begged me to keep the whole thing secret, but even as I promised her I would, I knew I was going to tell Jake.

He was my best friend, after all.

Of course, when we met up in the playground before school, Jake was full of what I'd missed yesterday afternoon in Starbucks. Apparently he'd got well into some girl while he was waiting for me.

'She was way fit, dude,' he said. 'All over me, as well.'

I rolled my eyes. I'd seen girls be 'all over' Jake before. It usually just meant they hadn't told him to piss off in the first ten seconds of him trying to chat them up.

'Listen.' I told him about my dad still being alive.

'Whoa, man. That is wild.' Jake stared at me intently.

I suddenly felt embarrassed. 'So d'you get that girl's number?'

'Maybe.' Jake grinned. 'D'you get your dad's?'

I explained what Mum had said about it being too dangerous to contact him. How she didn't know exactly where he was, but that he sent money every few months to pay for school. And Roy.

We crossed the playground, heading for the main entrance. We stopped behind the crowd of boys struggling to push their way inside.

'So what you gonna do then?' Jake tilted his head to one side thoughtfully. 'Just wait for your dad to get in touch one day?'

I looked at him. Jake isn't anything like me. He's shorter, for a start, with blond hair. And masses more outgoing. He's always saying it's good how different we are. How it means between us we'll attract a wider range of girls. But in spite of the differences, Jake knows me really well. I could see in his eyes that he knew I wasn't prepared to wait years to meet my dad. And suddenly I knew it too.

'I have to do something,' I said. 'I have to find out more about him at least.'

'Won't your mum tell you anything?'

'Nope.' I shook my head. 'And they don't email or speak on the phone and there's no information on our PC either. She told me.'

The queue eased and we pushed our way inside.

'Why don't you ask Max to help?' Jake said.

I considered this for a moment. Max is my other best friend and an amazing hacker. But I had no idea what would be helpful to hack into.

And then it struck me. The obvious place to start – and something I could easily do by myself.

Roy stared at me suspiciously. 'The library?' he said.

I nodded, as innocently as I could. It was after school and we were standing on the pavement outside the school gates. I'd already apologised to Roy for trying to run away yesterday.

And for punching him.

He'd shrugged it off, neither accepting my apology nor demanding that I was punished. I was grounded for a week, but at least Mum had climbed down from her earlier decision to have him wait outside all my lessons.

'Jake and I are doing a project on the Second World War,' I said. 'Air battles. We need books.'

'What's wrong with your school library?'

'Not big enough.'

That was a lie. The school library was out because I needed to go online and, at school, that was impossible without some teacher nosing into what you were looking at. And our PC at home was no good in case Mum tracked my internet search. She'd done that once before. Luckily all I'd done was take a look at this dodgy – okay, well, illegal – gaming website. Nothing too embarrassing, though she still went ballistic when she realised what I'd been doing.

Roy made the call to Mum. She said I could have half an hour at the library. Roy drove us as close as he could, then

33

we walked the rest of the way. It was cold and the light of the day was already fading. Roy walked slightly behind me, as usual, his eyes darting about, looking out for any trouble.

'How long d'you reckon before he puts his sunglasses on?' Jake whispered.

I grinned. This was a standing joke between us. Roy never went anywhere without his shades, even in the depths of winter – or today, chilly and grey and autumnal.

'Give it ten seconds,' I whispered back. I heard Jake counting under his breath. Then he turned round and looked over his shoulder. He suppressed a snort.

'Yup. Mr FBI Special Agent is looking cooool,' he said. 'I reckon he only wears them so he can stare at girls without them noticing.'

I shook my head. 'He's supposed to be looking out for me.'

The library was busy, but there were still a few free computers in the Young Adult section.

'I need to check something on the internet,' I said to Roy. 'Jake's going upstairs to look for the books we need.'

Roy grunted and positioned himself a couple of metres away from me at the foot of the staircase that led up to the library's first floor.

Five minutes later I was logged on and clicking on my Google search terms: *clinic* and *firebomb*.

I glanced over my shoulder. Roy was gazing around the library.

I looked back at the computer and frowned. Hundreds of

hits. I scanned quickly through them. Most of the results appeared to refer to abortion clinics in the United States. I added the words *genetic* and *research* and my dad's name, *Lawson*, to the search. Pressed 'go'.

Yes. There it was. That had to be it.

My heart thudded. I clicked on the hit.

A sharp prod in my ribs made me jump. I whipped round. Jake was grinning at me.

'What?' I snapped.

'How's it going, dude?' Jake sprawled into the chair next to me, his arms full of books. 'Hey there's a couple of babes upstairs looking at the CD section. Crap taste in music but . . .' He caught my eye. 'What?' His voice dropped to a whisper. 'You found something?'

I nodded and pointed at the screen.

We stared at it together.

It was a newspaper article, from *The Times* archive, dated from early September fifteen years ago, two weeks after I was born at the end of August.

RAGE firebomb kills ten at genetic research clinic

The bodies of ten scientists have been recovered from the wreckage of the Assisted Conception and Genetic Research Centre in central London, a police spokesman said yesterday.

Extremist right-wing group, the Righteous Army against Genetic Engineering (RAGE), has claimed responsibility for the firebomb, which exploded on the premises at 8.32 a.m. yesterday.

Richard Smith, an administrative officer at the Centre, heard the blast from nearby Elizabeth Price Maternity Hospital, where he was attending the birth of his daughter.

'I rushed over to the window,' said Smith. 'From the hospital I could see smoke rising. I knew at once it was a firebomb.'

'Hey, a firebomb, dude. That's hardcore.' Jake sat back in his chair. I could feel him staring at me. 'How did your dad get out, then?'

I shrugged, trying not to show how much finding out what had happened mattered to me. I scanned the rest of the article quickly, looking for my dad's name.

The ten victims of the firebomb include Elijah 'the Gene Genie' Lazio, the maverick geneticist and owner of the centre.

According to Smith, Lazio had received a number of death threats from RAGE in recent months.

'He thought they were empty threats,' Smith said. 'I was not directly involved in what he was working on. In fact, Lazio knew I was morally against his cloning programme. I gave notice I was leaving last month.'

Argentinian-born Lazio, 44, gained his nickname, the Gene Genie, two years ago after he claimed to have successfully cloned Andy – a rhesus monkey and the world's first cloned primate. However, Lazio has consistently failed to produce any evidence to substantiate his claims, and his results have never been published in a peer-reviewed journal or scrutinised by independent experts.

At the very end of the article was information about RAGE and a list of the other victims of the fire. *There*. The list included my dad – J. Lawson. Except that it wasn't true, of course. He had survived the firebomb. He was out there somewhere.

I let out a long, slow breath.

'Now what?' Jake said.

I glanced over at Roy. He was looking at me, tapping his watch and mouthing the words 'two more minutes'.

'I have to find this Richard Smith guy,' I said. I wasn't yet sure what I was going to say to him – how much of the truth I dared tell – but he knew my dad. That was what mattered. He'd known him fifteen years ago. Maybe he still did. *Jesus.* Maybe they were still in touch. My heart was hammering, just at the thought of it.

'Whoa.' Jake shook his head. 'First off – what makes you think he's going to tell you any more about your dad than your mum has? And second off – how are you going to track him down? Richard Smith's not exactly an unusual name.'

I thought for a minute. 'Look.' I pointed to the article. 'This gives us the exact date when his daughter was born.'

'So?' Jake frowned.

'So that means . . .' I paused, working it out in my head. 'That means she'd be fifteen, like us, but born in September, so probably only Year Ten. If we can find out where she goes to school, get hold of her . . .' I sat up, excited. 'Yes. In fact it'll work better that way. I can talk to her, use her to help me get to—'

'What are you talking about?' Jake frowned. 'How are you going to find out where she goes to school?'

'Annual Schools' Census.' I said. 'Max told me about it. Records schools have to submit to the government. Including the surname and date of birth of every pupil. If she's still in the country Max'll be able to find her.'

'Cool.' Jake's eyes widened. 'Wait. Are you saying that you think Max could actually hack into school records?'

'No.' I grinned. 'I'm saying that I know for a fact Max already has.'

8

Rachel

Two days passed. I forgot about the text. I mean, I forgot about what it said. I didn't forget that Dad had some kind of secret. I tried not to think about that. But it preyed on my mind. In fact, I was thinking about it when I arrived at school, when I would normally have been watching out for Jemima.

I was heading for the toilets, busting for a pee. I didn't see Jemima until I was almost at the door. She was with a couple of friends, giggling away across the corridor near the art room.

I hesitated for a second. Maybe she hadn't seen me. Anyway, it was too late to find another loo. I really needed to go. I pushed the toilet door open and hitched up my skirt as I scurried across to the cubicle. I was in and out really quickly, just splashing a bit of water over my hands after-wards. I reached the door. Pulled it open. And there she was. Jemima. Her pointy little face all sneering and cold. Amy and

Phoebe stood on either side of her. They're like copies of Jemima, except Phoebe's not nearly as pretty and Amy's got big braces on her teeth. But all of them are slim, with the same highlighted blonde hair.

Jemima nodded at Phoebe. 'Go on.'

Phoebe shoved me in the chest.

I stumbled back into the toilets.

'What were you doing in here?' Jemima sneered. 'Trying to make yourself look pretty or something?'

Amy giggled.

I shook my head. I wanted to say something. To shout at them. But it was like there was a barrier between me and the rest of the world, stopping me from speaking.

'Didn't work, did it, Phoebs?' Jemima went on. 'She looks as ugly as ever, doesn't she?'

Phoebe nodded.

I'm not ugly. I'm not. But the words didn't sound true, even inside my own head. I was ugly. Just as surely as Rebecca had been beautiful and Dad had a secret phone.

'So are you a virgin?'

What? I stared at Jemima. Why was she asking me that? She must know I was. Tears pricked at my eyes.

'Well?' Jemima prodded my shoulder.

'Maybe she doesn't know what the word means?' Amy giggled.

'I do.' The words ripped out of me – far too forcefully.

I caught the gleam in Jemima's eye. She knew she was

getting to me. She knew I was nearly crying. She was loving every second of it.

'So,' she said slowly. 'Are you or aren't you? Just say, then you can go.'

I clung to this. If I gave her an answer I could get away. But what was the *right* answer? If I said yes, I *was* a virgin, she would taunt me about being inexperienced. If I said no, I *wasn't*, she'd call me a slut and tell everyone I'd do it with any boy who wanted.

'I don't know,' I stammered.

No, Rachel. Stupid, stupid.

Jemima grinned.

'I mean . . .'

Too late. All three of them were laughing.

'She doesn't know.' That was Phoebe.

'Maybe she was drunk,' Amy giggled.

Jemima's eyes glinted. 'Maybe she couldn't tell it was happening.'

The others laughed even harder at this.

And now the tears really were coming. I bit down hard on my lip to hold them back, but it was no use. I pushed past Jemima and reached for the door knob, all blurry in front of me.

'Hey, freak show.' Jemima's voice was so commanding I stopped, my fingers outstretched and shaking. 'Maybe you'll work it out at the school disco . . .'

More snorts and sniggers from the other girls.

I grabbed the door knob.

'Don't forget you're my bitch,' Jemima sneered.

What's wrong with the ones you've got? I so wanted to say it. But I didn't have the courage. And I didn't trust my voice to speak. So I just turned the door handle and fled down the corridor.

9

Theo

Max said it would take thirty-six hours to find out the information on Richard Smith's daughter and that any communication between us should make no reference to either Richard Smith himself or my dad. Max is like that sometimes. Paranoid. Still, maybe hackers have to be.

The thirty-six hours crept by.

Even though it made me late for school, I was instant messaging at thirty-six hours and one minute.

From Big T, posted at 09:01 a.m.:

Any news?

From Maxitup, posted at 09:26 a.m.:

I think so. There were several Smiths born that day in the UK, but only one female who's still in London. Her name is Rachel.

From Big T, posted at 09:28 a.m.:

Okay. Where do I find her?

From Maxitup, posted at 09:31 a.m.:

Year Ten. Browning Wood. Girls' school in South

London. 186 Eastow Hill, SE26. When are you going there?

From Big T, posted at 09:32 a.m.:

This afternoon. Thanks. BTW, Jake thinks u r cool. Hah!

From Maxitup, posted at 09:34 a.m.:

Jake's a jerk. c ya.

10

Rachel

I spent the rest of the day drawing – a weird picture of tiny hearts, all red and bleeding, on a piece of paper which I kept transferring from one text book to another. I drew instead of starting an English comprehension essay, taking down history notes and making observations on some stupid science experiment. The only class where I couldn't totally zone out was gym – but I pretended I had my period and got the teacher to let me take it easy. I hate gym. I'm too clumsy and awkward to do any of it right.

That afternoon I left school promptly, as soon as the bell rang, so that there were plenty of people around as I walked out.

My school's on a hill, near the top. I came out of the gates and turned left to walk down the road as usual.

I'd only gone a couple of steps, looking round for Jemima the whole time, when Clara, this bushy-haired girl from my class, bounded up to me. Her eyes were all round and excited.

'Rachel, Rachel,' she gasped. 'There's a boy looking for you.'

I stared at her. I didn't know any boys. That is, I'd known some at primary school, but since I got to Browning Wood the only boys I'd met were other girls' brothers and a few guys from Princedale's at a couple of school discos.

'He's down by the bus-stop,' Clara continued. 'He wants to speak to you.'

I felt slightly sick. Who could it be? Surely not someone's brother? I hadn't been round to anyone's house for almost a year. Maybe the disco at the end of last term – I'd slow-danced with this horrible boy who'd given me a massive love bite on my neck. I'd had to wear high-neck tops for two weeks so Mum and Dad wouldn't see. His name was Fred or Frank or . . .

And then it hit me.

There was no boy. This was some trick of Jemima's. Some wind-up. I stopped walking.

Clara grabbed my arm. 'Come on. No one knows who he is. He won't say his name.'

I stared at her. Clara wasn't a mean person. She kind of got on with everyone. And she certainly wasn't part of Jemima's bitchy gang. Maybe she *was* telling the truth. I turned back. The downwards slope of the hill between where I stood and the bus-stop was filled with tartan skirts and tan jackets. The boy – if there really was a boy – must be either very short or inside the bus shelter.

I wandered ultra-casually down the hill. Clara was still

46

gabbling away beside me. 'He's not wearing a school uni-form. I saw him before anyone else. He's really fit.'

My heart started pounding. If it wasn't a wind-up it was a mistake. He was asking for the wrong Rachel. God, that would be so embarrassing. This little voice in my head was saying: *run away, run away now*.

But my feet kept on walking me forwards. The bus-stop really wasn't that far – maybe nine or ten metres, but it felt like a mile. As I got closer I caught sight of Phoebe, chatter-ing and smiling at someone inside the bus shelter.

No. No, no, no. There was Jemima. That settled it. Definitely a wind-up. I stopped walking again, just as Phoebe turned and looked up the road. She saw me. *No.* I couldn't move. Phoebe pointed at me. Jemima scowled. Then they stood aside, like they were making way for someone.

And this boy stepped out of the bus shelter.

He was tall, kind of rangy-looking. Wearing really nice jeans. Loose, but not too baggy or anything. He had dark hair – quite long round his face. He was turning, following Phoebe's pointing finger, looking up the road. At me.

Oh, God. He *was* fit. He was *really* fit. The way his hair framed his face, falling down round his eyes. His skin was olive and . . . and the lines of his face were all clear and strong.

Why did he want to talk to me?

It could still be a wind-up. Maybe Jemima had got some boy to pretend to like me or something. But it was too late to walk away now. The boy was coming towards me, staring intently at my face. Jemima and Phoebe were right behind him. I could feel other girls standing all round, watching us.

I fixed my gaze on the boy's top. It was dark blue with a pale-blue neck and sleeves and tiny writing on the chest. He was coming closer. Closer. Here. Now. Right here. Now.

'Are you Rachel Smith?' His voice was low. Intense.

I looked up. His eyes were dark brown. Very serious and deeply, deeply gorgeous.

I nodded. My mouth felt dry.

'Can I talk to you for a minute?' he said.

I could feel the girls around me shuffling, hear them whispering to each other. Sniggering. My face was burning. I suddenly felt completely humiliated. It *was* a wind-up. Tears sprang to my eyes. I'd rather Jemima had tipped my school bag over my head or called me any number of names. I started backing away a little, my eyes now on the boy's shoes. Trainers. Not flashy, expensive ones. But nice. Cool trainers.

'I have to go,' I mumbled.

'Please.' There was an awful urgency in his voice.

'Why're you interested in her?' That was Jemima. Really scathing. 'She's fat and she's so stupid she doesn't even know if she's a virgin.'

The crowd of girls surrounding us burst out laughing.

I swallowed hard, forcing the tears to stay down.

Then the boy reached out and touched my arm. He didn't grab me or anything, just pressed his fingers against my sleeve. It was like a million bolts of lightning zinging through me.

48

'I really need to talk to you,' he said in the same urgent voice. Though he now sounded massively embarrassed as well. 'Alone.'

There was a chorus of sarcastic *oohs* from the girls standing beside us. I looked up into his face. It was bright red. He looked as awkward as I felt. Which really confused me.

I couldn't see how this could be a wind-up. The boy seemed so genuine. And yet it didn't make sense. I must just be too stupid to work out what was going on.

I stood there, rigidly, unable to talk or move.

More giggles.

Then the boy took a deep breath. He drew himself up in this determined way. 'I've got a message for Rachel from her boyfriend,' he said, a new, don't-mess-with-me tone in his voice. 'I need to give it to her in private.'

There was something so definite, so insistent about the way he spoke, that I wasn't surprised when Jemima and the others started shuffling backwards. I stared at the pavement around me, watching all the black school shoes turning and walking away.

The boy let go of my arm. 'I'm sorry about that,' he said, quietly. 'I don't know your boyfriend really.'

I stared at the tiny writing on his top. *Just try it.*

Did he seriously think I might have a boyfriend?

Really?

'I'm Theo.' He smiled. 'Is there somewhere we can talk?'

11

Theo

The girl – Rachel – said nothing. Just stared at the ground.

'It's okay,' I said, feeling my face get redder. Why had I said that about her boyfriend? It sounded stupid. 'I'm not . . . I . . . I only want to ask you something. It's about my dad. He . . . er . . . he died . . . ages ago, but I think he might . . . might have known your dad once.'

I held my breath.

Rachel grunted something – I couldn't make out what. Then she started walking away, still staring at the pavement.

I followed her down the hill, taking short strides so as not to walk faster than her.

Crap. Now I was here, the whole thing seemed ridiculous. *I* was ridiculous. Taking all these risks and for what?

I'd escaped from school again – over the tree in the courtyard like before, but earlier on in the afternoon, to give myself time to change clothes and find my way across London to Rachel. I knew I'd be in massive trouble later – I

50

was missing school and skipping the detention I'd been given for going over the wall the first time.

Plus I was running away from Roy. Again.

But I had to find the girl and talk to her face to face. I couldn't see what else to do. I'd hardly slept last night thinking about it all.

And now, here she was. Rachel Smith. I glanced at her. My heart sank. I'd hoped that she'd be a tomboy kind of person. Easy to talk to. Straightforward. Confident. Though maybe not too confident.

But Rachel wasn't like that at all. She was all hunched over and awkward. *Man*, she couldn't even look me in the eye.

We walked for a couple of minutes, along a leafy road, to a roundabout in the middle of a fairly quiet intersection. There was a wooden bench underneath this big oak tree in the middle of the roundabout. Rachel sat down near one end. I sat at the other and looked at the sky. It was heavy with grey clouds, like it might rain any minute.

'Your friends were kind of embarrassing there.'

'Nahm af enz,' Rachel mumbled.

I stared at her. Her head was still bent over, staring down at the grass. I suddenly wondered if she was mentally retarded or something.

'What's that?' I said.

She looked up a little, not meeting my eyes.

'They're not my friends,' she said.

'Oh.' Of course they weren't. They'd been ripping the piss

51

out of her. *Get a grip, Theo.* 'I . . . I'm really sorry to just show up like this. I didn't know what else to do.'

Rachel nodded at the ground.

Somehow I managed to explain how I'd found her dad's name through my internet search. She didn't know about the explosion at the clinic, so I told her what the newspaper report had said.

'I think our dads must have worked together, at that clinic, before . . . before mine died,' I said.

Rachel looked up. Right up, at last, right into my eyes. I smiled. She was actually okay-looking. A bit shy and nervy maybe, but her eyes were bright and clear. As sane as I was, at least.

'So why did you come to see me?' She blushed. 'How did you even know where I was?'

I was ready for this. I knew I couldn't explain about Max hacking into the school records without landing both of us in trouble, so I'd made up a cover story.

'My dad mentioned you in these notebooks he kept,' I said. 'Mostly they were records of scientific conversations and stuff. But he also put in . . . things from when you were born, just after me. Like how your dad had everything planned out for you. Where you were going to school even.'

I ran my hand through my hair. Saying it out loud it kind of sounded ridiculous.

But Rachel was nodding. 'Sounds like my dad.' She shot me an embarrassed smile. 'He's a bit of a control freak. So's my mum. But ... um ... I still don't see why you're here ...'

'I ... er, I thought if I could find you, then ...'

'... You'd find my dad?' Rachel looked at me hesitantly. 'You want to meet my dad, then? You want to talk to him about *your* dad?'

Yes. Yes. That's exactly what I want.

I shrugged. 'If you don't mind me coming home with you.'

She started. 'What. Now?'

I wrinkled my nose. 'It's just I ran away from school to come here. And my mum'll go mental when she knows what I've done. I'll be grounded for weeks.'

Rachel frowned. 'Why ...? I mean ... I don't understand. Why didn't you just ask your mum about it all? I mean, if our dads were friends then ... maybe they *all* knew each other.'

I stared at her, my head whirling. What the hell did I say to that? I blushed. *Think, Theo. Come on.*

'Er ... er ... I can't talk to Mum about anything to do with my dad.' Inspiration struck me. 'She gets ... er ... really upset whenever I mention him. She was so in love with him, she can't say his name without crying. Even now.'

'Oh, that's awful.' Rachel pressed her lips together sympathetically. 'What *was* his name?'

'James Lawson.' I'd decided to lie about my school and home address – just to be on the safe side. But, obviously, I had to use Dad's real name in order to find out what Richard Smith knew about him.

Rachel nodded. 'My dad doesn't get home until late, so you'll have to stay for a while.' Her cheeks reddened again. 'I mean, if Mum says it's okay.'

Drops of rain fell on our shoulders.

'Thanks.' I stood up. 'I really appreciate this.'

Rachel shot me this nervous little smile. 'No problem. I just hope my dad remembers him.'

We crossed the road away from the roundabout and headed down a long, broad street with big trees lining either side.

Rachel looked round at me. 'I can't wait to hear what my dad says when he realises your dad wrote down all that stuff about him planning my life.'

I stopped walking. *Oh, man.* The chances of Rachel's dad having actually gone on and on about his plans for Rachel's life seemed so remote as to be totally laughable. Which meant Mr Smith would know there was no way I could have tracked him down through any notebooks recording those plans. Then I'd have to explain about Max hacking into the school records.

Why hadn't I thought this through better?

'D'you know what?' I said, thinking fast. 'I'm not sure we should say anything about the notebooks. For my mum's sake. Your dad might want to get in touch with her or something. And then she'll just get all upset about the past again.'

Rachel frowned. 'But what if my dad asks how you got his name?'

Crap. Crap. Crap.

54

I breathed out slowly, trying to push down the panicky feeling rising in my chest. There was only one way out of this. 'I won't say James Lawson's my dad,' I said. 'I'll say I'm doing a science project or something on the . . . on the history of genetic research. Get your dad to talk about the research going on at the clinic they both worked at back when they knew each other. Once he starts talking, I'll bring my dad into the conversation.'

Rachel was staring at me as if I was crazy.

'Right.' She looked away. 'But that means there's another problem.'

'What?' *Bloody hell*. This whole thing was turning into a gigantic nightmare. Now I wasn't going to be able to explain to Mr Smith why I wanted to know about James Lawson. And I was already unsure exactly what lies I'd told Rachel.

'Well,' Rachel stammered. 'How are we going to say you know me? I mean, it's okay me taking a friend home, but my parents might think it's a bit weird you turning up like this. I go to a girls' school. And you're a . . . a boy.'

'Oh.' I attempted a weak smile. 'Not much I can do about that.'

Rachel dipped her head. 'You know they'll think that we . . .' She stopped.

'What?'

'Nothing.' Her face was the colour of a tomato.

I suddenly saw what she was saying. Her parents were going to assume we liked each other. As in 'like'.

'Oh,' I said, thinking how much Jake would have loved being in my place. And how much I wanted to die, right now.

Rachel was staring down at the pavement again. 'Why don't we say we met at last summer's school disco. At my school. And that we bumped into each other just now. I mean, I'm not actually going out with anyone, so . . .'

'Okay.' I was staring at the pavement myself now.

The rain was getting heavier. Rachel sped up. We walked the rest of the way in silence.

12

Rachel

There was only one thought going through my head as I turned my key in the door.

I've got an almost boyfriend.

Okay. So he was a pretend almost boyfriend. But he was fit. With those lovely, serious brown eyes. And sweet. Trying to find out about his dead father like that. And not wanting to upset his mum.

Who knew what might happen?

I felt excited. Awake. Alive. Like I hadn't for . . . well, for as far back as I could remember.

13

Theo

Rachel's house was enormous. Red brick and detached with a huge brass knocker on the front door and smart bushes in the garden.

Inside, the hall was bigger than the whole of our ground floor. I followed Rachel across the criss-crossed wood floor. My trainers squeaked as I walked. We stopped as a door in the corner opened.

'Hiya, sweetie.' This weird-looking woman stepped out into the hall. She peered into the mirror opposite her. She didn't look at Rachel or notice me.

I stared at her. She was really old. Really thin. And her face was all stretched and shiny, like she was wearing a mask.

'Hi, Mum.' For a second, just as we'd come inside the house, Rachel had looked more normal. Less hunched over. But now she was shrinking down into herself again.

Her mum looked round and saw me. She jumped and gave a high-pitched squeal.

'Rachel, for goodness' sake. Who on earth . . .?' She stared at me, her eyes like little pebbles. 'What?'

'This is . . . er . . . this is Theo,' Rachel stammered.

I stepped forward and held out my hand. It's not that I'm used to meeting girls' mothers. Just that my school makes a big deal out of shaking hands – with teachers, before and after sports matches. That kind of thing. So I know what to do.

The woman took my hand. Hers felt like wire covered in thin foam padding. 'Mrs Smith,' she said. She gave my palm a brief squeeze then dropped my hand again and frowned. 'How do you know Rachel?'

I glanced at Rachel, but she was back to her whole staring at the ground thing. So I launched into the cover story Rachel had come up with, emphasising how we'd just bumped into each other on the street.

Mrs Smith led me into the kitchen – another massive room with lots of clear, pale wood surfaces. She sat me down at the table and started asking me questions. Where did I go to school? How come I'd been at the school disco last summer term when I didn't go to one of the invited boys' schools? She was all smiley and bright, but her voice sounded hollow.

My answers got shorter and shorter as I lied about my surname, the name of my school and where I lived.

I guess Rachel must have seen how awkward I felt, because after a few minutes she gave this nervy little cough from the doorway, where she was still standing.

'Theo said he would help me with my biology homework,' she said. 'He's doing a big project on genetics.'

Mrs Smith nodded. She had the weirdest eyes. They were set almost flat against the stretched-out skin around them.

'Fine,' she chirped. 'I'll leave you both to get on, then.' She narrowed her spooky eyes at me. 'I'll just be next door. Let me know if you need anything.'

She trotted out of the kitchen. I breathed out heavily.

'Sorry.' Rachel came and sat down opposite me. 'My mum's a nightmare.'

I shrugged, privately agreeing, but sensing it might be rude to say so. There was a big clock on the kitchen wall above Rachel's head. It wasn't even five o'clock yet.

'When does your dad get home?' I said.

'Not for a few hours.' Rachel looked up at me apologetically. 'Maybe we should work out what your project's about. Then I'll go and ask Mum if you can stay for tea.'

I groaned inwardly. At this rate I wouldn't be home until ten or eleven. Mum would be going mental. She might even call the police. Still, I was here now. I had to make the most of it.

My eyes fell on a framed photograph of a girl on the wall underneath the kitchen clock. She was smiling. Really pretty.

'Who's that?' I said.

Rachel stiffened. 'My sister,' she said, staring down at the table.

I raised my eyebrows, imagining what Jake would say if he was with me. 'When does *she* get home?' I said, trying to sound casual.

'She doesn't. She's dead.' Rachel got up and shuffled over to the fridge. 'D'you want a drink? I'm getting an orange juice.'

'Er . . . yeah . . . thanks.' I looked away, embarrassed.

After Rachel brought over our glasses, we talked through what my school project should be about. Still barely looking me in the eyes, Rachel explained more about what her dad did. It didn't sound as if he'd been involved in any kind of genetic research for a long time.

Mrs Smith came back into the kitchen and Rachel asked if I could stay for tea. Her mum looked annoyed.

'But won't anyone be expecting you at home, Theo?' she said.

I told her my parents were away on holiday and I was staying with cousins who were easy-going about what I did.

After so many other lies, I figured, how could one more hurt? Mrs Smith reluctantly agreed I could stay for tea.

Rachel's dad came home at about six-thirty. Rachel looked up, surprised, as his voice drifted through from the hall.

'He's back early,' she said. 'Mum must've called him.'

My heart hammered as heavy footsteps crossed the hall floor. Now Mr Smith was here, I felt terrified. I suddenly couldn't remember what on earth we'd agreed to say – how I was going to get him to talk about the past.

The door opened. A shortish, grey-haired man walked in. Like Mrs Smith, he was old. More like a grandad than a dad, really. He stared at me as if he'd never seen a boy before.

Man, this family were weird.

I stood up and held out my hand again.

But Mr Smith didn't seem to notice. He was still staring at my face. 'What's your name?' he said at last.

'Theo.'

Mr Smith shook my hand and kissed Rachel on the side of the head. He leaned against the kitchen table. 'My wife tells me you're helping Rachel with her homework?'

'I'm doing this genetics project,' I said. My mouth felt dry. 'The history of genetic research. Where science was and is and where it will be in five years' time.'

Mr Smith smiled. 'Bit ambitious for a Year Ten project, isn't it?'

'I'm Year Eleven,' I said, feeling uncomfortable. I glanced at Rachel. Surprise, surprise – she was staring down at the floor. She looked like she might be about to cry. I suddenly felt massively sorry for her. Okay, so my mum had her faults, but Rachel's parents were really weird.

Mr Smith was staring at me again. I plunged on.

'Rachel said you used to work at a clinic that did genetic research.'

Mr Smith shook his head. 'I don't know why she said that.' He glanced at Rachel and smiled. 'I'm a manager not a researcher. I've never been involved in actual genetic research.'

'But Dad,' Rachel muttered. 'You still worked at research clinics . . .'

'For goodness' sake, Ro.' Mr Smith rolled his eyes. 'I might have worked briefly at a couple of the clinics, but I had nothing to do with any of the genetic research they were doing. Look, I'm going to get out of my suit.' He turned away and strode out of the room.

Rachel and I stared at each other across the table.

'I'm sorry,' she said. 'I guess my dad isn't going to be much help.'

I nodded. But my mind was whirring away. I was sure Mr Smith knew more than he was letting on.

Rachel got out her school bag and appeared to be doing some kind of art homework. A weird picture of lots of tiny heart shapes – all red and dripping with blood. I bent over my English comprehension. We worked silently for a while. My mind kept sliding over the words on the page in front of me. I knew I couldn't leave here without asking Mr Smith about my dad. Somehow, I had to do it. Even if he refused to tell me anything.

My chance came an hour or so later. Mrs Smith had been bustling about in the kitchen making some kind of stew. It smelled delicious and I was starving. I usually had a couple of sandwiches when I got in from school, then a big tea later. But Rachel hadn't eaten so much as a biscuit yet – and no one had offered me anything either.

At last Mrs Smith told us to clear our homework away and set the table. Rachel brought out these shiny knives and forks, then some long-stemmed wine glasses and cloth napkins.

I was feeling more and more awkward. The last thing I wanted was to sit down with Rachel's weird parents and have some kind of formal dinner. On the other hand, I had to ask about my dad.

Plus, I was so hungry now it felt like my stomach lining was eating itself.

At last Mrs Smith plonked two bowls on the table – one, a steaming bowl of rice, the other full of a meaty mince dish.

'Richard,' she called. 'Supper's ready.'

She indicated I should sit on one side of the table. 'So what does your father do, Theo?' she said in this high, brittle voice.

'Er . . . er . . . my dad died,' I said. 'A long time ago,' I added, embarrassed by the wide-eyed look of concern spreading over Mrs Smith's face.

'Oh, I am sorry,' she said. Then she shouted 'Richard' again.

Mr Smith appeared grumpily in the door. 'Bit early, isn't it?' he said.

'Well. As you're home.' Mrs Smith gave this false-sounding, tinkly little laugh. 'And as Theo's here.'

Mr Smith glared at me as he sat down. 'When do you have to leave, Theo?'

The sub-text was obvious. *How quickly can I get rid of you?*

I took a deep breath. 'I'll have to go after dinner,' I said slowly. 'But I was wondering if I could ask you about the genetic research clinics you worked at again.'

Rachel's mum's mouth dropped open.

Mr Smith shrugged. 'I told you, I wasn't involved in any of the actual research.'

'I just wondered if you knew anyone else who was. Involved, I mean. Like one of the scientists. Maybe I could talk to them about the research they were doing back then.'

Mr Smith stared at me.

Crap. Even to my own ears I sounded phoney. I mean, I was good at science. I always had been. But the idea that I might be so into a science project that I'd actually go and interview real-life scientists was beyond ridiculous.

Still, now I'd started, I might as well go on.

'Did you ever meet that guy called the Gene Genie?' I said, trying to sound casual. 'I read about him on the internet. I think his real name was Elijah Lazio?'

Mrs Smith's shiny fork clattered onto her plate.

'Elijah Lazio?' Mr Smith shook his head. 'I know the name, but we never met.'

I was sure he was lying. He'd worked at the man's clinic, for goodness' sake.

I nodded. 'Okay. Maybe you remember some of the people he worked with.' My heart hammered. 'Er . . . there was one guy, one of the researchers I think.' I paused, as if trying to remember. 'James Lawson?'

Mr Smith pressed his lips together, then stretched them into a completely unconvincing smile. 'Never heard of him,' he said.

Again, I was sure he was lying. But why? And what did I say now?

I ran my hand through my hair. And then it happened. This look crossed Mr Smith's face. Immediately he covered it.

Turned away and started talking to his wife, who was still sitting rigidly at the end of the table.

I looked down at my plate. Suddenly my hunger had vanished. Because the look that had crossed Mr Smith's face was unmistakable.

Terror.

Pure, total, terror.

What the hell was going on?

14

Rachel

Theo left straight after dinner.

He stood at the front door, staring at me with those serious brown eyes, like he was trying to tell me something but couldn't because of Dad hovering nearby. Then he pushed a tiny, folded piece of paper into my left hand and squeezed my fingers tightly over it.

'See you,' he said under his breath. It was half a statement, half a question.

My heart thumped as he let himself out of the door. My hand where he'd touched it felt branded – like when they stamp animals to say who they belong to. Like Theo had marked me out as his.

Even if he didn't realise it.

I kept my fingers closed over the hard ridge of the paper as I turned round. Dad was behind me, watching – eyes hard, arms folded.

I was furious with him. Okay, so he didn't remember Theo's dad, but I couldn't believe how rude he'd been. I mean, I know

Theo wasn't telling him the whole truth, but that was just to protect his mum. The poor guy. He just wanted a bit of information and Dad had totally refused to talk.

I stomped upstairs without a word, still clutching the tiny piece of paper.

I unfolded it in my bedroom. My heart raced. It had clearly been torn out of some workbook. Next to the printed line of text, Theo had written his phone number. Not a mobile. A home number.

For a second I let myself imagine he'd given me his number because he wanted to ask me out. But this voice in my head told me not to be so stupid. He'd given me his number so I could let him know if Dad said anything about James Lawson.

I wanted to cry. How sweet that he cared so much. His life must be so hard. His mum in constant misery. Theo, himself, searching, yearning to know more about his father.

I lay on my bed, picturing his face. Remembering his eyes when he looked at me. But gradually my thoughts turned to how hopeless it was. I'd probably never see him again. And, even if I did, he would never be interested in *me*. Fat, ugly me.

And then I remembered how he'd asked about Rebecca. How his face had lit up when he'd seen her picture on the wall. A hole opened up inside my stomach. I was nothing. I was worthless. I was worse even than Jemima and her friends said I was.

I got off the bed and crept downstairs to the kitchen. I

walked quietly, not wanting Mum to see me. I found the cupboard I was looking for and reached inside for the round, steel biscuit tin. I eased the lid off and crammed a chocolate biscuit into my mouth.

The chocolate melted against my mouth – all rich and creamy. I crunched on the biscuit, letting my saliva smooth out the rough, sugary texture of the wheat. I swallowed it down. Then I took another. And another.

Five biscuits later, I shut the lid on the tin and slid it back in the cupboard. As I closed the cupboard door I filled up with misery again. Why had I done that? I was only going to get fatter and fatter.

And Mum would see. She would know what I'd done. Not that she'd say anything directly. She'd just start going on about carbs again.

I crept out of the kitchen as silently as I'd entered it. But this time as I passed the living-room door on my way to the stairs I heard Mum and Dad talking.

'I don't think you should do anything.' Mum's voice was sharp. 'He's just a boy.'

'But it was him. *Him.* I saw it when he put his hand through his hair.' Dad sounded terrified. 'We've got to do something or they'll find out about Rachel too.'

I paused, frowning. What was he talking about?

'I'm going to email Lewis,' Dad said firmly. I could hear him pacing across the room. 'He'll know what's going on.'

'No.' Mum's voice rose. Now she sounded scared too. 'No. Email's too risky.'

'Yeah, well.' Dad's footsteps stopped. 'I had to get rid of the secure phone, didn't I? So there's not any choice. Anyway, not doing anything's riskier. Didn't you hear the boy? He was talking about Elijah *and* he knew about James Lawson.'

My stomach gave a sickening lurch.

Mum knew about the secret phone too. Which Dad was now referring to as a *secure* phone for some reason. Worse, Dad had lied flat out. He *did* know Theo's dad. And that Gene Genie guy.

The footsteps suddenly got louder. Closer to the door. I scurried to the stairs. Raced up to my room. I stood just inside the door, panting, my heart pulsing in my throat.

Footsteps coming up the stairs. I peered through the crack in my bedroom door. Dad marched past, head down, making for his office.

I took a few deep breaths, trying to calm myself. Then I crept down the landing corridor and peered round the office door.

Dad was sitting in his big leather office chair, hunched over his laptop. He looked up. Saw me. Smiled, distractedly.

His hands pulled the lid of the laptop down a fraction, as if he was unconsciously trying to stop me from seeing what he was doing.

'Hi, Dad,' I said, awkwardly.

He frowned. 'That boy earlier,' he said. 'Theo. Did you really meet him at your school disco?'

I nodded, feeling myself blush.

'Then you didn't see him for months and he just turned up today?' Dad's eyes bored into mine.

I looked away, not wanting to lie, but also not wanting to betray Theo. 'I told Mum earlier,' I said. 'He came with a friend to the school disco. He was visiting the same person today – we just . . . just bumped into each other.'

Dad stared at me. 'I don't want you to see him again,' he said.

My mouth fell open. 'Why?'

Dad looked down at his laptop. 'Sorry, darling, I just think you're too young.' He sighed. 'No discussion. Now, I've got some emails to send.' He jerked his head towards the door, indicating I should leave.

Something was seriously wrong here. Dad was often pre-occupied with work stuff, but he hardly ever got really cross or . . . or dismissive like he was being now. And he never got heavy about boys. Not like some girls' dads. In fact, he was always encouraging me to go out and be more sociable. Like Rebecca had been.

I chewed on my lip. Dad definitely knew something about Theo's father. And he was emailing this guy, Lewis, to tell him that Theo had been in touch. I had no idea why it all mattered so much, or why Dad was hiding what he knew. But I was certain of one thing. Dad was scared. Really scared. I'd heard it in his voice earlier. And now I could see it in his eyes.

'I'm busy, Ro,' Dad said.

I nodded and shut the office door. I stumbled back to my

bedroom, my head spinning. My eyes fell on the scrap of paper that Theo had written his number on. I had to call him. Not right now. He probably wasn't even home yet. But later, or tomorrow, I was going to call him and tell him exactly what I'd heard my dad say.

I lay on my side on the pale-pink duvet. Gradually my heart stopped pounding and I shifted from wondering what Dad knew and hadn't told us, to thinking about Theo. About his face – about how strong he looked. And yet how vulnerable he must be, inside.

Maybe he'd want to meet up again, to discuss what I'd overheard. I bent my arm, snuggling down against the pillow.

Imagine if I looked like Rebecca – all slim and pretty and smiling. Maybe then Theo would want to kiss me.

This fluttery feeling fizzled up from my stomach, through my chest, into my throat.

I leaned forwards and pressed my lips against the soft, plump skin just below my wrist, imagining it was Theo's mouth.

15

Theo

I got home just after nine-thirty that evening.

Mum was completely hysterical. In my face before I'd even shut the front door.

'Where've you been?' she shouted. 'Do you realise that I've been out of my mind with worry? What is wrong with you?'

Across the corridor Roy's door was slightly open. I hated the idea of him hearing her. Hearing me being shouted at. I moved through the door to our living area, Mum still raging beside me.

I slumped onto the sofa.

'Roy says you are now on absolutely your last chance,' she shrieked.

I looked up. 'I thought last time was my last chance.' A grin twitched at the corner of my mouth.

Big mistake.

Mum moved into tenth gear. 'How *dare* you, Theodore. You think this is funny?' she spat. 'You are grounded. You are so grounded. For the rest of this year. For the rest of your life.'

'Hey . . .'

'No, Theodore. You have got to learn. I thought if I explained what was at stake, you would accept the need for protection. And instead you decide to disappear for hours.' Her lips trembled and her voice suddenly cracked. 'Don't you realise how terrified I've been?' she sobbed.

I stared down at the floor. For the first time, guilt flickered at the edges of my mind. I pushed it away. If Mum had been prepared to tell me more, I wouldn't have had to run off like that. If she'd been frightened it was her own fault.

Mum sank down beside me. She suddenly seemed smaller. Like all the energy had drained out of her. She touched my arm.

'Why did you do it?' she said. 'Why did you run off like that?'

The patch of carpet at my feet was threadbare. I scuffed at it with my toe. I knew I couldn't tell her. She'd go even more ballistic if she thought I was trying to find out about Dad.

'There was just something I had to do,' I mumbled, not looking at her.

She shook her head at me. 'What, Theodore? What did you have to do?'

I carried on staring at the worn patch of carpet. Why was it that Dad sent money for a posh school and a bodyguard, but not a big house or nice stuff? I ran my hand through my hair. There was just so much that didn't make sense. I glanced at Mum's face. Even if I asked her, she would refuse to tell me anything. Just like she had before.

'I was meeting someone,' I said. 'I skipped school so as Roy wouldn't be there. I hate him always watching what I do.'

'But . . .?' Mum frowned. 'Meeting someone?' Her eyes widened. 'You don't . . .? You mean a girl?'

I looked away, feeling my face growing hot.

Yes. But no. Not like you mean.

'Oh, Theodore.'

Oh, man.

I don't think I'd ever felt more embarrassed in my life. And yet, as I sat there squirming, it dawned on me that pretending to like Rachel would give me the perfect cover for seeing her again, in case she found out more from her dad.

Mum sat down beside me and squeezed my hand. 'So why didn't you tell me?' she said. 'I don't mind you meeting someone after school, so long as it's not somewhere open, of course. You could have invited her back here.'

I stared at her. She was being almost understanding.

'Mu-um,' I said. 'You can't just ask girls you hardly know to come back to your house. It sounds weird.'

She turned away and pressed her lips together, like she was trying not to smile. 'I see,' she said. 'I didn't . . . Anyway. So how did you meet this girl? What's her name?'

'Rachel. She's sort of a friend of Max's,' I lied.

Mum raised her eyebrows. 'Really?'

I could see why she was surprised. Max doesn't have many friends – of either sex. I nodded anyway.

75

'I hadn't realised you were . . . you know . . . you had . . .' Mum tailed off.

How embarrassing was this?

I shrugged, then sighed. 'Please don't ground me, Mum. At least, not for too long. I promise I won't run off again. I'll apologise to Roy.' I paused. Then I said it. 'You see, I'd really like to see her . . . this girl, Rachel, again. Soon.'

Ugh. Yuck. Puke. My whole face was on fire. I hoped it was worth it. That Mum would fall for my revolting lovesick jerk routine.

She did.

She tilted her head to one side. Then she leaned over and kissed my cheek.

Oh man, she was getting all soppy thinking I was getting all loved-up over some girl.

I resisted the impulse to wipe her kiss away.

'I'm still furious with you,' she said. 'But I do appreciate how hard it must be for you – having Roy around all the time.' She sat back on the sofa and stared at me. 'You're grounded for the rest of the week. And no friends here either. What you did was wrong. Skipping school. Not calling me. It was selfish and thoughtless.'

I nodded. A week wasn't bad. In fact it was brilliant, considering how angry she'd been when I walked in.

Mum smiled. 'So, what's this Rachel like then?'

16

Rachel

What was I supposed to do now?

As soon as I got to school the next day all the girls in my class had asked me about Theo. Even Jemima – though of course she made out he wasn't worth bothering with.

But it didn't work. Because everyone had seen him. Everyone had seen how fit he looked. I got a bit carried away, in fact. Hinting he was sort of into me. Hinting that he'd only pretended to have a message from my boyfriend because he wanted to ask me out himself. I mean, I didn't come out with an actual lie. But I hinted. I definitely hinted.

I thought about calling him all day, trying to work out exactly what to say. I did it on the way home from school. My fingers were shaking as I dialled his number on my mobile.

But it wasn't how I'd expected at all. First I got his mum, which was really embarrassing. And then Theo sounded really distant, like he didn't want to talk to me at all.

I got all confused telling him what had happened with

Dad. And my mobile kept cutting out, so he missed bits of what I was saying and I had to repeat myself.

And then it got worse. I couldn't believe what he asked me to do. As soon as he'd suggested it he took it back and said he couldn't expect me to do it. But I knew it was what he really wanted.

And I knew I was going to do it, even though part of me – a big part of me – knew it was wrong.

17

Theo

This was it. As soon as I put the phone down on Rachel, I knew. This was it.

I called Max straight away to set things up for Saturday week. That was the first weekend day we could all meet, when I wouldn't be grounded any more and Rachel would have the chance to do what I'd asked her to do.

If she was really prepared to do it.

I couldn't believe she would.

I mean, I hardly knew her.

But still. She'd said yes. She'd said she'd do it. If only she had the guts to carry it through.

I prayed that she did.

18

Rachel

Saturday morning finally arrived. I wandered into the kitchen and told Mum I was going out to meet up with some friends from my class.

'We're going to go shopping and then maybe get an ice cream or something,' I said, ultra-casually.

Mum pursed her lips and stared at me suspiciously. I knew what she was thinking. *What friends?* I hadn't gone out much all term and I never had people back to the house any more.

'It's Clara,' I said, saying the first name that came to me. 'And a few others. We're looking for stuff for the school disco.'

I had, of course, no intention of going to the school disco. Though, if I was honest, I'd spent quite a lot of the last week imagining being there with Theo.

Mum nodded. 'Have a good time, then,' she said. 'And sweetie, don't buy anything cropped. It's not a flattering look on you. Top or bottom.'

'Right.' Normally that kind of remark would have really

upset me, especially as we were standing in front of a picture of Rebecca looking stunning in these cut-off trousers Mum always referred to as clamdiggers. But today I was only half listening to her. Most of my mind was focused on what I had to do next.

I checked the time as I walked through the hall. Ten-thirty a.m. Dad was still at squash. He never got home before eleven. And I planned to be out of here long before that.

I could feel myself speeding up as I climbed the stairs. I just wanted to get this over with now. My mouth felt dry as I darted along the landing and into my room. Backpack. Make-up and hairbrush. Purse.

I had everything I needed.

Everything except the main thing.

I crept to the top of the stairs. I could hear Mum clattering about in the kitchen. I gritted my teeth and marched into Dad's office. His laptop was in its normal place beside the desk. I grabbed it and shoved it into my backpack. My hands were sweating as I zipped the bag up and swung it over my back. I sped downstairs, crept across the parquet floor and opened the front door.

Almost out.

'Sweetie.'

I spun round, my heart thumping.

Mum was staring at me curiously from the kitchen door. 'What on earth have you got that big rucksack on for?' she frowned.

' Er . . . school books,' I said, blushing. 'Stuff I borrowed off Clara. I have to give them back. She needs them for homework this weekend.'

Mum fluffed up her hair. 'Okay,' she said, turning to look at herself in the mirror opposite. 'I just wanted to say you should avoid buying anything yellow. Not a good colour for you. Go for blue or green. Bring out what colour there is in your eyes.'

Yeah, right, Mum. We both know my eyes are the colour of sludge.

'Fine,' I said, stepping outside. 'Bye.'

I shut the door and raced off up the road to the train station.

As I got closer to the North London address Theo had given me, I got more nervous. Up until now I'd only been worried about getting Dad's laptop out of the house. Now I started thinking seriously about what would happen when I arrived at the place we were meeting. It belonged to some friend of Theo's called Max.

A zillion anxious thoughts flooded my head.

What was Max going to be like? How was he going to hack into Dad's emails? I mean, Dad had a password I didn't know.

Anyway, suppose Dad had deleted the email after he'd sent it? Worse. What if I was wrong and the email was nothing to do with Theo? Or what if Dad had changed his mind and there was no email?

I'll feel so stupid if they can't find anything on the computer.

Then again, suppose Max *did* manage to find something? What if all Dad's files got destroyed or corrupted? How would I ever explain that?

By the time I reached the tube station closest to Max's house I'd been travelling for nearly two hours and felt all ugly and dirty as well as scared. I'd put on this pale-green top and was sure I was sweating into it horribly under the arms. I'd caught sight of myself in a shop window walking up from the tube station and, as usual, my hair looked awful – all lank and shapeless round my face.

I stood in a doorway and put on a little make-up. It didn't help. Now I just looked like an ugly girl with black-ringed eyes and overly glossy lips.

I found the right road and trudged down it. I rubbed some of the lip gloss off with my finger. Dad's laptop was pulling on my shoulders now and my back was aching.

I took a few deep breaths. At least I was going to see Theo. Even if he wouldn't go for me in a million years, I'd get to talk to him again. And it wasn't like there'd be loads of people there. Only this Max, who was probably just some geeky boy with spots.

I checked the address Theo had given me. I was here. A small, brick terraced house with a front garden full of weeds and peeling paintwork on the door. A thickset man was squinting at me from one of the windows, his arms folded. Who was that? Max's dad, maybe?

I rang the doorbell, fear surging through my stomach. The sound of dogs barking came from inside the house. Then the door swung inwards and two enormous, brown-haired mon-grels poked their heads through the gap. Theo was bent over between them, struggling to pull the dogs back by their stiff leather collars.

'Hi.' He flicked his head to get his hair out of his eyes.

'Hi,' I squeaked back, feeling my face redden. He was even more gorgeous than I'd remembered. I quickly clocked the jeans and trainers – the same ones that he'd worn before. But now he was wearing a black T-shirt. His arms were smooth and brown underneath, his muscles all tensed with the effort of holding on to the dogs.

'Sorry about the mutts,' Theo said. 'They're Max's. Hey, log off, guys. Log off.' The dogs stopped leaping about and stood obediently at his side. I stared at them. I like dogs, but Mum had never let me have any kind of pet, so I wasn't used to them. I reached forwards and carefully petted the smaller dog on the back. His fur was short and dark and rough. He sniffed at my shoes.

'That's Java,' Theo said. 'The other one's his mum, Perl.' Perl wagged her tail furiously. She had a long, intelligent face and almost looked like she was smiling at me.

I looked up at Theo. He glanced through a door to my left, where the thickset man I'd seen at the window was staring at us.

Theo saw I'd noticed. 'Er . . . that's Roy.' He shut the front door and propelled me towards the stairs. The dogs scam-pered after us.

I wanted to ask who Roy was, but Theo clearly didn't want to talk about him.

We climbed the stairs. 'Did you get it okay?' Theo said. His voice was low. It sent a shiver down my spine.

I nodded. 'It was fine. My dad was out and I don't think Mum suspected anything.' I shrugged the backpack off my shoulders as we reached the first floor. A long corridor stretched ahead of us, doors leading off on both sides – books and bags and dirty clothes were strewn all over the carpet. 'The computer's in here.' I handed Theo the bag.

'Thanks.' He stared at me. 'I really, really appreciate you doing this.'

I looked at the floor, embarrassed, not sure what to say. Then the smaller dog ran up again, licking at my hand.

'What did you say they were called?' I said, bending down to stroke him.

'Java and Perl. They're named after computer programs. They only understand computer-speak. If you want them to fetch stuff you have to tell them to defrag it. And check this out.' Theo leaned down and picked up a pink-and-white sock that lay on top of a heap of dirty washing next to us.

'Virus. This is a virus,' he said, holding the sock out to the dogs. He threw it into the air above their heads. 'Okay. Delete the virus.'

Perl and Java leaped for the sock. Each grabbed an end in their mouth and tugged hard. In seconds the sock was torn to shreds.

'Wow,' I said, transfixed by the dogs. 'They're amazing.' It was strange. All those anxieties I'd had. And now being here with Theo just seemed like the most natural thing in the world. He turned away from the dogs and smiled at me. A warm, generous, beautiful smile.

I could feel my heart liquefying and sliding into a puddle at his feet.

'Come on,' he said, patting the bag. 'Let's take this to Max.'

I followed him along the corridor. With any luck Max would be so geeky that he'd get completely wrapped up in hacking into Dad's computer and leave me and Theo to talk.

Not that I could think of anything to say.

Not that Theo would ever, ever be interested in me.

Perl and Java raced past us, barking happily as they bounded into a room at the end of the corridor. Theo stood back to let me go past him. The room was as messy as the corridor outside. Overflowing with wires and headphones and computer games, with heaps of clothes scattered across the floor. A pair of lemon-yellow curtains fluttered at the dusty window. A hunched-over figure was sitting at the desk in the corner, mostly hidden behind two precariously balanced stacks of DVDs and mini-disks.

'Max,' Theo said. 'This is Rachel.'

The figure uncurled itself and stood up.

Close-cropped, white-blonde hair. Pale, pinched face. Long, skinny legs in tight, massively ripped jeans.

My mouth dropped open.

Max was a girl.

19

Theo

I pulled the laptop out of the bag and shoved it at Max. She took it, then just stood there, staring at Rachel.

'Max,' I muttered. Why did she have to glare like that? I knew Max so well I didn't often stop to think about how strange she must look to someone who'd never met her before, with those jeans she always wore that were more rip than denim and her stony black eyes that bored into you.

Rachel was blushing, her forehead shining with sweat.

'D'you want a drink?' I said. 'Give Max a chance to examine the hard drive.'

'Yes, thanks.' Rachel smiled shyly at me. Then she turned back to Max. 'You won't . . . I mean, the computer . . . it won't show that you've been looking or . . .'

'Course not.' Max sniffed impatiently. 'Your dad'll never know anyone's been anywhere near it.'

'But he has a password,' Rachel stammered. 'I don't know what it is. Will you . . . I mean, how are you going to get past that?'

I could see Max bristling. She hates it when people question her hacking abilities. 'If I told you I'd have to kill you,' she said, completely straight-faced.

Rachel was now looking utterly freaked out.

'Hah, hah,' I said. 'Hilarious, Max.' I raised my eyes at Rachel. 'Don't worry. Passwords are one of Max's specialities.'

Max shook her head dismissively and shunted the laptop onto the desk. 'I'm looking for emails between this Richard Smith guy and someone called Lewis. Yeah?'

I nodded, ushering Rachel towards the door. 'We'll be back in a minute,' I said.

I took Rachel downstairs to Max's kitchen. She gazed round the room, her mouth falling open at the sight of the dirty plates piled up on every surface. It was a bit of a mess. Max's mum's an artist. Spends most of her time in her studio, painting and stuff. She's not massively into housework. And I doubt if Max even knows where the washing-up liquid is kept.

I walked over to the sink and rinsed out a couple of glasses.

'Water okay?' I said.

Rachel nodded.

We sipped our drinks in silence for a few moments. Rachel was still looking around, frowning.

'How . . . er . . . how do you know Max?' she said. 'Does she go to your school?'

I laughed. 'No way. Mine's just a boys' school. Max and

I've known each other since we were at nursery. Our mums met when we were little. Max and I are . . . we're like baby friends. I mean she's a bit weird. But she's all right underneath. Like my sister or something.'

For some reason this made Rachel smile. A big smile that lit up her whole face. It was the first time I'd seen her appear anything other than worried or embarrassed. For a couple of seconds she looked really pretty. Then she blushed and dipped her head.

The doorbell rang and the dogs started barking again.

'I'll go,' I yelled, unnecessarily. Like Max or her mum would even *hear* the bell.

I strolled down the corridor and restrained Perl and Java again while I opened the door.

Jake stood on the other side. He grinned at me. 'Both your birds here, then?'

Fantastic. Jake in full-on, babe-magnet mode.

Just what I needed.

'Stop it,' I hissed. But Jake pushed past me and the two dogs and strode over to the stairs. He had come with me to visit Max several times. I was pretty sure he had a fairly big crush on her. It was always hard to tell with Jake, of course, what with his habit of fancying anything that moved. But I knew he loved the way Max was always rude to him. Sometimes I wondered what Jake would do if a girl ever actually encouraged him. Probably collapse from shock.

'Hey, Max,' Jake called up the stairs. 'Wanna game of Deathmaster Battleground later? Bet I can kick your arse at it.'

'Yeah, right.' Max's shout dripped with sarcasm. 'I'm quaking.'

Undeterred, Jake spun round and mouthed, 'Where's Rachel?' at me.

I nodded towards the kitchen. 'Be cool,' I mouthed back.

Rachel was sitting at the kitchen table – which was covered with magazines and pencil sketches and old mugs of coffee – still sipping her water.

She looked up at Jake.

'Hey there, Rachel,' he said in what I knew was his attempt at a smooth and sophisticated voice. He slipped along the bench at the table until he was sitting directly opposite her. 'Wow,' he said. 'You have really pretty eyes.'

For God's sake.

I shuddered and marched over to the sink to pour myself some more water. Rachel said nothing. Out of the corner of my eye I could see her staring down at the table. She looked embarrassed. I suddenly felt massively annoyed with Jake. It was all very well him making a prat of himself with girls we didn't know at Starbucks. But Rachel was doing me a huge favour here.

'Hey, Jake,' I said fiercely. 'Why don't you—?'

'Theo.' I looked round. Max was standing in the doorway, grinning. 'I've done it. Come and see.'

We followed Max upstairs to her room.

'Richard Smith had deleted the email but I found it on the hard drive,' Max explained. 'He used a standard one hundred and twenty-eight-bit symmetric encryption.'

I stared blankly at her.

'High end for a domestic user, but fairly straightforward.' She ran over to the computer and jiggled the mouse. 'Look.'

Rachel, Jake and I lined up next to each other, peering over her shoulder at the email on the screen.

Apollo was here. In my house. I'm sure it was him. He came in with Artemis. She said they'd met by chance. But there's no way this is a coincidence. He was asking about that time. About James Lawson.

You know how dangerous this is. We have to stop anyone finding out about Artemis.

What should I do?

The email ended by giving the false name and school I'd told to Rachel's parents.

My heart thudded. Apollo? Was that me? Why was Mr Smith referring to me by some weird code name? And what did 'that time' refer to?

'Well, *that* makes sense.' Jake snorted.

I glanced at Rachel. 'D'you understand any of it?'

Rachel shrugged. She was staring intently at the email. 'Well Apollo is obviously you. And Artemis must be me. But why? And what is there to find out about me?' She paused. 'It would help if we knew what the names meant. I mean, Apollo and Artemis are two of the Greek gods, obviously, but . . .' She bit her lip.

Max twisted round. 'Obviously,' she mouthed up at me, sarcastically.

'Gods of what?' I said, ignoring Max.

Rachel shook her head. 'I don't know.' She hesitated, like there was something on her mind she wasn't saying.

'Okay.' I took a deep breath. 'Well, we can look up about the gods on the internet. But maybe the whole thing will make sense if we know who your dad was sending the email to. Who this Lewis is.'

'I already checked that out,' Max said. 'The recipient's email address is masked but I've got the header. Lewis Michael. He's working out of an ordinary domestic account. But I ran a check on the name and I'm almost sure he's connected to this organisation called RAGE. Quite a high-ranking member, I reckon. Does that help?'

My mind flickered back to the newspaper report I'd found on the internet at the library. RAGE. The Righteous Army against Genetic Engineering. The same group who'd blown up the clinic where Dad worked. Who'd killed nine people and sent Dad into hiding.

'What is it, Theo?' Rachel said.

I caught Jake's eye. I could see he was remembering the newspaper article too.

'RAGE is this extreme group that's against genetic research,' I said. 'This extremely violent group. They blew up that clinic your dad and mine both worked in.'

'But why's my dad emailing them?' Rachel frowned at me. I saw this awful look of realisation dawn in her eyes. 'You don't think he's . . .? He couldn't be.'

Long pause.

'He wasn't there that day. At the clinic.' My voice sounded strained.

The whole world seemed to shrink to Rachel's horrified eyes. Like we both knew the truth and neither of us wanted to face it.

But we had to.

'Your dad was the only person who worked at the clinic who survived the firebomb without becoming a RAGE target,' I said flatly.

'That doesn't mean . . .' Rachel's eyes widened. 'You can't be saying my dad was involved in killing all those people?'

I looked at a spot on the wall next to her face.

'But *your* dad was there,' she whispered. 'You're saying my dad killed your dad.'

There was a horrible silence. I knew Rachel was staring at me. I couldn't meet her eyes.

Then Jake put his arm round her shoulders.

'No way, babe,' he said cheerfully. 'Didn't Theo tell you? His dad's still alive.'

20

Rachel

I couldn't take it in. I stood there stupidly, my mouth open, just staring up at Theo. 'Your dad isn't dead?' I said.

His face went red. He wouldn't look at me. Couldn't look at me.

I dimly registered his friend Jake's hand resting lightly on my shoulder.

My attention was mostly on what Theo had just said, my mind ricochetting between the news that his dad – James Lawson – was alive and the suggestion that my dad could have ever, ever have had anything to do with blowing up that clinic.

But a part of my mind was horribly aware of the hand too. It felt awkward and wrong and embarrassing, just like it had when Jake had stared at me in the kitchen, earlier.

I shrank my arm down a little. The hand dropped away.

Theo slowly met my eyes and I knew. He'd lied to me. I'd stolen Dad's laptop and let his stupid weirdo hacker friend get all over it like a rash. I'd even put up with her staring at me like I was a bit of dirt.

And Theo had lied to me.

It didn't really matter what about or why. I could feel the itchy tingling of tears behind my eyes and nose. I grabbed the laptop and strode out of the room, down to the front door. I pulled it open and started running along the pavement. I'd left my backpack behind, but right then I didn't care. I felt so stupid for trusting Theo. I just wanted to get as far away from him as possible.

I could hear footsteps pounding after me. 'Rachel.' His hand grabbed my arm and pulled me round. 'Rachel. Please don't go.'

I stood, staring down at the pavement. My throat felt tight.

'I'm sorry I didn't tell you. I'm sorry.' Theo shuffled his feet. He let go of my arm. 'And I'm sorry Max was rude and Jake was an idiot and that somehow your dad's mixed up in—'

'My dad didn't do anything,' I snapped, blinking away my tears. But I couldn't be sure of that. My mind went back to the text Dad had sent me by mistake. GODDESS STILL IN HEAVEN. Was that somehow connected to the email with all the Greek god names?

Theo held up his hands, palms out. 'Okay,' he said. 'Maybe your dad didn't do anything bad to the clinic. But he definitely knew my dad, and he lied to both of us about that. Didn't he?'

I looked up at him.

That was true.

'Please come back inside,' Theo said. 'Let me tell you everything.'

Mum and Dad were out when I got home. I was relieved. I needed time to think, not have Mum wittering on in my ear about why I'd been shopping all day and come home empty-handed. And, of course, I needed to put Dad's laptop back. I slipped into his office and left it where I'd found it that morning. Then I lay down on my bed and closed my eyes.

It felt like a zillion different thoughts and feelings were careering about inside my head. I took a few deep breaths, trying to work it all out.

I'd forgiven Theo for lying to me about his dad before we'd even got back inside Max's house. He looked so miserable about upsetting me – his eyes all dark and sad.

I love his eyes. They're the sort of eyes you could totally fall into. Fall and keep falling.

Stop it. Focus, Rachel.

So. What else did I know? Everything Theo did. And I'd told him everything too – including about the text my dad had sent me by mistake. None of it made sense to either of us. My dad knew Theo's dad. And, for some reason, he was in touch with the bunch of lunatics who blew up the clinic where they'd both worked.

I sighed. Whichever way I looked at it, it was impossible to understand. I know Dad didn't approve of some of the genetic research that had been done at the clinic. That was clear from that newspaper report Theo told me about. But the idea that he felt strongly enough to murder people over it. No. No way. Dad was too conventional. Too normal. He had a job and a house and went to dinner-dances at the tennis club.

Anyway. He couldn't be a murderer. He just couldn't.

He was my dad.

I went over the email again. It was like a jigsaw with pieces missing: we'd found out that 'Apollo' was a sun god and 'Artemis' was a goddess – a hunter. But it didn't make anything clearer.

'Sweetie?'

I jumped as the door swung open and Mum's fixed blonde helmet of hair appeared. She clucked at me.

'Tired out from shopping?' she cooed. 'What did you get?'

'Mmmn,' I grunted. 'Didn't find anything I liked, actually.'

Mum's face fell. Or would have done, if it hadn't been artificially held in place by her latest face-lift. 'Oh, sweetie. I hoped you'd find something nice for that disco.' She raised her eyes. 'Shame Theo won't be going with you.'

She giggled. I swear, she giggled. I turned away, my face reddening. I'd forgotten about the school disco. It was less than a week away now – Friday evening. It suddenly occurred to me that Mum might not be the only person who assumed I would want to go with Theo.

Now I had another thing to worry about. *Honestly.* Why did life have to get so complicated?

I decided that as soon as I got to school on Monday I would somehow make it clear I was busy on the night of the school disco, before anyone could make out my decision had anything to do with Theo.

But, as usual, Jemima was way ahead of me.

Monday. The last day of November. Dad had left on a business trip to Germany that morning. For some reason I'd started working in class again. I hadn't meant to. I just found myself copying down stuff without realising it. Not that I was concentrating very much. I spent most of my time thinking about Theo. I was thinking about him when the bell rang for short break. I walked outside. It was freezing cold and everyone was huddled in groups, just trying to keep warm.

As I wandered across the playground I saw Jemima and her friends standing around in a giggling cluster, a couple of metres away. I scurried past them, intending to find a quiet patch of wall round the side of the school, where I could be by myself.

Someone grabbed my hair from behind. Yanked me backwards.

'OW!' I tried to turn round. Bodies pressed in on me from all sides. My chest tightened.

Jemima's face appeared in front of me, her eyes all narrow and mean. She glanced over my shoulder at whoever was tugging on my hair.

'Nice takedown, Phoebs.'

'Let me go,' I stammered.

'*Ooooh.*' The girls around me giggled.

'So. You know if you're a virgin yet?' Jemima sneered.

I looked down at my shoes. My heart pounded against my ribs.

'You see, I think you were lying about that boy,' Jemima said. 'I think you made up about him being your boyfriend just so you'd look like you weren't the total loser you in fact are.'

I blushed. Trust Jemima. This wasn't fair. I'd only hinted about Theo and me.

'I didn't say he was my boyfriend.'

Jemima pounced on this like a cat, her pointy face gleaming with delight. 'So he isn't then?' she said triumphantly.

I paused, unsure what to do. If I said Theo and I weren't going out now, I'd look unbelievably stupid. But if I said we were – and any of them ever found out . . .

'I know why you made it up,' Jemima said slowly. 'My mum told me you had a sister who came here years ago. Really pretty and popular. I bet *she* had a boyfriend in Year Ten.'

I stared at her, horror-struck. Jemima knew about Rebecca? Wasn't it bad enough to have Mum and Dad and the teachers talking about her all the time? Now everyone in my class would know how useless I was compared to her too.

I took a deep breath.

'Actually he *is* my boyfriend.' I stared Jemima in the eye. 'I saw him on Saturday. We were together all day.'

For a second, Jemima looked shocked. Like she wasn't really sure whether or not to believe me.

'Oh yeah? How far d'you go then?'

The girls around us sniggered. Then there was an expectant pause. They were all looking at me. I could feel Phoebe behind me, still tugging at my hair.

Jemima curled her lip. Any second now she'd start in on how I was making it all up again. I had to say something. Something convincing.

'We went to his friend's house . . .' I hesitated, my heart racing. No way could I add any imaginary details. 'We just did . . . stuff.'

Jemima snorted. 'You don't even know what people do, do you? Which isn't surprising. Who'd want to touch you? Ugh.' She screwed up her face. Phoebe laughed loudly behind me. I could feel her grip on my hair loosening.

'Actually he does want to . . . with me,' I said. It didn't sound like my voice speaking.

'Yeah right.' Jemima's eyes narrowed. 'You're making it up.'

My heart was beating so fast I thought it might explode. But it was too late to take back what I'd said now. 'No, I'm not.'

Jemima folded her arms and grinned nastily. 'Mmmn,' she said. 'We'll see at the disco, won't we? On Friday.'

Oh, God.

I guess I should have just come right out then and said I wasn't going to the stupid disco. That Theo and I were going to the movies instead, or something. But as I looked into Jemima's eyes I knew that was exactly what she was expecting me to say. And that she wouldn't believe a word of it.

'Yes,' I said, my face burning. 'You'll see on Friday.'

Jemima's mouth twitched with annoyance. She hadn't expected me to call her bluff. 'Fine,' she spat. 'Hey. I bet your sister didn't have to make up stories about having a boyfriend.'

Sniggers and giggles.

'Anyway, he's gonna dump you way before Friday.'

More sniggers. More giggles.

My eyes filled with tears. I tore away from Phoebe's loose grasp and pushed through the girls surrounding me. I ran hard across the playground, the tarmac blurring in front of me, the sound of sneering laughter ringing in my ears.

I'd just made things worse. Jemima still didn't believe Theo liked me. Which meant nobody did. And now I'd more or less staked the proof of it on whether or not Theo came to the school disco. Which he wouldn't. *Stupid, stupid.* I was going to look a total idiot.

Unless . . . unless there was some way I could get him to come.

21

Theo

I didn't speak to Jake for two days. I was too angry at him for telling Rachel about my dad being alive. I'd ended up explaining everything to her. She knew as much as I did now – more than Max and Jake, even. I felt I owed it to her to be honest, but I didn't like it. I really didn't like how it felt – trusting her with all that information.

Eventually I got bored of not talking to Jake. I went up to him at break on Tuesday and joined in his football game. We had to talk then, about passing the ball and stuff. So it was natural to just keep on talking afterwards.

He kept nagging me to organise another Saturday with Rachel and Max.

I didn't like that either. I mean, I'd expected him to bore on about Max. After all, he'd spent most of Saturday afternoon being beaten by her at Deathmaster Battleground. Grinning like an idiot while she insulted him.

But Jake kept talking about Rachel. 'I think she liked me,'

he said as we changed after games on Tuesday afternoon. 'Up for a snog anyway. Definitely.'

Rachel? I frowned. Max could look after herself, but the idea of Jake hassling Rachel for a kiss annoyed me. She was too shy. Too easily upset about everything.

I tugged my shirt on and started buttoning it up. 'You only think she likes you because she didn't tell you to piss right off,' I said. 'I don't want you stirring things up.'

'Then I'll go for Max.' He grinned. 'Don't you see? Between us we can't lose.'

'I didn't mean it like that,' I snapped. 'I'm not interested in either of them.'

It was true. I never thought about Max like that. And Rachel. Well. Rachel wasn't the sort of person you'd fancy.

'So who *are* you interested in outside of chicks in magazines and bands?' Jake rolled his eyes. 'D'you even *like* real girls?'

'Of course I do,' I said.

I did too. I'd got off with quite a few girls in the past year – at parties mostly, while Roy waited outside the front door. It was easy. You talk for a bit. Get into a snog. Go as far as they'll let you. Move on to the next one.

No problem.

'They're not creatures from another planet, you know.' Jake stared at me thoughtfully as he did up his tie. Then he grinned. 'Though Max is kind of weird. How come she knows all that stuff about encryptions and network protocols?'

I grinned back. 'She taught herself mostly. She's obsessed. Never does any schoolwork.'

'Good thing for you now.' Jake picked up his bag and slung it over his shoulder. 'Without her you wouldn't know about Rachel's dad. Or what he's going to do next.'

The smile slid off my face as I trudged after Jake to the main school exit, where Roy was waiting to take me home.

I'd been trying not to think about what Rachel's dad would do next. I knew it depended on how that guy, Lewis Michael, from RAGE replied to his email. Max had put some kind of blind copy trace on Rachel's dad's email address, which meant that if Lewis Michael responded, Max would see it.

I wanted to know. Of course I did. But at the same time I was scared. If RAGE knew I was James Lawson's son, I wasn't sure what they'd do.

Rachel had promised not to tell her dad any of the details that might lead them to me – like my real address or my actual school. My stomach clenched whenever I thought that my safety might depend on her keeping that promise.

Max phoned that night, about an hour after I'd got home from school. Her voice sounded strained. 'You'd better come round straight away,' she said.

I called Jake. It was only fair, I figured. Anyway, Rachel wasn't going to be there. We got to Max's house at just after six. As usual, Roy did a check round the ground floor for open windows and doors, then retreated into the front room with his paper. Max led Jake and me straight up to her room.

'Lewis Michael sent this to Rachel's dad this morning,' she said. 'It's kind of creepy, Theo.'

Zeus didn't send Apollo and He isn't pleased. Especially that you just let the boy go. When you're back from your trip, find out how much Artemis knows but don't make her suspicious. Zeus wants to keep it low key, not even telling Leto.

So long as Simpson doesn't know, all we have to worry about is shutting Apollo up, and Zeus is working out a way to do that – permanently. We'll make a move at the weekend.

The temperature in the room seemed to drop several degrees. I was Apollo and RAGE wanted to shut me up. Permanently. What did that mean? It didn't sound like it had anything to do with getting at my dad. It sounded like they wanted to kill me.

The same people who were after my dad, were coming for me. And by going to Mr Smith I'd walked straight into their hands.

My heart raced. It suddenly hit me how stupid I'd been. Mum had warned me, over and over, that I had to stay hidden. Why hadn't I listened to her?

I turned away from the screen to find Max and Jake both staring at me.

'Guess I'm not exactly Mr Popular.' I attempted a weak smile.

'What you gonna do, dude?' Jake said. His face was pale.

'I'll be okay,' I said, more confidently than I felt. 'I've got Roy, haven't I? And Mr Smith doesn't know where I live. I lied about everything – surname, school, address. Everything. I'll call Rachel – make extra sure she doesn't tell him the—'

'Like your pathetic lies are going to stop him finding out.' Max snorted. 'Theo, I think you should tell your mum what's going on.'

I imagined the conversation. Mum would be angry. And then upset. But most of all she would be scared. So scared she would probably never let me outside the house again. And she'd hire a new bodyguard. Three probably. Or else she'd insist we moved house. Immediately. Out of London. Maybe even out of the country.

I closed my eyes. I didn't want to tell her, but what choice did I have? This whole thing had got way, way too big for me to handle on my own now.

'Hey, Theo.' I opened my eyes. Jake was studying the email again. 'What d'you think this Apollo stuff's about?'

'It's their code name for James Lawson's son. Me.'

'I know.' Jake frowned. 'But why? I mean, I didn't think about it before, but Mr Smith mentioned James Lawson by name in that first email. And Simpson – whoever he is – here. So why use a code name for you and this Zeus guy? It doesn't make sense.'

I stared at the screen. Max had brought up the original email so that it was side by side with the second. Jake was right.

'And why use another Greek god's name for Rachel?' I said.

'Goddess,' Max said. 'Artemis was a goddess, remember?'

I nodded impatiently. 'It's too weird for me,' I said. 'How about we play Deathmaster Battleground? Three-player game?'

I didn't really want to play. I just wanted a few minutes to think, without Max and Jake looking at me like I was on the endangered species list. We started playing. I could tell Max wasn't really concentrating, but she still beat me and Jake so easily when we were all playing separately that after a few rounds Jake and I teamed up.

It didn't make much difference.

'Move your Secret Scyther,' Jake yelled. 'Theo. Move your . . . Oh, for God's sake, dude . . .' He threw his controller onto the floor.

'Sorry.' I stood up. 'Play without me. I need a pee anyway.'

I went down the corridor to Max's bathroom. It was piled high with dirty clothing. I sat on the side of the bath and looked down at my hands.

They were shaking.

This helix of panic whirled up through my chest into my throat.

We have to shut him up – permanently.

This was real. This was what my dad had been living with for years.

I thought about Roy downstairs. For the first time in my

107

life I was glad I had a bodyguard. I wondered if my dad had one.

I ran my hand through my hair. And it struck me. *Of course.* Suddenly I knew what I had to do next.

I strode back towards Max's room.

'You're the best girl I've ever met at this game,' Jake was saying in his 'smooth' voice.

I stopped in the doorway.

Jake had shuffled sideways across the carpet towards Max. He was smiling hopefully at her.

Max shot him a withering look. 'I should think I'm the best *person* you've ever met at this game,' she said. 'Being a girl's got nothing to do with it.'

'I'm going,' I said. Part of me wanted to tell them what I'd decided. Only a small part, though.

Jake and Max looked up from the floor.

'You okay, dude?' Jake said.

I nodded. 'I'm gonna go home. Think about what to say to Mum. D'you want a lift, Jake?'

He gave me a half-smile. 'Nah,' he said. 'I'm cool here.'

Max raised her eyes. 'So you don't mind being beaten by a girl then?' She sniffed contemptuously. 'Hardly anyone realises it, but women are actually naturally much better at computer games than men. And at hacking. Plus women hackers use what they do responsibly. Not like all those jerks who introduce viruses to screw up people's lives and steal money . . .'

I wandered back down the corridor. Roy drove me home in

silence. As soon as I got there, I took the cordless up to my room and punched in the number. My chest tightened as I heard her voice on the other end.

'Rachel?' I said. 'I need your help.'

22

Rachel

Theo's voice was low and intense, like something big was wrong.

'What's the matter?' I said, shutting my bedroom door.

'The guy from RAGE sent your dad an email.'

He explained what the email said. I sank onto my bed. This wasn't real. It couldn't be. Dad couldn't want to hurt Theo. Theo hadn't done anything.

'What are you going to do?' My voice was coming out all weird and hoarse.

There was a pause.

'Theo?'

He sighed. 'What I *should* do is tell my mum. But I can't. I just can't. She'll completely freak. And then she'll probably make us move away.'

'Oh.' There was so much I wanted to say. How I didn't want him to go away. How I was scared of what might happen to him if he didn't. How just the sound of his voice made my stomach twist into knots.

'So I'm going to find my dad,' Theo said.

What?

'But . . . but you don't know where he is,' I stammered.

'I know.' Theo sighed again. 'That's what I wanted to talk to you about. I'm planning to go tomorrow morning, after register. I'll go out over the wall at the back of school. I've done it before. If I'm not seen, I should have a few hours before anyone realises I've gone. But I need your help.'

'How? What?'

'I need you to go through your dad's stuff tonight. We know there isn't anything on the laptop apart from that email. And you said he'd got rid of his secret phone. But your dad has a PC too, doesn't he? And paper files? Maybe you could find something else about James Lawson there. Something that might help me work out where he is now.'

A million objections flooded into my head. If I was caught I'd be in massive trouble. Plus there was no way I could access the deleted files on Dad's hard drive. Not without Max's help. And I didn't even know where the key was for his filing cabinet.

'I'm going to go through my mum's paper stuff tonight,' Theo said. 'See what I can find. She said there wasn't anything. But maybe there's something she's forgotten she kept.'

He sounded desperate and my heart went out to him. But what he was suggesting – both the looking for information and the running away – was madness.

'Why don't you think about it for a bit?' I stammered. 'Maybe in the—'

'I can't wait,' he snapped. 'Don't you understand? RAGE are going to . . . to . . .' He tailed off.

I gulped. 'I do understand,' I said. 'But my dad's away at some conference in Germany this week. That's why that email says: *when you're back from your trip*. And . . . and there's that other bit about them moving at the weekend. It doesn't sound like they're coming after you *now*. You've got a few days to plan this through. Don't you see?'

There was silence on the other end of the phone.

'Theo?' I said.

'When's your dad back exactly?' Theo said.

'Saturday morning,' I said. An idea began to swim up through my mind. 'You know it's going to take me a few days to go through all my dad's stuff as well.' I stood up and paced across the room. 'I mean he's got loads of paper files and I won't get a chance to look at them until Mum's gone to sleep.' I leaned against my bedroom wall and looked out of the window. It was raining and the street lamp outside was flickering.

I don't want you to go away.

'Okay,' Theo said slowly. 'I guess a few days won't make any difference. It'll give me more time too. I've got to get all my money out of this building society account Mum set up for me. I've got a card and stuff – she gave it to me for emergencies, like if anything happened to her. But you can only take small amounts out a day. And I'm going to need as much as I can get.'

'I'll get you some money too,' I said quickly. 'You can have my allowance. I've been saving it up for months.'

'Um . . . No. I couldn't do that.' He sounded embarrassed.

'Yes you could. I'll meet you on Friday. After school.' I took a deep breath. 'In fact, that gives me another idea.' I was lying, of course. This was where I'd been heading all along. 'It's my school disco on Friday. You could come with me.'

There. I'd said it. I'd asked him.

'How does that help me get away from here?' Theo sounded confused.

'It goes on for three hours. You could come. Stay for half an hour. It'll be really crowded, so Roy won't be able to watch you all the time. There's this way out the back. I could show you. And the school's right next to the station. If we time it right you'd be on a train before Roy even realises you've gone.'

'Well,' Theo said slowly. 'I don't know.'

'Don't you see? It'll be dark – that'll help you get away. And there's less chance of anyone spotting you leaving. In fact, apart from Roy, why would anyone care if you did? No one at my school knows who you are.'

My heart was thumping. Everything I said was true. And yet it was all based on a lie. I wanted Theo to come to the disco to show Jemima and her friends we were together. I chewed on my lip, feeling guilty. Still, once I saw him face to face I'd be able to talk to him. Show him that running away and trying to find his dad was hopeless. And dangerous.

'Okay,' Theo said. 'What time does it start?'

23

Theo

'You're going to her school disco?' Jake said, enviously, the next day. 'At a girls' school? Can't I come too?'

'No.' I sounded angrier than I meant to. The wait was getting to me. Plus I was tired. I'd spent half the night rummaging through three huge cardboard boxes of Mum's that I'd lugged out of our living-room cupboard.

Jake slunk off to our next class without me.

I shoved my hands in my pocket and pulled out the leaflet I'd found halfway down the third box. It was a little brochure for the Assisted Conception and Research Centre. It didn't tell me much more than the original newspaper article had – just some stuff about how high their IVF success rate was and loads of bull on the owner: the Gene Genie himself, Elijah Lazio. It didn't mention James Lawson.

The only other information I'd found was a bundle of newspaper cuttings about Lazio's cloning claims. None of these were connected to either James Lawson or the fertility clinic.

I'd tried talking to Mum again. It was hopeless. She refused to discuss any aspect of my early life or my dad.

'I would never have told you he was alive if I thought you'd keep pestering me for information like this,' she said. 'You have to be patient, Theodore. One day your dad will be able to see you, but not yet.'

'Does he know I know about him?' I said.

Mum rolled her eyes. 'I'm not talking about it.'

'Okay.' I ran my hand through my hair. 'Just tell me if he's still working. You know, at a clinic. Doing his research stuff.'

Mum smiled at me. 'He'd rather be dead than not working.'

'So he's at a clinic, then?'

'Theodore, I've told you . . .'

'Just tell me which country, Mum.' I stared at her, trying to look as appealing as possible. 'Please. Then I promise I'll stop asking questions.'

Mum sighed.

'Come on, Mum,' I pleaded. 'If I knew even roughly where he was it would help me to deal with all this. Please.'

She stared at me. 'He's in Germany,' she said flatly. 'Okay?'

I stared at her, my heart pounding. Hadn't Rachel said her dad was at a conference in Germany? Surely that couldn't be a coincidence. Maybe he was on my dad's trail. A thrill of excitement shot through me. Now I had a plan. Some direction. I'd find out which town Mr Smith had gone to. Take the train there. Eurostar to Brussels. Then change to get to

115

Germany. Then I'd just go round all the fertility and genetic research clinics in whatever town it was until I found Dad.

I rushed upstairs to my room and dug out the photograph – the only picture I had of him. He was wearing a white, open-necked shirt and smiling. I stared at his face. His hair was dark and short and he had a dimple in his chin. I looked up in the mirror. I touched my own chin. No dimple. I'd always wished I looked more like him. But now it didn't matter. We had more important things in common.

The need to find him, to know him, was like this heavy weight in my chest. I felt a stab of anger at the people behind RAGE – especially Rachel's dad and that Lewis Michael guy. They had tried to kill Dad twice, forcing him to live apart from me and Mum. What had Mum said? *He sees himself as a soldier, though not in any conventional army.* Well I was going to be a soldier too. Fighting against RAGE's bigotry.

Fighting side by side with my dad.

24

Rachel

If I hadn't been so wound up about it myself, it would have made me laugh. Everyone at school was making out the school disco was going to be totally stupid. Yet by Wednesday lunchtime it was all anyone was talking about. Jemima kept on with these references to me and Theo all day. I knew what she was doing. She was making sure no one forgot I'd said I had a boyfriend, so that when he didn't turn up she could totally humiliate me.

On Wednesday evening Theo called to find out where my dad was in Germany. I told him: Cologne. Theo seemed to think that his dad was there too, working undercover in some genetic research clinic. He was more determined to run off than ever. Nothing I said made any difference.

I told myself it didn't matter, that I'd be able to convince him not to go, once we were face to face.

I spent the rest of the evening trying on clothes. Then Thursday evening trying them all on again. It was useless. I looked like a big blob in everything. In the end I decided to wear this knee-length blue skirt I'd had for a while. My bum was just too massive for trousers. I tried on every single top I owned with it. The only one I felt comfortable in was this big white smocky thing that covered me up completely.

Unfortunately, it made me look like a tent. No way could I wear it.

I still hadn't chosen a replacement by six-thirty p.m. on Friday evening. Every centimetre of my bedroom carpet was covered with clothes. I was starting to panic. I was supposed to be meeting Theo outside my school at seven o'clock and I needed to allow ten minutes at least to walk up there.

I shut my eyes and reached round on the carpet. *Please, please, let there be something here that I can wear.*

My fingers clutched at something silky. I opened my eyes. It was a black blouse. Short-sleeved, with buttons up the front. I pulled it on and turned to face the mirror. The shirt was fairly loose, though shaped in a little at the waist. At least it covered up the top of my stomach. I checked the time. 6.38 p.m. It would have to do.

I sped into the bathroom and cleaned my teeth. *How had I left so little time for my make-up and hair?*

I smeared on some eyeshadow, then carefully slid Mum's La Prairie mascara out of her make-up basket. She hates me borrowing her make-up – but it's good stuff. All designer. And I needed all the help I could get.

I stroked on some mascara, then placed the tube back exactly where I'd found it. I dabbed some of Mum's powder over my nose.

My face stared back at me from the mirror – anxious and ugly.

6.46.

I noticed a little arrow-shaped diamante hairgrip beside the sink and rammed it into the side of my hair. I tucked my hair over it, so the glittery bit didn't show up so much.

6.47.

I had to go.

I ran out of the bathroom and back to my bedroom. I grabbed the money I'd got out of my account the day before. I was still intending to talk Theo out of his mad attempt to find his dad, but I wanted him to know I'd meant what I'd said about giving him money.

I turned to leave. Then noticed my bare feet.

Oh, God.

Shoes.

I pounded over to my wardrobe. Trainers. Slippers. School shoes. Flat sandals. No, no, no and no.

I bent down and started hauling shoes over my shoulder, desperately trying to find something that would look nice.

6.51.

Suppose Theo got there before I did. Suppose Jemima saw him and started talking to him.

I pulled out a pair of black high-heels that Mum had bought me a few months ago. 'Elegant shoes,' she'd said. 'For special occasions.'

They were a bit grown-up at the front, but the heels were high and thin. I shoved them on my feet and stood up. I wasn't used to being three inches taller than normal. I walked across the clothes still strewn over the floor, onto the landing.

6.52.

I knew I was walking awkwardly, but there was no time to change the shoes. I took a deep breath and tottered downstairs, holding on to the stair rail to steady myself.

Mum was waiting in the hallway as I reached the front door.

I grabbed my coat and glanced up at her. 'See you later.'

'Have a nice time,' she said. She paused, her eyes flickering up and down my outfit.

How do I look?

I should have just gone, but I hesitated, really wanting her to say something encouraging about my appearance.

'Very nice.' She pursed her lips. 'Though a bit shop-girlish. I thought you . . .'

But I didn't wait to hear what she thought. I tore through the front door and up the road, walking as fast as my heels would let me, sniffing back the tears that threatened to smear mascara all down my cheek.

I just had time to catch my breath and put on a slash of lip gloss outside the busy school gates before Theo turned up. He was in jeans and a thick jacket, a backpack over his shoulder.

I stared at his face as he walked towards me, soaking up the shape of it, the way his hair fell round it, how perfect it was. He smiled at me.

I forgot that it was cold and my breath was misting in front of me. I forgot that there were people all around us, swarming in through the gates. I forgot everything except his face. I smiled back.

'Okay?' he said. I could see the anxiety behind his eyes. 'This is Roy. Remember?'

I shifted my gaze slightly to the right. The thickset guy who I'd seen peering through the window at Max's house was there. Theo's bodyguard. Standing right next to him.

I hadn't even noticed.

'Hi,' I said.

Roy nodded grumpily at me.

There was a pause. Theo appeared to be waiting for me to do something. Of course.

'Er . . . down here.' I led him and Roy through the gates.

My heart was pounding as we walked inside the school building. I wondered if Jemima was here yet.

The entrance hall was crackling with excitement. Nearest to us were several groups of boys, mainly from Princedale's I assumed, standing in line to show the teacher at the desk their invitations. Most of them were mucking about, shoving each other or else chatting loudly with their hands in their pockets – but I could see their eyes darting everywhere.

I looked round myself. *Oh God.*

I was *so* wearing the wrong clothes. Further inside the entrance hall, loads of girls were shrugging off their jackets, all talking at the tops of their voices. Most of them were wearing short skirts and really clingy tops. A few were in jeans – but they had the tightest tops of all – either cropped above the stomach, or low cut over their boobs. And they were almost all in high, clumpy shoes and wearing masses of make-up.

My stomach churned. Everything I had on was completely wrong. I glanced at Theo. He was staring open-mouthed at the girls across the hallway. Humiliation burned my cheeks.

Roy caught my eye. He dug Theo in the ribs with his elbow.

Theo jumped. Then blushed.

'Where's *your* invitation?' Roy said to him, roughly.

I pulled the one I'd taken for Theo out of my pocket and handed it to him. 'You better queue to sign in,' I said. 'I'll see you in the Assembly Hall.'

I shuffled off to the back of the entrance hall. I had to con-centrate really hard on walking so as not to fall over in my shoes on the slippy tile floor. I left my coat on while I walked down to the Assembly Hall. I wanted to put off being seen in my clothes for as long as possible.

Thankfully the Assembly Hall had an unslippery wooden floor. And it was darker in here than out in the corridor, just a few soft, yellow wall lights round the sides of the room, and flashing lights near the sound system. The DJ – this young black guy – was chatting away over the low beat of the first dance track. The rest of the room was clear, with chairs pushed back against the walls and a long table at the end, serving drinks. Someone had strung several rows of twisted paper streamers along the two long walls. You could almost taste the excitement in the room.

I felt my coat being wrenched off my shoulders. Falling to the floor.

'Oh. My. God. She looks like one of the teachers,' Jemima snorted.

I spun round.

She was standing in front of me – the same height as me for once, thanks to my heels. But just as evil-looking as usual, with Phoebe and Amy on either side of her.

'I saw your boyfriend earlier,' Jemima said sarcastically. 'Not exactly into you, is he?'

I stared at her. She looked amazing. Her hair was all swept up off a perfectly made-up face. And she was wearing an extremely short, tight, black dress that dipped at the front seam into a low V-shape.

'Well?' Jemima sneered at me. 'Has he gone off with someone else already?'

Phoebe and Amy laughed.

'He's just signing in,' I said, my heart hammering. 'He'll be here any second.'

At that moment the volume of the music rose dramatically and coloured lights started flashing across the room.

'Let's dance.' Jemima pointed Phoebe and Amy towards the sound system.

As they strutted past me towards the centre of the room, Jemima leaned across. 'I'll be watching,' she leered.

I bent down for my coat. The hall was already full of girls. Hordes of boys were now swarming in through the only open door. I folded my coat and shoved it under a chair. I stood

123

alone for a few minutes, watching Jemima, Phoebe and Amy dancing. I noticed most of the boys coming into the hall were watching them too.

And then I saw Theo, his backpack hanging from his arm. He'd taken off his jacket and was wearing that long-sleeved top he'd had on the first time I'd met him. The one with the tiny writing on the chest. He was too far away and it was way too dark for me to read what it said. But I remembered. *Just try it.*

Theo was looking round for me. I walked over.

We stared at each other for an awkward second. I wondered if Jemima was watching us.

'Where's Roy?' I said.

Theo's face relaxed a little. 'Outside. Your headteacher wouldn't let him in here – said there were plenty of adults as it was.'

I looked round the room, noticing five or six teachers for the first time.

'She also said no one could get into this room except through that door back out to the corridor,' Theo added. 'How am I going to get out of here if the other doors are locked?'

Oh, no. I'd been so fixated on what I was wearing and on Jemima seeing me and Theo together, that I'd forgotten all about Theo's main reason for being here.

How I'd told him I would help him.

And how I'd told myself I would try and talk him out of running away.

25

Theo

Rachel led me through the big hall. She pointed at the huge iron fire-escape door in the far wall. A stern-looking middle-aged woman was standing beside it.

'It's only bolted on the inside.' Rachel sounded nervous. Jittery. 'They'll probably open it later,' she said. 'They did at the disco last term, to let some air in.'

I stared at her. Last term would have been the middle of summer. It was hardly going to get as hot as that tonight, and certainly not in the next half an hour.

Rachel gazed up at me, clearly seeing the doubt in my face. 'If they don't, I'll just cause a distraction so you can pull the bolts and push it open. The door's noisy, but it's noisier in here.

It was true. The dance music was pounding away in my ears. I looked over at all the people dancing. I'd been to quite a few of these things before, but always with my friends. I'd never actually been to one *with* a girl before.

Not that this was a date.

I glanced down at Rachel. She looked nice. Not sexy like some of the girls here, but nice. And really quite easy to talk to. She seemed taller somehow. And I could see more of her face than usual, so she didn't look quite so hidden away.

She was looking out at the dancers, chewing on her lip. I followed her gaze to this fit blonde girl in a tight black dress. I vaguely remembered her from the first time I'd met Rachel. She had a pretty, pointy face and was gazing at Rachel, a mean expression in her eyes. She glanced across at me and raised her eyebrows.

I looked down, embarrassed that the girl had caught me staring at her. Rachel shuffled uneasily beside me.

'Look, Theo,' she stammered. 'I've been thinking. Maybe going after your dad's not the best idea. I mean, going to Germany and looking round fertility and research clinics on the off-chance he'll be working secretly in one. You've got to admit, it's a bit mad.'

I gritted my teeth. *Jesus*. The last thing I needed was somebody trying to talk me out of this. I was scared enough as it was.

'It's not Germany,' I said crossly. 'It's Cologne. A specific place. Anyway, I already know my dad's working in a clinic, from my Mum. *And* I know what he looks like.'

I moved away from her and sat down on one of the chairs against the wall. The picture of my dad, along with my passport, some spare clothes and a list of fertility and research clinics in Cologne that I'd got off the internet were all in my backpack. It was wedged under a nearby seat, next to Rachel's

126

coat. I'd left my jacket in the entrance hall cloakroom so that Roy wouldn't get suspicious. I'd have to do without it later.

My money – all seven hundred pounds of Mum's emergency fund – was tightly folded in my jeans pocket. I hadn't felt guilty about taking it out. After all, my dad had probably given it to her. And I was only using it to get back to him. I rubbed my sweaty palms down my jeans.

Rachel sat down beside me.

'Sorry,' she said hesitantly, not meeting my eyes. 'I was just worried about . . . about what was going to happen to you.'

I gazed out at the disco. There were groups of girls dancing everywhere, mostly giggling at the gangs of boys hanging round the edges of the dance floor. It struck me that there were relatively few couples in the room. There were some – dancing or chatting or snogging in chairs. But most people were definitely not with anyone. Yet.

Jake's parting words about Rachel went through my head. 'You might as well make a move on her, dude,' he'd said. 'Seeing as everyone else thinks you're her boyfriend already.'

What did he know about anything?

I checked my watch. Only seven-fifteen. Another fifteen minutes and I would leave. I was really nervous now. I just wanted to get going.

'Theo?'

I looked round. Rachel was holding out her mobile to me.

'Take it,' she said. 'You might need to be able to make a call. I've got some money for you as well.' She fished in her skirt pocket and pulled out a folded bundle of notes. 'One hundred and fifty quid. I've been saving up for ages.'

How amazing was that? She was offering me a phone and masses of cash. I frowned, feeling guilty for snapping at her earlier.

'I can't . . .'

'You'll need them.' She shoved the phone and the money into my palm. Her hand rested on mine for just a fraction, then she pulled it away.

Part of me wanted to give the mobile and the cash straight back. It wasn't fair, her helping me out like this. But on the other hand, it could take me ages to find my dad. I had the addresses of a couple of youth hostels in Cologne, but the more money I had, the safer I'd feel.

I pushed the money and the phone into my own pocket. 'Thanks,' I said. 'It's a loan. Okay?'

She nodded, staring out at the dancers again.

'I'm sorry I was rude,' I said. 'I'm just a bit freaked by everything.'

Rachel nodded again. She half turned back to me, not meeting my eyes. 'D'you want to dance?' she said.

What? God, no. 'Er . . .'

'It's okay.' She glanced away. 'I just thought, as you've got a few minutes . . .'

I gulped. 'Do you? Want to dance?' I said uncertainly.

Rachel shrugged. 'Whatever.'

Man. Still. It was the least I could do.

I stood up. 'Come on, then.'

26

Rachel

We walked over to the edge of the dance floor just as the song came to an end. My legs felt all shaky. I couldn't believe I'd asked Theo to dance with me. It was seeing that horrible, triumphant look on Jemima's face that had done it.

I could just imagine her next week, a cruel smile twisted round her mouth. 'Your boyfriend left early,' she'd say sarcastically. 'Couldn't bring himself to touch you, was that it?'

Another track started up and Theo and I began moving in time with the music, I decided I would have to leave with him. I'd tell him it was so I could show him where the station was. Then I could go straight home. I'd tell Mum I had a headache or something. At least that way I could make out Theo and I had left together.

I looked up at him. He was dancing opposite me, swaying in this cool, detached way and staring round at everyone. I caught sight of Jemima gyrating away on the other side of the room. She was with her friends and this big group of boys – maybe she'd forgotten about me.

No chance. Just at that moment she looked over. Her eyes narrowed. She shook her head.

I could see what she was thinking. What everyone must be thinking. Theo was looking everywhere but at me. He was dancing almost a metre away from me. He was not the slightest bit interested in me.

He was so, so obviously *not* my boyfriend.

Wham. Someone barged into me. I fell sideways. The floor flew up into my face. *Thump*. I landed heavily on my arm. *Ow*.

'Hey,' Theo shouted. 'Watch out.'

A male voice swore. Theo swore back.

I looked up, ignoring the pain in my arm. This stocky, dark-haired guy was shoving Theo backwards. I scrambled to my feet. Theo shoved the stocky boy back – hard.

The stocky boy clenched his fists. His friends were all glaring at Theo. Theo was glaring at them.

I didn't think. I just strode over and stood in front of him.

'Stop it,' I said. 'Get into a fight and you'll never get out of here.' I rubbed my arm – the pain was already fading.

Theo was still staring behind me, at the other boys, his breath all rough and shallow. I put my hands on his shoulders. They were hunched and tense. 'Relax,' I said. 'It's not important.'

He looked down at me. I felt his shoulders release their tension under my hands. 'Are you okay?' he said.

I nodded, suddenly horribly aware of how close we were standing to each other. My hands started shaking. Theo frowned. He put his arms round my waist. 'You sure?'

I gulped, nodding again. Now I had time to think I couldn't believe I'd spoken to Theo so forcefully. I looked round. The stocky boy and his friends had vanished. We were surrounded by people dancing. The music was still pounding away, but we'd both stopped moving. All I could feel was his hands holding me. My heart hammering like it would explode. My face burning.

I dipped my head so that my fringe brushed against his chest. I was only doing it so that he wouldn't see my red face, but he pulled me closer, into a hug.

I turned my head sideways, so my cheek lay against his chest. He was hugging me. It was amazing. It felt so *right*. His body all lean and muscular. His hands warm on my waist.

I could feel his heart beating. The swirly feeling that had been in my stomach since I'd seen him outside the school gates spread through my whole body. I'd never felt like this. Ever. I closed my eyes, only knowing that I didn't want him to stop holding me.

But he was bending down, whispering my name in my ear, pulling away slightly. I looked up.

His face was so close to mine I could have counted the long, dark lashes round his eyes. For one totally amazing moment I thought he was going to kiss me.

And then he let go of me and took a step back.

'I have to go,' he said. 'It's time.'

27

Theo

She'd looked so shaken that I'd hugged her.

I guessed that idiot barging into her had really upset her. I felt bad leaving right then, but I needed to get as far away as possible before Roy realised I was gone.

'I'm going for a pee,' I said. 'That way Roy'll see me. Then he won't think to come in here and check up on me. On my way back I'll grab my bag. Will you be ready to do whatever distraction thing you've got worked out?'

Rachel looked a bit dazed. But she nodded.

I strode off through the crowd. The toilets were opposite the hall door. Roy was sprawled in a chair outside them, his hands clasped behind his head. As usual, he looked phenomenally bored.

I indicated I was going for a pee. He nodded. When I came out of the toilets I hesitated. I was almost sure this would be the last time I ever saw him. I hadn't thought much further ahead than finding my dad – but I knew that Roy was unlikely to give me another chance if I ran off tonight, whenever I came home.

'Having fun?' he said gruffly.

'Yeah,' I said. 'Thanks, Roy.'

Back inside the hall, I grabbed my backpack and checked my pocket for the millionth time, feeling both tight wodges of cash – and Rachel's phone.

She was more or less where I'd left her on the dance floor, chatting with the pointy-faced blonde girl in the tight black dress. A much faster record was playing now and the place was heaving. I wove my way towards her.

She didn't see me. The blonde girl was sneering at her, turning to these two other girls beside her. All three of them were wearing short, skin-tight dresses.

Then the blonde girl caught sight of me and narrowed her eyes.

I walked up. Rachel and the other three girls all looked at me. I had a sudden vision of the expression on Jake's face if he could see me right now. Me and four fit girls. Well, three fit girls and Rachel.

Thinking of Jake reminded me of Max. And Mum. And home. Was running off like this really what I wanted to do?

I shifted my bag to my other shoulder. It had to be. RAGE were on my tail. After me to get to my dad. Which meant my dad and I were in this together. I had to find him. Waiting for him to come for me was not an option.

I turned to Rachel. 'Did you think of something?' I said, hoping she would understand I was referring to my need for a distraction while I slipped out.

'Yes.' Rachel looked down at the ground in front of her.

I stood there awkwardly for a moment. The pretty, pointy-faced blonde girl stared at me and rolled her eyes, as if encouraging me to agree to how useless Rachel was.

And then, suddenly, Rachel darted forwards. Grabbed the blonde girl's low-cut dress at the top. Gave it a violent tug. A loud ripping noise. The blonde girl started screaming.

I stood there, too shocked to even work out what had just happened. Rachel grabbed my hand and pulled me away. People were rushing past us, towards the girl, all crowding round to see what the screams were about.

'Her dress, it—'

'—just tore it right down—'

'Did you see her b—?'

I caught snatches of excited conversation as Rachel dragged me to the back of the hall. Suddenly we were right by the fire door. The teacher who had been standing nearby had vanished, presumably investigating the screams like everyone else.

I turned round. A huge crowd had gathered on the dance floor around the spot we'd just left. No one was looking at us.

'Come on.' Rachel dropped my hand and tugged at the bolt across the fire door. Seconds later we were outside in the cold, dark air.

28

Rachel

I pulled the fire door shut behind us. Theo stared at me, his eyes round with shock.

'I can't believe you just did that,' he said.

I stood, letting the cold air chill my burning face. I couldn't believe it either. I hadn't meant to. At least, not until about two seconds before I did it – when I caught sight of Jemima smirking at Theo. I'd looked down at her dress, at that front seam. And I'd just seen it ripping all the way down.

'You needed a distraction,' I said quietly. My ears hummed with the quiet of the playground. The dance music inside was a muted thump on the other side of the fire door. The only other sound was the whoosh of motor cars flying up the hill at the front of the school. 'Anyway. That girl's a toxic bitch.' I shivered, imagining what revenge Jemima would plan for me.

'Well remind me never to piss *you* off,' Theo grinned. 'Which way do I go now?'

I grinned back at him. This big, stupid grin. I couldn't help it. Of all the amazing, gorgeous things about him, his smile was the most heart-stoppingly amazing and gorgeous.

'This way.' I pointed past the jutting wall of the Assembly Hall. We set off across the tarmac. Round the corner and the school gates were visible about thirty metres away, dimly lit by a lamppost on the pavement beyond.

Theo turned to me. 'Thanks,' he said. 'For everything.'

I opened my mouth to say I'd show him to the station. There was no way I was even pretending I was going back to the school disco now. Then I caught sight of two men strolling towards us from the school gates. They were wearing hoodies, the tops pulled right over their faces.

One was sauntering along casually, his hands in his trouser pockets. The other looked more tense. He was glancing round, his arm stiffly held against his side. There was something in his fist, something dark and pointed. I squinted, trying to make out what it was.

And then I realised.

It was a gun.

29

Theo

I turned round to see what Rachel was staring at.

My heart skipped a beat.

The man nearest us raised his arm. He held out the gun. He wasn't pointing it at me. Just showing me.

I couldn't breathe. Couldn't move.

The man strode nearer. Right up to me. All I could see was the gun. It had a long barrel. Longer than I thought guns like that had. Some part of my brain registered that it was a silencer. I'd seen them in films.

My heart pounded.

'It's him,' the man said.

'Yup.' The guy next to him seemed horribly relaxed. Almost lazily, he caught hold of Rachel's arm. Whispered something in her ear. She froze, her eyes wide with fear.

I couldn't take it in. It wasn't happening.

'Get down,' the man with the gun hissed.

I looked up from the gun, into his face. I could only see his mouth. It was dark anyway, and the rest of his face was in the shadow of his hood.

'Down.' He cocked the gun with a click.

I sank to my knees. As I hit the ground my body started shaking.

No. This wasn't real. Couldn't be real.

'Please . . .' Rachel's voice was a gasp. The man holding her arm slapped his free hand across her mouth. I glanced up at her. At her terrified eyes.

The man with the gun took a step closer to me.

'You first.' His lips twisted into a horrible smile as he raised his arm. The metal pressed against my forehead.

Cold. Metal. Cold. Gun.

My whole body was shaking. Every cell. But it was like I was outside my body, watching it shake.

I knelt in the darkness. The ground was hard under my knees. The gun metal cold against my forehead. Somewhere far away, the music thumped and the traffic swooshed.

The man with the gun was going to shoot me.

I felt nothing. I was going to die. I felt nothing.

No fear. No anger. No sadness. Nothing.

'You freaks.' The man stood right in front of me, his legs firmly planted on the tarmac. Like he was about to take a leak all over me. 'You should never have been born. Either of you.'

I felt as if it was all happening to someone else, someone across the tarmac. Not me. Not here. Not now. The man straightened his arm. The gun pressed harder against my skin. Still cold.

Surely dying was supposed to be a bigger deal than this? Surely I should feel something now? I held my breath.

Waiting.

I closed my eyes. A second later this juddering ratchety noise filled the air. Then a loud thud.

My eyes snapped open.

The man with the gun was lying face down on the ground in front of me. The other man was kneeling down beside him, pressing his fingers into his neck. Checking for a pulse. Another gun – but smaller. Weird-looking. Some kind of stun gun. In his spare hand.

My mouth fell open. Rachel grabbed my shoulders.

'Theo? Are you all right?'

I nodded. Too dazed to speak.

The man with the weird-looking gun turned to me, pulling his hoodie down.

'Get up. Run. Back inside.'

I stared at him. He didn't look that old – early twenties, maybe. He had dark olive skin, his chin covered in stubble. My mind seemed to have stopped working. I couldn't make any sense of what was happening.

The man glanced at Rachel. 'Take him inside. The head's office. I'll meet you up there. Hurry. There are more of them.'

I could feel Rachel's hand tugging under my arms.

I stood up. My legs were shaky. Like they didn't really belong to me. None of this was real. Not what had just happened. Not the world around me. Not me, myself.

'Who . . . what's going on?' I said.

'RAGE.'

'How did they know we were here?' Rachel said.

'I'll explain later.' The man shoved his stun gun into his pocket, then picked up the real gun. 'Now, hurry.'

Rachel grabbed my wrist. Started dragging me back towards the fire door. 'Come on, Theo.'

Something about her voice pierced a little way through the numb wall around my mind. She sounded desperate. Like she needed my help.

I sped up. Rachel reached the fire door. She curled her fingers round the tiny slit of an opening.

I put my fingers next to hers. Together we hauled the door open.

The music hit me like a wave. How weird was that? Suddenly we were back with the disco. The DJ talking over a dance track. Groups of girls on the dance floor. Gangs of boys watching them. More couples now, I noticed.

Rachel shut the door behind us. The stern-faced teacher was standing next to it. She raised her eyes disapprovingly at me. I wondered vaguely what she thought we'd been doing.

'Come on.' Rachel set off round the dance floor. I followed closely behind her, my mind trying to make sense of what had just happened. The first man – a man from RAGE – had been about to kill me. Then the second man had . . . had knocked him out. Why?

Rachel sped through the Assembly Hall door and out into the corridor. Roy's chair was empty. Where was he? The question floated uneasily at the edges of my mind but it didn't feel real.

None of this felt real.

The entrance hall was virtually empty. A bored-looking woman was sitting beside the rows of coats and bags at the back.

Rachel stalked past her, towards the main staircase.

I followed.

'Hey,' the woman called out. 'Where are you two going?'

Rachel turned round. 'I'm just fetching something I left in my classroom,' she lied, this slightly haughty expression on her face.

'*He* should stay down here,' the woman said. She glared at me.

Rachel leaned closer. 'Wait till she turns round,' she whispered. 'I'll be at the top of the stairs. Hurry.' She set off, her heels clacking against the wide stone steps.

I stared after her. I still felt completely numb.

I sauntered across the hall, then turned and wandered back. As I reached the stairs again, a couple appeared, asking for their coats.

The woman on duty at the makeshift cloakroom promptly disappeared down a row of jackets.

I hurried up the stairs two at a time.

Rachel was waiting at the top, hanging over the bannisters. She turned away as I reached her, then led me silently down a long corridor, up another flight of stairs, down a few steps, along another corridor and into a carpeted area.

She opened a door marked *Headteacher's Office*.

She shook her head. 'I'm sure this is normally locked,' she said.

I followed her inside as she switched on a bright overhead light.

I screwed up my eyes against the glare, then looked round the room. A big desk. A few comfortable chairs. And loads of framed school photos on the walls.

Rachel sat down on one of the chairs and put her head in her hands.

I turned away, not knowing what to do or say. It was like there was some kind of barrier between me and what was happening. Like I couldn't reach out and touch any of it. I stared at the photos on the walls, not really taking any of them in.

Lots of girls in school uniform. That was all. Lots and lots of girls.

Across the room, Rachel started crying.

30

Rachel

I cried for several minutes. Great, big, racking sobs. The image of Theo kneeling on the tarmac with that gun against his head filled my mind. I could still feel that man's hand round my mouth. Hear him whispering at me to be quiet. See him shooting at that other man with . . . what was it? Like a laser gun or something. Sparks flying out into the dark. Then the other man falling to the ground.

And the worst of it was that somehow . . . somehow Dad was mixed up in it all.

After a while, Theo walked over and sat down next to me. I felt his hand on my back, patting me awkwardly. I glanced round, looking at him through my wet fingers. He wasn't looking at me. He was staring at the photographs on the wall opposite. Rebecca was in several of them, of course. Form-leader every year, sports captain of any sport, prize-winner of all prizes . . .

I sniffed hard, trying to stop crying, wishing Theo would hold me again. I felt his hand slide off my back. I wiped my eyes and sighed out the last of my sobs. He wasn't going to hold me. Not now. Not ever.

I looked up, into his eyes. They were blank.

'Why did that guy tell us to wait up here?' I said, my voice all croaky.

Theo ran his hand through his hair. He sat back in his chair and shook his head. 'Dunno.' He stared at the floor. 'I wonder why that other man wanted to kill me.'

I stared at him. He sounded like he was discussing a maths problem or something.

'I mean it doesn't make sense,' he went on. 'If RAGE wanted to use me to blackmail my dad, then why kill me seconds after finding me. And why did they want to hurt you?'

My mouth fell open. How could he talk about it so calmly? My own mind was jumping about like crazy, racing over what had happened, wondering if we were safe yet, wondering how we were going to get out of the school alive.

'And why did he call us freaks?' Theo mused.

I shrugged. Who cared what insults he'd thrown at us. He'd wanted to kill us. And now . . . now he was unconscious. Dead maybe? The image of his body on the ground flashed into my mind again. I felt sick.

Theo sighed. 'I reckon my dad must have been working on some really freaked-out stuff at that clinic that got fire-bombed. Genetic experiments or something. Maybe trials using us, you know, before we were born.'

What on earth was wrong with him? How could he be talking like that? He'd just had a gun in his face.

'Has your mum ever said anything about that? About when you were born?' Theo leaned forward.

I shook my head.

'Are you sure?' he persisted. 'Wasn't there *anything* unusual about it?'

For Christ's sake.

'Only her age,' I said. 'She was forty-seven when she had me, which is really old to have a baby and she did have fertility treatment to get pregnant but . . . but, Theo, how can you even be thinking about—?'

'Maybe that's the connection.' Theo's eyes widened. 'Fertility treatment. Maybe my mum had that too.'

I looked at his face. I could still see the gun there, the tip pressed against his forehead. I swallowed, trying to push the image away. 'But . . . but I thought you said your mum and dad weren't together that long?'

'So?'

'Well, people who hardly know each other don't usually go for IVF and all that.' I wiped my eyes. 'And your mum's young for a mum, isn't she?'

Theo sighed again. He looked up at the photograph on the wall opposite.

'Well, it must be something like that, or else—'

'We can talk about it later,' said a male voice.

I spun round. The man who had saved us was standing in the doorway. I hadn't even heard the door open.

'Come on,' he said. 'There's no time to explain now. Follow me.'

31

Theo

It all felt like a dream. Like it wasn't really happening. And yet, at the same time, I was hyper-alert. Totally in control. I could see Rachel hesitating, not sure what to do.

I grabbed her arm and pulled her towards the door.

The man looked at me. He had blue eyes – bright blue against his olive skin. There was this weird expression in them, like he was looking *for* something in my face. Then he held up his hand to stop us walking out past him into the corridor. He glanced up and down, then beckoned us after him. I scurried right behind him, still holding Rachel by the wrist. Her skin was clammy. She was trembling.

I wasn't. Not now. I wasn't afraid at all. I felt nothing.

The man led us to the fire door at the end of the corridor. He glanced at our shoes.

'Take those heels off,' he whispered to Rachel.

She gawped at him, blinking rapidly.

'Go on,' he said, 'they'll make too much noise on the fire escape.'

Rachel still didn't move, so I knelt down and started undoing the thin strap round her right ankle. Almost immediately she bent down and started working at the left shoe.

The man lifted the fire door bar and pushed the heavy door back across the top of the iron fire escape. How did he know his way round the school so well?

'What—?' I started.

'Sssh.' The man held his finger to his lips. He peered outside, his right hand reaching round and pulling out the gun tucked into the waistband at his back. I stared at it. It was a real gun.

He crept out onto the metal stairs, the gun in his hand, beckoning us to follow.

I could feel Rachel shaking beside me.

'It's okay,' I murmured.

She nodded and tiptoed after the man. It was even colder outside than it had been earlier. Her bare feet must have been frozen on the iron steps, but she said nothing.

Slowly, carefully, the man led us down the stairs.

I looked around. There was no sign of anyone or anything. But it was dark and there were many shadowy corners where people could have been lurking. I had the dim sense that this should have made me feel terrified. But it didn't. I was a machine. My only sensation was one of admiration for the man leading us down the steps. The way he moved without making a single sound.

As we reached the bottom of the staircase, a boy and girl lurched round the corner, their arms wrapped round each other. The man froze. His arm whipped out and pushed me and Rachel flat against the wall. Rachel gasped. Her shoes fell to the ground with a light thud.

The couple didn't seem to have noticed us. They wandered across the tarmac away from us, into one of the shadowy corners. I could just make out the girl leaning against the wall, the boy pressing against her. They started kissing noisily, their hands everywhere.

The man beckoned us forward again. He took us round the corner, down a narrow passageway, then across a wider space.

I had no idea where we were, or how far away the school exit was. Rachel was limping slightly now. I glanced down. Her shoes were no longer in her hands. She must have left them on the ground.

We rounded another wall and the dull thump of the dance music drifted towards us across the air. In the far distance I could just make out the school gates, their high, spiky bars silhouetted against the street lamps beyond.

'Lewis?' A low growl.

The man spun round. 'Sir?'

Another man stepped out of the shadows. He was dressed from head to toe in black, with a mask over his face. 'You've got them, Lewis?'

The man we were with nodded curtly. 'Yes, sir. Mr Simpson, sir.'

His voice was neutral, but I could see his hand tighten on his gun.

For the first time I sensed he was scared. I noticed this without feeling any emotion myself. I was just curious to see what happened next.

The masked man looked round. 'Where is he?'

Lewis said nothing. I guessed the man was referring to the guy Lewis had somehow knocked out. The one who'd almost shot me.

'Lewis?'

'I don't know, Mr Simpson.'

I frowned. Simpson. The name seemed familiar. In fact, so did the name Lewis. Where had I heard them before?

Beside me, Rachel shivered.

'Well, Lewis?' the masked man barked. 'What happened?'

There was a short, tense pause. Then Lewis swung his arm up and round. The movement was so quick there was no time for the other man to jump back. Lewis's hand – the hand holding the gun – slammed into his forehead.

The man staggered backwards, clutching his brow.

Lewis darted forwards and thumped the man on the upper back with the edge of the gun. The man fell to the ground.

'Oh . . . no . . . no,' Rachel whimpered beside me.

I stared at Lewis. How had he *done* that? His movements were so quick. So precise. Lewis stood over the man for two long seconds, his gun pointing at the man's chest.

It was like watching a film. I wondered if Lewis would shoot.

Rachel turned her face away.

Lewis stared down at the man. His arm shook.

149

Then he drew back his arm and tucked his gun in the back of his trouser waistband again. 'Hurry,' he said. He yanked on Rachel's arm, half dragging her towards the school gates.

I raced after them.

Through the gates, Lewis swerved to the right. He pounded down the hill, past the bus shelter where I had met Rachel for the first time. I flew after him. Rachel was stumbling, panting. Lewis holding her up.

We turned down a side road. A navy BMW with darkened windows was parked near the corner. Lewis clicked open the locks. 'In the back,' he ordered.

I pulled open the back door and bundled Rachel inside. Lewis was in the driver's seat, already revving the engine. I slammed my door shut and he zoomed off.

Silence.

I sat back against the leather seat, my hands in my lap. I realised with a jolt that I no longer had my backpack with me. I must have left it on the tarmac when . . . when . . . I suddenly flashed back to the gun barrel pressed against my forehead. I could feel the cold metal against my skin.

Don't think about it. I tried to remember exactly what was in the bag. Clothes. Toothbrush. My picture of Dad. My only picture. Something twisted in my gut. *Don't think about it.*

'My passport.' *No.*

'Don't worry, we'll get you a new one,' Lewis said.

Had I spoken out loud? I looked at him. Who was 'we'?

'Who are you?' I said.

'Lewis Michael.' He half turned round to give me a quick look.

I felt Rachel stiffen beside me. I remembered the name now. Lewis Michael. The person who'd written the email to Rachel's dad about 'shutting me up'. That's where I'd heard the name Simpson too.

My stomach twisted again. *The gun. Pressing against my skin.*

'But you're with RAGE,' I stammered. 'We saw your email. You said you were going to kill me. *Shut him up – permanently*. That's what you said.'

Lewis Michael snorted. 'Shut you up as in stop you talking. Which you were doing far, far too much of.'

He turned a corner. We were driving quite slowly, through heavy traffic. I had no idea where we were.

I glanced at the door nearest me. It was locked. 'But RAGE want to kill me. And you're with them.' The twisting feeling was filling my stomach now, swelling inside me. I had this strong sense that I had to keep it down, that it was way, way too big to let out.

'I was working undercover. You saw me taser that guy earlier – knock him out.'

'Taser?' Rachel's voice sounded weak. She was huddled in the far corner of the car, her arms wrapped round her body. Her face was pale and scared and tear-stained.

'Electric stun gun,' Lewis said. He looked round at me again. 'I work for your . . . your dad.'

'My dad?' I sat forward, trying to ignore the panicky feeling

151

that was growing and growing inside my stomach. 'You work for my dad?'

Lewis nodded. 'That's why I'm here. He sent me to rescue you.' He sighed. 'Even though it meant blowing my cover.'

'What about *my* dad?' Rachel said.

'We're in touch with him.' Lewis reached for some kind of mobile phone set into the dashboard. 'We'll let him know you're safe as soon as we can. And your mum, Theodore.'

'It's Theo,' I said, absently.

'Theo.' Lewis pressed the phone. 'Zeus?' There was a distant crackle from the receiver. A few indistinct words. 'Gods are safe in heaven. Over.' Lewis said. He switched off the phone.

Rachel nudged me. 'That's what my dad's text said,' she whispered. '*Goddess still safe in heaven.*'

'That's right, Rachel.' Lewis glanced over his shoulder. 'It's our code message to confirm you guys are safe. Your father was supposed to send me the text every week. If it didn't arrive we'd know to check it out, make sure you were okay.'

'But how did you know where we were?' I said.

Lewis sighed. 'RAGE got suspicious as soon as your friend Max started hacking into the RAGE membership list.'

'They know about Max?' I said.

'They'd been keeping tabs on her since then, trying to work out why a fifteen-year-old girl was hacking into their data. It took them a few days to make the connection with you. And then with Rachel. They've been tracing Max's calls – that's how they found out about tonight. Some friend of yours – Jake something? He called Max. Told her you were meeting Rachel here.'

I shook my head. Jake and his big, girl-impressing mouth.

'I found out RAGE were planning to catch you here about an hour ago. I got word to your dad, but by then there was no alternative but to scope the school, go in with them and get you both out. Before they took you out.'

Took me out.

The image of the gun against my head filled my mind. I could feel it too, pressing cold against my skin. Then the click.

The wait.

Without warning the twist in my stomach exploded into this shattering fear that threaded through every vein in my body. Panic surged up from my gut. Spiralling through me. All that I was. All that I knew. I started shaking uncontrollably. My breathing all shallow and jagged. *Help me. Help me.* So scared. I was going to piss myself I was so scared.

I bent forwards, pressing my hands together, trying to stop the shaking.

'What happened to Theo's bodyguard?' Rachel was saying.

Roy. I'd completely forgotten about him.

Lewis Michael gave a little cough. 'I had to get him out of the way, but he'll be fine.'

I hunched further over, closing my eyes, focusing on pushing away the panic that filled me. Silent tears were streaming down my face. I had no idea why I was crying.

I never cried.

I felt Rachel's hand on my shoulder. 'Theo?'

Oh, man, she'd seen me bawling. How embarrassing. I turned away from her, determined to make myself stop. But I didn't seem to be in control of my body any more. I wanted to pee. To shit myself. To vomit.

And I could not stop shaking.

32

Rachel

I caught Lewis's eye in the rearview. He looked concerned. My hand felt awkward on Theo's shoulder. I wanted to help him so much, but he was turning away, turning his back on me.

I sat back in my seat. At least my dad had nothing to do with RAGE. He wasn't a murderer. He hadn't helped kill all those people.

I breathed out. A heavy sigh of relief. Outside we were moving onto a faster road. It was raining – cars whooshing past.

'Theo.' Lewis's voice was low and commanding. 'Theo, buddy.'

I opened my eyes. Theo was still hunched over at the other end of the back seat.

'Theo.' Lewis's tone was sharper now. 'That was some hardcore stuff back there. You were seconds away from dying. There's no shame in how you're feeling now. You were brave when you needed to be. D'you hear me? Now it's time to let the bad stuff out.'

Theo said nothing.

'Theo. Listen to me,' Lewis said. 'I've been where you are now. It's better you let it out. I promise you.'

Theo shifted slightly. His hands were pressed together but I could see they were shaking.

'Do you trust Rachel?' Lewis said.

Theo looked up at last. Tears shone on his cheeks. More leaked out of his eyes. He nodded.

It was like a fist squeezing my heart. A feeling that somehow made total sense, that I recognised even though I'd never felt it before.

Love. I loved him.

'Let Rachel hold you,' Lewis said. 'Let it all out. Right now. She won't laugh at you. I won't. If you like, we'll never mention it again. Just let her hold you. It'll help.'

Theo shook his head, but only half-heartedly. I reached out and put my hand over his. I gave it a gentle tug and he turned, his head bent down. He wound his shaking arms round me and laid his head against my shoulder.

And then he cried and cried and cried.

33

Theo

Gradually I stopped shaking. The tears dried up. Rachel was still holding me, stroking my hair. Lewis had been right. Being held had helped. At least it had helped when I'd been all weird and shaking. Now, I just felt embarrassed. I mean, I was beginning to think of Rachel as a friend. A good friend. But I hadn't cried like that since I was a little kid. Not even with Mum.

I sat back, hoping Lewis had meant what he said about not mentioning me bawling ever again.

I wiped my face with my sleeve and stared out the window. We were speeding down a motorway.

'Er . . . where are we going?' I sniffed.

'A safe house. Somewhere RAGE won't find you.'

The sudden thought was like a punch in the gut. 'What about my mum?' I sat forward, gripping the seat in front. 'Is she in danger? What—?'

'Your mum's going somewhere safe too. So are Rachel's parents. It's better they don't know exactly where you are right now. But you'll be able to talk to them from the safe house.' Lewis sighed. 'There's no other choice, I'm afraid. You're both in too much danger.'

'What about my dad?' I said. 'Do RAGE know where he is?'

'No,' Lewis said. He glanced over his shoulder at me. 'Look, I know you have a lot of questions,' he said. 'Both of you. But I'm not the right person to answer them.'

Rachel and I exchanged glances. 'So who is?' I said.

Lewis smiled. He suddenly looked very tired.

'Your dad, Theo,' he said. 'That's where we're going now. To meet your dad.'

Part Two

Scotland

34

Rachel

I woke up. We were still in the car, travelling over a bumpy road. I was lying slumped sideways, my head resting against something hard. With a jolt I realised it was Theo's shoulder. It was damp where – *oh no* – where I must have dribbled onto it. I opened my eyes and sat up, wiping away the crusted spit from round my mouth.

Yuck. How embarrassing.

Ow. My neck was all cricked. I rubbed it and glanced at Theo. He was still asleep, his head nodding forwards. Lewis looked at me in the rearview mirror. He yawned.

'Not far now,' he said.

I looked out of the window. Lewis had switched the head-lights on full. We were driving down a narrow lane, with what looked like moorland on either side of us. The night sky was clear and wide, stars shining all across the horizon.

'Where are we?' I said.

'Scotland.' Lewis smiled. 'Just.'

We'd changed cars earlier, not far out of London. The

second car was much bigger. Lewis had brought sandwiches, water and blankets out of the boot. I must have drifted off some time after that.

I checked the dashboard clock. It said 2:41 a.m. We had been driving for over six and a half hours. A few minutes later Lewis took a right turn onto an uneven track. He slowed down as we jolted towards a small building in the distance. It was a stone cottage – set in isolation in the heart of the wilderness we were travelling through. A single light was on in one of the downstairs rooms. As we pulled up, the front door opened. A woman in a baggy sweater stood in the doorway, her arms hugging her chest. She was black, with straightened, shoulder-length hair.

'Where are we?' Theo said groggily, stretching out his arms.

'Home.' Lewis answered, his eyes on the woman in the doorway. 'For now.'

I opened the car door. A blast of icy wind whistled past my face. I put my bare feet onto the bumpy ground outside. They'd warmed up inside the car and the stones were cold and hard against my skin. I stood up. *Ouch*.

Lewis walked over to the woman in the cottage doorway. There was something about the way he leaned into her – close but without touching – that made me think he knew her well. Really well. I limped round the side of the car.

'Hey, Lewis.' The woman had an American accent. She looked over at me, then back at him. 'Be a British gent, why don't you? Girl's got no shoes on.'

She smiled warmly at me. I relaxed a little. I was glad there was a woman here. Lewis glanced round at me. 'Sorry, Rachel,' he said. 'D'you want me to carry you over the stones?'

No. I shook my head, hoping the darkness would cover up the fact that I was blushing furiously. Theo appeared next to me.

'I'm fine,' I said firmly, striding across the stones and trying to ignore the sharp pains stabbing at my bare soles.

'Hey, there,' the woman said. 'I'm Mel.'

She had a striking face – beautiful, with strong, broad features. It was hard to say how old she was, maybe a little older than Lewis.

'You've had some night, haven't you?' Mel put her arm round my shoulders and guided me inside. The front door opened into a small living room. There was a long sofa down one wall and two armchairs. The floor and walls were made of stone, with a large empty fireplace in the middle and a red patterned rug in front of it. It felt warm and cosy, though my bare feet were still cold.

'Hey.' Mel turned away from me to welcome Theo. 'I'm Mel. I . . . I'm your dad's friend.'

Theo stared blankly around him, like he was having to force his eyes to stay open.

I didn't feel tired at all.

'You guys must be wiped,' Mel said. 'Why don't we get you settled for tonight? We can talk in the morning.' She led us across the living room to an open doorway in the opposite corner. A set of narrow stone steps led up to a tiny landing. I climbed them.

Upstairs the cottage smelled slightly musty.

'Don't worry,' Mel said. 'We'll only be here a few days. Coupla weeks at most.'

I whipped round. *A couple of weeks?* What about Mum and Dad? What about school? Mel must have seen the concern on my face. She smiled.

'Sorry,' she said. 'We'll talk in the morning. Get some sleep for now.'

I felt less tired than ever as she herded me through one of the four doors that led off the landing. It contained a small single bed and a chest of drawers. A nightgown lay on the bed. I walked over and picked it up. It was blue and silky with thin little straps – really elegant and grown up.

'It's a spare one of mine,' Mel smiled. 'We'll get you some clothes tomorrow.'

I was desperate to ask her some questions. When was I going home? Why was I even here? It was Theo RAGE wanted to kill. But Mel was hovering by the door, giving off very definite don't-ask-me-any-questions vibes. Looking at her big, baggy jumper, I couldn't imagine her in a girlie nightie like the one in my hands. Yet there was something graceful about her – and something shy too.

'Restroom's next door,' Mel said. She yawned. 'There's a towel and a toothbrush in there for you. Pink ones.' She smiled. 'Get some sleep, babe.'

She backed out of the room and shut the door.

164

I sank onto the bed, the silky nightdress in my lap. For the first time since we'd left London there was absolute silence. I could hear my own heart beating loudly. This was all so strange. So scary.

Tears pricked at my eyes. My questions slid away and all I wanted was to be in my bedroom at home, with all my familiar things and Mum and Dad next door.

I sniffed back the tears and went out onto the landing, hoping I would see Theo. A minute later he staggered out of a room opposite. He blinked at me, then yawned. He looked so tired he could barely stand up.

'Well, this isn't weird. Much.' He raised his eyebrows, sleepily. 'Lewis took your phone off me, by the way. He said we couldn't call anyone for now.'

I stared at him.

He yawned again. 'You okay?'

I nodded. *No*.

'Want the bathroom?'

I shook my head. *I want you to hug me, like you did before. Make me feel safe.*

'Night, then.' Theo stumbled into the bathroom and shut the door. I went back to my room and lay on the bed. A tear trickled down my face.

I heard the sound of running water on the other side of the bedroom wall. I closed my eyes. I was never going to sleep.

I woke with a start some time later. I had no idea how much later. The bedside lamp was still on, and I was lying on top of the bed, clutching the silk nightdress. I was freezing cold. The house was silent. I checked the time. Only 3:15. I'd been asleep for less than twenty minutes.

My heart sank.

I wriggled under the covers and lay still for a few minutes. I wasn't warming up. It was just too cold. And I needed the bathroom.

Outside on the landing, the two doors opposite were shut. I went next door, and spent several minutes wondering whether or not to flush the toilet. The house was so small I was worried I'd wake everyone up. On the other hand . . .

Then I heard a laugh from downstairs. Mel. I left the toilet unflushed and stood on the landing.

I could hear her voice – soft and low. But not what she was saying. I crept down the narrow stone stairs to where the door at the bottom opened into the living room.

'I know, but I couldn't kill him.' That was Lewis. He sounded bitter. 'I just couldn't do it. Not in cold blood like that.'

I held my breath. He must be talking about the man from RAGE. Simpson. The one he'd called 'sir'. The one he'd hit with the gun, but hadn't shot. I peered through the crack in the door. Lewis and Mel were sitting at opposite ends of the sofa. Mel had her back to me, her straightened hair shining in the lamplight. Lewis's bright blue eyes were fixed on her face.

'He'll be furious,' Lewis said. 'I had to blow my cover and I didn't take a single one of them out before I went.'

Mel sighed. 'Don't tell him,' she said. 'Make like you had to choose between rescuing Apollo and killing Simpson. Say it was a time thing.'

Lewis frowned.

'Seriously, babe.' Mel shifted a little in her seat. She lowered her voice. 'He doesn't need to know. He'll be all over Apollo tomorrow anyway. Not interested in what went down to bring him here.'

Apollo. She was talking about Theo. Who was the 'he' they were referring to? Theo's dad? My heart raced.

'So what are they like?' Mel said. 'The kids.'

Lewis shrugged. 'Confused,' he said. 'Scared.' He smiled at her. 'Not that different from how I'm feeling right now, actually.'

Mel turned her face away. 'Undercover work's tough,' she said softly.

Lewis moved closer to her.

'Being here with you, when you're with him, is tougher.' He reached out and touched her arm. His eyes were still fixed on her face. If he'd looked up he would have been staring straight at me.

But he didn't look up.

'You should get some sleep.' Mel's voice was almost a whisper.

'I'm not tired.' Lewis leaned nearer to her. At last she looked back at him.

I suddenly felt really embarrassed, like I shouldn't be here, watching and listening like this. Like they would both be mad if they knew I was there. I turned round and padded silently back upstairs to bed.

I didn't think I would be able to rest at all, but I fell asleep as soon as I'd crawled under the covers.

35

Theo

The gun was at my head, cold against my skin. I wanted to move. To run away. But I was paralysed. Unable to make my legs work.

The click filled my head. The gun was cocked. The shot was coming. It was coming. It was . . .

'AAAAH!'

I came to with a jolt. I was sitting up in a strange bed, drenched in sweat. Where was I? Where was the gun?

My heart pounded. I looked round the room. A second single bed against the opposite wall. Bare stone walls and floor. Flowery curtains drawn at the tiny window. Sunshine beyond.

Sunshine. It was daytime. There was no gun.

Everything that had happened the night before flooded back. I looked over at the other bed again. It was Lewis's. He'd told me last night we'd be sharing. A blue duvet was smoothed across the bed. It didn't look as if anyone had slept in it.

The door opened. Lewis peered round. His eyes crinkled with concern.

'You okay, buddy?' He came over and sat down on the other bed. 'Heard you yelling out. What was it? Nightmare?'

I nodded.

Lewis grimaced sympathetically. 'That'll pass.' He turned round and punched a dent in his pillow. Then he shifted around on the bed so that the duvet got crumpled. I frowned. Why was he deliberately messing up his bed, making it look slept in?

He pointed to the chest of drawers by the door. 'Help yourself to my clothes. I'm going out now, but Mel's cooked some breakfast if you're hungry.'

He stood up and left.

I pulled on my jeans and found a fresh T-shirt in the chest of drawers. Lewis was only a bit bigger than I was. The T-shirt fitted fine. I dragged open the curtains. Wow. Empty moorland for as far as the eye could see. The landscape was flat and scrubby with a few trees dotted about. Mostly dull greens and browns with occasional flashes of purple. The sky was wide and blue – though dark grey clouds threatened in the distance.

Downstairs, I wandered through the living room towards the sound of Mel's voice and the sizzling noise of something frying. It smelled like bacon. And I was starving.

Mel was standing by the cooker in the little kitchen, prodding at a frying pan. My mouth fell open as I clocked her sweatpants and tight white vest. She had the hottest body – all curves and sleek muscles. There was a butterfly tattoo on her right shoulder.

'So, when d'you think he'll get here?' That was Rachel. She was sitting at the little table in the middle of the room, sipping from a mug.

'Who?' I said.

They both spun round to look at me. Rachel immediately dipped her head, her hair falling over her face. Mel smiled.

'Hey, Theo. Bacon sandwich?'

'Thanks.' I pulled out a chair from under the table and sat down opposite Rachel. 'Who were you talking about?'

'Your dad.' Mel took a plate from the cupboard above her head. 'He called about half an hour ago. He'll be here this evening.'

My dad. I was going to meet him. Everything I didn't understand about my life was going to be made clear. My heart pounded with excitement. I stared down at the table, not wanting Mel or Rachel to see how much the idea of meeting my dad meant to me.

'Where are we?' I said.

Mel slapped a slice of bread onto the plate. 'About a hundred miles north of the Scottish border. The nearest village is five miles. The nearest big town is twenty. Lewis has gone there to get you both some clothes.'

I nodded. 'And *why* exactly are we here?' I could feel Rachel looking at me now, but I kept my eyes on Mel. To be honest, it was hard to look away.

'We're hiding you from RAGE,' she said.

171

'But why?' I persisted. 'Why do they want to kill me?'

'Wait for your dad, Theo.' Mel raked three slivers of bacon out of the frying pan and laid them on top of the slice of bread. 'He'll explain everything.' She pressed a second slice of bread on top of the bacon and sliced the sandwich in half. Then she plonked the plate on the table in front of me.

I stared up at her.

She sighed. 'I guess this is all really weird for you guys, but RAGE are serious business. They won't stop looking for you now. You both need to be real clear about this – your lives are going to be different from now on. We're working on relocating your families. To keep you both safe.' She put her hand on Rachel's arm. 'For you it should just be a few weeks while your parents move. You'll be able to speak to them after Theo's dad's got here. You'll be with them again, soon, somewhere new. With a new name. New school.' She turned to me. 'For you, Theo, I just don't know. But I'm sure your dad has it figured out.' She looked at me intently – just like Lewis had last night, like there was something she was trying to see in my face.

'Why though?' I knew I sounded belligerent, but I didn't care. This woman was a complete stranger to me and yet she seemed to know more about what was happening to me than I did. '*Why* are RAGE after me? What did my dad do that makes them hate *me* so much?'

Mel's face hardened. 'I can't tell you.' She paused. 'Look. Forget about it this morning. Your dad suggested, and I thought it would be a good idea, if I gave you guys some combat training. You know, just in case. Why don't we start in one hour?' She hesitated. 'I'm afraid you can't go outside. The door's made from reinforced steel and it's locked three ways. And all the windows are bulletproof. They don't open either.'

She strolled out of the room.

I turned to Rachel. 'This is starting to piss me off. Why won't anyone tell us what this is really about?'

Rachel shook her head. 'D'you think everyone at home is really safe?' she said.

'Sure.' I suddenly remembered Max and Jake. What would RAGE do with them? 'That guy who rescued us yesterday. Lewis. He knows how to handle himself. I'm sure they've got people who are looking after things at home.'

Home. With a jolt I realised that if what Mel said was true, I would never see my home again.

An hour later we trooped into a back room that I hadn't noticed yesterday. It was small, but so bare there was plenty of space to move around. Just some handweights in one corner, a rowing machine and a punchbag. Mel was pounding it, wearing boxing gloves.

'Cool,' I said. 'Will we learn to shoot as well?'

Rachel looked at me, shocked.

'No.' Mel grinned. 'Let's start with this.'

She pulled off the gloves and handed them to me. Then she slid a thick black pad over each hand and held up her arms. There was a small red circle – about the size of a pingpong ball – in the centre of each pad. 'Hit the red,' she said. 'Hard as you can.'

I pulled on the gloves. They felt sticky with sweat inside. I held my hands up by my face, like I'd seen boxers do.

'Good job,' Mel said encouragingly. 'Now this is as much about balance and co-ordination as building muscle. Stand hip-width apart, left foot in front . . . Awesome. Now. When you jab, swing from your back heel, so all your bodyweight goes into the punch. Same with the cross. Swing round from the heel.'

She took a moment to correct my stance. Then nodded. I clenched my fists inside the gloves. I was as tall as Mel. And I knew I was strong. I wondered if I should hold back on my punches a little. I couldn't see how those pads would protect her hands enough.

Thump. I punched the red circle with a satisfying *thwack*. Mel's arms didn't flinch.

'Good,' she said encouragingly. 'Again.'

Thump. Thump. Thump. Thump. It was harder than it looked to hit the red circle precisely every time. And I quickly realised my right arm was stronger than my left. But as I jabbed and crossed I could feel all my frustration welling up and pouring out. I pounded at the pads, really getting into a rhythm.

'Reach forward. That's it. Keep your guard up. Retract the punch. Sharper. Faster.' Mel kept shouting instructions at me. Then she showed me how to swing up for an uppercut and round from the side for a hook. I punched hard at the pads for several minutes. It was deeply, deeply satifsying.

At last Mel stood up and shook off the pads. 'Nice work,' she said. She wiped her forehead with the back of her hand.

'I didn't hurt you, did I?' I said, suddenly worried that I'd hit the pads too hard for her. I mean, she looked strong. But she was only a girl, after all.

Mel grinned. She shoved the pads at me. 'Put them on.' She pulled on the gloves and took up a ready-to-punch stance.

I held out the pads like she had and tensed my arms.

Wham. Before I was even aware Mel's arm had moved, she had rammed it so hard against my left pad that my whole arm was thrown back, from the shoulder down.

I heard Rachel giggle beside me. My face reddened.

Mel's grin deepened. 'Don't worry about hurting *me*, babe,' she said.

Then she handed the gloves to Rachel. 'Your turn,' she smiled.

36

Rachel

We must have worked out for about an hour. I was exhausted at the end of it. We did rowing and boxing and skipping. I hated it, but Mel said I needed to do some intensive cardio work. I think she meant I needed to burn off some fat.

Theo seemed to love it all. Most of the time I felt stupid. I disliked the boxing most of all. It hurt my hands and tired my arms and I could never create the same satisfying noise that Mel and Theo made when their gloves made contact with the pads.

It didn't help that I had bare feet and was wearing Mel's sweatpants. She was at least a head taller than me – with far, far longer legs – so my trousers were all rolled up at the bottom. Of course they were still tight round my huge, fat arse. Unlike hers, which hung, elegantly, from her high, perfectly rounded bum.

Now she'd taken off that great big jumper I could see what an amazing figure she had. No wonder Lewis fancied her.

Theo probably did too.

We took it in turns to shower after we'd worked out, then Mel gave us cheese-and-pickle sandwiches. I helped her make them. I noticed Theo disappeared up to his room until it was time to eat. He didn't offer to wash up afterwards either. I half expected Mel to order him to help or something. But she didn't. She kept looking at him through the doorway, at where he was sitting on the living-room sofa. It was the sort of look you give people when you think you know them from somewhere, but you can't place them.

We both asked her about Max and Jake, but she was as evasive about what had happened to them as she had been about everything else. 'They're fine. Just wait,' was all she would say. She wouldn't answer any of our other questions either.

Lewis arrived back after lunch, laden with shopping bags.

'I hope it all fits,' he said anxiously. 'Mel and I went over the sizes this morning before you woke up. But even so . . .'

I peered into one of the plastic bags. I could see trainers and jeans and some pale-green combats. I pulled out a long-sleeved blue-green jumper with a scalloped neck. I held it out. It was such a pretty colour. I loved it.

'This looks great,' I said, smiling at Lewis. He blushed and glanced over at Mel.

'Nice work, gent,' she grinned.

Lewis held up two final plastic bags. 'Got you some magazines too.' He handed one bag to Theo. 'I know what kind of magazines fifteen-year-old guys like,' he said, his eyes twinkling.

Theo took the bag, blushing slightly.

Lewis handed the other bag to me. 'For you I had to guess a bit.' He smiled. 'Hope there's something there you can read.'

I said thank you and took everything up to my room. I tried it all on. The trousers fitted okay – though neither pair was particularly flattering. The blue-green jumper was lovely though. It was a bit clingier than I'd normally wear, but the colour was gorgeous.

I spent the afternoon flicking through the magazines. Lewis had bought five. A *Vogue* – which was full of stick-thin models and boring fashion articles, two gossip mags which looked quite good, a Manga-style comic which wasn't at all my kind of thing, and a teen magazine called *Sensa*. I read it from cover to cover in about two hours. It was full of articles on healthy dieting and finding the right clothes for your shape and how to survive a first date. I was just starting on the problem page at the end when Mel poked her head round the door.

'He's here.'

I didn't have to ask who she meant.

Theo's dad.

I scrambled off the bed and raced to the window. It was getting dark outside. A large, four-wheel drive car bumped up the uneven track and stopped outside the cottage. Two men got out either side of the back. They each made three-hundred-and-sixty-degree turns, scanning the horizon. They looked like bodyguards. I was sure neither of them was

Theo's dad. Then the driver emerged. Smaller than the other men. He held open the second back passenger door. Someone else must still be in the car. Him.

'Come on, babe.' Mel sounded apprehensive. 'Downstairs.'

I followed her down to the living room. Theo was in there already, standing beside the sofa.

The atmosphere in the room was taut. I could feel Mel all jumpy beside me. Lewis was nearest the front door, reaching out to pull back the bolts. Were his hands actually shaking? My own heart was beating fast. *God*. If it was this big a deal for the rest of us, imagine what it must be like for Theo. Meeting his dad for what was, really, the first time.

I took a step over to him. He was staring at the door. I badly wanted to put my arm round him. But, frankly, I would have found it easier to have cartwheeled across the floor.

I looked up as the door opened.

37

Theo

This was it. This was really it. My mouth felt dry. I was going to meet my dad.

I could feel, rather than see, Rachel right beside me. She seemed almost as tense as I was. My eyes were fixed on Lewis, pulling back the door. It was dark outside. I could only see a silhouette of a man. Tall. Well built.

He stepped into the light and smiled at me.

It wasn't my dad.

James Lawson had been in his early twenties when I was born. That's how he looked in my photograph. Which meant he would now be in his late thirties.

The man in front of me had to be way older than forty – his tanned, leathery face was heavily lined. Plus James Lawson had blue eyes and a long, oval face with a dimple in his chin, whereas the man in front of me was dark-eyed and square-jawed. No dimple.

We stared at each other.

I could feel the tension in the room building. Everyone

was looking at him, waiting for him to move or speak. You couldn't help it. There was this aura about him – of power or confidence or something. And he took his time. He kept on looking at my face, poring over it like a map, then his serious, brown eyes flickered over my whole body.

I shuffled, feeling self-conscious. He ran his hand through his slicked-back hair. Rachel gasped beside me. He glanced at her briefly, smiled, then looked back at me.

'Theodore,' he said. His voice was deep and strong. American, with the trace of a Spanish accent. He smiled – a warm, charming smile. 'It is the great happiness of my life to see you here. Now. Today. Safe.'

But you're not my dad.

I didn't know what to say.

The man raised his hand and made a light, flicking gesture with his little finger. 'Leave us,' he said.

Lewis melted away towards the kitchen. I could hear Mel and Rachel crossing the room behind me. The kitchen door shut. We were alone.

The man waved me towards the sofa. As I sat down, he took off his coat. He was wearing a dark suit underneath – it looked expensive – and a crisp, open-necked white shirt. He strode over to the nearest armchair and eased himself into it.

'Theodore. Theodore,' he said, still staring at me.

'Theo.' I looked down.

Several long seconds passed in silence.

'My name is Elijah Lazio,' the man said.

The Gene Genie. The man who owned the clinic where my dad worked. Except . . .

'As you can see, I did not die in the firebomb attack.' The man smiled. 'The press were as easy to fool as the police were co-operative.'

I realised my mouth had fallen open. I closed it.

'Call me Elijah,' he said. 'I think I would prefer it to Daddy.'

'But . . .' I didn't know what to say.

You're not my father.

'You know me as James Lawson.'

'But you're not him,' I said. 'I have . . . I had a picture. He . . . he looked different.'

'James Lawson was a cover. Always.'

I stared at him.

'Do you understand, Theodore? James Lawson. Elijah Lazio. A different face. A different name. A different past. But the same *person*.'

'The same person?' The world started spinning inside my head. What was he saying? 'You mean, my . . . my . . .?'

A lazy smile crept across Elijah Lazio's face. 'Ah, the ego-centricity of youth. All others are the planets around your sun. Still, yes, I do mean partly that.' He chuckled. 'Anyway, you *are* the sun. Apollo. The god of the sun. And therefore, in a way, truly my son.'

I had no idea what he was talking about. I gritted my teeth.

Elijah Lazio leaned forwards in his chair. 'Do you not see it, Theodore? Do you not see it in my face?'

His eyes laughed at me.

Suddenly my temper reared up. How dare this man talk in riddles to me? I'd been sold a pack of lies about who he was for years, then nearly killed when I tried to find him. At the very least I was owed a straight explanation of who he was and why – thanks to something *he* had done – RAGE wanted me dead.

'No. I don't see it,' I snapped. 'I don't see at all. Who are you? What did you do to me and Rachel when we were babies? And if you are my dad, why has everyone been lying to me about you all my life?'

Elijah Lazio's eyes widened. For a second he looked shocked. Furious, even. And then he laughed. A deep, rich belly laugh.

'Perfect,' he grinned. 'You are perfect. And I am, truly, a genius.'

'Yeah, and modest with it,' I spat.

'Okay. *Vale*.' Elijah Lazio ran his hand through his hair again. 'Let us begin at the beginning. In this sense you are my son: since you were born I have cherished you. Provided for you. Protected you. But genetically no, you are not my child . . .'

'Then who . . .?'

'Genetically we are more like twins.'

I stared at him. How could we be twins? The man was at least forty years older than me.

'Don't you see, Theodore? The truth is in your name – it means "Gift from God". I am far more than your father. I am your creator. I gave you life in a way no father could.'

183

What the hell was he talking about?

'Come on, Theodore. I know you have nearly guessed the truth. You know something special happened around your birth. Yours and Rachel's.'

'Rachel?' My mind was spinning.

'Yes. In fact . . .' Elijah turned towards the closed kitchen door. 'Mel,' he barked.

Mel poked her head round.

'Send Rachel out.'

A few seconds later, Rachel stumbled into the living room, her head bowed. Mel stood behind her, her hand on Rachel's shoulder.

Elijah introduced himself, then stood up.

'I shall tell you together,' he grinned. 'Oh, Theodore. My first full success. My bright, shining boy. My past, my present and my future. Do you not see how alike we are?'

I stared at his lined face. What did he mean? Then I looked into his eyes. And I saw.

It was like looking into a mirror.

'Yes,' he nodded. 'Yes. You are a clone, Theodore. My clone. A clone of me.'

38

Rachel

I stood there, shaking, vaguely aware of Theo sitting on the sofa, his mouth open in shock. Mel squeezed my shoulder.

Theo was a clone? A genetic replica of this man? It was crazy. Ridiculous. And yet the way Elijah had run his hand through his hair before – it had made me gasp precisely because I'd so often seen Theo make the exact same gesture.

I looked into Elijah's eyes. I didn't need to look over at Theo to make the comparison. They were exactly the same colour.

Elijah moved closer to me. 'How are you, Rachel?' His voice was smooth and confident.

I forced myself to hold his gaze.

'Do you know who *you* are?'

I shook my head, my mind spinning.

'Well . . .' He smiled. 'I created you too. I cloned you from your parent's dead child, Rebecca. I did it for them. They were my friends and they had suffered such a terrible loss.'

I stared at him, unable to speak. Unable to take in what he was saying.

'I was at your birth. That is how I avoided the firebomb.'
Elijah glanced at Theo. He was still sitting on the sofa, his head in his hands.

'*Guapa?*' Elijah nodded at Mel.

Mel nodded back, then glided away, towards the sofa.

Elijah put his arm round my shoulders. His presence was overpowering. Like a tidal wave.

'You must have wondered about your sister, no?' he said. 'How alike you are?'

I stared at him. *No way*. Rebecca had been beautiful. I wasn't. Even if cloning was possible, we simply didn't look the same. At least . . . I remembered how much like her I had been as a little girl.

'I didn't think it . . . that you could . . . that it was . . .' I tailed off.

Elijah glanced at Theo again. Mel was talking to him, but his hands were over his ears, his eyes cast down at the floor.

Elijah cleared his throat. 'All my life I wanted to be someone who made a difference. I became a doctor. A specialist . . . driven to help people who are denied the greatest gift of life – a child. I became obsessed with the power and the beauty of somatic cell nuclear transplantation – what the world knows as cloning. I was the first scientist to clone a primate – and I knew that I was close to creating a human embryo.' He sat back in his chair. 'Despite the creation of embryos used for stem cell research, no one else has yet successfully managed full reproductive cloning of a human. Do you know why that is?'

I shook my head.

'Because it is hard.' Elijah smiled. 'The understanding is there. The technology . . . though making it work is another matter . . . But what really held – holds – science back is fear: fear of the genetic and physical defects that all cloned animals so far have demonstrated – chromosomes with shortened telomeres or . . .' He flicked his fingers impatiently. 'But never mind that. The important area is that of methyl molecules. These are molecules which attach to DNA in all cells, controlling the functions of the DNA to an extent. Do you understand?'

'Er . . . not really.' I blushed, feeling stupid.

'Well, anyway.' Elijah took a deep breath. 'This process – the methylation of DNA in adult cells – happens unpredictably. Not at all like the way DNA is formatted in eggs and sperm. I knew that if I could find a way to control this process I could control the vulnerability of cloned subjects to genetic deformities.'

I frowned, trying to make sense of what he'd just said. 'You mean . . . you mean you worked out how to stop the clones you made from being deformed?'

'Yes, the discovery . . . I did it almost by accident,' he said. 'Of course this now minimised the risk of the human cloning, and I pressed on with my experiments until finally Theodore – and then you – were created.'

My head felt like it was too full, like I couldn't take in what he was saying. I was only dimly aware of Theo standing up, crossing the room and disappearing up the stairs.

Elijah and Mel exchanged looks. 'Leave him for a minute,' Elijah said. He took my arm and led me over to the sofa. We sat down.

Elijah sighed. 'I did not want to make any claims for my creation until I was sure Theodore was viable. I wanted my work to be properly verified by independent experts, of course, but I knew my life would change forever if I had succeeded. Look at the controversy surrounding the unsubstantiated claims of Pavel and Andropovich in past years, for example. And of course reproductive cloning is also illegal in the UK – though the initial stages of the process are identical to thera-peutic cloning, which is not. Anyway, I tried to keep what I was doing a secret. But even before Theodore was viable, RAGE discovered his existence. They tried to alert the press but their claims were ridiculed. The death threats started. But I kept going. I created you, for your parents. My friends.'

My heart thudded. Elijah smiled at me again. 'You know your mother was a beautiful woman, Rachel. And your father was a good friend to me. Not a geneticist. That is why he was never, individually, a RAGE target. But a good friend, never-theless. He knew much of what happened, though not the details of where I sent Apollo. And he told no one. So, then the firebomb, which I escaped, and the running away to Germany where RAGE found me and tried again to kill me. And I realised that I would be running for the rest of my life. And I nearly killed myself, Rachel. Maybe you cannot imag-ine that suffering. I was alone and despised with no money, no backing, no resources. No life. It took me nearly ten years to find a way to build back my research. And all the time I thought of Theodore, whom I was keeping carefully hidden from RAGE – and of you, whom they didn't realise even existed. My two precious creations.'

There was a long pause. Elijah Lazio held me with his eyes. They were like laser beams, probing right inside my head.

'Why do you not believe, Rachel?' he said softly.

His eyes were somehow drawing the truth out of me.

'Because Rebecca was beautiful.' Tears welled up, a twisting, miserable sensation in the pit of my stomach. Mel had been standing near the kitchen door. Now she walked over and squatted down beside me. She squeezed my hand.

Elijah sat back in his chair. 'Interesting,' he said. 'I wish I could show you to those *idiotas* at RAGE. You are proof, all the proof needed, that a clone is not a carbon copy of another individual. That each fresh unit is a new creation and that, if given a different environment to grow in, even one where the parents are the same, it will develop differently from the original – both physically and mentally.'

Each fresh unit?

He sounded as if he was delivering a lecture or something. I stared at him uncertainly. His eyes had glazed over, as if he were thinking about something far, far away. Then he snapped back to attention and I felt the full force of his gaze again. Mel let go of my hand and stood up.

'Go to the bathroom, Rachel,' he ordered. 'And this time look – really look – in the mirror.'

189

I did as I was told. The way Elijah spoke, you didn't feel you had much choice. There was no sign of Theo on the landing – his bedroom door was shut. I wondered vaguely how he was feeling – but my mind was mostly focused on Elijah's command.

In the bathroom I stared at the dark-edged mirror above the cracked enamel sink. An anxious, plump-faced girl with lank, skank hair stared back at me.

My heart sank. Somehow Elijah's words had sounded so powerful I'd almost imagined I would look in the glass and see Rebecca. But it was just me.

A clone.

I let the word sink in.

What did it mean? That I was a copy of another life? Second-hand? Yes. I was a replacement for my dead sister – never wanted in my own right.

It was hard to feel those things. And yet, they made sense. They made sense of my life up to now. The way I was always being compared to Rebecca. The way I didn't really fit in at home. Or anywhere.

There was a soft rap at the door. Mel appeared. She smiled sympathetically. 'You okay?' she said.

I shrugged. I didn't know what to say.

'This isn't easy stuff to deal with,' she said hesitantly. 'For either of you.' She paused. 'I think Theo's having a hard time with it, too.'

I nodded. 'It *is* hard. But in a funny kind of way it's like, somehow, I've always known too.'

Mel came over and put her arm round me. She was holding a piece of thin white card in her hand.

'Elijah's an amazing man,' she said. 'He found me on the streets. He turned everything around for me.'

There was something hollow in her voice, but I was too preocupied to think about it. She turned the card in her hand round. On the other side was a photograph of Rebecca – a copy of the one on our kitchen wall at home. In it Rebecca looked smiling and glamorous, with all her hair swept back.

'Elijah gave me this to show you. Here.' Mel handed me the photo. I held it under my chin so that it was reflected in the mirror, next to my own face.

Then Mel stood behind me and pulled my hair away from my head, like Rebecca's was in the picture. 'Smile,' she said.

I forced my mouth into a curve. I stared at our faces. Mine and Rebecca's.

Mel tilted her head to one side. 'Mmmn,' she said. 'Your face is a little fuller, of course, and your eyes are greener, though that could be the top you've got on, and the different light. Maybe you just look prettier because you're alive and she's only in a photo.'

I stared at her. She thought *I* was prettier than *Rebecca*?

Mel let go of my hair. 'You should wear it off your face more,' she said. 'You have great bone structure.'

She grinned at me, then walked out of the room.

I turned back to the mirror and stood there staring for a long time.

191

39

Theo

It was like the world was spinning round and round and my feet couldn't find the ground. Mel came into the bedroom. Tried to talk to me. But I couldn't focus on what she was saying. I pushed past her and went downstairs. I could hear Elijah and Lewis in the kitchen. No sign of Rachel. She must be as freaked out as I was.

Man.

I sat on the sofa for a minute, but the living room was closing in on me. I had to get out of the house.

The front door was no longer bolted shut. I guessed there was no need. I'd seen at least three security guards staked outside the house. I opened it and stepped outside. It was freezing. My breath rose in a mist around my face.

This was what I needed. Cold, clear air. One of Elijah's security guards was standing beside the front door. He looked at me suspiciously. I could hear him talking in his radio, asking for orders, as I stomped off across the gravel.

I hadn't been out of the house all day – and now it was

night time again. Away from the house, tramping across the nearest field, the darkness closed down around me like a net. I could hear footsteps behind me.

'Go away,' I yelled.

The footsteps stopped. More muttering into a radio.

I sank down onto the damp ground. What was the point in walking any further? I didn't know where I was or where I was going.

I put my head in my hands.

My dad was not my dad.

I had no dad.

My mum had lied to me all my life. My heart clenched up like a fist when I thought of how often I'd stared at that photo of James Lawson – the face of my made-up father. A man who didn't even exist. Or maybe did exist, but who had nothing to do with me.

And then another thought struck me like a blow, almost winding me. My mother wasn't really my mother. If I was a clone of Elijah, then I wasn't even related to her. Was I? I pressed the heels of my hands into my eyes. It was too much. Everything I thought I knew was being taken away from me.

More footsteps behind me.

'Theodore.' Elijah's voice was low and calm.

I ignored him.

'Theodore. Please come inside. I do not want to talk in the freezing cold.'

'Tough,' I muttered. 'And it's *Theo*.'

Elijah gave a heavy sigh. 'You have questions, no? Well, ask.'

I turned round. He was standing a few metres away from me, silhouetted against the lights from the cottage. There was no sign of the security guard who'd followed me.

'Why did you do it?' I got up and walked over to him.

Elijah looked surprised. 'Because I could,' he said. 'And because it is beautiful science.' He paused. 'You know, RAGE and many people think I am a monster because I play God. And in some ways I like this. I play along. Like with the code names. Did you work those out?'

I stared at him.

'I am Zeus, the father of heaven. Apollo and Artemis are two of Zeus's children. My creations. But it is a joke. What I do, really, is not so different from any fertility treatment. It is to—'

'How can you say that? I don't know who I am any more. My mother isn't even my mother.' My voice cracked.

'Of course she is your mother,' Elijah said crossly. 'You saw in the email – Leto, Apollo's mother.'

I stared at him blankly. He rolled his eyes.

'For what am I paying out all that money on your education if you do not have the most basic knowledge of classical culture?'

I looked away. 'I still don't see how she's my mother,' I said stubbornly.

Elijah sighed. 'Because she cares for you. And because she bore you in her womb – gave birth to you. What did you think? That I grew you in some sort of bell-jar?'

'I don't know what to think,' I snapped. 'I don't even know who that man is in the picture that I thought was my dad for fifteen years.'

Fury boiled in my stomach. Mum had lied to me. Lied and lied. And it was this man's fault.

I clenched my fists, barely containing the impulse to hit out at him.

Elijah waved his hand dismissively. 'A man from a magazine. Some photo agency. A nobody your mother and I picked to—'

'Did you care about her?' I said, suddenly gripped by a new thought. 'I mean, was she just a . . . a place to put me, or . . . or . . .?'

Since Mum had told me my dad was alive I'd imagined them as a couple. Kept apart by forces outside their control, maybe, but still a couple.

I ground my teeth. *Man*, how stupid was I?

Elijah sighed again. 'Your mother and I were something,' he said evasively. 'I think maybe she loved me once. Women do. Like they will you.'

'You don't know that,' I said. 'You don't know anything about me.'

The wind whistled through the small copse of trees at the far end of the field. It pierced through the jumper and jeans I was wearing – new stuff that Lewis had bought me.

'I know how you do at school.' Elijah folded his arms. 'That you are particularly good at math and science. Like I was. It is interesting to see how far the genetics take root. How far environment makes a difference.'

195

'What do you mean?' *Jesus*. I clenched my fists harder. He was talking about me like I was some kind of science experiment.

'When I knew I could not keep you with me, that I had to hide both of us from the murderers who would hunt us down and kill us like animals, I decided to give you an upbringing as close to my own as possible until you were old enough to join me. That meant a single mother. A good education, but being poorer than the other boys.' Elijah smiled. 'My parents – who, in a genetic sense, are your parents too – were victims of the war. The Second World War. I assume you know about this from your history lessons?'

I nodded, curtly, but inside my head was spinning almost out of control. How the hell could I have parents who'd been alive during the Second World War?

'They escaped from Germany in 1944,' Elijah said. 'I was born soon after. But my father killed himself when I was very young. We were extremely poor for a while. But we survived. And I was hungry to better myself. To be rich. To be successful.'

My mind somehow twisted away from the impossibility of such parents, to what Elijah had just said.

'I don't care about being rich and successful,' I said.

Elijah narrowed his eyes. He took a step towards me.

'Maybe not,' he said. 'But I recognise things in you that were in me when I was your age. Like your temper. Your recklessness. Your lack of fear. The way you don't let people in too close.'

'What?' My hands were freezing now. I shoved them in my pockets. 'I'm not like that.'

'No?' Elijah ran his fingers through his hair. 'You bullied your mother to tell you I was alive. You ran away from school to find Rachel. You took risks to find me. You didn't think how any of it would worry or hurt your mother.'

'I did . . . I . . .'

Elijah held up his hands in surrender. 'Very well. Maybe you do care about your mother. But you can't deny you behaved selfishly when you ran away, can you?'

I said nothing.

'Then you pick friends who make you look good – who show you the image of yourself that you like – like Jake and Max. Yes, I know about these friends. Jake with his hopeless girl-obsession. Max with her computers. You, Theodore, would never let yourself become so out-of-control as to let a girl or a hobby take over your life. No. Like I say, you let no one in too close. You stay in control. Looking down on the rest. No one is allowed in. Not even your mother. Not even that girl inside the cottage who clearly likes you so much. You make sure you feel superior to everyone.'

I stared at him. Well, *that* wasn't true. Jake might be a bit of a loser with girls and Max was a total nerd, but I liked them. They were my friends. I certainly didn't look down on them. Or Rachel. And I loved my mum. If anyone looked down on people it was Elijah.

'You've got no idea what you're talking about.'

Elijah smiled, which really pissed me off. I opened my

mouth to point out one thing he was definitely wrong about. Rachel. No way did she 'like' me in the way he meant. Anyway, he'd met her about five minutes ago. How could he know?

Then another thought struck me. Part of what he said – the earlier bit – *was* true. I had to admit it.

I didn't let anyone get too close. Not really.

I felt sick. Numb. All the anger was draining out of me.

'Come inside.' Elijah put his hand on my shoulder. It felt warm through the jumper. 'We will talk more while my beautiful Mel is preparing our meal.'

I didn't have the heart to resist any longer.

Without speaking, I let him guide me back to the house.

40

Rachel

When I came downstairs they were all sitting round the kitchen table. Elijah was telling some story, his arm round Mel's shoulders.

Were they an item? *Ew.* He was old enough to be her grandfather. And what about how she'd been with Lewis last night?

Lewis himself sat opposite. He was smiling with his mouth, but his eyes kept flickering to where Elijah's hand was stroking Mel's arm.

Theo was slumped in a chair at the end of the table, slightly turned away from the others. He was the only one who didn't look up when I walked in.

'Wow, Rachel. You look real nice,' Mel beamed.

I gave an embarrassed shrug. After she'd gone, I'd got my little arrow-shaped, diamante hairgrip and experimented with ways of pinning back my hair. Right now a long strand was holding back most of the rest of my hair on the left side of my head.

Elijah pointed to the hairgrip. 'Artemis the hunter.' He smiled. 'You know I see a lot of your father in you.'

I wanted to ask him more, like how well he knew Dad. But there were too many people in the room.

'Would you like to speak to your parents?' Elijah said.

'Yes.' I nodded eagerly.

Elijah glanced at Lewis, who sprang to his feet and herded me back out to the living room. He bent over a bulky cordless receiver.

'It's a safe line.' He handed me the phone. 'Go on. It's your dad.'

Lewis went back into the kitchen. I held the phone to my ear. My palms were sweaty against the plastic.

'Hello?'

'Hi, Dad.'

'Rachel?' I could almost feel the relief in his voice. 'Oh, Rachel, are you all right?'

'I'm fine.' I hesitated.

'Oh, Ro.' Dad's voice broke. 'I thought . . . we were so afraid . . . let me get Mum. She'll—'

'Wait.' I stared at the empty fireplace. 'I know, Dad. About . . . about everything.'

I let the words hang in the air.

'I know you do,' Dad said finally. 'Elijah told me he was going to have to tell you.' He took in a shuddering breath. 'I'm so sorry, Ro. I'm so sorry if it feels like we were lying to you. So sorry that you've been through all this. It wasn't how I wanted you to find out. But once we're together again I promise we'll make it up to you . . .'

There was another long pause. I sat down and leaned back against the armchair.

'Ro?'

'Why?' I said. This lump lodged itself in my throat. 'Why did you do it?' I knew the answer. I just needed to hear him say it.

Dad's breath quickened.

'Okay,' he said. 'I don't know if you can understand this, Rachel, but when Rebecca died it nearly killed us, your mother and me. And, maybe it sounds crazy, but we both thought that if we could just have another baby, it would help. It wasn't that we wanted to replace her . . .'

Yeah, right.

'. . . but your mother was too old to conceive naturally, so I talked to Elijah. I mean, I knew about his work on the methylation of DNA in adult cells – not that I understood the half of it – so I knew how far he'd come to getting over the problem of genetic disabilities. And I knew about his . . . about Apollo. Not details. Just that he existed. Anyway, Elijah persuaded us he was ready to clone again – and what more perfect scenario than ours? I think he thought the public would be sympathetic to our situation. We were planning on making an announcement once you were born, but . . .'

'RAGE,' I said.

'Yes. When they firebombed the clinic everything changed. Elijah went into hiding. We knew RAGE knew about Apollo.

We had to keep you a secret. We were scared if RAGE knew you existed they would . . . they wouldn't let you live.'

'But now they do know about me . . .' I remembered what Elijah had said in the kitchen.

Artemis the hunter.

Artemis the hunted.

'Yes. Thanks to that stupid boy who started sticking his nose—'

'He's my friend, Dad.' I glanced back at the closed kitchen door. 'He was just trying to find out the truth.'

'I know.' Dad sounded more subdued than I'd ever heard him. 'I'm sorry, Ro, you have every right to be angry.'

Another long pause. Then Dad spoke again.

'You know there were several reasons why we didn't tell you how you were born. At first because we couldn't risk you telling someone else. But also because we didn't want you to feel you were growing up under Rebecca's shadow, always being compared to her.'

I wanted to laugh and cry at the same time. Could he really not see how he and Mum had made comparisons every day of my life?

'I know everything must seem terrifying right now, Ro,' Dad went on. 'But please don't worry. We'll keep you safe. Elijah's making all the arrangements for our relocation. We're in a safe house too. We thought it would be better this way. RAGE will be looking for a family, not a couple. And soon they won't be able to find us at all. We'll have new names. A new home. A new school for you . . .'

A new school. I sat there, the possibilities of my new life trickling through my mind – energising, awakening me. I could reinvent myself. I could become the Rachel I wanted to be. It was a second chance. A chance of a new life.

Dad and I talked a bit longer. Then he put Mum on. She was all brittle and edgy, calling me sweetie but sounding angry underneath. At first that upset me, then it occurred to me that it wasn't actually me she was angry with – more that, if we relocated, she would have to give up her whole life, all the tennis club dinner-dances and the little lunches with her friends.

None of that was my fault.

After I hung up I sat in the armchair for a while. Then Mel called me in for the meal she'd cooked. It was some kind of vegetarian curry. Not too spicy, but full of delicious flavours. I ate hungrily. So did Elijah.

The others hardly touched theirs.

Theo still sat, hunched, at the end of the table. He looked miserable and completely lost in his own thoughts. I tried to catch his eye a few times, but he barely looked up from his plate.

Mel was trying hard to be cheerful, laughing at Elijah's stories and gazing up at him with this fixed smile on her face. But, to me, it was clearly put on. Lewis was even more obviously miserable. He listened and laughed too. But he prodded his food with a fork, eating very little. And his eyes were full of resentment.

'So Mel, *querida*,' Elijah said. 'I must leave after this meal. Will you come with me? Back home?'

Mel bit her lip. Lewis stiffened in his chair.

It struck me that if I could see they were behaving oddly, then maybe so could Elijah. It was pretty gross thinking that he and Mel were together. But still. A girlfriend was a girlfriend. I couldn't imagine Elijah would be very happy if he realised how much Lewis was into her.

'I think I should stay with Rachel,' Mel said awkwardly. 'It would be better for her with a woman around.'

For a second Elijah's eyes grew cold and hard. Then they softened again. He glanced at me, his eyebrows raised.

I nodded, blushing. 'I'd like Mel to stay,' I said.

Elijah looked from me, back to Mel. 'Fine,' he said neutrally. He stood up. 'Now I must speak to the men.'

He strode out of the room. Seconds later we heard the front door slam shut. The atmosphere round the table suddenly relaxed.

'He's leaving.' Lewis let out a long sigh and smiled tenderly at Mel. She blushed and smiled back.

Could they make it any more obvious?

Embarrassed, I looked at Theo. He was still staring at his plate, apparently oblivious to everything around him.

Elijah came back after a few minutes. 'RAGE are heading north,' he said. 'They know about our airstrip.' He looked at Lewis. 'It's deeply unfortunate your orders to save Theo prevented you from killing Simpson.'

Simpson. The man from RAGE Lewis could have shot. But hadn't.

'You know your next assignment?' Elijah said.

'Yes, sir.' Lewis stood up.

But Elijah turned to Mel. 'Come with me,' he commanded.

She bent her head and followed him out of the room. Lewis slumped back down in his chair. A minute later the floor above us creaked. I made a quick assessment of which room that was. Mel's bedroom. I suddenly realised what Mel and Elijah were probably doing. Lewis kicked at the chair opposite him, where Elijah had been sitting a few minutes before.

I walked over to Theo and put my hand on his arm. 'You okay?'

'I guess.' He shot me this beautiful, sad smile.

My stomach flipped over. I wanted to talk to him about everything. Later, I wished I had. But at the time, with Lewis brooding away at the table beside us, it seemed impossible.

Elijah and Mel came back down after twenty minutes or so. Elijah's eyes were cold as he commanded us to go into the living room. I stood between Theo and Lewis, staring at Mel. She seemed to have shrunk into herself, and was standing close to Elijah with her head bowed.

One of the security guards appeared at the front door.

'We're ready, sir.'

Elijah nodded towards two large bags on the ground beside him. I stared at them uneasily. What was in them? As far as I'd noticed, Elijah hadn't brought anything into the house with him.

'Mel?' Lewis stared at the bags. His voice was uncertain. They were *her* bags. Mel didn't look up.

Lewis took a step towards her.

'Stop,' Elijah barked.

The atmosphere in the room tightened. Lewis stepped back.

Elijah flicked his little finger and the security guard strode over from the door and picked up the bags, then turned and went outside.

Gripping Mel's hand, Elijah walked towards us.

'Say goodbye to everyone,' he said.

Mel looked up. I gasped. There was a dark red bruise under her right eye. Lewis let out his breath in a hiss.

I stared at Elijah. Had he hit her? Had he realised about her and Lewis? Fear spiralled up into my throat. I took a step backwards. Into Theo. We stood, our arms touching, watching Elijah.

It happened too quickly for me to take in. Elijah raised his hand. Something glinted in his fist. He pointed whatever it was at Lewis. Electric sparks. The same ratchety, thudding noise that I'd heard when Lewis had knocked out that man at my school. It took seconds. Lewis swayed slightly. Toppled forwards across the arm of one of the chairs.

I stared, unable to breath.

'*No.*' Mel. Half a gasp. Half a groan.

Elijah ignored her. He pulled a real gun from inside his jacket. Pointed it at Lewis's unconscious body. Then he glanced at the guard who had reappeared in the doorway.

'Take them outside. All of them.'

The guard grabbed my arm and marched me to the door.

206

He shoved me through. The wind sliced across my face. The guard vanished. Seconds later, Theo stumbled out beside me. Then Mel, her eyes wide with horror.

My mouth fell open in disbelief. Elijah wouldn't. He couldn't be going to . . .

A shot echoed out from the cottage.

For a second everything froze. Then I turned towards Theo, just as he turned to me. Our arms reached out. Clutching at each other, holding each other. *No. No. No.* I buried my face in his chest. His face was down too, pressed against my hair.

I could hear Mel whimpering.

I held Theo tighter, my eyes squeezed shut. He was clinging to me like he was drowning.

Footsteps. The front door opening. Elijah's voice – a low growl. The beep of the car unlocking. Mel falling silent. More footsteps. *No.* Someone wrenching Theo away from me. *No. No. No.*

Inside my head I was screaming. But I knew I was making no sound. Theo was yelling though, gripping my arms, his fingers being prised off one by one. I opened my eyes and watched him kicking out at two security guards – one on either side of him. They were dragging him to the car.

Another guard spun me round and shoved me backwards into the house. The front door slammed shut in my face.

I stared at the closed door. Heard the car engine starting up. The scrunch of tyres on gravel.

Silence.

They were gone. They had all gone. It didn't make sense. Elijah had gone and left me here alone with . . .

I turned round, my heart bumping furiously in my chest, and stared at Lewis's body slumped over the armchair.

41

Theo

I yelled until I was hoarse. My head felt like it was exploding. Like I was going mad.

Elijah had shot Lewis. Why? It made no sense. And now I'd been bundled away from Rachel, my arms twisted behind my back by the guards – across the gravel, into the warm seven-seater Toyota. Mel was already in there, sitting behind me, her bruised face in her hands. Elijah had done that too. Why?

And what was he doing with me?

I understood none of it. All I wanted was to get back to Rachel. She was the one fixed point in the chaos. The one person I was sure I could trust.

One of the guards sat beside me, holding my arms. I kicked out at the seat in front. At Elijah.

'Why did you shoot him?' I yelled. 'Where's Rachel? Where are you taking me?'

'Quiet,' Elijah ordered.

'No.' I swore at him, kicking the seat again. Fury blasted,

red hot, into my head. 'What are you going to do with me? Kill *me* too?'

'*Mierda*.' Elijah twisted round, his face contorted with rage. 'Stop, Theodore. Stop. I have a phone here, for you to call your mother. Now, stop.'

'No.' I pummelled the seat with my heels, swearing in long, loud strings of words – the worst words I could think of. The guard was twisting my arm up high above my back, trying to stop me. But I was off my face with rage – so furious I could barely feel the pain.

Elijah barked out some orders in Spanish. A few seconds later one of the other guards appeared over my shoulder, a syringe in his hand.

'No,' I shouted, struggling even harder. 'No.'

But they were too strong. The guard holding my arm wedged me against the side window, while the one with the syringe tore at my top. With a sharp prick the needle pierced my upper arm. I felt something cold seeping into me. And then I felt sick and everything went black and I was sinking down, down, down . . .

I woke up disoriented, icy air whipping round my face. I was slung between two guards, being hauled across tarmac with lights on either side, like a runway.

I lifted my head a little. *Man, that hurt*. I felt sick. Groggily I lifted my eyes and looked around. It *was* a runway. Round lights ran for hundreds of metres down either length of it. And there was a small plane at the far end. A white Lear Jet, stood in front of a brightly-lit building. Like a warehouse or . . . of course . . . an aircraft hangar.

My stomach heaved. I groaned.

'Kid's gonna barf,' said one of the guards holding me. He had an American accent.

Both guards slid out from under my arm. I stumbled, trying to find my feet, but my legs were too shaky. I dropped to my knees and puked over the tarmac.

I sat back on my heels, shivering, and wiped my mouth on my sleeve.

'What a waste of Mel's delicious food.' Elijah's voice above my head was cold.

I looked round. He was standing beside me, holding Mel by the hand, staring down contemptuously. Then he turned to the guards. 'Get him on the plane.'

He strode forwards, tugging Mel after him. The guards stepped around my vomit and hauled me up by the armpits. They started dragging me roughly again, but apart from my groggy head, I felt better for having been sick. Stronger. My feet fumbled against the ground. Then I took a proper foot-step. And another.

By the time we reached the plane I was starting to think more clearly. The guards shoved me up the steps. Inside there were five, maybe six, rows of seats. More like little sofas than ordinary aeroplane seats. Two guards were already strapped into their seats at the back. A third was walking through to what looked like the cockpit.

Elijah was standing in the aisle.

211

'Sit with Mel,' he ordered. I made my way towards her. She was near the front of the plane, hunched over, looking out of the window.

I sat down next to her. Elijah eased himself into the seat opposite. He held out the large phone I'd noticed before.

'This is your last chance to call your mother,' he said. 'I would like you to speak to her. I promised her you would. It may be some time before you see her again.'

'Why?' I snapped. 'Where are you taking me?'

A look of exasperation crossed Elijah's face. 'We can speak about it after you've talked with your mother.'

'Back to Germany?'

Elijah laughed. 'Was that where your mother told you I was?'

I looked away. Mum had even lied about that. Fury flooded through me.

'She was just trying to protect you, Theodore.' Elijah tutted. 'Is that where you were going when RAGE and Lewis found you?'

I said nothing.

'I see. You made the connection with Richard Smith, who *was* in Germany,' Elijah said, slowly. 'Clever. And not really a coincidence. I did live in Germany for a long time. And Richard *was* there on business for me. Clever of you, Theodore.'

I couldn't bear the patronising tone of his voice. 'So where are we going then?'

'Somewhere safe,' he said. 'Now, please speak to your—'

'What was wrong with where we were before?' I clenched my jaw. 'Why is Rachel still there?'

Elijah pressed his lips together so tightly they were almost white.

'Your mother,' he said, firmly, holding out the phone.

I sat back and folded my arms. 'No. Not till you tell me where we're going.'

'Señor Lazio.' The second of the two guards who had dragged me across the tarmac materialised beside us. He said something in Spanish.

Elijah flicked his fingers in a gesture of irritation. '*Vale.* Okay.'

He looked at me and pocketed the phone. 'I will speak to her myself. Explain you are angry with her.' He leaned forwards and lowered his voice to a whisper. 'Because you *are* angry with her, Theodore, aren't you? You are not thinking about your mother's fears at all. Only how she deceived you about me. Only how you don't need her. Or anyone.'

Then he drew back a little and smiled at me – a cold, hard smile.

'You see, I was right about you,' he said.

He stood up and strode off down the aisle.

I sat there for a minute, staring down at the seatbelt in my lap. Elijah was right, of course. I *was* angry with Mum. But I had refused to speak to her only because he had wanted me to do just that. Because I thought it would annoy him. And yet somehow he'd turned it around to make it sound like he'd always known that's how I would behave.

213

'Sometimes it's hard to work him out,' Mel whispered. 'He's the cleverest person I've ever met.'

I looked round at her. The bruised skin round her eye was swollen now.

She saw me staring and turned her face away.

'It was my fault,' she said.

'That he hit you?' I said. 'No way. He . . .'

'No.' Her lips trembled. 'My fault about Lewis.'

She drew back into her seat and turned to the window again.

I didn't know what she meant. But right now why Elijah had shot Lewis was not the most burning question in my head. I wanted to know where we were going. I wanted to know what was going to happen to Rachel. And, most of all, I wanted to know what Elijah was planning to do with me.

The plane's engine started whirring. I could hear voices outside. Shouts. Commands.

I was sure of only one thing. I was going to need a friend in order to survive whatever was about to happen to me. I glanced over my shoulder. Elijah was walking back towards us.

'Mel?' I whispered.

She looked round, her cheeks shining with tears.

I made a fist and thumped it into my other hand – like we'd done with the boxing. I wanted her to see it as a gesture of strength. Of solidarity between us.

I think she got it. She nodded. 'Talk later, babe.'

She turned back to the window as Elijah swung himself

into the seat opposite me again. The plane doors slammed shut.

'Fasten your seatbelt, Theodore,' he said.

I did as I was told. There was no point fighting and yelling over stuff I couldn't control. I had to make my priority getting some answers, then getting away from Elijah.

I gripped the side of the seat as the plane chugged slowly round in a circle and began taxiing down the runway.

I could survive this. I *would* survive it.

Whatever happened.

I was trying to be strong. But as the plane took off, all I could think about was how I wished I'd spoken to my mum when I'd had the chance.

42

Rachel

My whole body shook.

I edged towards the chair. Lewis was slumped over the arm, his face pressed into the seat, his right arm dangling down to the stone floor below. It had occurred to me that I should make sure he really was dead. I mean, maybe he was only unconscious. I wasn't sure what I would do then – dial nine-nine-nine for an ambulance, I guess. If I could find Lewis's mobile. If RAGE didn't trace the call and get here first.

But I was scared. He was lying so still I was sure I was wrong. He had to be dead. And I'd never even seen a dead body before, let alone touched one. I took another tiny step, then crouched down. His nose was creased, pressed sideways against the rough chair fabric. The tip beyond the crease almost white. I looked behind him, at the chair. I frowned. There was no blood.

I glanced quickly round the chair. If he'd been shot, surely there should be blood somewhere?

I reached out my trembling arm and touched Lewis's

neck – like I'd seen him do when he was checking the guy he'd tasered at the school disco. His skin was warm.

I pushed my fingers in under his chin. I had no idea exactly where the pulse would be.

He groaned. My hand shot back.

'Lewis?' My voice was hoarse. 'Lewis?'

The arm dangling from the chair twitched. A single blue eye opened and stared at me.

'Lewis? Are you okay?'

He groaned again, then tried to push himself up off the chair. I put my arms under his and helped him stand. He lurched unsteadily towards the sofa and collapsed backwards onto it, breathing heavily.

I knelt on the stone floor beside him. 'Lewis?'

'Water,' he whispered. 'Please.'

I scrambled to my feet and raced into the kitchen. When I returned with a glass of water slopping in my still-shaking hands, Lewis was sitting slightly more upright, his face grey, clutching his forehead.

He took a sip of water.

'Man, I've got a mother of a headache,' he muttered.

After a few moments his face started to get some colour back.

'What happened?' I said. Tears of relief pricked at my eyes. 'I thought you were dead.'

Lewis's lips curved into a gentle smile. 'Not me,' he said. He pointed to one of the sofa cushions. A bullet-sized hole was torn through its cover. 'Elijah's latest game.'

He closed his eyes as if it was hurting them to talk.

I stared at the cushion, then back at Lewis. Why had Elijah only pretended to shoot him?

'Did you see what he did to her?' Lewis's face creased. 'Did you see . . .?'

He was talking about Mel – the bruise round her eye. I sniffed back my tears.

'Don't think about it now,' I said. 'Go to sleep.'

A minute later his breathing grew deep and steady. I fetched a duvet from upstairs and laid it over him. Then I sat curled up in the armchair and wept.

I cried and cried.

In the end I didn't even know what I was crying for – for the shock I'd just been through, for learning I really was a freak – a clone – that people wanted dead, for how unloved and unhappy I'd been for years, for missing Mum and Dad, and for Theo, whose arms I wanted to feel round me more than anything else in the world.

Lewis slept on as my gut-wrenching bawling gave way to softer, shakier sobs. Finally, completely exhausted, I fell asleep too.

When I woke up, a thin grey light was filtering in through the window. The duvet that I'd laid over Lewis was tucked in around me, tickling my neck – and the sofa was empty.

I sat up, feeling curiously empty. Like I'd shed some terrible weight I'd been carrying around my whole life. And I was starving hungry.

Toast smells drifted towards me from the kitchen.

As I stretched out my arms the door from the kitchen opened. Lewis appeared, balancing a mug of tea on a plate of toast.

'Breakfast?' he smiled.

We sat in silence for a while, munching on the toast. Lewis looked lost in his own thoughts. My own pressed down on me.

'Will Theo be okay?' I said.

Lewis nodded. 'Elijah's not going to hurt him. I'm more worried about Mel.' He looked down at the floor.

'What do you think all that was about . . . yesterday?' I said, timidly. 'Pretending to shoot you, I mean.'

Lewis shrugged.

'D'you think . . .' I paused. 'D'you think he wanted Mel to think you were dead in order to . . . to punish her . . . to punish you both for . . . for . . . being together?'

Lewis put down his toast. 'How did you know?'

I looked away, remembering how I'd seen them on the sofa that first night. 'Er . . . well . . . you looked like you hated it when he was touching her,' I stammered. 'I mean it was quite obvious you liked her.'

'God, then Elijah must have realised . . . Oh God, I messed up my bed so he wouldn't . . . but . . .' Lewis groaned. 'That means it's my fault he hit her.' He held his head in his hands. 'Oh God.'

'No.' I sat forward. 'No. She looked like she hated him touching her too. And it was really obvious how much she was into you.'

Lewis looked up at me. 'Was it?' He grinned like a little kid, suddenly looking incredibly pleased with himself.

I rolled my eyes. It was weird but now the two of us were on our own, it felt different, like we were more equal. It was hard to remember how in awe I'd been of Lewis just two days ago, when he'd rescued us from RAGE. Now he seemed more like I imagined a big brother might.

'I don't understand though,' I said. 'Why make her think you were dead? Why not just punch you? Or say something?'

'Elijah's like that. Full of complicated games,' Lewis said. 'Maybe he thinks she'll stop caring about me if she thinks I'm gone. Maybe he just wanted to show us both he's more powerful than we are.'

I nodded. It all fell into place. Elijah was a bully. Which meant what he wanted most of all was to make other people feel weak.

'I expect he *is* planning to kill me, anyway,' Lewis added, bitterly. 'He just needs me to complete my next assignment first.'

'How can you be so sure?'

'Elijah saved my life years ago,' Lewis said. 'As far as he's concerned I owe him everything. *Everything*.'

'What d'you mean?'

'I was nine going on twenty-nine,' Lewis said. 'Living on the streets of Buenos Aires, hanging with a gang. I already knew how to use a knife and a gun. If Elijah hadn't rescued me I'd have been dead within a year. He taught me how to read and write and how to move without making a sound. He made me learn English from an English tutor so that I would have no trace of a Spanish or American accent. So I could pass as British, here, where RAGE is based.'

My mouth fell open. 'He did all that so he could send you into danger?'

Lewis laughed. 'I was an investment. Expendable. As he sees it, he "created" me – just like he "created" you and Theo. Though not in the same league of course. And what he created is his to destroy.'

A shiver went down my spine.

'So what's your next assignment?' I said.

'Deliver you to your new home,' Lewis said. 'Elijah is making a considerable effort to protect you. He must owe your father an awful lot – or else . . .' He smiled. 'Maybe he still hopes one day RAGE will collapse and he'll be free to show you off to the world. Be recognised for the genius he undoubtedly is.'

I shrugged, uneasily. I was beginning to realise that my life would be tied to Elijah's for as long as we both lived.

It wasn't a happy thought.

'What about Theo?' I said. 'D'you think Elijah will let me know where he relocates him and his mum?'

Lewis sighed. 'From what I've picked up, Theo won't be going back to his mum. Elijah's planning to keep him.'

I stared at him, horrified.

'We can't let that happen,' I said. 'Theo won't want that.'
And I'll never see him again.

221

Lewis sighed again. 'It's what Elijah wants that counts.'

'We have to get him out.' I sprang up, sending my plate of toast flying.

'And what about RAGE?' Lewis shook his head. 'They're closer to finding Theo than they've ever been. I don't think you appreciate how much danger both of you are in from them.'

The image of Theo kneeling on the tarmac, that gun pressed against his forehead, forced its way into my mind.

I sat down again slowly. 'I do realise,' I said. 'It's just . . . none of this is his fault.'

A few minutes later, Lewis had finished his toast and went upstairs to shower. I curled back up in the duvet and let my mind drift off, thinking about Theo. His sad smile last night in the kitchen. How he'd held me outside the cottage. At the school disco. Then further back, to how we'd met up at Max's house. How gorgeous he'd looked when he opened the door. How he'd told Jake off for hassling me in Max's kitchen.

I sat bolt upright. Jake and Max. After Mel had told us they were safe, I'd forgotten all about them.

Of course. An idea flowed, fully-formed, into my mind.

Yes. Max was the key. If she really was all right. If she'd only agree.

If Lewis would agree too.

By the time he came back downstairs I had a plan.

Part Three

Washington, D.C.

43

Theo

We took off just before three a.m. Mel wrapped herself in a blanket and appeared to fall asleep almost immediately. Elijah soon after. I moved to the window seat in the row behind them and looked out at the dark sky. My mind raced. I couldn't sleep.

Where were we going? What was Elijah planning to do with me? What was happening to Rachel? I went over and over these questions in my head, my imagination finding no answers that brought me any peace.

My thoughts kept returning to what Elijah had told me yesterday. I was a clone. More . . . I was Elijah's clone. But what did that mean? How much of Elijah was really in me? I didn't want to be like him. He was cold and cruel and violent. And yet he was also powerful – not just because of the guards he was surrounded by. In spite of myself, I had to admire the way he commanded a room by walking into it.

Then again, he was also a scientific genius, which I certainly showed no sign of becoming.

How could we be made from the same DNA and yet appear to be so different? What had Elijah said? That when he realised he couldn't have me with him because it was too dangerous, he'd deliberately arranged my upbringing to match his own as far as possible. Why had he done that? Was it to try and make me like him? He'd said he always intended me to join him at some point? What was that for?

I shivered. Outside the aeroplane was empty space. We were a tiny white dot, flying through the blackness. Elijah had said his parents were dead – that made me an orphan too. Technically.

I felt like one. I felt like a plane crashing. Spinning through the sky – unseen and alone.

I thought about Mum. I thought about Rachel, on her own in that cottage with Lewis's body. I thought about Lewis – how impossible it seemed that he could be dead. That Elijah could have killed him.

Hours passed. The night seemed to go on forever. I had no watch, so I walked over to where Elijah slept to look at his.

One of the guards was immediately at my side, pushing me away.

'I just want to know the time,' I said.

The guard grunted. 'Fifteen after six, UK time.' He had an American accent, like the guard on the tarmac before.

I frowned. If it was still so dark that meant we must be flying west, into the night, and not east, into the morning.

I tried to imagine what lay west of Britain.

America.

Of course.

We were going to America.

I fell asleep in the end, waking stiff and cold and still tired as the plane bumped along the landing runway. As it taxied to a halt, Elijah stood up and walked past, talking very fast in Spanish to one of the guards.

Mel's head appeared over the seat in front. The bruise round her right eye was darker now. She gave me a weak smile. 'We're here.'

'Where?' I said. All I could see out of the window was a distant row of trees.

'Virginia,' Mel whispered, glancing at Elijah's back. 'Just outside Washington D.C. That's where we're going now. D.C.'

Elijah turned and she shut up.

We were heading for the capital of the United States? I frowned. That didn't make sense. Why would Elijah work in such a busy area? His life depended on RAGE not being able to find out where he was. For the first time I wondered what Elijah did day to day. Did he really work in some clinic? Or had that been a lie too?

It was good to feel the bright morning sunshine on my face as we crossed the landing strip. I followed Elijah and Mel towards a waiting limousine with darkened windows. The American guard I'd spoken to in the night opened the back door for me. I slid across the long, leather seat.

Elijah settled himself next to me. 'Feeling better?' he asked.

I resisted the temptation to bite his head off.

'Why don't I need a passport?' I said, as calmly as I could.

Elijah smiled. 'You do.' He flicked through the pile of documents in his lap and pulled out a small dark-blue book. A United States passport. He opened it and handed it to me.

There was a photograph of me. I was called Theodore Lawson, an American citizen. Lawson – the name I'd *thought* was my dad's. How many times had I fantasised about taking that name – and about meeting my dad. How proud I'd thought I would feel.

Elijah rapped on the glass barrier that separated us from the driver. 'I thought you would appreciate the name,' he chuckled.

I wanted to tell him I thought it was a pretty sick joke but, again, I stopped myself. The limousine glided towards the edge of the landing strip. Through the front of the car I could see wasteland in front of us, leading to a wide road beyond.

'It's just a formality of course,' Elijah said. 'I bribe the official here anyway. But officials everywhere – corrupt or not – do love to see paperwork. No?'

He beamed at me, clearly thinking he'd made some fabulous joke.

I forced myself to smile back.

'Is Rachel all right?' I said. The limo started bumping over the wasteland. We were clearly heading for the road. I held my breath. I think if he'd told me anything had happened to her I might have lost it again. But he didn't.

'Rachel will be fine,' he said coldly. 'Someone is looking after her. They will make sure she is reunited with her family in the next few weeks.'

I nodded. Of course I had no idea whether he was telling the truth, but I was reassured nonetheless. In the clear, crisp daylight it seemed unlikely that Elijah would have gone to such great lengths to rescue either of us from RAGE only to kill us himself.

As the limo swung out into the road, it occurred to me that if Rachel was settled with her family under a new name – possibly even in a new country – then I would probably never see her again.

My throat tightened. I didn't want to think about that. I peered out of the window as we flashed past a signpost. I didn't catch the name.

'What do you do here?'

'My work.' Elijah waved his hand, vaguely. 'Genetic research.'

'Cloning?' I said.

He shook his head. 'No. I do not wish to put more lives at risk. Now, Theodore, for your own safety I do not wish you to see where we go now. I must ask you to accept a blindfold.'

I let one of the guards tie a black band round my eyes. Elijah made a few more comments about his work – what a great man he was, what a terrible waste of his talents RAGE had brought about years ago by denying him the opportunity to carry on developing his research.

I said nothing. Apart from the fact that I thought the man

was a pompous idiot, I refused to carry on a discussion with anyone while suffering the indignity of not being able to see them.

Soon Elijah lowered his voice and started murmuring in Spanish to Mel.

My thoughts turned to my real parents. My genetic parents: Elijah's mother and father, who had escaped from Germany towards the end of the Second World War. Elijah had called them victims of the war. The main victims of the war that I knew about from school, were the six million Jews killed when Hitler tried to wipe out the entire race from Europe in the Holocaust. I guessed that was a kind of sick genetic engineering. Was that why Elijah had studied so hard to become a geneticist? In revenge for what had been done to his race?

My race?

If my genetic parents were Jewish, did that make me Jewish too? At home I hadn't been anything. Well, British – but no religion. Now I was . . . what? German? Jewish? I had no idea.

I was lost. In absolutely every sense of the word.

I lost track of how long we'd been driving too. At last I sensed the car slowing and tilting downhill. I was sure from the muffled outside sounds we were driving through a tunnel. It seemed to go on a long time.

Finally we stopped. I felt hands tugging at my blindfold. Mel's face appeared in front of me. She looked calmer than she had last night.

'We're here.' Smiling, she leaned into my ear and whispered, 'It'll be okay, Theo. Don't worry.'

And then she turned away to get out of the car – and I caught sight of the weirdest place I'd ever seen in my life.

44

Rachel

'Of course it will work,' I said.

I was so fired up I wouldn't listen to any of Lewis's objections.

'It's masses of work. *And* it's insanely risky,' he said.

I shook my head. 'So what do you want to do? Leave Theo at the mercy of a man he doesn't even know? Leave Mel with someone who hits her?'

Lewis looked across the moorland. We were outside, taking a walk around the cottage. I couldn't bear to be cooped up indoors for another second. It was fantastic to feel the wind whipping through my hair, burning my cheeks.

'I don't want to put you in any danger.'

I glared at him. 'It's the only way.'

'Okay.' He sighed. 'Explain it to me again.'

'You take me to the RAGE headquarters. You pretend Elijah was blackmailing you to rescue me and Theo from RAGE. But you were only going along with it until you could get away from him, that you were really working for

RAGE all along. That *that* was why you didn't kill Simpson and that other guy.' I focused on Lewis's bright blue eyes, willing him to accept what I was saying, to believe in my plan. 'You explain that you can get RAGE right inside Elijah's compound – all the way to Theo – on the pretext of delivering *me* to Elijah.'

'As I said, it's insanely risky.' Lewis sighed. 'But it's the next bit that's the problem.'

'No.' I turned into the wind, letting it surge against my face. 'No. It's perfect. While RAGE and Elijah's guards are battling it out, we find Theo and Mel and escape.'

Lewis rolled his eyes. 'You have no idea what that kind of scene is really like. It's total chaos. Impossible to plan for.'

'But you know Elijah's compound. You know where he'll have Theo. Roughly, at least. You can direct RAGE some-where else.'

Lewis strode on ahead. I let him go. I sensed he needed some time to think through what I was suggesting. He'd already told me about the Washington D.C. compound where Elijah lived. Lewis knew the place inside and out. If anyone could get us in there, it was him.

The wind died and the sun emerged from behind a cloud. I tipped my face upwards, enjoying its warmth. I wondered how Theo was. Whether he was thinking of me.

Lewis walked back.

'Even if Max is as good as you say, she may not want to have anything to do with this,' he said. 'And I'd need her help. I'm no computer expert.'

'But there's no reason why we shouldn't ask her,' I said.

'I guess.' Lewis paused. 'It's just RAGE picked up Max and Theo's friend Jake on Friday evening, trying to find out what they knew. Only for a couple of hours, but still . . .' He tailed off.

I nodded. I could just imagine how frightening that must have been – being questioned by the people who'd held a gun to Theo's head.

'But they didn't know anything,' I said. 'RAGE must've realised that. Max and Jake didn't even know Theo was planning on running away. And they certainly had no idea about all the cloning stuff. Don't you see, so long as RAGE don't realise we've contacted them, they're not at risk. And if Max does all the work in internet cafés, they won't be able to track her like they did on her home computer.'

'Which they'll definitely be monitoring,' Lewis added.

'I know.' I waited while he paced off again.

My plan was that, while Lewis and I worked out how we would infiltrate the RAGE headquarters and attack Elijah's base in Washington D.C., Max – under Lewis's direction – would research the basic stuff we needed for a successful secret relocation. Not the one Elijah had come up with for me and my family. But three whole new packages. I had this idea we could all end up somewhere close to each other. Me, Mum and Dad – Lewis and Mel – and Theo and his mother.

I hadn't mentioned this particular detail to Lewis yet.

'Rachel.' Lewis shook his head. 'The whole thing is totally mad.'

'But you'll do it?' I said eagerly.

Lewis grinned. 'For Mel and Theo, yes. But there's one condition.'

45

Theo

I got out of the car and stared at the building.

The two huge steel doors that the car had just driven through shut with a clang. We were completely underground – concrete walls on either side and a low ceiling above our heads. The building in front of me was built right into the concrete. Squat, with a curved glass front and sturdy steel pillars. But it wasn't the outside of the building that caught my attention.

I couldn't take my eyes off what was inside.

Through the glass was a huge room that looked . . . well, it looked like a *park*. It was unbelievable. A carpet of grass. Trees and flowers instead of furniture.

Elijah led Mel, me and two of the security guards through the first set of sliding doors. They shut immediately behind us. He punched some numbers into the screen beside the next set. After a few seconds these doors opened too and we walked into the indoor park.

I gasped. It was like stepping into the country. The glass

walls that led out to the concrete exterior had vanished. Instead were images of trees and distant fields that vanished into a faraway horizon. I knew they must be projected pictures – holograms – but they were more convincing than anything similar I'd ever seen before. Above was what looked like a clear blue sky, the occasional cloud drifting across it. A few people were walking about. I could even hear children playing in the distance. And the air smelled different – sweet, somehow, like real country, with a light breeze.

'The Outdoor Room. It's all smoke and mirrors,' Elijah said, clearly enjoying the stunned look on my face. 'We use holograms and sound tracks and modified air con to create the illusion of an outside world. It's our main recreation area. A prototype for the sort of thing they'll build in space one day.'

He led me across the field and over a small bridge that spanned a stream. Elijah noticed me gawping at the sparkling water. 'It's on a loop,' he said. 'Like a fountain.'

We passed an exit sign pinned to a tree – the only incongruous element in the whole scene – and came to a large wooden shack. Elijah entered some numbers into a pad next to the door. The door slid open. Inside were tables and folded table umbrellas.

'There's a café outside at weekends,' Elijah smiled. 'And some people prefer the shade. Not that you'd burn in our sun. No harmful UV rays.' He laughed.

The door we had just walked through slid shut again. Elijah pressed some buttons to open the one in front. 'So what do you think?'

'It's incredible,' I said, truthfully. 'But why is it here?'

'I have powerful friends.' Elijah ran his hand through his hair. 'And there's a staff of over a hundred here – scientists, security, plus all the service staff – catering and cleaning and so on. And all their families. We have an elementary school and a children's play area. Most people only leave for holidays. Our biggest security risk is when the doors open to let people in and out.'

I tucked this piece of information away in my head for possible future use. I was impressed by the Outdoor Room, but there was something about it that I hated too. Maybe the idea that it was entirely fake.

There was no time to think about it. The door in front of us opened. Elijah strode off along a long, clinically-white corridor. Rooms led off on both sides. We rounded a bend and went through two or three more security doors. Several harassed-looking men and women scurried past. They all greeted Elijah with the same mix of respect and fear.

'Tell me again what kind of work you do here?' I said.

'Cutting-edge work in genetics. PGDT techniques, mostly.' He smiled. 'That's pre-implantation genetic diagnosis – when you screen embryos for genetic diseases. All good, helpful, scientific work.'

I stared at him. 'Why's it all so secret then? Why does it have to be underground?'

The smile slid off Elijah's face. He cast me a withering stare. 'I wonder if some of my DNA was corrupted when you were created,' he snapped sarcastically. 'Perhaps you have forgotten the people who tried to kill you? RAGE? Well they have been attempting to assassinate me since you were born – and nearly succeeded twice. So being underground keeps me safe.'

I frowned. All this amazing technology – just to protect Elijah? There must be more to it than that. I wondered uneasily who was paying for the compound. Elijah had mentioned powerful friends. Who were they?

He stopped beside a door marked *Private*.

'Mel will take you to a room,' he said, without looking at me.

He stood in front of a small pad and a light beam scanned his eye. The *Private* door opened and he disappeared.

I stood there for a second, not quite sure what had just happened.

Mel touched my arm. 'He didn't exactly graduate charm school,' she said. 'Though he can turn it on when he wants.'

I nodded. I still had no idea why Elijah had brought me here. Okay, so he wanted to keep me safe from RAGE. But this was clearly a working compound – a place designed for scientific developments. How did I fit in with that? In fact, so long as he couldn't show me off as a scientific achievement, why was he protecting me at all? No way did he see me as a son. I was pretty sure all I was was a successful genetics experiment to him. Nothing more.

Mel led me through more doors and corridors. At last we reached a long line of apartments.

'You've got your own studio,' she said, pushing a door open. 'I'll show you the main dining area later.'

It was a large room with a bed at one end, a tiny bathroom off to the side and a sofa and little kitchen area nearer the door. Everything was smart and clean – like a hotel room.

I looked around, my mouth dry, then wandered across the wood floor towards the sofa. The whole room was actually bigger than the living area Mum and I shared in our house. I had a flashback to my messy bedroom at home. I missed it all desperately. Not just Mum herself, but my whole life – school, my friends, even Roy. I couldn't get my head around the fact that they were all in another country. Another life.

I sat down on the sofa, a lump in my throat.

Mel perched next to me and put her arm round my shoulders. 'You'll get used to it,' she said.

'I don't want to.' I gritted my teeth. 'I don't understand why I'm here. Why can't I be relocated, like Rachel?'

'For some reason Elijah wants you here.' Mel squeezed my arm. 'Like he wants me here. And what Elijah wants, he always gets.'

'So I'm a prisoner?'

Mel sighed. 'My best guess is that he wants to train you up to take over from him. I mean, he had this really bad virus last year. Left him with some godawful heart condition that he's on loads of meds for. Don't get me wrong, he's fine now, but I think being ill like that showed him he wasn't going to live forever. I think he likes the idea of someone, literally in his own image, taking over from him.'

I stared at her. 'But there's no way I could do any of the

240

stuff he does here. He was probably dissecting dogs when he was ten.'

Mel laughed.

'Are there even any other people my age here?' I said.

She shook her head. 'There are some younger kids. But for high school most families send their children away during term time. Blindfolded, of course. Hardly anyone knows where we actually are. Somewhere underneath D.C., obviously. But I don't know exactly where. I get blindfolded too.'

'He doesn't trust you?' I said.

'Not about that.' Mel shook her head. 'Especially not now.'

I wondered what she meant. Something to do with why he'd hit her, I guessed.

'Get some sleep, babe.' She stood up. 'The door's automatically programmed to lock when I shut it. I'm sorry, there's nothing I can do about that, but I'll come back in an hour or so . . . and Theo?'

I looked up.

'You're going to be okay. He's actually nicer with you than I've ever seen him with anyone.'

And, with that, she gave me a sad smile and slipped away, leaving me feeling more alone than ever.

46

Rachel

Lewis's condition for going ahead with my plan was that we should both be fully prepared before we contacted RAGE. And part of being prepared, he said, was being physically fit.

'If you are going to come with me to the RAGE headquarters and Elijah's complex in D.C., you must be able to look after yourself . . .' he said, '. . . for when I can't look after you.'

This meant several days of workouts. They were far tougher than the couple of hours Theo and I had spent with Mel on our first morning. Lewis made me row on the rowing machine until the sweat was pouring off me, and my arms and legs ached. Then he showed me some martial arts moves.

'It's not about brute strength,' he said. 'It's about balance and using your bodyweight.'

He showed me how to pivot on one foot, thrusting the other leg into a kick. We did the same move over and over until I was completely exhausted.

Then he stood over me while I did a hundred curl-ups, grinning down at me and yelling encouragement.

After I was done, he cooked steaks while I soaked in a bath.

'I can't do anything fancy,' he smiled as I sat down at the little kitchen table half an hour later. 'But when you've worked hard you need good food.'

My arms were so tired I could barely lift my knife and fork, but the steak and potatoes and salad tasted great.

'This is great,' I grinned. 'Easily as good as Mel's veggie curry.'

As soon as I'd said her name I wished I hadn't.

Lewis's face darkened. He pushed his plate away.

'Sorry,' I said awkwardly.

'It's okay,' Lewis sighed. 'I just can't bear thinking about him hurting her again.'

I nodded, to show that I understood. It was funny – no one as grown up as Lewis had ever talked to me so openly before, like an equal. I mean, he wasn't exactly in the same age bracket as my parents. But he was still a good few years older than me.

'Do you love her – Mel?' I said timidly. Two days ago I would never have dared ask anyone such a question. But now, well, now I wanted to know. And there didn't seem to be any reason not to ask.

Lewis looked across the room. 'I think about her all the time. How amazing she is. I remember when I saw her the first time in D.C., I just stared and stared. I couldn't believe how she looked.' He laughed. 'I was terrified of talking to her. She was so out of my league, she was practically orbiting another planet. Plus, she was Elijah's girlfriend. But I had to talk to her. *Had* to. And then when I did, it was so easy. We got on really well. She's like this really strong person, but really shy too . . . Anyway, we had to be careful because of Elijah, so we didn't have much chance to . . . to spend time together before I had to go undercover with RAGE for six months.' He smiled at me. 'I've never felt like this about anyone. It's kind of awesome and awful at the same time. You'll see when it happens to you.'

I stared down at the last piece of steak on my plate and said nothing.

After we'd eaten, Lewis sketched an outline of the Washington complex on a piece of paper.

'Recreational areas across the front, then staff quarters and Elijah's private rooms behind to the west. The labs are in the block to the east. No one ever goes into them except Elijah and the scientists. There's some hardcore security built into the doors, but that's where we direct RAGE. Keep them away from the staff quarters as much as possible, yeah?'

He looked at me as if he was expecting me to make some kind of intelligent comment on his plan.

I attempted a smile. I was starting to feel rather overwhelmed by what we'd agreed to do.

'Are you sure about this, Rachel?' Lewis said. 'I have to get Mel anyway. But there are other—'

'Of course I'm sure,' I said fiercely. 'It was my idea, wasn't it?'

The truth was I was scared. More scared than I wanted to admit. But Elijah had Theo. He wasn't giving him up.

Which meant I couldn't either.

And I decided another thing too. Maybe Theo was never going to feel about me like I did about him. But I had to find out – one way or the other.

Lewis and I talked for a little longer about the best way to contact Max. Lewis was sure RAGE would still be tapping her phone and monitoring her emails.

'Why don't we send her a postcard?' I said. 'Snail mail. We could tell her to meet us somewhere.'

Lewis frowned. 'Where? She's probably being followed by RAGE. They know how close she is to Theo, they'll be expecting some kind of contact attempt. Where could she go that wouldn't look suspicious?'

I grinned at him. 'I have the perfect place in mind,' I said. 'It's crowded, it's full of teenagers and we'll be able to talk to each other without anyone noticing.'

47

Theo

I explored my room while I was waiting for Mel to come back. It contained some pretty cool stuff – computer, games console, big plasma screen TV, music station.

I went online and tried to send Mum an email. But the computer blocked my attempt to log onto my account. Then I tried to access the chat rooms Max and I often used. Also blocked. After half an hour I had to accept that I had absolutely no way of contacting anyone.

Rage and fear paced round my head like wild cats trapped in a cage. I couldn't see a way out. Couldn't see any way back to any part of my old life. At least I knew Mum and Rachel were okay – or safe from RAGE anyway. My thoughts turned to Max and Jake. Mel had said she was sure they were fine – but what if RAGE had caught up with them?

'D'you know if they're really all right?' I said to Mel when she turned up an hour or so later.

She nodded. 'Elijah reckoned RAGE would pick them up, interrogate them, discover they knew nothing of any importance and let them go. And, as usual, he was right. He's been monitoring them.'

'Monitoring?' I said. 'Why not protecting? Elijah sent Lewis for me and Rachel. Why didn't he send someone to rescue them?'

Mel sighed. 'Elijah took a calculated gamble that RAGE wouldn't harm them.'

'But—'

'RAGE have a specific agenda which doesn't include murdering innocent kids. They want you and Rachel because of what you are. You in particular, because in their eyes you are a replica of Elijah. There's no reason for them to hurt your friends.'

'But Elijah couldn't have known that for sure,' I said, my temper rising. I couldn't believe it. Max and Jake had nothing to do with the argument between Elijah and RAGE, and yet Elijah wouldn't lift a finger to help them.

'Despite what you see here, he doesn't have unlimited resources,' Mel said. 'And to be fair, it wasn't his fault they got involved. Listen, buddy, Elijah doesn't want you to leave this room yet, but you've got to eat. So I'm going to take you to the dining hall.' She handed me a baseball cap. 'Put this on and pull it over your face. It's not likely to happen, but we don't want anyone connecting you and Elijah. Don't look at anyone directly and keep your mouth shut when you're there. Okay?'

I pulled on the cap and followed her down the long corridor. Was she saying it was *my* fault Max and Jake were at risk now? I thought about it. I had involved both of them. But I hadn't known how dangerous it would be. Then it hit me. I *had* known. Mum had told me the first night we talked about my dad being alive still. And yet, thoughtlessly, I'd led both of them – and Rachel – into terrible danger.

The dining hall was at the end of my corridor – a cafeteria full of people and long rows of trestle tables. A weird mix of pale, middle-aged men and women, who I guessed must be Elijah's scientific staff, and some seriously beefy guys in security-guard uniforms. A few small kids trailed by bored-looking younger women wandered around a little play area in the corner.

We ladled portions of macaroni cheese onto our plates. A couple of the security guards wandered over as we found a table.

'Remember,' Mel hissed, 'keep your head down and your mouth shut.'

As it turned out, the security guards weren't interested in me in the slightest. They barely glanced in my direction as they tried to get Mel to chat to them. She kept her head bowed, so you couldn't see that bruise round her eye, and answered in monosyllables. They soon drifted off.

Mel and I ate in silence.

I started thinking about Jake and Max again. How I'd involved them without thinking. I had been very hungry, but suddenly I couldn't eat any more. How could I when I didn't know if my friends were still safe?

I saw Lewis in my mind's eye, slumped over that armchair in the cottage. Elijah had done that.

And I was Elijah.

I couldn't bear it.

'I'm going back to my room,' I muttered.

Mel nodded. 'I'll call in on you later,' she said. 'Don't talk to anyone on the way.'

I stumbled back along the corridor. A lump lodged in my throat. Nothing made sense any more. A week ago I'd been Theo Glassman. A popular, powerful fifteen-year-old boy with a home and a mum and friends and no real worries at all. And now I had been stripped of everything that made up the life I knew. I didn't even know who I was. There was absolutely nothing to hold on to. Nothing real. And nobody who could understand how it felt.

Except Rachel, maybe. She was like me. A clone. She would understand.

I suddenly missed home so hard it was like a physical pain in my chest. I stopped in the corridor and leaned against the wall, my eyes closed against the terrible ache of it. Holding Rachel had been real. Less than twenty-four hours ago I had stood outside the cottage and hugged her. To comfort her. To comfort myself. And she had hugged me back. That was real. That was genuine. I had to remember it.

'Theodore?' Elijah's voice snapped my eyes open.

He was towering in front of me, a frown on his face.

'Do you feel all right?' he said. For the first time since I'd met him I heard real concern in his voice. 'What are you doing here?'

'I'm fine,' I said. 'And it's *Theo*.'

Elijah's eyes narrowed. 'Well, I want you to have a full medical examination tomorrow, anyway. It's standard procedure for newcomers to the compound.'

I stared at him. 'Tell me why I'm here.' Maybe I could get him to talk. To tell me his plans.

'You're here because this is where you belong, Theodore.' Elijah smiled and leaned back against the wall. 'I was always going to send for you, once you'd finished school. You might have forced me into moving faster than I was planning, but I always wanted you here to . . . to help me.'

'What d'you mean, "to help you"?'

'To learn about what I do.' Elijah stopped. My heart beat faster. So Mel was right.

'Is that it?' I said. 'You want me to somehow take over your work? Because—?'

'Where is Mel?' Elijah pushed himself away from the wall and looked down the corridor. 'I told her I didn't want you to leave your room unaccompanied.'

I stared at him. I still needed answers. 'Tell me what you want me to do.'

'Not now. Not here.' Elijah folded his arms. 'Back to your room.'

My temper rose like a volcano.

'Tell me!' I shouted. 'Tell me or I'll tell everyone who I am.'

Elijah whipped round, his eyes blazing. 'You will do no such thing.'

'I will,' I shouted. 'I'll go back to the dining hall and stand on a table and—'

'You've been in the dining hall?' Elijah glared at me. 'I told Mel to keep you away from all the public areas.'

My heart pounded. *Crap.* Now I'd got someone else into terrible trouble.

'It's not Mel's fault,' I said quickly. 'She told me to go back to my room. But I . . . I don't want to. I don't want to be a prisoner here. I want to go back to London. I want to go home.' I fought an impulse to cry. No way was I showing any emotion in front of this man.

Elijah stared at me. He suddenly looked tired. Exhausted, even. He pulled a pot of pills out of his pocket and popped one in his mouth.

'If you're keeping me here because you're going to die one day and you want me to take over from you, there's no point,' I snapped. 'I've got as much chance of becoming a genius scientist as I have of turning into a bunsen burner.'

A look of shock crossed Elijah's face, then he smiled. 'Okay, Theodore,' he said slowly. 'I'm sorry. This must all seem quite bewildering to you.' He put his hand on my shoulder and started walking me back towards my room. 'I do want you to learn about what I do here. And yes, my hope is that you will be able to follow in my footsteps. But I do not intend to force you into anything. Right now, all I ask is that you give me and my work a chance.' He squeezed my shoulder. 'You know I was angry that you disobeyed your mother and set off to find me in that reckless way you did, but I was also touched. Proud that you wanted to know me.'

I looked away, remembering how I'd imagined us as soldiers, fighting side by side against RAGE's bigotry. That seemed a long time ago now.

We reached my room.

'We will talk again soon, Theodore,' Elijah said. 'Okay?'

He patted my back. For a split second I felt that gun pressing against my forehead again.

I nodded slowly.

'Good.' Elijah opened my door. 'Now, please, inside and rest.'

I walked into my studio. The door clicked shut behind me.

I was locked in.

48

Rachel

It was late Friday afternoon. The Starbucks near where Theo lived was packed with teenagers. I'd guessed it would be, from the way Theo had described hanging out there with Jake.

Lewis and I had driven down from Scotland that morning. We waited in a shop opposite, watching out for Max.

Our postcard to her had read: *Starbucks. Friday. Five p.m. Say nothing. Baby Friend.*

Baby friends was how Theo had described him and Max to me the first time I'd met her. I'd hoped the phrase would make sense to her. I also hoped she wouldn't be too pissed off at us pretending the postcard came from Theo.

The truth was, I wasn't sure if Max would turn up for anyone else.

She arrived at 4.55 p.m. Lewis scanned the street up and down as she walked into the café.

'She hasn't been followed,' he said.

'How can you be so sure?'

'Because I am. Plus I'd recognise anyone from RAGE. Or the people they use to do this kind of thing.' Lewis glanced at me. 'I worked with them for six months, remember?'

We waited five minutes, then crossed the road.

I spotted Max as soon as we walked in. She was sitting at the back, beside the toilets, drumming her fingers on the table. I started threading my way through the throng of teenagers clustered around the order and collection points.

Lewis kept his hand protectively on my shoulder. I noticed a number of girls checking him out and shooting me envious glances. In spite of how nervous I was feeling, I smiled. Lewis was tall and really fit, with amazing blue eyes. I mean, I didn't fancy him myself, but the idea that anyone would think I was old enough or pretty enough for him to be interested in was kind of nice.

Max stood up as I reached her table.

'Where's Theo?' she said. 'What's happened to him?'

She caught sight of Lewis beside me and frowned. 'Who are you?'

'This is Lewis,' I said. 'He saved Theo's life. And mine.'

Max looked back at me. 'Where *is* Theo?' she repeated.

I explained what had happened. I didn't mention the whole cloning thing. Just that RAGE had come after us and Theo's dad had sent Lewis to rescue us.

'They came after us too,' Max said. 'Me and Jake.'

'Are you talking about me?' said a smooth, familiar voice.

I jumped. Jake was standing right beside me, a leering smile on his face.

254

I felt Lewis's hand grip my shoulder more tightly, drawing me away from him. I kicked myself mentally. Why hadn't I thought about it? Jake was bound to be here.

'Who's this?' Lewis asked.

'Just Jake.' I blushed. 'Another friend of Theo's.'

'Hey, Rachel. Good to see you, too,' Jake purred. 'What have you done with Theo? Max and I have been in this total nightmare. The guys from that weirdo organisation your dad's mixed up in are seriously evil.'

'Oh, shut up, Jake,' Max snapped. 'You don't know what you're talking about.'

Before anyone could say anything else, I introduced Lewis properly and we all sat down at the table. I went over what we'd just told Max, again. Then Max explained how the night RAGE came for Theo and me, they also picked up Jake and her.

'They took us together to this abandoned building. Left us for ages.'

Lewis nodded. 'They would have been waiting to see what you knew. What you said about Theo.'

'Then they interrogated us separately,' Jake went on. 'It was really scary. They were dead threatening. I mean they didn't hurt us or anything, but I bet they had guns.'

I opened my mouth to tell him I was sure of it. But Lewis laid his hand on my arm.

'We had to tell them what we knew,' Jake said. 'They kept asking where Theo was now – but of course we didn't know.'

Lewis cleared his throat. 'The point is that although

Theo's dad rescued him, now he wants Theo to stay with him,' he said.

'But we know Theo won't want that,' I added. 'We're going to get him out.'

'How?' Max asked.

Lewis glossed over the details of our rescue plan – he'd made it clear earlier that, for their own safety, the less Max and Jake knew the better. Then he outlined exactly how Max could help with the relocations. 'I need you to find some old identities for us,' he said. 'People who died as children but who would be the same age as me and Rachel and Theo . . .'

'And this friend of Lewis's called Mel, and my mum and dad,' I added.

Lewis and I had called Mum and Dad from a payphone. We hadn't told them about our proposed attempt to rescue Theo and Mel, though. It was too risky. Dad was bound to try and stop us. He might even tell Elijah what we were planning.

'We need basic information – name, age, where and when they were born . . . that sort of thing,' Lewis went on. 'And you'll have to use computers in internet cafés so nothing can be traced back.' He fixed Max with his clear blue eyes. 'Can you do it?'

She stared from him to me, then back to him. 'Sure,' she said. 'But what will you do with all the data?'

'Well, I won't be able to sort out jobs or schools or anything like that,' Lewis said. 'But I've got a contact who can get some basic I.D. done. New passports, driving licences. Stuff like that.'

Jake whistled. 'This is major.'

Lewis turned to him. 'It's also a matter of life and death. Ours and Theo's. You can never tell anyone. *Ever.*' His eyes shone hard.

Jake nodded. 'Whatever you say.'

The four of us left Starbucks for a nearby internet café where Max started searching for the information she needed. While she and Lewis were poring over the computer screen, Jake pulled me to one side.

'That Lewis guy's way too old for you, the big perv. Though I have to say –' he grinned, '– you're looking good, Rachel . . .'

I blushed. I was sure I didn't look any different than I had when Jake had last seen me.

'Lewis isn't like that,' I said. 'For a start he's madly in love with the girl he mentioned earlier. He's like . . . like my big brother or something . . .'

'Oh?' Jake raised his eyebrows. 'Oh, well then . . .'

'Hey.' Lewis was back. 'Max has made a start but she can't do it all today. Rachel and I need to split now. We'll meet you back here same time Tuesday. No contact in between, okay?'

Jake looked a little disappointed, but he didn't say any-thing. Two minutes later Lewis and I were outside the café, our hoodies pulled up, striding down the high street.

'Where are we going?' I said, tugging my jacket round me.

It was nearly as cold here as it had been up at the cottage and I knew Lewis had very little cash – just enough for the petrol down here and a few days' food.

'To find a squat,' Lewis said. 'Some abandoned building where we can stay while we get all this stuff sorted out.'

'How do we do that?'

'Easy.' Lewis grinned at me. 'We head for somewhere run-down and look for boarded-up doors and windows. I spent the ages of six to nine living in squats. Though I don't remember it being this cold where I grew up.'

He was right. It *was* easy. By ten o'clock that night we had found an abandoned flat on a council estate and broken into it. Someone had obviously been living there before because they had left some blankets and a stained mattress behind on the floor.

'You take that,' he said, putting down the two torch lanterns we'd brought from the cottage. 'I can sleep on the floor.'

I looked around the largest room. There was no furniture, just a pile of broken bottles in one corner. I could see my breath in front of my face, it was so cold. Paint was peeling from the walls. And I already knew that the kitchen and bath-room were filthy, with no running water.

In short, it was by far the most revolting place I'd ever anticipated spending the night in my life. And yet the prospect of staying here for a few days filled me with far less horror than I'd felt for months every morning before setting off for school.

'I'm sorry it's so dirty. We'll get some stuff and clean up a bit tomorrow,' Lewis said, clearly misinterpreting my silence for disgust.

I smiled at him.

'This is fine,' I said.

I meant it. Being without Mum and Dad was hard. And thinking about what we were planning to do in order to rescue Mel and Theo was terrifying. But for the first time in my life I felt truly alive. I knew I would be safe here with Lewis. I knew he could and would protect me.

And, if everything went as we were planning, I knew that soon I would see Theo again.

49

Theo

After a few days of being shut up in my room I was climbing the walls. Despite what Elijah had said about talking to me soon, he had hardly come near me since our encounter in the corridor. I didn't see him the next day for the medical exam, though it felt like I met half the compound's staff. An endless stream of doctors prodded and poked at me for most of the morning. I had blood taken, my height and weight measured and my blood pressure checked. Then I was hooked up to all sorts of machines including an ultrasound scanner which showed my liver, kidneys and bladder and an E.C.G. machine which checked out my heart. All perfectly healthy, apparently.

I'd been in my room ever since.

Mel brought me meals and stayed to talk to me too, as often and for as long as she could. But she had work to do on the compound – I discovered that as well as being part of the security detail, she ran body combat classes for all the staff. *Elijah insists everyone attends*. And then, of course, she had to spend time with Elijah – most of the evenings and all of the nights, I was guessing. The dark bruise around her eye had faded now, though a mark still remained.

It was clear to me by now that Mel didn't want to be with Elijah. And equally clear – as it must have been to anyone who knew him – that he wasn't going to let her go until he no longer wanted her around.

When I wasn't focused on Elijah and Mel, I thought about Mum and Rachel. I asked Mel several times if I could call Mum, but she said I'd have to talk to Elijah about it – and, so far, I hadn't had the chance. I spent a lot of time wondering about him and Mum, though. Things like how much they'd really cared about each other, and whether they still did, and whether he'd ever hurt her – like he hurt Mel.

And I worried a lot about Rachel – if she was okay with whoever Elijah had sent to sort out her relocation.

Apart from that, I browsed online, watched TV and slept.

I was more bored and miserable than I'd ever been in my life.

Mel could see how bad I felt, and on the fourth morning she appeared early with my breakfast: toast and bacon and grilled tomatoes.

'I've persuaded Elijah to let you try out my body combat class,' she said. 'It's like an exercise class, but we go through combat moves. There's one every morning at ten a.m. Everyone who lives in the compound has to come at least once a week. Elijah says you can do it, provided you wear a cap and I'm with you the whole time and you don't speak to anyone. You'll just look like someone's visiting older kid.'

It was a sign of how desperate I felt that my spirits rose at the prospect of prancing about in some exercise class with a bunch of macho security guards and ancient scientists.

'Okay.' I grinned. 'Thanks.'

Mel beamed at me as she put down my tray.

On the underside of her arm, where the skin was paler, were four oval bruises. They looked like fingermarks.

Anger surged through me. 'Has he hurt you again?' I said.

Mel's cheeks flushed. 'It's since he found out about me and Lewis. He didn't do it before.' She looked up at me, her eyes dark and defiant. 'Don't worry about me, Theo. I'll find a way to get out of here. Now remember, my class starts in an hour. I'll be back just before then.'

She left. I sat at the table and ate my lonely breakfast. It hadn't occurred to me before that Mel and Lewis might have been seeing each other, but now she'd said about Elijah 'finding out' about them, it made sense. It explained at least why she had been so upset at Lewis being shot and why Elijah had got so angry. Not that it justified him hitting her.

Nothing justified that.

The exercise class was far better than I'd expected. It was held in one of the big rooms near the Outdoor Room. There were about twenty or thirty other people there. A mix of ages. Out of their uniforms it was hard to tell which of the twelve or so younger men and women were professional security guards and which worked in the labs.

Mel began by getting us all to jog round the room, then we

262

did some shadow-boxing and kick-boxing to music. It was all fairly easy to be honest, though some of the older guys looked a bit out of breath at the end. Then she paired us up. I was with this smiley, fair-haired woman about Mel's age. I felt a bit self-conscious then. I mean, it was one thing to ponce about to music when everyone else was looking in the mirrors that lined the side of the room, but I didn't fancy doing it in front of a pretty blonde.

Thankfully Mel turned the music right down and started talking us through the detail of what we were doing. Each pair took it in turns to attack. We ran through a series of moves in slow motion. Kick. Block. Punch. Block. Uppercut. Block.

Then we practised in our pairs, with Mel coming round correcting our moves and yelling out encouragement.

'Nice, Laura,' she said as she passed my partner. 'Get him in his six-pack.'

The two women laughed. I blushed. I wasn't sure whether Mel was teasing me or whether she thought I might really have incredibly toned abs. Which, of course, I absolutely didn't.

I redoubled my efforts, determined not to look stupid.

Once Mel was convinced each partner of each pair was sure of the routine, she made us stand slightly further apart, so there was no danger of us actually hitting each other, then speed up.

I really started to enjoy what we were doing then. Laura was good. No doubt about it. She was well co-ordinated and springy on her feet and managed to block all of my moves without breaking sweat.

When it came to my turn to block her, she was too fast for me at first. Every time I raised my arm she'd whip her fist past it. It was frustrating but fun too. As we kicked and punched at each other, following through the routine, I could feel adrenalin starting to pump through my body. The release of tension was fantastic. By the time the class finished I was feeling better than I had for days.

I waited while everyone left, then Mel walked me back to my room. We talked through the moves from the class. I asked for more information about the decoy gambit she'd shown us that I hadn't really understood.

As we got close to my room, Mel laughed. 'So you enjoyed it, then?'

I nodded eagerly, practising a punch, then a cross in quick succession.

'Can I do it every morning?'

'Sure thing, babe.' Mel smiled. 'Though I guess I'll have to check with Elijah first. He's off compound today.'

'Oh?' I raised my eyes. 'In that case would you mind if I went down to the Outdoor Room? I could do with some fresh air, even if it isn't real. And I promise I won't talk to anyone.'

Mel hesitated.

My face fell. 'There aren't security cameras, are there?'

She shook her head. 'No. At least only on the front entrance. There's no need for them inside, it's so secure.'

'What then?'

She bit her lip. 'There are always at least four guys by the front door, Theo. You're not thinking of trying to get outside, are you? It's just . . .' She tailed off, looking embarrassed.

I suddenly saw what she was worried about.

'I won't do anything that draws attention to myself.' I touched the peak of my cap. 'And I'll keep this on, promise. The last thing I want is to get you into trouble. I'd just like some fake sunshine.'

'Okay.' Mel's face softened. 'Okay, but I can't come with you,' she said. 'I'm on duty in half an hour and I've got to shower first.'

'No worries,' I said. 'I know the way.' I turned and walked away before she could change her mind.

'Hey, Cinderella,' Mel called after me. 'Elijah'll be back by one at the latest. Make sure you're in your room well before then.'

I waved my hand to show that I had heard her, and walked on.

Ten minutes later I was hopelessly lost. All the corridors looked completely alike to me, and I'd been out of my room so little – and, then, mostly to the cafeteria at the end of my row – that I really had no idea where anywhere was in relation to anywhere else.

I passed a few people but didn't dare break my promise to Mel about not speaking to anyone and asking them the way to the Outdoor Room. I passed a wall clock. 11:33. *Man.* At this rate I'd still be wandering about when Elijah came back.

I paced up and down a couple more corridors, feeling more and more frustrated. The lab-room doors were labelled with symbols that I didn't understand, while the ones in the living area were named after flowers. I'd already passed my own – which was called *Begonia* – twice. There was no sequence of numbers anywhere to help me get my bearings.

I walked on and on. Left down one corridor. Right down another. Past *Tulip* and *Iris* and *Rose*. I turned down another long, empty corridor. Only one door, halfway down. A door which had neither a flower name or a symbol. It was simply labelled: *Private*.

I stopped, my heart thudding. This was where Elijah had gone on that first day. I was certain of it.

I stared at the little iris-recognition screen on the wall beside the door. Nowhere else on the compound had that level of security.

And that's when it hit me. If I was genetically identical to Elijah, then surely my eye would open the door, just like his had.

My heart hammered against my throat. He wasn't here. And Mel had already told me there weren't any security cameras.

What did I have to lose? All I was doing was trying to open a door. If it didn't work, I'd just carry on looking for the Outdoor Room. I took a step up to the little pad. Tall for my age though I was, Elijah was several centimetres taller. I stood on tiptoe, trying to remember whether the scanner had run down his left eye or his right.

From the way he'd been standing I was pretty sure it was the right eye.

I leaned closer towards the pad.

It whirred into action, running a bar of light down my face. I held my breath.

With a smooth swish, the door in front of me opened.

50

Rachel

Several days passed. Lewis and I stayed mostly in the squat – going out for jogs and to buy food only after dark and with our hoods up.

We washed in the public toilets at the end of the road. Lewis bought a bucket and told me to take it into the ladies with some soap and a handful of paper towels. The water was cold, but at least it meant we could stay clean. After we'd both washed, Lewis would fill the bucket with drinking water and we'd haul it home.

Home. The squat was a bit less smelly now – we'd bleached the floors and walls – but no lighter or warmer.

I lugged the thin, hard mattress into a corner of the room. That first night I hardly slept, it was so uncomfortable. But soon I got used to it, though I did start dreaming of luxurious four-poster beds and being able to soak for hours in a hot bath.

Lewis lay on the floor. He chose a different part of the room every night, but always placed himself between me and the door. I asked him once why he didn't pick a single spot and stick to it.

'Habit's a dangerous thing,' he said. 'When something becomes familiar, it's much easier to let your guard down.'

I guess he never did let his guard down. He slept lightly, waking at the slightest noise. And when he moved, it was always stealthily, like a big cat. The only time I ever saw him remotely out of control was when he woke, screaming, from a nightmare on our second night in the flat.

The noise woke me instantly, but I was so bundled up in my blanket that he didn't see my eyes open. Across the room I saw him sitting, hunched over on the floor, panting. Then he got up and went over to the window. We had pulled one plank of wood away to let in daylight and right now a sliver of yellow street lamp was gleaming through, casting a thin line of light across the floor.

Lewis leaned against the wood and peered out through the crack. Sweat glistened on his forehead.

I heard him whisper her name. 'Mel.' It was almost a sob.

I squeezed my eyes tight shut, not wanting him to know I'd seen and heard him.

During the day Lewis trained me to fight – how to defend myself from attack and how to throw my bodyweight behind kicks and punches. I hated it at first, but I worked hard – partly because I knew being able to look after myself was important, but mostly to please Lewis. He made me feel special, like no one ever had. Like I was a little sister he wanted to look out for. He told me he had never known his dad, and his mum had died when he was eight years old. I couldn't imagine what it must be like to have no family.

'So, d'you think of Elijah as your dad?' I asked him one day.

But he shook his head. 'No. Elijah was always fair, but he never showed me any affection.' He smiled at the look of horror on my face. 'But I had carers. Kind people who cuddled me and listened to me when I was younger. So I didn't do so bad.'

We met up with Max every few days. Lewis insisted we used different internet cafés each time, to reduce the risk of RAGE discovering us. Max had found new identities for me and Theo and Lewis now. I was Alice Stewart – dead from meningitis as a toddler. It felt weird to be thinking about new names. I still hadn't asked Lewis about us all relocating near each other. I knew him well enough now to be pretty sure he would say it was too risky. And I didn't want to hear that. I didn't want to hear that I might be separated from him – or from Theo.

I thought about Theo a lot, playing out endless fantasies in my head where we met up by running into each other's arms and kissing passionately. I knew I was probably being stupid to even think it would happen, but I couldn't stop myself from imagining it. By Thursday afternoon, we had all the identities sorted. I stayed in the squat while Lewis visited his friend to order all the paperwork we were going to need. He was planning to get Max to hack into one of Elijah's online accounts at the last minute to get the money to pay for the passports and certificates his friend was forging for us.

That whole side of things seemed slightly unreal to me. I was happy to let Lewis deal with it and stay behind to concentrate on the simple martial arts moves he had taught me.

I was so focused on what I was doing that I didn't hear Lewis come back into the squat. When I turned round he was standing in the doorway, watching me. He tossed a pack of sandwiches on the floor. I made a face. I was fed up of eating nothing but sandwiches.

'You look good, Rachel,' he said. 'Seriously. You're really starting to be able to handle yourself.'

I blushed, more pleased than I could put into words. I hadn't seen myself in a mirror for days – the one in the public toilets had been ripped off the wall – but I knew I'd really toned up because my trousers felt looser and my arms didn't get so tired any more when I worked out. Plus, my hair had started to annoy me all round my face, so I'd started tying it back into a ponytail. But none of those physical things seemed to matter so much any more. What counted was feeling strong and confident.

And, with Lewis around, I did.

I grinned at him, then bent down to pick up the sandwiches.

Egg mayonnaise.

'They'd run out of ham,' Lewis said apologetically.

I straightened up. Something was different. Lewis seemed a little on edge. Anxious even.

271

'What's up?' I said.

'I've contacted RAGE,' he said. 'Told them I've got you and I want to talk. They're bringing us both in. Tomorrow night.'

51

Theo

It's instinct, isn't it? A door opens in front of you. You look inside.

I looked. And saw a smart, comfortable living area, not that different from my own, complete with sofas, table, and TV. On the left-hand wall were two doors. On the right was a desk and one of those large holographic panels like they had in the Outdoor Room, showing a moving scene of trees waving in some imaginary breeze.

Everything was neat and ordered. No sound of anyone nearby.

I stepped into the room.

I didn't think about it. I just did it. The door immediately swished shut behind me. My heart bumped in my chest. There was no way I could kid myself any more. I was somewhere I wasn't supposed to be. Doing something I wasn't supposed to be doing.

I crept across the room to the doors on the left-hand wall. Eased the first gently open. A bedroom. Large, steel-frame bed. Black silky cover. A picture of Mel on one of the bed-side tables.

If I hadn't been completely sure before, I was now. I was in Elijah's private quarters. I opened the second door. A grey-and-white marble bathroom. Again, everything neat and ordered.

I couldn't see any more doors leading on from the bedroom and bathroom. I frowned. Was this all the space Elijah had? It didn't make sense. He used a private jet. Surely, at the very least, he'd have some kind of kitchen or dining area.

I shut both doors and walked across the living area to the large desk. I scanned the surface – a slim computer, a bundle of papers and a large, scuffed leather diary. Clearly Elijah liked old-fashioned ways of keeping track of his schedule.

Glancing round me again, I shuffled through the papers. A few incomprehensible reports on some scientific research. My medical report was there too. I flicked through it. I hadn't actually seen it written down, but as far as I could tell there was nothing in it that differed from the information the doctors had given me at the time of the examination.

I put all the papers back as I'd found them, then opened the leather diary. I scanned the pages. Some were completely blank, others full of entries. They were all written in black ink, in old-fashioned, looping writing. I turned to this week's page. Under today's date it said: *Med. Exam.*

Was that my medical examination? But that had been yesterday, not today. Anyway, why was it logged in Elijah's personal diary?

I slammed the book shut, feeling annoyed. I placed the diary carefully back on the desk, beside the bundle of papers. There wasn't much else to explore.

My frustrated sigh sounded loud in the silence of the room. And that's when I noticed. The computer in front of me had silently switched on. A digital clock in the upper right corner of the screen was flashing.

Return in 119 seconds

Return in 118 seconds

Panic seized my throat. What did that mean? Had the computer realised I was in the room? I stared stupidly at the screen. It was covered with tiny folders.

Return in 112 seconds

Return in 111 seconds

The words sank in. Elijah was on his way back to his room. He obviously had some way of priming his computer to be ready for him.

Shit. Shit. Shit.

I started backing away, my eyes still fixed on the screen. I had to leave. But this was Elijah's personal PC. All his private files were on here. All his secrets. All his plans . . .

I scanned the folders, desperately searching for something that might refer to me. Most of them were labelled in code. Or with boring, financial-sounding titles.

Return in 95 seconds

Return in 94 seconds

Then I saw it. A file labelled: *Hermes Project*.

Hermes.

I was sure that was another Greek god name. It had to be connected.

Connected to me.

Return in 82 seconds

Return in 81 seconds

I dragged the mouse so that the on-screen cursor hovered over the *Hermes Project* folder.

Return in 77 seconds

Return in 76 seconds

No time. No freaking time.

Shit. My heart raced. Elijah would be inside the room in just over a minute. My breathing was loud and ragged in my ears. I let go of the mouse. Checked again that the papers and diary were as I'd found them.

Then I turned. Ran to the door. Pressed the exit button. Slipped out. Tore down the corridor.

As I reached the corner I looked back. Elijah was coming into view, striding towards his room, his head bent over some papers.

I sped off. The way back to my room seemed as obvious now as the route to the Outdoor Room had been confusing earlier. I was inside *Begonia* in less than a minute. I raced over to my computer and went online. I checked out the name Hermes. *Yes.* Hermes *was* another Greek god. More. Hermes was another of Zeus's children. Just like Apollo and Artemis.

My stomach tightened. Did that mean Elijah was planning more clones? He had said he wasn't cloning any more, but then he'd said a lot of things. How did I know what to believe? I switched off my computer and sighed. Even if the Hermes Project was something to do with another clone experiment – what did that have to do with me?

There was only one way to find out.

Somehow I had to get back into Elijah's private room and look at the file properly.

52

Rachel

We waited just outside Victoria Park. It was almost midnight and I was shivering from the cold.

Well. Not just the cold.

I was more scared than I'd ever been in my life. Far more scared than I'd felt at the school disco. Then I had no idea what was going on and everything was happening too fast for me to take it in.

Now I knew exactly what was going to happen. Or at least what Lewis and I wanted to happen. And we'd been waiting for hours.

'How much longer?' I murmured for the tenth time.

'Soon,' Lewis said calmly. 'They're probably watching us right now.'

I shivered again.

Lewis was acting all casual, like he had when Theo and I had first seen him sauntering down from the school gates. He was slouching against the park entrance, his hands in his pockets. But he was making this little hissing noise under his breath. It wasn't a big deal, but he didn't normally do it. I was sure, now I knew him better, that he felt more tense than he was letting on.

'Lewis?' A harsh male voice behind us.

Lewis and I spun round.

A pale-skinned man in a thick, hooded jacket was standing on the other side of the park gates. He was staring at me as if I'd just crawled out from under one of the park's many small bushes. My heart pounded.

'That you, Franks?' Lewis said. 'D'you want us over the gate?'

Franks nodded. 'If freak-girl can make the climb.' He glanced contemptuously at me. I glared back. The park gate was high and made from steel bars. Two weeks ago there was no way I could have climbed it. But now . . .

'I'll be fine,' I said.

Lewis helped me onto the first bar. I scrambled up to the next, then swung first one leg, then the other over the top of the gate. Lewis clambered up beside me like a monkey. Together we let ourselves down the other side of the gate as far as we could. Then Lewis let go.

I heard him land with a gentle thud.

'Rachel,' he said. 'Come on.'

I let go too. Lewis half caught me as my feet touched the ground. He gave my arm a gentle squeeze before gripping my wrist. 'Where now?' he said.

Franks beckoned us across the park. It was kind of creepy in there in the dark. The wind whipped round our faces, tearing through the nearby trees. All around bushes rustled. I was so spooked I half expected masked men to jump out at us at any moment.

We made it to the other side of the park and climbed out over the fence there. As we passed under a street lamp Franks gave me a long, scornful look. I shivered, glad Lewis was with me.

After a couple of roads we reached what looked like the edge of some kind of industrial estate. It was completely deserted. Franks stopped us and insisted we put on blindfolds. 'Simpson's orders,' he snapped.

Lewis nodded. 'Fine. But remember I'm doing you the favour. And I've been putting up with freak-girl here for nearly a week. I haven't got much patience left.'

I swallowed. I knew Lewis was going to have to talk about me like that – after all, he had to convince RAGE that he was on their side and double-crossing Elijah – but I still didn't like hearing it.

'Just do it,' Franks barked.

I tried to breathe in and out slowly as I tied the blindfold behind my head.

'Walk,' he said.

I stumbled forwards, reaching out with my hands, trying to feel my way.

Franks swore. Then grabbed my wrist, like Lewis had done, only much more roughly. Close to, he smelled of sweat and tobacco. He dragged me after him for several minutes. I lost all sense of what direction we were walking in.

At last we came to some steps. I fumbled my way down them, feeling the air around me get damper. There was a strong smell of urine. The sound of bolts being dragged back. Whispering. A door scraping.

I was pushed forwards, out of the cold. Indoors. The door slammed shut behind me. Fingers fumbled at the knot in my blindfold. I could see bright light through the black of the material.

The material fell away. I screwed up my eyes against the sudden glare, trying to see around me.

We were in some kind of underground room. Bare walls, bare concrete floor, no windows and a fluorescent striplight in the ceiling. Computers were set up on trestle tables all around. A handful of men and women were sitting at the tables. They were all staring at me, their eyes showing naked curiosity. And disgust.

'New H.Q.,' Lewis said flatly. 'I see you moved.'

'We had no choice, thanks to you.' The speaker was a man with long, grey hair tied back in a short ponytail. I recognised his voice straight away.

He was the masked man Lewis had hit, but not shot, when we were escaping from my school disco. He strode towards us, his glassy eyes intent on my face.

Lewis took a step forwards.

'Mr Simpson—'

'Quiet,' the man barked.

Two burly men appeared from nowhere and grabbed Lewis by the arms. The man who'd walked with us from the park – Franks – moved closer to me. I could smell his breath, rank from stale cigarettes.

'Wait. Please, sir.' Lewis's voice was urgent.

Simpson glared at him. 'You have thirty seconds to convince me not to kill you both,' he snapped. 'Starting now.'

'I can get you to Apollo,' Lewis said quickly. '*And* I can get you to the heart of the compound in D.C. Destroy that and you set Elijah Lazio's research back by ten years.'

Simpson's eyes narrowed. 'Why didn't you tell me all this six months ago, when you came to me, asking to join the army?'

Army? And then I remembered. RAGE: Righteous Army against Genetic Engineering. My heart pounded.

'I didn't know any of it then,' Lewis said. 'Elijah Lazio only contacted me last week, just before the school attack. He had my girlfriend. Said he'd kill her if I didn't save Apollo and Artemis. So I went along with it. Later he took Apollo and told me to wait here with the girl, until—'

'Why didn't you come straight to me as soon as he contacted you?' Simpson snapped.

'I was waiting to make sure my girlfriend was safe,' Lewis said. 'Lazio won't release her until I deliver this piece of filth.' He pointed at me and a completely convincing look of fury crossed his face. 'I don't trust the bastard. He's going to kill my girlfriend. Kill us both. I hate him. Hate his work. Hate everything he stands for. You *know* that.'

'What about Bains?' Simpson said more slowly. 'He's not here now, but I know he's eager to see you again.'

I held my breath. I knew from our conversations that Bains was the man Lewis had tasered. The man who had been going to shoot Theo.

'He got in the way,' Lewis shrugged. 'At the time it was him or my girlfriend.'

Simpson drew a gun from his jacket and pointed it at Lewis's head. The two men beside Lewis tightened their grip on his arms.

'You're pathetic,' Simpson said. 'Putting your personal shit before the cause.'

I could see the faintest flicker of panic in Lewis's eyes. He opened his mouth. 'Wait. Listen. I—'

'Shut up.' Simpson's shout cut off Lewis's words. The atmosphere in the room grew tense. I held my breath. Simpson cocked the gun. 'Write down exactly where the compound is,' he snarled at Lewis. 'Address. Right now.'

Someone put a pen and paper in front of Lewis. He bent over, scribbling an address. 'But you can't just walk in through the front door,' he said as he wrote. 'I can draw you a detailed schematic. I—'

'SHUT UP!' Simpson roared.

I could see Lewis's heart beating furiously against his chest. For some reason his fear made me feel more afraid than seeing the gun pointed at his head.

'All we need is Artemis.' Simpson glanced at me. 'She's our ticket inside. We don't need you, Lewis.'

'No . . .' I gasped.

'Quiet,' Simpson snapped.

Lewis looked at me. His eyes said he was sorry.

My heart was in my throat. I couldn't survive this without Lewis.

Do something.

Simpson sucked in his breath. He steadied his arm. The tip of the gun pressed against Lewis's forehead.

Lewis closed his eyes.

'Wait,' I said. 'Lewis is right. You won't get inside the compound without him.'

'What do *you* know about it?' Simpson sneered.

'I've seen the plans,' I said, desperately trying to remember the rough drawing of the compound Lewis had shown me. 'It's completely underground. The only way in is through the tunnel and the front gates. There are two of them. With cameras showing exactly who's approaching. The guards won't let anyone through whose face they don't recognise.'

I was pretty sure all that was true. But I didn't care. All that mattered was keeping Lewis alive.

Simpson hesitated. 'And why do *you* care so much about us getting inside the compound?'

I thought fast. 'I don't,' I said. 'But . . . but I care about Theo. If you're going to kill us then I'd rather we were together. And anyway, once we're inside the compound anything can happen.'

Simpson stared at me. He shook his head, slowly. 'What's

going to happen, you little freak, is that we're going to blow that disgusting abomination against humanity into the next century.' He lowered his gun. 'Very well,' he said to Lewis. 'You get one more chance. Make it count.'

53

Theo

'So is Elijah going to see me today?' I tried to sound casual, but I was sure I wasn't fooling Mel.

She put down my breakfast tray on the low table and gazed at me sympathetically.

'I don't think so,' she said softly. As she stood up I noticed a fresh bruise on her cheek. My chest tightened. I wanted to say something to her – something about Elijah being a bastard, and about how sorry I was and how, if I could, I'd knock him into the next century for her.

But I didn't know how.

Anyway, it was obvious Mel didn't want to talk about it.

It was early Saturday morning, two days after I'd sneaked into Elijah's private rooms. I hadn't told Mel about that, mainly because I was aware of how much trouble she'd be in if anyone had found me and I was worried she'd be cross. I had asked her some questions about his work, but her knowledge appeared to be limited – stuff picked up from overhearing conversations that she didn't fully understand, rather than any in-depth information about his scientific research.

It was up to me. Me alone. Somehow I had to get back into Elijah's room and get another look at his computer. I was sure that his files – especially that Hermes one – would answer all my questions.

I picked up a slice of toast.

'So what's he doing today then?' I said.

Mel sighed. 'When he left my room he said something about heading straight into a heavy day of experiments. That means he'll probably be in the labs all day.'

My heart raced. If Elijah was in the labs all day, I'd be able to get into his room no problem.

Provided I could get out of mine.

I glanced at the clock above the door. 8:55. I knew Mel was due on security duty at nine a.m. I kept her talking as long as I could. When she finally looked at her watch she jumped up in shock.

'Damn,' she said. 'I should have been in the cafeteria two minutes ago.' She darted across the room, 'I'll call for you for combat, babe. Gotta go.'

As she flew through the door I raced after her. The door was so heavy it always took a few seconds to swing fully shut. I got there just as the nub of the lock brushed against the door frame. I pressed my toe against the door, preventing it from shutting fully – and locking me in.

I grinned as I counted to ten, slowly, under my breath.

Mel's footsteps disappeared into the distance.

I slipped out into the corridor. Lots of people were striding up and down. No one gave me a second glance. I crept towards Elijah's private door. Round the first corner. Round the second. I was a metre away. But the corridor was busy. Too busy. I waited impatiently beside the door. My mouth was dry.

Come on. Come on.

Suddenly the corridor emptied. I turned round, ready to stand on tiptoe to put my eye to the scanner.

'Theodore.' Elijah's booming voice made me jump about three metres in the air. As I turned round he was there, looming over me, his face practically purple with rage. 'What the hell are you doing?'

'Going to combat class,' I stammered.

Elijah glanced at his heavy gold watch. 'It doesn't start for nearly an hour,' he shouted. 'And how did you get out of your room?'

I stood there, silently, not wanting to reveal Mel's carelessness in rushing away and not properly shutting the door.

'No combat class today,' he said sternly. 'I'm taking you back to your room.' He marched me down the corridor, his fingers like pincers round my shoulder.

I thought of the bruise on Mel's cheek and gritted my teeth.

'Why do you keep me shut up in there?' I said. 'If you want me to take over your operation one day, why do you keep me away from everything to do with it?'

Elijah tightened his grip and muttered in Spanish under his breath.

My temper rose. 'You're a bully!' I shouted. 'You hit Mel. You keep us both prisoners here.'

With a roar Elijah stopped and raised his free hand above my head, a look of absolute fury on his face.

I flinched.

But the blow didn't come. Instead Elijah was moving again, pushing me along the corridor. Seconds later we were outside *Begonia*. Elijah unlocked the door and shoved me inside.

I stumbled across the floor, then turned to face him.

'What makes you so special?' I yelled. 'What gives you the right to keep me locked up like this? Not even letting me talk to Mum.'

Elijah ran his hand through his hair. 'I don't have time for this,' he said, clearly making an effort to speak calmly. 'I will arrange another call to your mother, if you like. She knows you are here with me and safe and well. But right now there's someone I have to speak to . . . some test results I'm waiting for.' He smiled. 'You know, no one has dared to shout at me for many years, Theodore. In spite of the fact that it goes against my most profound beliefs, I am forced to conclude that you are more like me than I would have predicted.'

'What beliefs?' I said. 'And if you didn't want me to be like you, why did you bring me up like you said – like *you'd* been brought up. A single mum and a good education, all that?'

Elijah stood looking at me for a moment, then he folded his arms. 'That was part of the experiment,' he said. 'I knew I couldn't give you the same upbringing I had. It would be a different country, a different generation. A very different mother. Plus you needed a bodyguard. But I wanted to see what would happen if there was some common ground. My belief was that a cloned child is no more or less connected to its clone original than an identical twin. My belief is still that, in fact. You and Rachel prove it. Though, with you and me, our similarities sometimes make me question the parameters of my original theorem.'

I shook my head in disbelief. 'Is that all I am to you? An experiment? A theorem?'

Elijah sighed heavily. 'There's plenty of time for us to talk about your role here. I'm sorry I've been so busy the past few days.' He turned towards the door. 'Maybe you should come to the labs with me. Next week perhaps. Now if there isn't anything else . . .'

'There is,' I said quickly. Annoying though the man was, I didn't want him to leave. If anyone had asked me I wouldn't have been able to say why. Maybe it came down to the fact that in spite of what I'd seen him do to Lewis, in spite of what he was still doing to Mel and me – part of me couldn't help but feel connected to him. We shared the same DNA, for God's sake. I wanted to know him. I struggled to find a neutral topic that would keep him inside the room.

'Who pays for all this?' I said. 'The compound and everything?'

'The government,' Elijah said, turning back to me. 'Or a branch of it.'

'That's who your powerful friends are?' I frowned. 'Why does the government care so much about keeping you protected here?'

'*Mierda*, Theodore. Do you understand so little?' Elijah rolled his eyes. 'The US government is publicly against much of the work I do here. Stem cell research and other . . . other, more complicated experiments. So officially I do not exist. But there is a government department that funds most of my research and provides the security we have here. I—'

'Do they know about me and Rachel?' I said.

Elijah was silent for a minute. I studied his face. The lines on his forehead. The dark shadows under his intense brown eyes. The slope of his nose. Was that nose really the same as mine? Was that face, in front of me now, how mine would look in fifty years' time?

'No,' he said finally. 'I could not risk them putting me under pressure to do more clone experiments.'

I stared at him. He wasn't telling the truth. At least, he wasn't telling the whole truth. I was certain.

Elijah coughed and pressed his hand against his chest. 'I have kept you alive, Theodore. Do you not see it? I gave you life. And I have sustained your life.'

I thought of the Hermes Project. 'So there aren't more like . . . like me and Rachel?'

A flicker of a smile crossed Elijah's face. 'No, sadly.' He

turned away again. 'Just three gods. Zeus the all-powerful. Artemis the hunter. And Apollo – the shining son.'

My heart hammered. He was talking. He was opening up, really starting to tell me stuff. I had to keep him here. There was too much I needed to know.

'Tell me about your parents,' I said. 'I mean, they're my parents too. Technically.'

Elijah rested his hand on the door handle. He bowed his head slightly.

'If you like,' he said wearily. 'There is not much to say. They were German, as you know. Hard on me,' he said. 'My mother was, anyway. Nothing I did was ever good enough. That is, she adored me, but she was deeply, deeply ambitious that I should become a doctor, like my father.'

'He was a doctor?' I said.

Elijah turned round. To my surprise there was a look of pain in his eyes.

'He died before I had a chance to know him, when I was very young. He couldn't live with his past. My mother told me he was a hero. That he had been a great scientist. But then when I was older, fifteen years old, I found out . . .' He looked up and caught my eye. 'I must go . . .'

'No. Wait.' I rushed over and grabbed his arm. 'What happened then? What did you find out? Was he tortured or something? Was he in one of those death camps? The concentration camps? Where the Nazis killed the Jews?'

Elijah frowned. 'What?'

'In the war?' I pleaded. I had no idea why I was so desperate

292

to know all this stuff. I only knew that when Elijah talked about his parents I felt less lost.

This is where I'm from. This is who I am.

'Please tell me,' I whispered.

'I think,' Elijah said slowly, 'that my father was a weak man who did bad things without questioning what he was being told to do. My mother believed in it all, though. The day I found out, I knew I would never speak to her again. I left home. Changed my name. Everything. That discovery changed my life. It made me who I am today.'

I let go of his arm. My head was spinning, my heart drumming against my throat. What was he talking about?

'I don't understand,' I stammered. 'What did they do? You said they escaped from Germany. You told me they were victims of the war.'

'There are many victims in wartime,' Elijah said. 'The losing side are victims too, are they not? Forced to leave everything they have known and owned and held dear.'

No.

I shut my eyes. I could feel the cold metal of that gun against my forehead. Everything around me was spinning out of control.

'But they were *Jews*,' I said hoarsely. I opened my eyes and backed across the room. 'They were per . . . persec . . .' I couldn't think of the rest of the word. My attention was focused on Elijah's eyes.

'No, Theodore.' Elijah shook his head. 'My parents believed in the supremacy of White over Black and Asian and Jew. They believed in using violence to achieve and maintain political power. They believed in their right to silence anyone who questioned their opinions.' He stared into my eyes. 'My parents . . . your parents . . . were Nazis.'

The floor seemed to slide away from my legs. I slumped down, into the chair behind me.

Elijah paced across the room. 'My father did unspeakable things in the name of science. Experiments and . . .' He shuddered. 'He took away people's lives and their dignity. That is why I became the scientist I did. To cancel out his evil.'

I stared at my lap. I was the child of Nazis. I was the clone of a man who beat his girlfriend and shot his staff. A man who was cruel and cold and utterly self-deluded.

These things were who I was.

'It is the great irony of my life,' Elijah went on, 'that so many consider me a monster, when my whole working life has been about creating and sustaining life. Helping parents who are desperate for a child. Using stem cells to find cures for terrible diseases. These are not the acts of a monster. Are they?'

For a moment he looked as if he was really asking me.

I couldn't speak.

He stood there for a few seconds, then he turned and left the room.

My mind seemed to shut down. I forgot about the Hermes Project and my desire to find out why Elijah wanted me here.

I had never felt so lost. The old reality of my life was gone forever. Nothing from the past was true. I was the child of Nazis.

Unwanted images rushed through my mind. I saw Mum, lying to me over and over about my dad. I saw Elijah's face in the cottage when he saw me for the first time. I saw the bruises on Mel's face. I saw Lewis lying, crumpled, over that chair.

It was all hate or lies or fear.

And then I remembered how Rachel and I had held each other. How I had pressed my face against her hair, terrified, but somehow stronger because I knew she was terrified too. How we had helped each other.

That was real. That was real.

I curled up in my chair, my head in my hands, clinging to the memory as if it was all that would save me from going mad.

54

Rachel

The RAGE 'soldiers' left me in a side room for hours. It was cold and bleak – but I was used to that from the squat. Two low campbeds laid out with grey blankets stood on either side of the room. I sat on one. After the lumpy mattress I'd been sleeping on for the past week it felt ridiculously soft and comfortable. But there was no way I could rest. Too much was happening outside. Lewis was with Simpson, going over the plans of Elijah's compound. I caught snatches of their conversation. Simpson kept talking about 'fire power' and 'body counts'.

It struck me that if RAGE raided Elijah's compound, people were going to die. Innocent people – like the security guards and admin officers who worked there. People like my dad. Lewis had explained to me how big and self-sufficient the compound was. That meant there must be people living there whose only job was to provide food for the others, or keep the place clean.

From what I'd seen of RAGE I didn't imagine they

would care much if people like that got caught in the cross-fire.

And it had all been my idea.

The door opened. Franks was in the doorway, staring down at me. I shrank back, self-consciously. There was something unnerving about the way his eyes bored into mine. And his skin was so pale. It looked clammy under the dim light.

'Get some sleep, freak show,' he sneered.

Perhaps if he hadn't been so repulsive I might have been upset by this. As it was, it just made me angry.

'Why do you call me that?' I said. 'I'm not a freak. I'm just a person, like you.'

Franks snorted. 'Not like me,' he said emphatically. He came over and sat at the end of my bed. I drew my feet up, away from him. 'You're an example of everything that's wrong with the way people interfere with nature. Playing God. Desecrating the planet for commercial gain.'

I stared at him. I could almost feel the hate radiating off him.

'But I can't help how I was born,' I said. 'I mean, I can understand you all being against animal testing or doing research on embryos or whatever, but none of it's *my* fault.'

'You're missing the point. *You* don't really exist. You're just an imprint – an echo – of someone else. In your case, someone who died a long time ago.'

My heart skipped a beat. Did he really believe that? That I didn't really exist?

297

Franks stood up. 'It isn't nuclear power's fault that nuclear power exists,' he said. 'But that doesn't mean it's a good thing.' He narrowed his eyes. 'That doesn't mean it should carry on existing.'

He walked out, shutting the door behind him.

I hugged my knees to my chest. If I hadn't been sure before, I was now. RAGE would try to kill me as soon as they had used me to gain entry to Elijah's compound.

How scary was it that people could hate you that much, not for anything you'd done, just for how you were born?

For the first time it occurred to me that if my plan to rescue Theo didn't work, RAGE would certainly kill him too. The weight of what Lewis and I were doing pressed heavily on my chest. This was real. And there was no turning back.

I stood up and went through the combat moves Lewis had taught me.

Theo's face was in my head as I turned and lunged and kicked and punched the air.

He was the only other person in the world who carried this same accident of birth. This blood tie to another person. The one person who could truly understand how it felt.

I wondered where he was right now. What he was doing.

I wanted to be with him so much that it hurt.

Lewis came in about an hour later. He looked exhausted. He barked something angry in my direction, then quickly strode over and whispered in my ear.

298

'We're on. We're going to D.C. tomorrow morning. You remember what you have to do?'

I nodded.

Lewis's blue eyes crinkled into a smile. 'You're amazing,' he said. 'Don't ever forget it.'

55

Theo

I spent a whole day in my room without talking to a single person. Mel came in with my lunch, then, later, my dinner. She tried to talk to me, but I didn't want to speak to her. I didn't want to speak to anyone. Not even Mum.

I just wanted to forget. Especially who I was and where I came from.

Mel turned up the next morning – Sunday – to collect me for her combat class.

I was still in bed. I hadn't got to sleep until about four a.m. 'I'm not going,' I groaned, looking blearily up at her from my pillow.

'Elijah says you have to.' Mel walked towards me. Yesterday's bruise had faded a little, but her face still looked swollen and sore.

I sat up crossly, the sheets tangled around my waist.

'Who cares what he wants?' Irritation itched at my skin like a rash.

Mel frowned. 'You've got to take this opportunity to learn

to fight. You may need it.' She sat on the end of my bed. 'Theo, I don't know why Elijah wants you here, but I know *him*. He has a reason, believe me. He always has a reason.'

I stared at her face. 'Does he have a reason for hitting you?'

Mel winced. She looked down at the sheets.

I was too angry to feel bad that I'd embarrassed her. I was fed up with caring about other people's feelings.

'He feels betrayed by me,' Mel said quietly. 'He thought I loved him. And now he knows I don't. He hits me because he gets angry and he can't stop himself. Then afterwards he feels guilty. Says he won't do it again.'

'That's crap,' I said.

'I know.' Mel gave a heavy sigh. 'But I'm as trapped here as you are. We mustn't give up, Theo. You have to keep fighting. Please. We'll find a way out.'

I glared at her. 'I'm still not going to your stupid combat class. And Elijah can't make me. If he was going to hurt me he'd have done it by now.'

'Right.' Mel stood up. There was something deeply sad about the way she crossed the room, her head bowed and her hair just brushing the tips of the butterfly tattoo on her shoulder. As she reached my bedroom door it occurred to me that Elijah might hurt *her* if I didn't show at the class.

Resentment tussled with guilt in my head.

'Wait,' I said. I threw back the sheets and got out of bed. I was in my sweatpants already. I reached out for a T-shirt. 'I'm coming.'

301

Mel turned round. 'Good.' She smiled at me. 'After all it'd be a shame to lose that six-pack.'

'Ha ha,' I said. 'Very funny.'

I followed her down the corridor to the workout room. The usual assortment of beefy security guards and tired-looking scientists were gathered, waiting for Mel. Or maybe it was the scientists who were the beefy ones and the guards who looked tired. How would I know? How could I know anything for sure any more?

We started the warm-up and I let my body go through the moves it knew so well by now. It was good to have something mindless to focus on. My head was too full of angry thoughts. Against Mum. Against Elijah. Against his – our – past.

As Mel organised us into pairs, most people took a swig of water. I watched my partner: male, slim – a scientist, I guessed – glugging at his bottle. The sight of the clear liquid seemed to clear my own head.

Just a few weeks ago I was a child, imagining my father was a brave soldier who had died for his country. Now I knew the truth. My fathers – both Elijah and my genetic father – were bullies and killers. They were my past. They were my present. How could they be anything other than my future?

I hated them both.

We started on the slow-motion attacking and blocking moves. I stared at my partner. He *was* a scientist. I was sure of it. He had thin arms and greying hair and a slightly timid expression.

302

I snarled at him, letting all the hate inside me well up. Then I edged closer, punching within a few centimetres of his face.

'Ready to speed up?' Mel's voice sounded far away.

Hate was pumping through my veins. I moved faster. Closer to the man in front of me.

Hadn't Elijah said he was fifteen when he found out that his father was a cold-blooded murderer? How ironic that I should be the same age. *No.* I gritted my teeth. That was no accident. It was part of Elijah's plan. Part of his stupid experiment to see how alike we were.

I moved even closer, slashing and jabbing and kicking for all I was worth. All I could hear now was the blood pounding in my head.

Hate was in my genes. It *was* my genes. It was who I was.

'Theo.' A hand gripped my arm. 'Theo. Stop.'

I was so flooded with adrenalin I couldn't focus properly. Then the room rushed back into view. I was panting, completely out of breath, my fist less than a centimetre away from my partner's face. He was backed completely against the wall, his eyes staring, terrified, into mine.

'Stop.' Mel's voice was sharp. Insistent.

It was her hand on my arm. Her strength stopping me from punching the man in front of me.

'This isn't real, Theo,' Mel whispered urgently. 'This man hasn't hurt you. Let it go.'

Suddenly all the fight went out of me. My whole body released.

'Nothing's real.' I turned on her. 'Nothing's real now.'

I tore away and strode out of the exercise room, only barely aware of the hushed voices and pale faces behind me.

As I marched down the corridor I thought of Mum. I wondered how much of Elijah's past she had known. How she could have agreed to him cloning himself. It was sick. He was sick.

I was sick.

'Theo!' Mel was calling out. I could hear her footsteps behind me. I broke into a run. I didn't know what I was doing or where I was going. I only knew that I didn't want to speak to her. Didn't want to speak to anyone. Didn't want to go back to my room and be alone with my thoughts.

I dived left and right and right and left. As I ran I tore off my cap and chucked it down a corridor going in the opposite direction. I hoped this would throw Mel off my tracks. After a few minutes I stopped and leaned against the wall, panting. I looked back the way I'd come. No sign of Mel.

I knew I should feel guilty. She would be worried about me. She might even get into trouble again if Elijah discovered I'd run away. It struck me that if Elijah knew how much attention I'd drawn to myself in that combat class today, I would never be allowed out of my room again.

Who cared?

Screw Mel.

Screw Elijah.

Screw everybody.

I looked round me. I wasn't far from Elijah's private

rooms. I had no idea if he was there or not. I didn't care. I was going to go in there and find out about the Hermes Project. Find out why I was here. Maybe even find a way out of the compound. Well, why not? I'd escaped from school, hadn't I?

I strode towards Elijah's rooms.

I'm Theo Glassman.

I need no one.

It was liberating. I didn't care about anyone any more. I didn't even care what happened to me. I reached Elijah's door. I didn't look round to see if anyone was watching. I stood in front of the iris-recognition pad and let the bar of light stroke my face.

The door opened.

The room was empty.

I headed straight for the desk and switched on the computer. The screen took a couple of seconds to flash into view. I dragged the mouse so the cursor was over the Hermes Project file. Clicked.

Password required

I stared at the box on the screen.

Crap. What would Elijah choose as a password? I tried his name. No. I tried mine and Rachel's – both our real and code names. I tried Mel.

Nothing.

I looked round the room, my frustration building. Everything was as it had been before. Just the two closed doors leading to the bedroom and bathroom, the sofas and

TV and the holographic wall panel, its leafy trees swaying in imaginary sunshine.

I thumped my fist against the desk.

Bastard. I gripped the computer with both hands. Lifted it off the desk. If I couldn't see inside it I was going to smash it to pieces. Who cared about the consequences. If Elijah was going to hurt me, let him.

Let him freaking well try.

I raised the computer higher, pulling against its wires, tugging it towards the edge of the desk.

'What are you doing?' A child's voice.

I twisted round, almost dropping the computer in shock.

A little boy – maybe five or six years old – was standing just a metre away from me, in front of the holographic wall panel.

'Who are you?' For a second I was so freaked out I wondered if I was imagining him.

The little boy wrinkled his nose. 'I'm Daniel,' he said.

I stared at his face. It was even-featured – little snubby nose, olive skin, short dark hair, big, brown eyes. My heart skipped a beat. I knew this face.

I had been this face.

I set the computer back down on the desk.

'How did you get in here?' I said.

'Through the magic wall.'

'What?' Okay, now I was in serious danger of losing it completely. Either another clone of Elijah was standing in front of me, actually talking about magic walls, or else I had flipped out to planet nut-job proportions.

Daniel pointed behind him to the holographic wall panel. Then he bent down and prodded at a little pad I hadn't noticed at the base of the wall. The holographic panel slid silently open. A room was beyond it. I could just make out a low kids' table and a few kids' chairs set round it.

I stared. A magic wall. Leading to a hidden room.

Daniel stepped inside the room. He turned round and stuck his tongue out at me. Then he pressed something I couldn't see on the wall beside his head. The holographic panel started closing in front of him.

No. 'Wait! Stop!' I walked towards him.

Daniel grinned.

The holographic panel slid shut in my face.

56

Rachel

Lewis held out his hand, the fingers together, the palm flat and facing down. He glanced round. Franks was in the plane toilet. Simpson was asleep across the aisle.

'Later, when I do this –' he dipped his hand, pointing the fingers to the floor of the plane '– get down. As low as you can. Okay?'

I nodded. 'Don't worry,' I whispered. 'I know the signals.'

Lewis sat back, an anxious frown on his face.

'Hey,' I smiled. 'Don't forget this was my idea.'

Lewis didn't look reassured. I knew he felt guilty about taking me into so much danger. The thought of what we were about to do – storm into Elijah's heavily guarded compound, find Theo and Mel and escape with them – made my stomach churn.

I turned away and looked out of the window. The seat-belt signs had just come on and we were close to Washington D.C. now. The plane had taken off at about ten o'clock this morning, Sunday, but because of the five-hour time difference it was still, now, only midday, seven hours later.

The greens and browns of the fields below were giving way to rows of cream and white houses with brown roofs. From way up in the sky they looked like toy houses. It was hard to imagine real people living in them.

The sun glinted off the river flowing wide beneath us. I stared at the water, going over the plan in my head. *If* we got through the two sets of steel security doors, to the front of the building, and *if* Lewis managed to convince the guards to let us into the compound itself, then the attack would begin.

How it would work made no sense to me. There were only four of us. Me, Lewis, Simpson and Franks. How did RAGE think it was going to overpower Elijah's entire complex with just three men? And me. Not that I would be a part of it. Before either side could shoot me, I had to somehow make my way to Mel's room. Lewis had explained exactly where it was and what the number entry code was. He had told me to wait there for him. It sounded impossible.

Lewis left his seat and crossed over to where Simpson had just woken up from his doze.

I fingered the passport in my hands. It was the real thing. Franks had taken me back to my old house to fetch it. He had to break in because the whole place was shut up. It was weird being back there. It made me really miss Mum and Dad. My bedroom was a total mess. Clothes and shoes everywhere. It took a moment before I remembered why. Was it really only a couple of weeks since I was in here last, worrying myself sick about what I was going to wear to the school disco? It seemed laughable now.

'Cabin doors to manual.' The pilot's drawling instruction made my heart skip a beat. We were about to land.

It was time.

We got through Dulles Airport security with no problem, which amazed me. I mean there were questions at the desk – Lewis and I pretended to be a half-brother and -sister – and we each had to have our photograph taken and our fingerprints digitally recorded. But all that was clearly standard procedure. None of the airport officials seemed in the slightest bit suspicious of any of us.

Lewis caught my look of surprise. 'No criminal records,' he explained quietly. 'Except for some ancient assault charge on Franks.' He lowered his head nearer mine. 'RAGE are good at what they do. Don't get careless.'

I didn't need the warning. My heart was already in my throat as we took a taxi along wide open roads towards Washington. The taxi dropped us at some huge supermarket car park. Mothers with little kids kept arriving and parking, then disappearing inside the shop. The four of us waited by the exit – standing silently in the cold, sunny air. Even Simpson seemed tense. I asked what we were waiting for, but no one answered me.

Half an hour later I found out.

A grey van pulled slowly into the car park. It didn't park properly, just did a loop and pulled up where we were waiting.

Simpson opened one of the back doors a crack and bundled me inside. It was dark – I could hear breathing sounds, but I couldn't make out any faces. I felt someone – Franks maybe, or Lewis – pushing in after me. I moved forwards and stepped on someone's toe.

'Sorry,' I said.

'Quiet,' Simpson barked behind me. A hand on my arm guided me to the side of the van. My eyes adjusted to the darkness and I could see that the van was lined with men sitting on benches. They all seemed to be wearing black, with black wool masks over their faces – completely covered apart from slits for eyes.

One of them squeezed sideways to let me sit down.

I could feel the press of his leg against mine. I wanted to shrink away, but there was literally nowhere to shrink to. Lewis, Simpson and Franks sat on the floor of the van between the two benches, the four small bags we had between us at their feet. The door slammed shut. Some kind of infrared light came on. I looked round the van interior. Altogether there were twenty men.

And each one held a handgun in his lap.

57

Theo

'Daniel.' I thumped my fists against the holographic wall panel. 'Daniel. Let me in.'

Silence.

My heart raced. I had to get inside that hidden room. I had to talk to the little boy.

I peered closely through the holographic trees. Behind the panel I could just make out another room. Low tables and little chairs. Daniel standing beside them. I thumped the panel again, so hard it shook.

'Daniel,' I shouted. 'If you don't let me in Elijah will be cross.'

This seemed to do the trick.

'You can let yourself in.' He sounded sulky, but scared.

'How?'

'There's a number pad. You have to put in numbers.'

I bent down and found the pad at the base of the wall. 'Which numbers?' I shouted.

'050414,' he called. 'That's my age and my birthday. I'm

five, then the four is for April because it's the number four month in the year. Elijah told me. And my birthday's April fourteen.'

I pressed in the numbers. The panel opened.

Daniel was backing away from me across the room. His eyes were big and round. I looked round quickly. There were two low kids' tables. Four little chairs round each one. But it wasn't any kind of kids' room. Nothing on the walls. And a desk and filing cabinets down the left-hand wall.

I glanced down at Daniel. Mum had a picture of me at about the same age on a shelf in our living room. My hair had maybe been a bit longer, but otherwise we looked identical. There was no doubt that he was another clone of Elijah.

Daniel stared back at me defiantly. I suddenly realised how scared he was. Scared of me. I smiled and squatted down so I was closer to his height.

'How old are you?' I said.

'I just told you,' Daniel said. 'I'm five. Five and four-sixths.' He ran his hand through his hair. 'I learned fractions the other day. I'm the only one in the research group who understands them. Brad Cummins can't even count above thirty.'

I raised my eyebrows, wondering if Elijah's brains had finally found their way to the surface of his DNA. Not to mention his arrogance. Although . . .

'Wouldn't that be two-thirds, not four-sixths?' I grinned.

313

Daniel made a goofy face, twisting his mouth and crossing his eyes. 'What's your name?' he said.

'Theo.' I sat down on the floor. 'I know Elijah too.'

Daniel nodded solemnly. 'Everyone does.'

There was a pause.

'Do you live here?' I said.

Daniel nodded again.

'With your mum and dad?'

He shook his head. 'I don't have a mommy or a daddy. I have Kelsey. She looks after me. We live through there. Elijah comes too, sometimes. Kelsey's asleep.' He pointed to a door on the opposite wall. My heart leaped. The door must lead to the rest of Elijah's apartment. Maybe even another way out.

Daniel made a goofy face again. 'You won't tell Elijah I was out here, will you? I'm not supposed to unless someone's with me.'

'Sure.' I thought rapidly. 'Hey, Daniel. Tell me about the research group you're in.'

Daniel wandered over to one of the little tables and reached across to the pot of pens that stood on top of it.

'What do you have to do?' I said.

Daniel picked out a red felt-tip pen. 'Different things.' He held the pen out in front of him and squinted down its length like a gun.

'Okay.' The holographic wall panel was still open; Elijah's room in plain view. *Jesus*, he could walk in at any second. 'What did you do last time? Were you on your own?'

314

'No.' Daniel pointed his pen-gun at me. 'There were six of us. We did drawing.'

This was hopeless.

'*Bang* – you're dead.' Daniel grinned.

I put my hands in the air and fell over sideways. 'Ya got me.'

Daniel appeared above my head. 'I know what it's called.'

I sat up. 'You mean your research project?'

He nodded. 'I saw the letters on the front. Elijah has a big book about it. I read the letters,' he said proudly. 'I can read better than anyone else in the research project. That's because the project's about me. Elijah told me.'

My heart skipped a beat. 'What did the letters say?'

'We-ell.' Daniel pulled away and pointed the pen-gun at me again. 'The first one was a hairy hat man.'

'What?' I stared at him, completely bewildered.

'A "ha".'

I scrambled over to the little table. I pulled a pen out of the pot and reached for a scrap of paper from the pile. I wrote down the letter H. 'Did it look like that?'

Daniel nodded.

Yes. I wrote the rest of the word. I showed Daniel.

'Is this what it said on Elijah's book?'

HERMES

Daniel shrugged. He lined up the pen-gun again. 'Maybe. *Pow*. I think so. Hey, I said you were dead.'

Thump. Thump. Thump. I jumped as a rapid series of knocks sounded on Elijah's outer door. *Thump. Thump. Thump.*

315

My mind whirled. The Hermes Project was about Daniel. Hermes must be Daniel's code name. Which meant it *was* connected to me. I was Elijah's clone too.

Thump. Thump. Thump.

'Theo, if you're in there, please open the door.' Mel's voice.

I scrambled to my feet. 'Stay here,' I hissed at Daniel.

'PLEASE.' The thumping was louder than ever. 'THEO.'

Crap. She'd have half the security staff here in a minute. Not to mention waking up Daniel's nanny.

I strode back into Elijah's living area and opened the door that led out onto the rest of the compound.

'Mel?'

Her face was twisted with fear. 'Theo, listen.' She barged into the room. 'Elijah knows you ran off. He's looking for you. Looking for me. You have to go back to your room.'

'No.' I turned and pointed to the holographic wall panel. 'See? There's loads of hidden rooms through there,' I said. 'I need to look around. There might even be a back way out of the compound.'

'Hi, Mel.' Daniel ran out from behind the holographic panel, which swished shut behind him. He flew across the room and hurled himself into Mel's arms.

'Hi, Daniel,' Mel said distractedly. 'Theo, you—'

'You *know* him?' I stared at her, shocked. 'You *knew* about him?'

Mel frowned. 'Only that he's in this research group of Elijah's. Please come with—'

316

'Why didn't you tell me?' Fury tore through me.

'Tell you what?'

'You *know*.' I glared at her. 'How he's the same as me.'

Mel's eyes widened as she took in what I was saying. 'Are you sure? I didn't . . . I mean, Elijah just said . . . it never occurred to me . . .' She tailed off, staring at Daniel.

I could see in her face she was telling the truth.

She turned to me. 'I didn't know, Theo,' she said urgently. 'But what I *do* know is that Elijah could come back here any minute.'

I swore. 'Is there any way outside through the rooms behind that?' I pointed to the holographic panel.

Mel nodded. 'There's a back way out. But it's locked. Only Elijah has the key. He keeps it with him all the time. Puts it in a safe when he goes to bed.'

It didn't matter. I had to try. I marched across the room.

'No,' Mel said.

'You can't stop me.' I glanced round, but Mel wasn't looking at me. She was staring at the computer on the desk. It had switched itself on and was counting down. I stared at the screen in horror. How hadn't I noticed?

Return in 10 seconds

Return in 09 seconds

Mel started backing away from the door towards the little bedroom that led off from the living area. She gripped Daniel's hand tightly.

'What's the—?'

'Sssssh!' Mel and I spoke together.

Return in 06 seconds

Return in 05 seconds

Mel opened the bedroom door behind her. She pushed Daniel into the room. Then she caught my eye, just as the main door opened.

58

Rachel

No one spoke as we drove. It was hot in the back of the van and it smelled rank. Sweat and that horrible boys' changing-room smell you get of old trainers.

I kept looking across at Lewis, but he was avoiding my eye.

I knew it was all part of keeping our cover, but it just made me feel more scared. I rubbed my sweaty palms on my combats.

Without warning the van swerved right. We bumped along an uneven track for several minutes. I had to press myself against the side of the van to stop myself from being hurled forwards into somebody's lap. And then the van stopped.

Immediately, the door at the back swung open. The men stood silently and filed out. I followed, jumping down onto the ground. We were surrounded by trees, in some kind of clearing. Two cars were parked nearby, their windows darkened. I could hear the distant roar of traffic, but the uneven track we were on bent round, hiding the road we'd just driven along from view.

All the men except Lewis and Franks were now lined up opposite the van. I could feel twenty pairs of eyes on me. I retied my ponytail, then folded my arms self-consciously, trying to hide the fact that my hands were shaking.

Simpson was talking in a low voice with the van's driver. He had two black masks in his hand. He strode over and handed one to Franks.

'First five,' he barked. 'Go.'

Four of the men plus Franks walked over to the van. One of them pulled down a narrow metal shutter below the van's back door. He crawled on his stomach into the space that opened up. I stared in horror. The space was less than half a metre deep and only as wide as the van. The first man disappeared from view. Another crawled in after him.

'As soon as the gates blow, the back-up teams follow. The signal for amber is the first gunshot,' Simpson barked.

My legs were shaking so badly I could barely stand.

What had I done? What had I started?

Franks was now crawling in after the last man. Someone must have given him a gun. It glinted in his hand as he inched his way across the narrow gap.

Simpson came right up to Lewis. 'You wired up okay?'

Lewis prodded the tiny stud in his ear that doubled as a microphone. 'Yes, sir.' His voice echoed through the walkie-talkie strapped to Simpson's arm.

'The back-up cars will be following you the whole way,' Simpson said. 'And I'll be able to hear everything. So no tricks. No detours. No deviation of any kind from the plan. Got it?'

'Yes, sir.' Lewis stared Simpson straight in the eyes.

'We have ten minutes' air down there,' Simpson said, leaning closer to Lewis. 'Don't screw me on this or the cars behind will take you out.'

'No, sir.'

Simpson drew a stopwatch from his pocket and clicked it on.

He turned to the remaining line of men. 'As soon as we're away, get in the cars.' He scrambled into the metal space under the van. One of the other men pulled up the shutter. Once it was closed there was no way you could see an opening, or even suspect there was one.

'Come on.' Lewis dragged me up to the front of the van.

'I'm glad we're not travelling like them,' I whispered.

'Yeah?' Lewis jumped into the driver's seat and turned the key in the ignition. 'Don't be so sure. You and I are the ones who'll get shot first if the guards at Elijah's compound suspect anything.'

I sat down and put on my seatbelt. My heart was in my mouth as we bumped back down the unmade track. The other cars followed right behind. Lewis turned left onto the main road and we continued on our way.

In ten minutes we would be there.

In ten minutes it would be make or break.

In ten minutes I might be dead.

59

Theo

Mel slipped backwards into the bedroom.

I turned and faced Elijah. He stood in the doorway, his face grey with tiredness, his eyes blazing with rage.

'What are you doing here?' The coldness of his voice sent a shiver down my spine. Out of the corner of my eye I could see Mel's face in the shadow behind the bedroom door.

With a jolt I realised that Elijah would almost certainly hurt Mel if he found her here. Guilt flooded my head. She had begged me to leave and I'd stayed because I was angry. But it wasn't her fault. It wasn't anything to do with her.

I had to keep Elijah away from the bedroom. I forced myself to look him in the eyes.

'I am angry, Theodore. Very, very angry.'

'Yeah? Me too. And it's *Theo*.'

We stared at each other.

'Tell me about the Hermes Project,' I said.

Elijah's eyes narrowed. 'You've been looking through my files?' His voice was low and threatening.

'Only because you wouldn't tell me anything.' I strode over to the desk, more to keep his eyes off the bedroom than for any other reason. I grabbed the leather diary and opened it at this week's page. An entry for yesterday caught my eye.

Dr M. Results.

What was that about?

Elijah strode up behind me and slammed the diary shut.

'Well, I have something to tell you now, Theodore,' he said. 'There's been a change of plan.'

60

Rachel

We were driving through the streets of Washington. Houses had given way to big office blocks and shops. We passed through a very smart area with wide streets, then into a dingier, more built-up neighbourhood.

Lewis was making that hissing sound under his breath again. My heart was thumping so hard, I thought for sure he would hear it.

He glanced at me as we turned a corner, then drew a tiny, folded piece of paper out of his pocket. He laid it on the dashboard and pushed it towards me. He put his finger to his lips. I remembered the microphone in his ear and how Simpson could hear everything we said.

I nodded to show I understood, then unfolded the paper.

If anything goes wrong, just get out of the building. Head for the Jefferson Memorial. I'll find you there.

I gave Lewis a thumbs up, trying to ignore the churning, sick feeling in my stomach.

Lewis blew out his breath. 'We're here.'

I looked around. I could see nothing that remotely resembled a scientific compound. Just some boarded-up buildings and a disused car park with a notice in front: *KEEP OUT. THIS BUILDING IS UNSAFE. Dept. of Public Works.*

Lewis turned into the car park. He drove over a series of speed humps.

One. Two. Three.

I wondered how being bumped like that felt for the men hidden under the van.

Lewis turned through an archway down a long, dimly-lit tunnel. Shadows from the van played against the concrete walls. In the distance I could see a tall steel gate that spanned the whole width of the tunnel. It didn't appear to be manned, though what looked like some kind of intercom screen was on the wall this side of the gate.

Lewis slowed the van slightly, then pulled up beside the screen.

He reached out and pressed his hand against the glass. 'Lewis Michael,' he said, 'to see Elijah Lazio.'

61

Theo

'What change of plan?' I said. 'What do you mean?'

Elijah hesitated. 'Nothing. It's not important.'

He was lying again. I could feel it. And it was something to do with the Hermes Project, I was sure.

'You told me there were no more clones,' I said.

'I had to.' Elijah stared at the floor. 'Only three people know about Hermes. Four now, including you. Not even RAGE.' He paused.

'Go on,' I said. 'What were you going to tell me about?'

He ran his hand through his hair. He looked tired. But also irritatingly reluctant to speak. In fact he looked torn – uncertain what to do. I'd never seen him look so . . . so weak.

'Well?' I said.

'I haven't been fair on you, Theodore.' Elijah met my eyes at last. 'I thought if you spent enough time here you would begin to see how important my work is, maybe want to emulate me, even.' He looked away. 'But I was wrong. And I'm ready to let you go. There's something. . . I need to have an operation. Soon – within the next few weeks. I won't be able to spend as much time with you as I'd have liked for a while. I need you to trust me though, trust that once I'm better we will begin our work together in earnest.'

I stared at him. '*What* work together?'

Elijah walked across the room. 'Just let me change my shirt and I'll explain . . .'

'No.' I couldn't let him go into the bedroom. Couldn't let him find Mel. 'No. Stop.'

He turned and frowned at me. He looked more tired than I'd ever seen him. 'Theodore, I thought—'

A shrill ringtone cut through Elijah's words. He frowned and pulled the tiniest of mobile phones from his pocket. No. Not a mobile. Some kind of walkie-talkie.

He flipped it open. 'What?' he barked.

'Sorry to disturb you, sir,' said a fuzzy male voice. 'You're needed at the front gate. Code seven.'

Elijah flicked his fingers impatiently. He motioned me towards the door. I had no choice but to follow him through it. At least he hadn't seen Mel.

We walked down the corridor, Elijah still talking into the hand set.

'Who is it?' he barked.

'Lewis Michael,' the fuzzy voice said.

I stopped in my tracks. Elijah stopped too.

'Are you sure?' he said.

'Yes, sir,' the voice continued. 'With a girl. Wouldn't give her name but told me to tell you: Artemis. Is that some kind of pass—'

'Quiet.' Elijah glanced sideways at me.

My stomach knotted. Lewis was here? With Rachel? But Lewis was dead. I'd heard Elijah shoot him. And Rachel was supposed to be somewhere safe with her parents.

Elijah raised the receiver to his mouth again. 'What does he want?' he said.

'To bring the girl inside, sir,' the male voice said.

'Make sure they're alone and unarmed, then let them through, but only to the front gate,' Elijah said, shortly. 'I'm on my way.'

He snapped the walkie-talkie shut, then beckoned me towards him.

'Come with me,' he said. 'We'll carry on our discussion in a minute.'

Together we headed for the main entrance.

62

Rachel

The steel gates opened and we drove slowly through. Two men appeared, long guns slung casually round their necks.

We were still inside the tunnel; another identical steel gate a few metres up ahead. Lewis stopped the van and switched off the engine.

'They'll search the van here,' he said. 'Before they let us through to the front of the building.' He glanced at me. 'How you doing?' he mouthed.

'Fine,' I lied. I sat on my hands so he wouldn't see they were shaking.

The door beside me opened. One of the gate guards jerked his head at me.

'Out,' he commanded. I got down from the van. The guard patted up and down the sides of my body and legs. I could see Lewis on the other side of the van submitting to a similar examination.

'Wait here.'

I nodded, then held my breath as both guards marched to

the back of the van and opened up the doors. If they found Simpson and his men now . . . I shuddered, imagining the gunfight that would take place. We were virtually trapped here, between the two gates. It was not a big space and, apart from the van itself, there was nowhere to hide. On top of that, Lewis and I had no weapon. I couldn't imagine surviving any battle that took place here.

The guards stamped about inside. Then they got out and waved some sort of metal baton and then a hand-held device, like a BlackBerry, along the van's underside. Lewis walked round to where I was standing. His posture was still relaxed, but his breathing was tense and shallow.

'Heat sensors,' he whispered. 'And state-of-the-art technology for picking up traces of explosives and stuff. The van's designed to block all of them.' He squeezed my arm, then mouthed. 'Stay low. Find Mel. Okay?'

One of the guards strode up. 'You can go through,' he said.

I scrambled up into my seat and watched as the big steel doors in front of us swung open. Lewis started the engine and drove slowly forward.

Through the gates, I could see the concrete and steel frame of the compound. As Lewis stopped the van again, the doors behind us closed.

Oh my God. We were here. We were finally, actually here.

63

Theo

Elijah walked fast through the corridors. I had to take extra steps to keep up with his long legs. He started coughing as we went through the acclimatisation shed that led into the Outdoor Room.

As we stood inside, waiting for one set of doors to close and the other to open, I noticed beads of sweat standing out on his forehead. He leaned against the wall, breathing heavily.

'It's rude to stare, Theodore.'

I carried on staring as he looked up. Again, I saw the weakness in his eyes. I took a deep breath.

'As I've already told you,' I said. 'It's *Theo*. And I wouldn't want to work with you if you were the last man on earth. You're a bully and a coward.'

Elijah's eyes pierced through me, then he smiled. 'Fine.' He coughed and pressed his hand against his chest.

'What's the matter?' I said, as aggressively as I could. 'Indigestion?'

The door in front of us slid open.

As we crossed the open space of the Outdoor Room I marvelled again at the smell of fresh air, the way clouds scudded on their holographic loop across the sky and at the distant bird sound.

'How can Lewis be here?'

'Smoke and mirrors,' Elijah said.

I stared at him. He didn't appear in the slightest bit shocked to find Lewis was actually alive. Which meant he must already know.

Still. I got the distinct impression he had no idea why Lewis had turned up at the compound. With Rachel. My chest tightened. I couldn't see beyond the hologram walls of the Outdoor Room, but she must be out there.

As we reached the front gate, this strange fluttering feeling started up in my stomach. I realised that I was nervous about seeing her. Maybe I was just picking up on Elijah's nerves. He was sweating worse now and frowning as he muttered to the security guard on the door. He peered at the intercom screen.

'What the hell are you doing here?' he barked.

He was standing in front of the screen so I couldn't see Lewis's face, but I could hear his voice.

'The relocation was compromised. RAGE have been on our tail since Scotland,' he said. 'I had to bring Artemis here.'

Elijah said something in Spanish. It sounded like he was swearing.

He stood in front of the eye scanner. The door opened.

Lewis appeared on the other side, his lips pressed together. He looked worried.

And then Rachel stepped out from behind him. She looked completely different from the last time I'd seen her. Strong and determined. Not all bowed over herself, like she used to be, apologising for existing. And her hair was tied back off her face.

Her very pretty face.

She met my eye for just a second, then looked at Lewis.

'Well, come on,' Elijah said impatiently. He stepped away from the door so that Lewis and Rachel had room to walk inside.

They stepped inside. Lewis raised his hand with the palm flat, the fingers together. He held it steady for split second, then dipped the fingers downwards.

And then several things happened at once.

Rachel dived forwards and grabbed me, pulling me down beside her onto the floor.

Elijah yelled out – an incoherent roar of frustration.

A gun fired behind Lewis. Then another.

One of the security guards rushed past me to the door. I turned my head in time to see Lewis twisting the man's arm behind his back, forcing him to the ground.

'Run,' he hissed.

More gunfire. Elijah was trying to shut the main gate. Rachel was dragging me across the ground – half crawling like a snake.

'What's happening?' I yelled. Gunshots were ringing out,

deafeningly loud in the enclosed concrete passage outside. Then a huge explosion.

I froze. 'What the—?'

'RAGE.' Rachel tugged at my arm. 'They've bombed the gate. The second car'll be coming through. Come on.' She scrambled to her feet and rushed into the Outdoor Room.

An alarm screeched out all around us, piercing through the gunshots.

Security guards flooded past us. There was no sign of either Elijah or Lewis.

I raced beside Rachel through the Outdoor Room. Her eyes were wide, staring all around her as she ran.

More security guards were rushing towards us. RAGE's gunfire boomed behind.

'Oh, God,' Rachel said. 'We're right in the middle.'

I grabbed her hand. 'This way.' I ducked sideways into a clump of trees, then wove my way right round to the stream. The shooting sounded close. Screams and yells echoed all around us.

The shed that led back to the main part of the compound was open – more security guards hurtling through it.

We reached it. I pulled Rachel after me. In one side. Out the other. Even in the corridor you could still hear the fighting.

'Lewis said we should go to Mel's room,' Rachel said urgently. 'He told me where . . .'

'She's not there.' I pelted down the corridor towards the lab areas. We had to get back to Elijah's room. Mel was

334

there. Daniel was there. And neither RAGE nor Elijah's security guards would be able to follow us.

The alarm blared out as we swerved round the corner. *No*. Ahead the lab area was blocked off with a large corrugated-iron shutter from floor to ceiling.

We skidded to a halt.

'Is there another way?'

I nodded, then sprinted back down the corridor, trying to remember the other – longer – way round towards the living quarters. The sound of the fighting grew closer again. I sped up. Left round the corner. Right down another corridor.

Left. Left again. Blood pounded in my ears. A final right turn. Rachel ran lightly beside me, her trainers sounding a tapping beat on the vinyl floor.

'You came here with RAGE?' I panted.

'To rescue you.'

What? I stopped. 'But RAGE want me dead.'

'I'll explain later,' Rachel gasped. 'How much further?'

'We're here.' I pointed to Elijah's private door. I stood in front of the eye scanner. The bar of light flashed down my face. The door opened.

I knew as soon as I walked inside that Mel had gone. The logic of it hit me like a brick round the head. Of course she'd gone. Why would she hang around here waiting for Elijah to come back and find her? I strode across the main room, flinging open the doors to the bedroom and bathroom. Then I crossed over to the holographic panel, squatted down and punched in the access code. The panel slid back. The room inside was empty too. I strode across and through the door leading out into the rest of the private apartment.

'Mel?' I yelled. 'Daniel?'

Nothing. My heart hammered in my chest, loud in the silence of the room. The sound of the fight going on at the front of the compound had completely vanished.

Rachel ran up beside me. 'What are you doing? Where is she?'

'I don't know.' I thought quickly. 'Maybe she went back to her room? Maybe she went to see what the alarm was for?' No. As I said it, I was sure she wouldn't have done that. Not with Daniel with her. Unless she'd taken him back to his nanny first.

I stepped out into the hallway that led to the rooms where Daniel had said he lived. 'DANIEL!' I roared.

Not a sound.

'Why isn't Mel here?' Rachel's voice rose in panic. 'Where is she? And who's Daniel?'

'I don't know where she is,' I snapped. I was mostly angry with myself. It was so obvious Mel wouldn't have stayed here. She must have taken Daniel and . . . *man*, and the nanny too, probably, somewhere she thought they'd be safe.

I walked back into the main living area. 'Look we'll be okay here for a bit. No one can get in.'

Except Elijah.

'We can't just hide. Mel might need our help.' Rachel turned away and paced up and down a few times. 'Oh, God, I hope Lewis is all right.'

I frowned. This wasn't the Rachel I'd been remembering.

The Rachel who'd clung to me, needing me to comfort her.

'Why do RAGE want to rescue me?' I said.

'They don't.' Rachel stopped pacing. 'Me and Lewis went to them. The plan was that if we brought RAGE here to get you and destroy the compound, then Elijah's men would fight them. And . . . and while they were all busy we would find you and Mel and get you out.'

I stared at her. I couldn't quite believe what she was saying.

'Whose bloody idea was that?' I said. 'How on earth did you think we'd get past all those people shooting the crap out of each other?'

Rachel jutted out her chin. 'Lewis said the fighting would move further inside,' she said defiantly. 'If RAGE gets the advantage, that is. Which they should because they're heavily armed, they know the layout of the building and they have the element of surprise on their side.'

My eyes widened. 'Since when did you turn into a walking military tactics textbook?'

I meant it to sound like a joke. But the words came out all harsh and hard.

There was a horrible silence. Then Rachel bowed her head. 'I haven't.' She pressed her lips together, like she was trying not to cry.

I ran my hand through my hair. *Shit*. Rachel had come here to get me out, to help me. What was I doing getting angry at her?

'What *is* this place?' Rachel's voice was all shaky and embarrassed. She still wasn't looking at me.

I wanted more than anything to walk over and hold her. But I couldn't. It just felt too awkward. Anyway, after what I'd just said, she'd probably push me away. The thought turned over in my stomach like a dead weight.

'Elijah's private quarters,' I said, flatly. I told her about Daniel. 'I don't know what the Hermes Project is exactly, but from what Daniel told me it sounds like Elijah's doing tests that compare him with a bunch of other kids. God knows why.' I tried to smile. 'Maybe he's hoping more of his genius scientist brains will have come through in his later clone model.'

Rachel didn't smile back.

'Look,' I said, indicating the door that led through to the rest of the apartment. 'There's a way out of the compound down there. Mel said it would be locked, but maybe we can find a way through.'

Rachel opened her mouth.

'Once we've found Mel,' I added quickly.

'And Lewis.' She met my eyes. 'He told me he'd meet us in Mel's room.'

I nodded, wondering just how close Rachel had got to Lewis while I'd been stuck in Elijah's compound. She seemed to be going on about him a lot.

'Okay,' I said. 'Well, maybe we won't need to find a way through here. Maybe RAGE will be further inside the compound now, like you said. Mel's room isn't far. If we can reach her, maybe we'll be able to get round them and out the front without anyone seeing us.'

338

We walked across the room and out into Elijah's living area. Rachel stood beside me as I opened the door out onto the corridor.

The sound of gunfire was closer now.

Gritting my teeth, I led Rachel towards it.

64

Rachel

He was different.

My heart constricted in my chest. Theo was different from how he'd been before. There was something harder about him. Something rougher.

I glanced at him as we ran down the corridor. At his beautiful, strong face. I didn't understand. It was like he was angry with me.

We turned a corner. Practically collided with two of the RAGE soldiers.

One of them looked down at me. His face was completely covered by his black mask. He grabbed my arm.

The other man sucked in his breath. He was staring at Theo. 'This is Apollo,' he breathed. 'Apollo. We've got him.'

Both men now fixed their eyes on Theo. He backed away a step. The man nearest to him reached out to grab him too. Theo darted sideways.

Taking advantage of the fact that neither man was looking

at me, I raised my free hand, made a fist and punched the guy holding me in the throat.

He let go of me, choking, clutching his neck. I squared up and drove my knee hard between his legs.

'Aaaah!' The man doubled over in pain.

Yes!

Theo ducked as the other guy made a grab for him, then darted up and punched him in the stomach. The man stumbled backwards. Theo grabbed my hand. 'Come on.'

We raced down the corridor. Gunshots fired. A loud hiss passed my ear. And another. *Oh, my God.* Were those bullets?

Theo pulled me round corner after corner. The corrugated-iron gate that had previously barred our way through to the labs was in pieces across the corridor. Theo pelted round the biggest bits of iron, then turned left down another long corridor. He was running so hard I could barely keep up. Noise was all around us. The piercing screech of the alarm. People yelling. Gunfire. A group of Elijah's security guards ran across the corridor ahead of us. They didn't see us.

We swung round another corner. More rooms. More doors. *Lily. Ivy. Hyacinth. Acer.*

A massive bunch of RAGE masked soldiers powered across the corridor ahead of us.

'In here.' Theo opened a door on the right. A cafeteria. Huge. Full of long tables. Empty.

I raced inside. The alarm was still screeching, the sound piercing through my head.

Theo slammed the door shut. We both leaned against it.

Euphoria flooded through me. We'd fought off two RAGE soldiers. I bent over, panting. 'Man, that was a rush,' I gasped.

I straightened up. Theo was grinning at me. 'Good use of the element of surprise,' he said. 'Where did you learn to fight like that?'

For a second it was like seeing the Theo I remembered again – his gorgeous smile and his brown eyes almost melting me.

'Lewis,' I breathed, trying desperately not to blush. 'He taught me when we were in this squat, before we went to RAGE.'

Theo's eyes hardened. 'Oh.' He turned away.

No. What had I done to upset him now?

'We sorted out new identities too,' I said, quickly, trying to make whatever was wrong, right. 'For Mel and Lewis, you and your mum, and me and my parents. Max and Jake helped.' I gabbled on, explaining how Lewis and I had worked to give us all a chance of a new life free from both RAGE and Elijah.

Theo listened and nodded. But he didn't smile at me again.

It was like a barrier had come down between us.

At last my words dried up. I stood there, staring stupidly at him.

'Do you think they've gone now?' I said. 'Those RAGE soldiers?'

Theo nodded. He opened the door and peered onto the corridor. He beckoned me after him.

We didn't see anyone else as we ran down the last few corridors. The sound of fighting grew more distant.

'How much further to Mel's room?' I said.

Theo stopped outside a room labelled *Poppy*. 'This is Mel's,' he said.

He pressed a buzzer beside the door. I could hear it ringing inside the room. No one came to the door. He pressed it again, then stopped. Seconds ticked by, the only sound the alarm screeching. Theo ran his hand through his hair.

'It's okay,' I said. 'Lewis gave me her room code.' I punched in the numbers. 'Let's go in. Work out what to do.' I opened the door and stepped inside.

'Theo.' A female voice called out from the end of the corridor.

Theo turned. I peered round the door. Mel was running towards us, a little boy floppy in her arms. Her face was grimy.

She didn't see me inside the room, her eyes were fixed on Theo.

'They've set the labs on fire.' Her voice shook. 'I was trying to get to the front of the building with Daniel and Kelsey – that's his nanny. She got across but we got trapped . . .' She coughed. 'So much smoke . . . Daniel breathed it.'

I stared at the little boy in her arms. It was unmistakably the Daniel Theo had mentioned. The same glossy brown hair as Theo. The same smooth, olive skin. The same shape eyes. Exactly the cute little boy I would have imagined Theo had once been. And because of me, because of my idea, he was unconscious.

The alarm stopped.

'Oh God,' Mel said. 'They've disabled it. And they must have turned off the whole sprinkler system too.'

My chest tightened. RAGE wouldn't care who died, so long as the whole compound was destroyed.

'We have to get back to Elijah's room,' Theo said. 'We can—'

'What about Lewis?' I interrupted, stepping out into the corridor.

'Rachel?' Mel's eyes widened. 'What—?'

'No time,' Theo shouted. He pointed up the corridor. Black smoke was pouring through an open door. Through it I could just make out the outline of a masked RAGE soldier. 'Come on!'

65

Theo

We made it back to Elijah's private room, no problem.

Here, the fighting noises were more subdued. Without the alarm piercing through the air, it was easy to imagine everything was over. Easy, except for the acrid smell of burning chemicals that drifted towards us. And the distant crackle and hiss of flames.

I closed the door, my heart thudding.

I grabbed a couple of the sofa cushions and shoved them along the bottom of the door. Maybe they would keep the smoke out for a while.

Rachel sagged against the wall. 'Oh, God. All those people working here.'

'Maybe they got out in time,' I said.

I didn't believe that.

I was pretty sure Rachel didn't either.

'Is Lewis here?' Mel was asking her. 'Is he really . . . I mean . . . he's alive?'

Rachel nodded.

'I hate to break up the Lewis fan club meeting,' I said, trying to smile, 'but we can't wait for him. We have to get out of here.'

Mel nodded. 'Can you get hold of him, Rachel? Let him know what we're doing?'

Rachel shook her head. Her lips trembled as she looked at Mel. 'I don't want to leave him,' she said.

'I don't either,' Mel said. 'But Lewis can look after himself. He'd want me to get you two and Daniel out safely. And this is the only way. Elijah's private apartment is totally separate from the rest of the building. This is the only way out to the front without going through the fire.' She looked at me. 'We just have to find a way through the door that leads outside. It's always locked.'

I nodded, looking round for something, anything, that we could use to break it down.

Mel carried Daniel over to the couch and laid him down. His eyes flickered open and he coughed. She bent over him. 'He's okay,' she said after a few moments. 'I'll fetch some water.' She disappeared into the bathroom.

There was nothing in the living room that could possibly break down a locked door. Maybe there'd be something in the kitchen of the hidden apartment. I strode over to the hologram door and opened it

Boom. The sound of a gun firing made me jump. It sounded close. As if it had come from beyond the room, somewhere in the rest of the private apartment.

Rachel appeared at my shoulder. 'What was that?'

We stared at the closed door opposite.

The handle twisted.

I stepped back, out of the hidden room, dragging Rachel with me.

The hologram panel slid shut in front of us. I leaned forwards and stared through it. The door opposite was opening.

Lewis walked into the hidden room. Elijah was behind him, a gun in his hand.

66

Rachel

I stood next to Theo and stared through the holographic panel. My heart was beating fast. *No*.

'Lewis.'

'Sssh,' Theo hissed.

Inside the room, Elijah pointed to one of the little kids' chairs beside the low table. 'Sit down.'

Lewis sat, his big legs looking all awkward on the tiny plastic seat. His eyes were flickering everywhere. I knew he was working the room, trying to see if there was anything he could use to get away. At least his hands were free.

'Oh God,' I whimpered under my breath. 'Oh, God, oh God.'

I could feel Theo tensing beside me. I glanced round. Mel was still in the bathroom.

'I gave you everything.' Elijah's voice was low and furious. 'And you have brought those evil madmen in here, destroying my work . . . everything. You've got no goddamn idea what you've done.'

Lewis said nothing.

'Before I kill you,' Elijah went on, 'tell me why.'

My mouth was dry. *Please don't do this. Please.*

Lewis looked up. 'I came to get Mel.'

'How gallant,' Elijah sneered. 'How pointless.' He aimed the gun.

I didn't think. I just knew I couldn't stand there and watch Lewis killed.

'NO!' I shouted, banging my fists on the panel. 'NOOO!'

Elijah and Lewis both looked up.

Keeping his eyes on Lewis, Elijah strode towards me. He pressed something on the wall beside the panel.

I held my breath as it opened.

67

Theo

What the hell was she doing?

I backed away so that Elijah wouldn't see me.

'Rachel?' I heard the triumph in his voice.

I flattened myself against the wall. *Jesus.*

'Don't hurt Lewis,' Rachel pleaded.

'How did you get in here?' Elijah sounded suspicious. He was going to work out I'd used the eye scanner any second. Then he was going to realise I was here too. My heart pounded. *Think, Theo. Think.* I ducked down behind the long couch where Daniel was lying.

The bathroom door opened. Mel appeared, a small glass of water in her hand. She did a double take as she saw Elijah.

'And how did *you* get in here?' Elijah's voice was icy. 'And why is Daniel with you?' No one spoke. 'Get over here.'

Mel disappeared from my sight.

What the hell did I do now? Maybe if Elijah came out looking for me, I could jump him somehow. Get the gun off him.

I could hear Mel explaining about Daniel breathing in smoke. Then Rachel appeared across the room. The tip of Elijah's gun was pressed against her neck. Her eyes were wide with fear.

My stomach heaved. For a second I thought I was going to be sick.

Elijah's walkie-talkie beeped. 'Yes,' he snapped.

The man on the other end coughed. His voice was muffled, hoarse. From where I was hiding I could only make out a few disjointed words: *doors . . . stock . . . destroyed*.

Elijah sagged back against the wall. 'Everything?' His voice was a whisper. For a moment he closed his eyes.

Now. Rush him now. I hesitated. The moment passed. Elijah looked up, his eyes now desperate. He looked round the room.

'Theo?' He said it gently. 'Theo? I know you're in here and I don't want to hurt you.'

Yeah, right.

He moved across the room. 'Theo. If you don't come out I will shoot Rachel.'

He wouldn't. He wouldn't do it. He wanted to save Rachel – that's why he'd arranged the whole relocation thing.

Smoke was seeping in under the door. Elijah dragged Rachel over and peered out. A gust of black smoke billowed into the room.

Elijah coughed. 'Theo, I'm not joking. There isn't much time. We have to go. *Now*.' He cocked his gun.

I could see Rachel's face. Hear her ragged breathing. I clenched my fists.

Oh shit. Oh shit.

'Theo. I don't want to kill Rachel. But I will. You are more important to me than she is. If you give me what I want, I will let her go.'

He wasn't coming any closer. Even if he did I didn't see how I could get the gun off him and get Rachel away from him in one movement. Still. I could try.

'Theo. I'm counting down from three. Three . . .'

The only sound was Rachel's breathing and my heart thundering in my ears. Why wouldn't he walk over here? Just walk over here. *Over here.*

'Two . . . If you give me what I need I will let her go.'

Long pause.

'One.'

I jumped to my feet, holding my hands in the air. 'Okay, okay,' I shouted. 'Okay, I'm here. Tell me what you need.'

Elijah lowered the gun from Rachel's neck. He narrowed his eyes and, again, I saw them harden and set, as if he were deciding something.

'I need time, Theodore,' he said simply. 'I need you to come with me for just one more day. To give me time to . . . to think. After that, you and Rachel will be free. Free for-ever.'

68

Rachel

Was Elijah serious? One more day and then he'd let us go? And what did he mean about needing time to think. Think about what?

It was obvious from Theo's expression that he had no more idea than I did.

My whole body was shaking. Elijah brought the gun up again. It pressed cold and hard against my neck. He looked at Theo.

'Stand by the wall,' he ordered.

Theo moved away from the couch.

Elijah came closer to Daniel, still pressing the gun against my neck. Daniel's eyes were closed but he was breathing steadily.

'Mel, give Rachel the water,' Elijah commanded.

Mel stumbled towards me, the water slopping over her fingers. She handed me the glass, then backed away. I bent over Daniel, lifting his head a little. My hands shook as I tipped the glass against his mouth. My entire being was fixed on the metal of the gun, still pressed against the back of my neck.

'You could at least take that gun off her,' Theo said.

Elijah pulled the gun back. I glanced gratefully up at Theo, but he wasn't looking at me. He was staring at Elijah. I coughed. Acrid smoke fumes were starting to seep into the room.

Daniel's eyes stayed closed, but he sipped at the water, then spluttered some of it back up.

'Not too much,' Elijah barked.

I set the glass down and laid Daniel's head back on his cushion.

Elijah flicked out his walkie-talkie.

'Williams? Esposito?' The machine crackled back at him. 'Anyone?'

'Sir.' A faint voice could be heard above the static. 'All the staff are out. Fire trucks on their way.'

Daniel coughed. I stroked his hair and looked up at Theo. He was still staring at Elijah, an expression of complete confusion on his face

I shivered.

'And the labs?' Elijah said. 'Williams said they were . . .'

'Destroyed,' said the voice. 'Totally destroyed. Where are you, sir? Are you all right?'

Elijah snapped the walkie-talkie shut. His face was drawn – for one second he looked utterly defeated. Then he coughed and clenched his jaw.

Daniel moaned and opened his eyes.

'Theo,' Elijah barked. 'Pick Daniel up. Over your shoulder. Now.'

He pulled me upright and pressed the gun so that the tip was right against my temple. He walked me over to the open hologram door. Lewis and Mel were standing together. Elijah stared at them contemptuously, then glanced back as Theo came up behind us, Daniel slung over his shoulder.

'Go through the door opposite.' Elijah pointed to the door that Theo had said led to a passageway to the front of the complex.

Theo walked past us. Elijah inched after him, not taking his eyes off Lewis and Mel.

'Move a muscle and I *will* kill Rachel,' he said. 'I don't need her. I only need the boys.'

My heart thudded so loudly the noise filled my head.

I met Lewis's eyes. He was watching us every step across the room.

We reached the door. Theo and Daniel were already through. Elijah turned and faced Lewis and Mel.

'I wish I had time to make this painful,' he said viciously.

I looked at Lewis. He caught my eye, then made a tiny motion with his hand so that his palm was held flat, parallel with the floor, fingers together.

I shook my head. I wasn't diving out of the way this time. I held my hand in the same position as his and moved it sideways.

Lewis gave an imperceptible nod as Elijah pulled the gun away from my head and pointed it at Mel.

'Now,' I yelled. I shoved Elijah sideways as hard as I could. If he'd been expecting it I'd probably have bounced straight off him. As it was, I took him by surprise and he stumbled, the gun waving dangerously in the air.

Lewis leaped like a panther. He drove his fist against Elijah's arm, knocking the gun onto the floor.

'Go!' he yelled.

I didn't need to be told twice. I ran out of the room, almost colliding with Theo. Together we hurtled along a carpeted corridor. Open doors led off on both sides. Kitchen. Bathroom. Bedrooms.

'Which is the way out?' I gasped.

'No idea,' Theo panted. Daniel was bumping along over his shoulder, groaning more loudly now.

We turned a corner and came to a fire door. The lock was completely blasted away. My heart leaped. That was the shot we'd heard before. Elijah must have had to shoot the lock off to get inside. I pushed the door fully open. The remains of a large steel bolt lay on the concrete floor. The air smelled clearer and colder out here.

'This has to be it,' I said.

We ran hard.

Harder.

The corridor behind us was silent.

The air was much colder now. I guessed we were coming closer to the front of the building and further from the fire at its heart. Sirens nee-nawed in the distance.

At last we reached a door marked *Emergency Exit*. Theo

pressed down on the long metal bar and the door opened. Inside was a sort of garage. Dimly lit, with at least four huge cars lined against the far wall.

I ran to where chinks of light were coming in under the rolldown door opposite. 'This must be the way out.'

Theo's breathing was uneven. 'I can't see a switch or a button or anything that would—'

'Maybe some light would help,' said a male voice.

I froze. Elijah was in the doorway, one hand flicking at a light switch by the door. The other gripping his gun.

He pointed at the nearest car – big and black, like a taxi.

'Get in,' he said.

'What have you done to Lewis and Mel?' I said.

'Locked them into the fire,' Elijah said simply. 'They can die together, since being together is what they wanted so much.'

'No.' My voice came out as a hoarse gasp.

'Yes,' Elijah snapped. 'Now get in.'

I stumbled over to the car, standing numbly by while Theo laid Daniel across the back seat

I got in next to him and slid his little head onto my lap. Theo went round to the other side and got in next to his feet. Tears were streaming down my face. I saw Theo notice them, but I didn't care. For once I didn't care what he thought of me. I couldn't see how Lewis and Mel could get out of the building any other way than we had. Guilt filled me, choking me.

It was all wrong. Coming here had been the most stupid,

destructive, wrong thing I'd ever done in my life. Lewis and Mel were going to die. Goodness knows how many innocent compound workers already had. And I would have to live with it for the rest of my life.

Which probably wouldn't be a very long time.

Elijah revved up the engine. There was some kind of thick plastic barrier between us and the front seats – like you get in cabs.

'We'll be there in about fifteen minutes.' Elijah was clearly shouting, but we could barely hear him through the plastic.

I could feel Theo's eyes on my face.

I turned and looked out of the window.

The doors in front of us opened. Brilliant light flooded into the room. How could it still be daytime? I felt as if it was about two in the morning.

I put my head in my hands and wept.

69

Theo

The sunshine almost blinded me. How long had it been since I'd been outside? A week? Two?

It was weird seeing buildings and blue sky again. Real blue sky.

I tried the window control and the door handle beside me. Both were locked.

I sat back and looked at Rachel again. Her face was in her hands now. She was crying and trembling and I didn't know what to say to her.

I looked down at Daniel. He seemed to be breathing steadily. At least he was safe. And Mel and Lewis couldn't be dead. They would find a way out through the fire. I was sure of it.

I sat back and let my mind go over what Elijah had said about needing me for one more day, then letting me and Rachel go free. Was that just a way of getting us to go along with him while he escaped? Or did he mean it?

I glanced at Rachel. She had stopped crying and was

stroking Daniel's hair, smoothing it softly off his face. She looked so sad. I guessed she must be thinking about Lewis.

'Rachel?' I said.

She looked at me, her eyes a fierce blue against the raw red skin from her crying.

'If anyone can survive a building on fire, it's those two.' I smiled.

Rachel smiled weakly back at me. 'I know,' she said. 'It's just . . .' She gulped. 'All Lewis and I wanted to do was rescue you and Mel. And . . . and now so many people are . . . have been killed and you're not even free and . . .' Her lips trembled.

'Listen,' I said. 'What you did was the bravest thing anyone's ever done for me. And you don't know if *anyone's* actually been killed. I mean all the security guards wear bulletproof vests and that guy Elijah spoke to said all the staff got out. Didn't he?'

I stared into her eyes. She looked down.

'Hey, how did you and Lewis sort out that dive thing you did?'

She smiled sadly. Something twisted in my chest. She liked Lewis.

A lot.

'It was just this move he taught me.' Rachel held her hand flat in front of her, then dipped it so the fingers pointed at the floor of the car. 'Dive.' She sighed.

'Rachel?' I had to ask her.

She looked up.

360

'D'you think Elijah will really let us go?'

Rachel shook her head. 'I don't know.' Her eyes filled with tears and she reached over and touched my arm. 'I'm so sorry this has gone all wrong.'

I squeezed her hand, wishing more than anything that I could make her feel better.

'Theo?' Daniel's voice was barely a whisper. 'What's happening?'

I tore my eyes away from Rachel and smiled at him. 'Hey, how you doing, big guy?' I said.

'My throat hurts.' Daniel stared down at my hand over Rachel's. He looked back up at me and made his goofy face. 'Why are you holding hands?'

70

Rachel

'We're not holding hands.' Theo laughed and pulled his hand off mine.

I let go of his arm and turned to look out of the window, hoping he couldn't see me blushing.

For a moment it had felt like Theo and I had been close again. Those things he said were so sweet and kind.

But maybe that was just because he *was* sweet and kind. And it wasn't about me at all.

We appeared to be driving through central Washington. Wide, busy streets. Big office buildings and smart-looking shops on either side. Men and women strode purposefully past.

In the distance I could see the tip of a pointed stone tower.

'The Washington Monument,' Elijah called from the driver's seat.

I remembered Lewis's instruction to meet at the Jefferson Memorial. I wondered if it was anywhere nearby. Then the tears welled up again. Theo had sounded positive earlier and it was true that if anyone could escape a burning building it was Lewis. And yet . . .

I looked down. Daniel was gazing at me, his brown eyes all big and round and serious.

'Hi.' I tried to smile. 'I'm Rachel.'

Daniel carried on staring. I turned and looked at Theo. The same eyes were gazing at me. Except they weren't the same, I realised. Theo's eyes were strained – like he'd seen too much. There was no innocence left in his eyes.

'It's so weird seeing you and Daniel together,' I said. 'You look so alike. And yet different too.'

Theo nodded. 'This whole thing's weird.'

'Where are we going?' Daniel said.

'We don't know,' I told him.

The car swerved sharply left. I looked out again. We were driving down a wide, six-lane road. Shops on either side. A little shoe shop. A book store. A shop called Pottery Barn with brightly-coloured plates and glasses in the window.

The people strolling by looked groomed and relaxed, enjoying their shopping. They were only a few metres away outside the car.

It felt like they were on a different planet.

'This is Georgetown,' Elijah called out. 'We're nearly at the house.'

I turned to Theo. 'Why's he telling us all this?' I whispered.

Theo held my gaze. 'Maybe because it doesn't matter what we know now. Maybe because he's not planning on ever letting us go again.'

363

Oh God.

A few minutes later Elijah pulled the car up at the back of a large brick house. It looked old compared to most of the houses we'd passed on the drive, though not much different to the houses round where Theo lived in London.

Elijah ordered us out of the car. He patted his pocket. The metal tip of the gun handle was poking out. 'Be careful,' he said.

I helped Daniel walk to the front door. He started coughing. Elijah stared at him anxiously.

Inside, the house was simply furnished. Plain walls and polished wood furniture. Elijah led us through a large open-plan living room into an equally spacious kitchen with gleaming steel surfaces and glass French doors giving out onto a trim back lawn.

Theo immediately strode over to the doors. 'They're locked,' Elijah said wearily. 'And the glass is reinforced. And before you look, there's no phone in here.'

He withdrew with Daniel, leaving us alone in the kitchen. I heard a key click in the door.

Theo was still staring out onto the garden, his hands pressed against the glass.

I wandered over to the huge double fridge. A pack of bright pink ham and a slab of plastic-wrapped cheese lay on the middle shelf. There was a loaf of bread on the counter, beside a notepad, pen and a thick leather address book.

'D'you want something to eat?' I said.

'Please.' Theo didn't turn round.

I made two large sandwiches. I couldn't find a knife to cut the bread, so I had to tear off what I needed with my finger-nails.

'They look a bit rubbish,' I said, 'but . . .'

'Thanks.' Theo strode over and picked up one of the sandwich slabs. He turned away again, shoving it in his mouth.

I tried desperately to think of something to say to him.

'What was it like, in the compound with Elijah?' I said.

Silence.

I sat down on one of the stools at the counter and took a small bite of my own sandwich. My hands were still shaking slightly and the bread tasted like cardboard in my mouth. I rested my elbows on the counter, suddenly overwhelmed with tiredness. The clock above the oven said it was two p.m. Which meant it was seven p.m. at home. Still really early for me to feel this tired.

Theo stared out of the window again.

'It was weird,' he said. 'Being in the compound, I mean.' He sighed. 'I found out things. Not nice things – about who I was, where I come from.'

'You mean about being a clone?'

Theo nodded. He still hadn't turned round.

'For me it made sense of things.' I picked a piece of bread out of the sandwich and rubbed it between my fingers. 'For me, knowing I'd been made with Rebecca's DNA explained why Mum and Dad were always comparing me to her.'

Theo turned round at last. He walked towards me, his eyes burning.

'But didn't that make you feel weird? Like somehow you'd lost any idea of who you were any more?'

'No way.' I held his gaze. 'I'm not like Rebecca at all. It's like Elijah said, being a clone doesn't make you a xerox copy. Rebecca was smart and sporty and confident and beautiful. And I'm ... well ... I'm just not those things. So finding out about being her clone; it's like finding out we were twins instead of sisters. Weird. But not really that big a deal.'

Theo leaned on the counter, facing me. He was frowning, his eyes deeply troubled. 'D'you really mean that?'

I nodded.

His face was so close to mine, I could have reached over and kissed him.

He looked as if he wanted to say something else.

Don't start babbling. Let him say it when he's ready.

He was still staring at me, examining my face. I could feel it reddening by the second. The tension built.

Don't start babbling.

'Would you like another sandwich?' I babbled. 'There's plenty more ham. And cheese. Though more ham, I think.'

Theo looked down. 'No thanks.'

Then he turned away and went back to the window.

Brilliant, Rachel. Just brilliant.

71

Theo

I wanted to tell her about Elijah's parents. My parents.

They're in my genes. They're in my DNA. All that evil is in me.

But I couldn't.

For one thing, I wasn't sure she'd understand. I mean, what was all that about her sister being smart and sporty and confident and beautiful? What on earth did Rachel think *she* was?

I couldn't believe she really didn't see it.

But it was more than that. I couldn't tell her just how bad my genetic parents had been. The truth was I was ashamed. Ashamed of being connected with them. Ashamed of all the hate and anger that was inside me.

Several hours passed. Elijah came in to tell us Daniel was fine and sleeping. We each had to see the doctor as well. My examination took ages. I had my blood pressure taken and my lung capacity tested and masses of other stuff.

When I came back downstairs Rachel was in the living room, her face pressed against the kitchen door.

'What are—?'

'Sssh.' She beckoned me over. 'Elijah's talking on the phone,' she whispered. 'It's something about tomorrow.'

I stood next to her, my ear flat against the door.

'It *has* to be tomorrow,' Elijah insisted. 'I have no security here. RAGE will be looking for us.' There was a pause. '*Hijo de* . . . for God's sake, Dr Munsen, it's the same operation, just a slight change of. . . okay, okay, I know . . . *I know* . . . do you think I would be even considering this if there was an alternative? You're the one who told me I'm on borrowed . . .' Another pause. 'Of course Apollo doesn't know.'

Elijah's voice was low and intense. There was a desperation in it I'd never heard before. I glanced at Rachel. She looked as confused as I felt. What was Elijah talking about? 'I'm on borrowed . . .' meant 'borrowed time', didn't it? And what operation was he talking about?

'Yes. No. Very well. Nil by mouth. I know, Munsen. I *know*.'

Footsteps sounded across the room.

Rachel and I darted back from the door. I pulled her onto the sofa and wrapped my arms round her.

I was only trying to stop Elijah from thinking we had overheard him. But once I was holding her, I didn't want to let go. She felt good. All soft and curvy.

Except . . . except her back was rigid. Her arms too – all tense and awkward by her sides. And it struck me – she was hating me holding her. Hating it.

368

I twisted round. Elijah had crossed the room and was disappearing through the door out to the hallway. It didn't look like he'd even noticed us.

I sat back, my face reddening.

'That was close.' I pulled a cushion into my lap and pretended to be interested in the intricately embroidered pattern on the cover.

Rachel looked away. 'What does "nil by mouth" mean?' She sounded embarrassed. 'I'm sure I've heard someone say it before.'

'I don't know.' A thought struck me. I put the cushion down and went over to the kitchen. 'Keep a lookout. Okay?'

I found the address book beside the torn loaf of bread on the counter. I thumbed quickly through to M.

Dr Munsen
Attending physician, Cardiothoracic surgery
Transplant Programme Director
Mercy Hospital
Georgetown
Washington D.C.

Transplant programme?

My hands shook. Why was Elijah phoning a doctor involved with a transplant programme? What did cardiothoracic surgeons transplant, anyway? And what did that have to do with me?

'Theo.' There was a warning note in Rachel's voice. I put the card down, feeling numb, and walked back to her.

She was sitting on the sofa, where I'd left her.

'Elijah's at the front door,' she whispered. 'Saying good-bye to that doctor. And I think I know what nil by mouth means. It's for when you have an operation and you're not allowed to eat or drink anything beforehand. My mum's had to do it loads of times when she's had her face-lifts and stuff.'

I sat down beside her.

'What is it?' she said.

I looked into her eyes. They were a mix of grey and blue and green. The colour of the sea. It felt like years since I'd seen the sea.

'What does cardiothoracic mean?' I said.

'Cardio is something to do with the heart, I think.' Rachel frowned. 'Why?'

'That man Elijah was speaking to – Munsen – he's a doctor. A heart doctor. He does . . . it says . . . he . . . he runs a transplant programme.'

Rachel's frown deepened. 'Is that what they were talking about? Heart transplants? But why . . .?'

'Elijah has a heart condition . . .' My breath caught in my throat. I saw it, like a picture coming into focus. In that moment it all made sense. All the jigsaw pieces fitted together – Elijah being on borrowed time; Elijah having a heart condition and the references in his diary to *Med. Exam.* and *Dr M.*; Elijah planning an operation tomorrow; Elijah needing me for just one more day.

'He wants my heart,' I said.

Rachel screwed up her face. 'What d'you mean?'

'My actual heart.' My voice cracked. It was impossible to get my head round. That someone could actually imagine what Elijah was planning. And yet I knew it was true. 'That's what he wants. My healthy heart in place of his sick one.'

She stared at me. 'You mean . . .?'

I nodded. 'A heart transplant.'

Rachel's eyes widened. 'But that means you . . . you'll . . .'

'I'll die.'

'No.' Rachel sprang to her feet. 'No. We have to find some way out of here. He can't get away with this.'

'Get away with what?' Elijah said suspiciously.

I whipped round. He was standing in the doorway, leaning against the frame. I stared at the dark rings under his eyes. The greying face.

'You can't take my heart,' I said, as evenly as I could.

'It's murder.' Rachel stood up.

I pulled her back down. This was my fight.

Elijah sighed.

I suddenly realised I should have kept quiet. That would have given us – what had Rachel called it – the element of surprise?

'I do not want to kill you, Theodore,' Elijah said calmly. 'I want you to be part of what I do here.'

He was lying. I could see it in his eyes. It gave me that weird feeling I'd had before. I suddenly saw what it was – he looked exactly how I felt when *I* lied.

371

'You have to let us go,' I said.

Elijah swore. 'You are so stubborn, Theodore. I am trying to protect you. Keep you safe.' He paused. 'It is incredible. You are so like I was when I was your age. Reckless. Arrogant. Uncaring—'

'I'm not those things,' I shouted. I turned away, my head pounding with rage. 'I'm *not* you.'

The very hate in my heart told me I was lying.

Rachel put her hand on my arm.

'It is true that you are a genotype, not a phenotype. Yes,' Elijah said in that vague way he had when he was focused on some scientific discussion. 'But you are more like me than I had believed possible. And Daniel too.'

Daniel. I wondered what Elijah had in store for him.

I caught Rachel's eye. I could see she was thinking the same thing.

Whatever we did, however we got away, we had to take Daniel with us.

'How long will we be here then?' Rachel said politely.

'Only until tomorrow.' Elijah checked his watch. 'It is nearly six o'clock, which means for you, Rachel, it is nearly eleven p.m. UK time. There are rooms upstairs where you may sleep. Please do not attempt to escape. The windows are all reinforced and I will be locking you in for the night.'

'I'm not tired,' Rachel said quickly.

'Well I am,' Elijah snapped. He raised the gun in his hand. 'Upstairs please.'

72

Rachel

I sat on my bed. I couldn't see how we were going to escape. Elijah had locked me in. I knew that Daniel was on one side. Theo on the other. But we had no way of getting to each other.

I lay back on the pillow and closed my eyes. How could Elijah be planning to kill Theo? It wasn't possible that anyone could . . . could do such a thing. Lewis's smiling face flashed into my mind. There was this terrible, empty feeling in the pit of my stomach.

I pulled the pillow down and hugged it, trying to feel less alone. When Theo had held me earlier I had wanted to believe it meant something to him. Even though I knew it was just his way of making Elijah think we hadn't been listening to him.

I wished I'd hugged him back. But it had all happened so fast. Anyway, what did it matter? Lewis was probably dead. Theo wasn't into me at all. I *was* alone.

More alone than I'd ever been in my life.

I turned over. I couldn't give up. Somehow we had to get away and make it to the Jefferson Memorial, wherever that was. Lewis had said if everything went wrong he would find me there. I had to try it, at least.

I put the pillow I was holding under my head and lay back again, trying to work out how we could escape. As my pulse gradually slowed, my mind felt like fog. I couldn't think. The tiredness that had been with me all day was weighing my whole body down. My eyes felt unbearably heavy. I yawned.

The pillow was blissfully soft.

Maybe if I just rested my eyes for ten minutes, then I would be able to see what I needed to do . . .

73

Theo

Anger and adrenalin flooded through me. How dare Elijah do all this.

I didn't care what I had to do. He was going to pay. And I was going to get away.

I looked round my room. Thick, reinforced glass windows with crisscrossing lines running through the panes. A bed with a flowery counterpane. A rickety-looking chest of drawers. A sink. No mirror. No glass.

Glass would've been better.

Still, I looked back at the chest of drawers. I strode over and pulled open the top drawer. It was made of cheap, thin wood. Nothing special. I ripped the front off. It was glued onto the sides of the drawer and came away easily in my hands.

Quickly I held one end of the long flat plank in my fingers, rested the other end on the floor and stamped hard in the middle. The wood snapped with a satisfying splitting noise.

I examined the jagged edge. It was sharp and splintery. It would do.

I drew the wood across the inside of my arm, just above the wrist. It grazed the skin, but didn't break it.

I gritted my teeth and pressed down harder. *Yes.* A bead of blood bubbled to the surface. *Again. Again.* The graze deepened. A dribble of blood trickled down my arm.

I realised I was holding my breath and let it out heavily. This was no good. I needed to be bleeding badly.

I leaned back against the wall and braced my legs, wishing I had something sharper to use. Something quicker.

Then I sawed at my arm again. But this time it was Elijah's arm I was carving into. *Harder. Harder. HARDER!*

'Aaaagh!' I muffled a roar as the wood dug painfully across my already broken skin.

I could feel I'd left splinters in my arm. The wound was sore. *Do it again.*

I groaned and pressed down again, sawing into the bleeding gash.

Yes. Blood – bright red – was seeping out of the wound.

Again. My hand shook. I hesitated. The jagged line in my skin was already throbbing. I couldn't hurt myself any more. *You have to.* I pressed gently on the wound. *Ow!*

Do it. Do it now. Don't think about it.

I tried to summon Elijah's face again. But it wouldn't come. All the hate seemed to be seeping out of me along with my blood.

Do it for Rachel. You know he's only kept her alive to make you do what he tells you. Which means once you're gone, he'll have no more use for her.

This time I let myself roar.

'AAAAGGH!' Adrenalin flooded through me as I sawed through the open wound. 'AAAGGH!' Blood poured down my arm.

I could hear movement outside. I raced to the door and banged against it.

'Elijah. Elijah,' I yelled. 'Help me.'

I looked down at my arm. At the blood. I felt sick.

A key turned in the lock.

Elijah appeared in the doorway, his face lined and anxious. 'What?'

I carefully held my hand over the wrist just below the cut. My arm was so covered in blood now it was impossible to see where the cut actually was.

'I slit my wrist,' I said hoarsely. 'The blood's pumping out. It hurts.'

Elijah's eyes widened. 'Sit. Hold your arm in the air,' he ordered. He rushed to the bed and started ripping at the sheet.

My hands were still shaking and my cut arm was throbbing painfully. But this was my chance. I darted outside the room, slammed the door shut and turned the key.

'NO!' Elijah gave a great roar. 'Open this now!' He banged on the door with his fists.

I raced next door. 'Rachel?' I yelled.

No reply.

I turned sideways and hurled myself at the door. It shook, but didn't give way. I threw myself at it again, putting all my weight behind my shoulder.

This time it burst open.

Rachel was lying on the bed, fast asleep.

For a second I stared at her incredulously. How could she be sleeping?

I ran over and shook her shoulder. 'Rachel? Rachel?'

She opened her eyes and looked up at me blearily. 'What . . . what's . . .?'

Then she registered the open door behind me. She sat bolt upright. 'Theo. We've got to meet—'

Bang. The thud of Elijah hurling himself against my door made us both jump.

I pulled Rachel to her feet. 'Get your shoes on,' I said.

I ran out into the corridor, raced to the next room and heaved myself at Daniel's door. *Ow*. My shoulder was really bruised and my arm was hurting so badly now it was painful to move it.

Boom. Elijah must be close to breaking that door down. He was yelling too. Spanish. It sounded like swearwords.

'Theo.' Rachel's voice cut sharply across the yells. 'What are you doing?'

'Door. Daniel.'

She pointed to the lock. 'Try turning the key.'

I stared down. The key was in the lock. I reached out with my uninjured arm and turned it.

Rachel gasped. 'Your arm!' she shrieked.

I looked down. My arm was drenched with blood all the way down to the hand.

I stormed into Daniel's room. He was asleep too, spread-eagled across the counterpane. I picked him up – ignoring the pain in my cut arm – and carried him outside.

Thud. Snap. The frame of Elijah's door splintered.

Rachel appeared in the doorway of her room. She held out what looked like a pillowcase to me. 'Wrap this round your arm,' she said.

'In a minute,' I nodded. 'Let's get out of here first.'

I pounded down the stairs, Daniel a dead weight in my arms. I was feeling faint now. I wasn't sure I could carry him to the street, let alone any further. I stumbled to the front door, then stared stupidly at it. Locked. Of course.

Rachel ran up, the pillowcase over her arm, a bunch of keys in her hand.

'They were on the table,' she panted.

The sound of splintering wood echoed down the stairs.

'Hurry,' I urged. I rested against the wall, trying to shake Daniel awake. He didn't even murmur.

Rachel was turning keys, pulling bolts. 'God, it's like a bank safe.' Sweat beaded on her forehead.

Footsteps thundered along the landing.

Rachel turned a final key. Pulled the door open.

Footsteps on the stairs.

Rachel sprinted outside. I lumbered after her. I had no idea which way to go. My cut arm was bleeding furiously now, the wetness soaking into Daniel's T-shirt. The pain of it was all I could think about.

Rachel hesitated for a fraction of a second, then turned left and raced along the pavement.

Breathing heavily, my head spinning, I chased after her.

74

Rachel

All I could think about was getting away from the house as quickly as possible.

I flew towards the nearest corner. Whipped round it. Then took the next left. Quick. Then the next right. It was all houses. Old, brick houses with neat lawns. It was dark now. Hardly anyone about.

I had to find a main road and some directions. Or someone I could ask directions from.

Panting, I stopped and looked over my shoulder. Theo was a few metres behind me, half running, half staggering towards me. Daniel hung limply from his arms, half asleep.

With a jolt I realised that Theo's arm was dripping blood onto the pavement.

'You're leaving a trail,' I shrieked.

He stared at me in this weird, unfocused way.

'Put Daniel down,' I ordered.

Theo sank to his knees and deposited Daniel on the

pavement. He sat back on his heels, breathing heavily. I knelt beside him and shoved the pillowcase into his hands.

'Wrap that round the wound. Tight.'

I hauled Daniel to his feet and shook his shoulders. 'Daniel. Wake up.'

He moaned a little.

In the distance I could hear running footsteps. Elijah wasn't far behind.

There was no other option.

I drew my hand back and flung it against Daniel's left cheek. *Slap*.

'*Ow!* What?' Daniel grumbled sleepily.

'Wake up,' I said. 'Now.'

Daniel opened his eyes. 'What *is* it?'

I glanced at Theo. His face was strangely pale in the street lights. I hauled Daniel to his feet.

'Get up, Theo,' I said.

He stumbled to his feet. Blood was starting to show through the pillowcase on his arm, but at least it wasn't dripping out of him any more.

'Now run,' I said.

I dragged Daniel after me. He was still half asleep and having to run hard to keep up with me.

We reached another corner. I ploughed down it. But I knew we were going too slowly.

'Come on, Daniel. This is a race,' I panted. 'Beat Theo and there's a big prize.'

What?' Daniel whined.

'Anything you want,' I gasped, clutching with my free hand at a stitch in my side. 'We'll go to a toy shop and you can choose. Anything you want.'

Daniel said nothing, but I could feel him running harder.

Suddenly we burst onto a main street. Smart shops and restaurants all lit up. Theo pounded up behind us.

'I won,' Daniel said gleefully.

'Not over yet,' I said.

I tugged him after me to the next crossing. I had no idea if we were heading in the right direction. My first aim was to make sure we'd lost Elijah.

A red light was flashing at me from the other side of the road. Beside it, also in red neon, numbers were counting down. *Four. Three. Two. One.*

A green neon figure appeared. *Walk.* I tugged Daniel across the road and looked round. Theo was beside us, paler than ever. He leaned against a lamppost. A smartly-dressed woman passing by gave him a wide berth. I looked round. No sign of Elijah.

'Wait here a sec,' I said. I let go of Daniel's hand and darted over to a couple holding hands outside the nearest restaurant. 'Where's the Jefferson thing?' I said. 'Please?'

The couple stared at me. The woman was young, blonde, pretty. The man older and wary-looking.

'The Jefferson Memorial?' The woman smiled at me.

I nodded.

She pointed up the road. 'Follow M street up to Pennsylvania. Then hang a right down Connecticut and follow the signs.'

'Thanks.' I darted back to Theo and Daniel. Theo was bent over, his forehead beaded with sweat.

'This way,' I said.

He straightened up. We jogged on. I felt we should still be running hard, but it was obvious Theo was in no state to do so any more. Daniel was now wide awake.

'What's happening?' he whimpered. 'Where's Elijah?'

We were at another crossing. The red neon numbers were counting us down again. *Ten. Nine. Eight.*

I looked over my shoulder and gasped. Elijah was only a few shops away.

I turned back. 'Hey, Daniel. Another race. Okay?'

Cars were still flying past. *Six. Five.*

There was no time to wait.

'Cross,' I yelled.

Dragging Daniel after me I dodged between the cars, horns screeching in my ears.

On the other side of the pavement I broke into a faster run. I could hear Theo panting beside me. I didn't dare look back. I whipped down a side road, then turned right and right again to come back out on the main road.

No sign of Elijah.

On and on we raced.

I followed the directions the woman had given me as best I could, weaving down and round what I hoped were blocks leading me back to where I'd been – small diversions, in case Elijah was still on our tail.

The area we were running through got quieter, then busier

again. Cars whooshed past. The whole city was buzzing. Alive.

At last we arrived at a small park. It wasn't enclosed or anything, just a patch of trees and bushes set off the main road.

'Are we nearly there?' Theo said hoarsely.

I bit my lip. The truth was I was lost.

'I think so,' I lied.

'Good,' he said. Then he slid to the ground and passed out.

75

Theo

I was lying on something hard. It smelled damp and earthy, rough against my face. And I was cold. Shivering with cold.

Something heavy was lying across my chest, like a thick rope. I tried to move but I was wedged between two solid objects. No. Not objects. They were too warm and soft for that.

I opened my eyes. Earth. I was lying on the ground. My arm was throbbing. Daniel was curled up in front of me, his breathing deep and even. I tried to twist round. Something was rustling above me. Green. A bush. It was really cold. There was frost on the leaves. The sky filtering between them was a greyish-pink colour.

I had no idea how I'd got here. I could remember slashing at my arm, getting out of the house. Running and running, with Daniel in my arms. And then . . . nothing.

I moved my frozen hand to touch the heavy rope across my chest. It was an arm. I twisted round some more. Rachel's arm. And it was her whole body, I realised, that was pressed into my back. Her whole soft, curving body.

It felt good, her holding me like that. Safe.

But more than that. Much more.

She stirred. 'Theo?'

'Hey.'

'Oh, Theo.' Her voice dissolved into tears. I could feel the wetness against my neck.

'Hey,' I said again, trying to twist round to face her.

She tightened her hold on me. 'I thought you were going to die,' she sobbed. 'When you collapsed I didn't know what to do. I was so scared.'

With my uninjured arm I pushed Daniel forwards a little, so I had room to turn round properly. The side of my face that had been pressed into the earth felt ridged and gritty.

Rachel's face was glistening with tears. As I turned towards her she buried it in my neck.

I stroked her hair.

I was freezing cold, my whole body stiff and sore, and my arm where I'd cut it was pulsing with pain. The man who had created me wanted to kill me to take my heart. If I escaped from him, an army of ruthless anti-cloner terrorists were waiting to tear me apart. My mother had lied to me. I could imagine nowhere in the world where I would be safe.

And yet, at that moment, I don't think I'd ever been happier.

'You did it,' I whispered. 'You got us away.'

Rachel looked up at me. Her eyes were shining. 'You hurt yourself,' she whispered. Her breath was white mist in the cold air. 'To save us.'

387

'To save myself too,' I grinned.

Like the Nazi I am.

The smile fell from my face.

'We should go.' I pulled back a little.

Who am I kidding? I don't let people in.

That's who I am.

'The Jefferson Memorial, yeah?' I frowned, trying to remember what Rachel had said the night before.

Rachel nodded. 'Lewis told me to go there if we got separated. If he's alive, that's where he'll be.'

I sat up, colliding with the bush leaves. My head spun. 'Let's go.'

'Are you okay?' Rachel's voice was full of concern.

'Sure.' I closed my eyes, fighting the nausea that swelled inside me. 'We have to find Lewis. Get started with the relocation stuff you said Max had worked out.' I took in a deep breath. It helped. The air was crisp and cold.

'Theo?'

I opened my eyes. Rachel was sitting up beside me.

'How's your arm?' she said gently.

I looked down. The pillowcase was a mess of dried blood, stuck to my skin. I tugged part of it away, exposing a centimetre or so of jagged flesh. *Ow.* I felt sick again.

'That looks nasty.' Rachel made a face. 'Maybe we should get you to a hospital.'

'I'm fine,' I lied. 'Anyway, I'm not going near any hospital. If Elijah finds me in one he'll have all my internal organs out before you can say *clone-boy.*'

388

Rachel smiled. *Man*, she was so pretty when she smiled.

'Hey,' I grinned. 'Maybe having my heart'd make him a nicer guy.'

Rachel gave a sort of hiccupy laugh. I put my hand on her cheek and stroked the dirt off her face with my thumb.

'We'll be okay,' I said. I bent my head so my nose almost touched hers. Her eyes were shut, her lips slightly parted. I could feel her breath, warm against my mouth.

My heart was beating fast. I wanted to kiss her.

I'd never wanted anything so much.

Too much.

I don't let people in.

I pulled away, then twisted round and stood up carefully, using the bush we had slept under for support.

'Come on.'

I stretched out my good arm to her. The sun was an orange disc on the horizon. The air was still. The distant hum of traffic the only noise.

Rachel stood up, silently, ignoring my offered arm. She kept her face turned away from me too, or maybe that was just a coincidence.

Then, together, we dragged a complaining Daniel to his feet and set off to find someone who could tell us how to get to the Jefferson Memorial.

76

Rachel

'I'm hungry,' Daniel said for the tenth time.

I took his hand. 'Won't be long now,' I said.

We had been walking for what felt like hours, though it couldn't have been that long really. The sun was properly risen now, and there was loads of Monday morning traffic. Commuters were bustling about the busy Washington streets. Apart from the many people I'd asked for directions to the Jefferson Memorial, no one had taken much notice of us, even though it must have been obvious we'd slept outside. Our clothes were creased and dirty, and Daniel's face in particular was covered with specks of earth.

I guess big cities are the same everywhere. It's easy to ignore what you don't want to see.

I didn't know what to say to Theo. When he'd moved so close to me earlier my heart had practically stopped beating. For a minute I almost let myself believe that he liked me. As in 'liked'. Big time.

But then it was over and since we'd left the little park area he'd hardly said a word. I had no idea what I'd done wrong. Maybe when he got up close to my face he'd realised how ugly I was under all the dirt. Maybe he was just worrying about finding Lewis. And it was obvious his arm was hurting him badly. He held it gently, using his other arm like a sling.

'I'm hungry,' Daniel whined again.

I was hungry as well, but I was more tired than anything. I'd hardly slept all night what with the cold and worrying about Theo and being terrified by the rustling noises all around us. I glanced at Theo. His face was drawn and horribly pale. He must be hungry too.

We passed a busy pretzel stand on the corner of two busy streets in a business district.

'Let's sit down for a minute,' I said.

Theo slumped to the ground and leaned against the wall of some office block. He closed his eyes. I watched men and women in smart suits buying coffee and pretzels from the stand. Then I shuffled forwards, slightly away from the building we were resting against. I held out my hand and dipped my head.

I had never begged before in my life, but I'd seen plenty of people do it at home in London. Sometimes they had cardboard signs round their necks saying they were hungry or homeless. I had to rely on my dirty face – and on Daniel, who huddled pitifully against me as I sat there. He was shivering from the cold air, even though the sun was really quite fierce now.

A few minutes passed.

Somebody pressed a coin into my hand. Change clattered down onto the pavement beside me. I quickly gathered the money into my lap and held out my hand again.

It took about fifteen minutes to collect three dollars. Armed with this, I bought two large pretzels and shared them between us. The guy on the stand gave us further directions to the Jefferson Memorial. It wasn't far now. We just had to keep going down Fourteenth Street, past the turn onto Independence Avenue, right down to something called the Tidal Basin – a little bay that the memorial stood on the edge of, apparently.

We trudged on. Daniel was munching on his big pretzel, holding my hand. I could see trees and water up ahead. Then Theo pointed.

'That's gotta be it.'

Set against the clear blue sky was a raised stone structure. At the top of some steps was a huge statue, covered with a roof and flanked on three sides by tall columns.

We walked closer. There was hardly anyone about. It must still be very early. I walked round the base of the memorial. There was no sign of Lewis.

'If he's . . . he's probably sweeping for us,' I said as I reached Theo and Daniel again. 'It's what he'd do. Sweeping the area every hour or so to see if we're here yet.'

Theo squinted down at me, shielding his eyes from the sunlight. I couldn't read his expression.

'Let's go up to the statue,' I said. The air was still as we walked up the steep stone steps. The sun disappeared as we entered the memorial itself. The figure of Jefferson loomed high above our heads.

'Who's he?' Daniel asked.

'One of the American presidents, I think,' I said. There was still no one about. 'Why don't you race round the monument ten times, Daniel?' I said. 'Warm you up. I'll count how quickly you do it.'

Daniel shoved his last bit of chewed up pretzel into my hands. 'How fast will you count?'

'Like this.' I drummed a beat on my hands. 'One. Two. Three. Yeah?'

He nodded, then dashed off.

Theo wandered over to the wall on the right far side of the statue. Some writing was carved there, in large, clear letters.

He read out loud: 'We hold these truths to be self-evident.' He turned to me. 'What does that mean?'

'It's obvious,' I said.

Theo raised his eyebrows. 'Not to me, smart-arse.'

I blushed. 'No, that's what it means: "To us the following is obvious". And then it goes on to say *what's* obvious . . . that all men are created equal.'

'Well, that's a load of crap.' Theo snorted. 'People aren't equal. Some have money and talent and power while—'

'No,' I said. 'It says "created equal" as in "start out equal", deserve equal rights to . . . to . . .' I searched the writing again. 'To those things it says right there . . . life, liberty and the pursuit of happiness.'

Theo stared at the words.

'This is from the American Declaration of Independence,' I burbled on. 'They wrote it when they got independence.'

'Independence from what?' Theo asked.

'From us. From Britain. Hundreds of years ago.' I rolled my eyes. 'Don't you study history at your school?'

Theo shrugged. There was an awkward pause. 'Bet they didn't have clones in mind when they wrote that.'

I looked round at Daniel. He was still hauling himself round the statue. I could hear him checking off laps under his breath. *Three. Four.*

'Hey, Rachel.' Theo grinned at me, but the smile didn't reach his eyes. 'I've got a history lesson for you.'

77

Theo

I told her everything that Elijah had told me. I don't know why. Once I started I couldn't stop myself. It was a relief to get it off my chest. She listened silently. Sympathetically.

Daniel ran up. 'How long did I take?' he panted.

'Two hundred and twenty-three seconds,' Rachel said instantly.

I smiled. I was sure she hadn't been counting.

'Can we go to the toy shop now?'

'Later,' Rachel said. 'Why don't you do ten more laps? See if you can beat your record.'

He ran off.

Rachel looked at me. 'All that, about who Elijah is and who his parents were. You know it doesn't mean anything, don't you?'

'Of course it means something. All that terrible stuff they did is in me too, like it is in Elijah.'

'Who says?' Rachel frowned. 'Anyway, didn't you just say that Elijah hates his parents for what they believed?

For what they did. That he's tried to create life, not destroy it.'

'Exactly.' I clenched my jaw, feeling a terrible rage boiling up inside me. 'He's tried to be different, but he's ended up exactly the same. Prepared to play God and experiment with people's lives. Even to kill me to save himself.'

Rachel shook her head. 'No, Theo. That's not the same thing. Who you are is up to you. It's down to the choices you make, the things you decide to do with your life.' She pointed at Daniel, still padding round the monument. 'He's got the same genes as you and Elijah. Look at him. He's just a little boy. Not a murderer.' She laughed. 'Exactly when do these killer genes kick in?'

'You don't understand.' The anger ripped out of me in a shout. 'I *am* like Elijah. I'm tied to him by . . . by the exact same blood, even. I don't care about other people. I look after myself. Only myself. Other people don't matter. I hate other people.'

I stared at Daniel as he disappeared behind the monument. The pain in my arm was intense. I felt like driving my fist into the stone walls of the memorial.

'If that's true,' Rachel said scornfully, 'then it's because that's how you *want* it. Not how it *has* to be. But I don't think it is true. I think you just feel sorry for yourself, which is—'

'How *dare* you say that. You don't know anything about . . .' I stopped. Daniel hadn't reappeared round the other side of the monument.

I paced forwards.

'What is it?' Rachel was at my side. 'Did you see Lewis?'

'Daniel?' I called out.

There was no sign of him round the sides or front of the statue. I strode to the top of the steps and looked round as far as I could.

'DANIEL!'

Rachel clutched my arm. I swivelled round and followed her pointing finger.

There, emerging from behind one of the columns opposite, was Daniel, his arm tightly gripped by a man with a short, grey ponytail and cold, blue eyes. My stomach flipped over. The man's hand was over Daniel's mouth. Daniel's eyes shone wide and terrified above it.

There was no sign of Lewis.

'That's Simpson,' Rachel breathed. 'The man from RAGE.'

He beckoned us towards him.

Rachel's hand slid off my arm and I took it in my hand. I could feel her shaking as we walked over and stood in front of Simpson and Daniel.

'Where's Lewis?' Rachel said.

'In the car.' Simpson pointed beyond the memorial grounds to the street. Several cars were parked in a row. It was impossible to see if anyone was really inside them. 'If you don't walk down there quietly with me now, my men have orders to shoot him. There are also people positioned all around the memorial who will catch you if you try to escape.'

'Is Lewis really okay?' Rachel let go of my hand. 'What about Mel?'

Simpson stared at her. 'Both fine,' he said shortly. 'We found them half conscious as we were leaving the building. They've told us a lot.' He looked meaningfully down at Daniel, whose face was creased with terror. 'An awful lot.'

I froze. 'Lewis and Mel wouldn't tell you anything.'

'To stop us hurting the other, they would tell us everything,' Simpson sneered. 'Come on.' He gave Daniel a little shake. 'I told you, I'm going to take you home.'

He turned and trotted down the memorial steps, still clutching Daniel by the arm.

Rachel and I stared after him.

'If we get in that car we're dead,' I said.

She nodded. 'I know, but what about Lewis and Mel? What about Daniel?' She started walking down the steps after Simpson.

I raced after her and grabbed her arm.

'We don't even know if Mel and Lewis are really alive.'

Rachel shook me off.

'I'm not giving up on them now. And anyway, we can't leave Daniel. It's obvious RAGE knows who he is – he's in as much danger as we are.'

She walked on, down the steps.

The memorial was busier now. A coachload of tourists was spilling out in front of the cars. Several elderly couples were puffing their way past us up the steps.

The sun shone harsh on my face. My cut arm felt hot and heavy and sore. I looked at Rachel. She had reached

Simpson, who was halfway down the steps. He stopped and stared back at me, impatiently.

I looked beyond him towards the water in the distance. Something glinted behind one of the trees. I couldn't work out what it was. It moved. The sun flashed off it again. It was long and narrow and . . . *Jesus*, it was a gun, the barrel clearly pointing towards Simpson, Daniel and Rachel.

My heart leaped into my throat. *Not Rachel. Not her.* I swerved my gaze back to them. Lewis's hand sign flashed into my head. I caught Rachel's eye and held my hand out flat. I dipped my straightened fingers.

Dive.

For a second her eyes widened. Then she got it. Just as Simpson turned, she grabbed Daniel and threw herself at the ground.

BANG. The shot was like a bomb going off. Simpson crumpled to the ground. Daniel started kicking and screaming. People were rushing over. A big man in outsize jeans rolled Simpson over. He jumped back. 'OH MY GOD!' he yelled. 'HE'S BEEN SHOT!'

Rachel was still on the ground, holding Daniel down. I raced down the ten or so steps that separated us and yanked her up by the wrist. More people were surging round now.

'What?' A male voice.

'Oh my Lord!' A woman.

A pool of blood was seeping out from under Simpson's head, surreal against the stone steps. Daniel's screams pierced through everything. I let go of Rachel and grabbed his arm. Hauling him up, I ran down the steps, looking round for Simpson's men.

Rachel was beside me. She stumbled on the bottom step. I reached out for her with my cut arm. As I flexed the muscles to hold her up, the pain that shot through my arm was indescribable.

'RUN!' I yelled, fighting the nausea that swelled in my stomach. I turned right onto the pavement.

Rachel was pulling against me. 'No,' she said. 'RAGE.'

I looked up the road. Men on either side of the street were running towards us. Only metres away. I turned, tugging sharply on Daniel's arm, and pelted in the opposite direction, towards the water, towards the trees.

I was half carrying, half dragging Daniel, who was still screaming hysterically. Rachel pounded along beside me. Ignoring the throbbing agony of my arm, I gripped her wrist tighter and pulled them both forwards.

'This is where the shot came from,' I said.

'Doesn't matter,' Rachel panted. 'No choice.'

We dived into the trees, weaving in and out of the bare trunks. Across a bridge. At least two men were still following us. More trees. A bigger space.

I ran on and on. More shots rang out in the distance. Rachel tripped and stopped running for a second. I hauled her forwards again. I could hear Daniel gasping for breath. At least he'd stopped screaming.

Pain drove through me. I ran on and on, focused only on

the uneven ground beneath my feet and the pulsing agony in my arm.

I looked over my shoulder.

Sirens were screaming in the distance. I could hear raised voices from the direction of the memorial. But no one was here. No one was following us.

I dived down behind the biggest tree I could find and sank to the ground, breathing heavily, finally letting the pain take me over.

Daniel's screams started up again, louder than before.

'Be quiet.' I grabbed his shoulders. 'Stop it.'

Daniel looked up at me with terrified, tearful eyes. 'I want . . .'

I slapped the hand of my good arm over his mouth. He struggled furiously.

'Theo, stop.' Rachel wrenched Daniel away from me and hugged him, stroking his hair like she had in the car. He was still bawling, but the noise was muffled against her top. She was whispering in his ear. '*Sssh.* It's all right.'

I sat back against the tree trunk, watching them.

Watching her.

Gradually Daniel's sobs subsided.

Then there was silence.

'Did you see where any of the shots came from?' Rachel whispered over Daniel's head.

'Further back, I think. It's hard to say from this angle.' I peered round the tree again. No sign of anyone. 'Why aren't

401

those men from RAGE following us? They must have seen us run over the bridge.'

Rachel frowned. 'And who did the shooting?' Her lips trembled. 'They killed Simpson. Back at the memorial, didn't they?'

I nodded, my mouth dry.

'Was it him they were aiming at?' she said, shakily.

'I think so,' I said. But the truth was I wasn't sure. I wasn't sure of anything any more.

'I wish I knew if Lewis was all right.' A tear trickled down Rachel's face. 'D'you think he and Mel managed to get away?'

'You like him, don't you?' The words were out of my mouth before I could stop them.

Rachel frowned. 'Of course I like him. He looked after me when . . .' Her eyes narrowed. 'You mean like as in "like"?' She stared at me incredulously. 'No. He's, like, *years* older than me.'

I shrugged. 'Whatever.'

Daniel disentangled himself from Rachel's arms. 'I want to go home,' he sobbed.

She patted his head. 'Soon,' she said. She glanced at me. 'What do we do now?'

I looked around. The park area around us was pretty empty. I could see a few people now in the distance, but no one nearby. A wave of uneasiness swept through me. What *had* happened to all those guys from RAGE? Where were Lewis and Mel and whoever had shot Simpson? And was Elijah still following us?

Without Lewis and Mel, I couldn't see how we could possibly deal with our relocation plans ourselves. All the work Rachel and Max had done would be for nothing without Lewis's expertise.

We were totally trapped. Even if we could somehow get out of this park without being spotted, both Elijah and RAGE would always be on our tail.

'We have to go to the police,' Rachel said. 'That's what Lewis would want me to do if he didn't show up at the memorial.'

I stared at her. Had Lewis not explained to her where Elijah got his money from? If we went to the police, the government would find out. And the government were on Elijah's side.

I started to speak. 'Rachel—'

'Rachel.' The other voice was like an echo. Deeper. More urgent. 'Rachel.'

78

Rachel

'It's him.' I jumped to my feet. 'It's Lewis.'

I looked around.

There, emerging from one of the tall bushes nearby, were Lewis and Mel. Lewis looked strained and anxious, but his blue eyes twinkled as I flew into his arms.

'You okay, Rachel?'

'Fine.' I hugged him tightly. 'How did you get away?'

'Once Simpson was shot, RAGE panicked. Mel and I got the guys who had us, then the ones following you.'

'I thought you were dead.' I gave him another squeeze, then turned to Mel and hugged her too. Over her shoulder I could see Theo explaining who Daniel was to Lewis. There was a weird – slightly resentful – look on Theo's face. I flashed back to that question he'd asked me earlier.

Do you like him?

It suddenly struck me. Theo was jealous. *No*. I must be wrong.

'We have to get out of here,' Lewis said.

Daniel shuffled up beside me, his little hand creeping into mine.

'Oh, Theo, what happened to your arm?' That was Mel.

I followed her gaze to Theo's arm. The pillowcase was drenched with fresh blood. Theo shrugged, looking embarrassed.

'He did it so we could escape from Elijah,' I said.

'Where are RAGE now?' Theo asked. 'What's left of them, that is.'

'I think we lost them.' Lewis's face coloured. 'But beforehand, last night, they got all the relocation information out of us. I'm sorry.'

My heart sank. The relocation plan was our only way out.

'We'll just have to start again with it,' Lewis said. 'It'll take a few days but RAGE'll be—'

'Actually, I've got a better idea,' I said.

'Listen, Rachel.' Theo's voice was urgent. 'There're things you don't understand.'

'Not now, six-pack,' Mel grinned at him. 'Whoever shot Simpson is still out here somewhere.'

Six-pack?

I met Lewis's eye. 'D'you think it was Elijah?'

'Has to be,' Lewis said. 'He must have picked up your trail this morning.'

I shivered, thinking of all the people I'd stopped and asked for directions to the Jefferson Memorial.

'Let's go,' Mel said.

405

We set off across the park, away from the memorial. Lewis carried Daniel in his arms.

As we got closer to the highway up ahead, we could see a police roadblock in the far distance. The police officers stationed there appeared to be stopping all the cars passing through. Other officers were swarming into the park. None were coming in our direction.

'We have to get to the police,' I insisted. 'That's what I was trying to say earlier. We get them to protect us. Get the government to relocate us. It's the only—'

'Won't work,' Theo said.

I looked at Lewis. He was scanning the rest of the park.

'Why?' I frowned. 'I—'

'Elijah works for the government,' Theo said.

'So?' I raised my eyes. 'I bet they don't know half of what he gets up to. I bet they'll do anything for us if we tell them everything we know about what he does.'

Lewis turned round. He and Mel exchanged looks.

A twig snapped behind me. I spun round.

'A good idea. Except none of you understand anything about what I do.'

I froze, as Elijah stepped out from behind a tree.

79

Theo

Elijah had a rifle in his hands. 'I know none of you are armed. So no stupid sudden movements, okay? You saw Simpson. You all know how well I shoot with this.'

Lewis set Daniel onto the ground. He moved closer to Rachel, pushing Daniel behind him.

Elijah walked towards us, his eyes flickering along the line of us, from Mel to me to Rachel to Daniel. His eyes rested on Lewis.

'Ah,' he said softly.

I heard Rachel suck in her breath, but before any of us could move, Elijah whipped a smaller gun with a silencer attached out from behind his back. It was almost a careless movement. A swift glide upwards. A second to position. Then he fired.

Straight into Mel.

She was standing the closest to him. The bullet ripped through her throat. Even with the silencer it was an explosion. Then Mel seemed to fly backwards in slow motion, like it wasn't real. Then *thud*, onto the ground.

My brain shut down, like it couldn't make sense of what it was seeing. For a few seconds all I was aware of was my arm hurting and the air, cold against my face.

And Rachel standing beside me.

Lewis rushed forwards. '*NO!*'

'No.' Elijah pointed the gun at him. 'No more noise.'

Lewis stopped, his breathing ragged and hoarse, his eyes on Mel. Elijah indicated the road and the police block in the distance. 'No noise, or you'll all be dead before they get here.' He held out his hand. 'Daniel, come here.'

Daniel stared up at him, his brown eyes wide with shock.

'Now!' Elijah barked.

Daniel scurried across the grass. Elijah reached out and pulled him close. Daniel huddled behind his legs.

'Now,' Elijah said. 'Who's death will hurt you most next, Lewis?' He smiled at me, then shifted the gun to focus on Rachel.

I held my breath.

'Yes,' Elijah said. 'You seem to have become attached to her, Lewis.'

'But you created her.' It was my voice. I hardly recognised it. 'You don't want her dead. You've tried to keep her alive.'

Elijah snorted. 'That was before she decided to thank me by helping RAGE hunt me down and destroy everything I've worked for for the past ten years. To destroy me.' He looked at Rachel. 'Not a wise move, Artemis.'

Rachel was shaking, her whole body trembling.

408

'Everybody deserves life,' I said. 'You don't have the right to take—'

Lewis leaped forwards. Elijah spun round and fired. The shot pierced Lewis's jacket. He fell backwards, banging his head against the tree behind. He slumped to the ground.

'No,' Rachel sobbed. '*No.*'

I stood there, numb.

It wasn't real. They weren't dead. Not Mel. Not Lewis. It wasn't real.

Elijah was breathing heavily. I fixed my eyes on him. My senses seemed hyper-alert. I was aware of the ground under my feet, the whisper of wind in the trees. 'You can't kill us,' I said.

'I've got no intention of killing *you*, Theo,' he said smoothly. 'But you must see that Rachel has betrayed us.'

'Us?' I frowned. 'There is no "us". And don't go kidding me about not killing me. I know what you're planning. You're going to take my heart out of me and put it in you. And then you'll move on to Daniel.'

Elijah's eyes were fixed on mine. If I could just keep him talking maybe he wouldn't shoot. Maybe the police would find us.

'What happened to you wanting me to take over from you? What happened to that . . . *Dad*?' In spite of myself, my voice shook.

'Oh, Theodore. Do you still understand so little?' Elijah ran his hand through his hair. 'That was my plan. And if RAGE had not destroyed my laboratories, that would *still* be

409

my plan. But everything I needed to live was in them. My life was literally in those labs . . .'

'What life? What d'you mean?'

'My heart. Clones of my heart. And other organs. All developed over years in my laboratories. All destroyed in minutes by the monsters that she –' he pointed at Rachel '– that she brought here.'

Rachel gasped.

'Yes.' Elijah laughed, his eyes dark and furious. 'Do you see what you've done, Rachel? In coming to deliver Theo from the terrible fate you imagined, you have only succeeded in sentencing him to death.'

'It's not Rachel's fault they destroyed your . . . your bloody body parts,' I yelled. 'And it certainly doesn't justify you taking *mine*.'

Elijah shifted impatiently. 'My heart is too weak to wait. I could be dead in weeks. I didn't mean this to happen, I swear, but your heart is a perfect genetic match, no risk of my body rejecting it and—'

'So what?' I said. 'You've got no right to take my life, just because yours is ending.'

Elijah's eyes burned into me – sad and fierce and deeply troubled.

'I am not doing this for myself, Theodore. In ten years' time, believe me, with you trained and my powers fading I would make a very different decision. But, right now, I am at the forefront of scientific endeavour. My work on PGDT techniques alone . . . there's no one in the world to touch me.

410

I cannot put my personal feelings before scientific progress. I must be able to continue with my work, with my experiments . . .'

I shuddered. He really believed what he was saying. He thought he was in the right over killing me. A cold, hard weight settled miserably in my stomach. I was alone. I was completely alone.

'That's bullshit,' Rachel shouted. 'We're not experiments. We're people. *You* told me that.'

Elijah's face clenched. 'You're missing the point.' He raised his gun and steadied his gaze. His eyes grew hard, like dark stones. 'If you think about it, Rachel, it's only fair,' he said. 'I gave you life. Now it's your turn to give it back to me.' He straightened his arm and levelled the gun at her heart.

Rachel gasped, her eyes round with shock.

It was going to happen. He was going to shoot her.

In that moment every terrible emotion I'd ever felt swept through me. A tornado of feeling.

Hate. Anger. Betrayal. Pain. Shame. Fear.

Especially fear.

They whirled through me as I stared at the gun. And then they whipped away and I was left with one thought.

One feeling.

I would rather be dead, than watch her die.

I stepped in front of Rachel.

'Go ahead,' I said. 'Shoot.'

80

Rachel

'Get out of the way, Theodore,' Elijah growled.

'No.' Theo's voice was calm and steady.

I peered round him. Elijah's face screwed up with anger. He had his gun in one hand, a shaking Daniel in the other.

'I want to go home,' Daniel whimpered.

I put my hand on Theo's back. It was the only way I had of letting him know how I felt. How much I felt.

Shouts nearby. My heart leaped. The police. Getting closer. I could feel Theo's back stiffening under my hand. He'd heard them too.

'Theo.' A note of panic had crept into Elijah's voice.

I couldn't see Theo's face.

'Okay. We'll leave Rachel,' Elijah said. 'But you must come with me.'

'No.'

'Then I'll kill Daniel.'

My heart thudded.

Theo answered straight back.

'No you won't. You need him. He's as valuable to you as I am.'

'No he's not,' Elijah insisted. 'His heart is not mature enough.'

'Exactly.' Theo sounded triumphant. 'You need to keep him alive until he's useful.'

More shouting in the distance. I could see Elijah's eyes darting everywhere.

Please let the police be coming. Please.

Suddenly he turned and ran, dragging Daniel after him.

Behind us, dogs barked. People yelled.

Elijah – hauling Daniel – weaved in and out of the trees.

Shouts. More dogs barking. People thundering past.

And Theo. He turned round and stared down at me. There was so much feeling in his eyes that I couldn't breathe.

Of course it didn't shut me up.

'I thought you didn't care about anybody?' I whispered.

He put his arms on my shoulders and leaned his forehead down onto mine.

'I care about—'

'BACK AWAY FROM HER WITH YOUR HANDS IN THE AIR!'

I jumped. Theo sprang away from me, his hands raised.

I looked around. We were surrounded by police officers in flak jackets and helmets. Five or six were in a semi-circle on the ground in front of us.

Someone laid a hand on my shoulder. 'Please spread your arms and legs so I can search you.' It was a female voice.

413

Polite. It reminded me of Mel's. I stared at her lifeless body on the ground and all the energy drained out of me. My whole body shook as I stood with my legs apart and my arms raised.

The woman who had spoken patted up and down my arms and legs, then walked round in front of me. She was young, not much older than Mel had been.

'Hey,' she said. 'It's over now. Nothing to be scared of any more.'

But I couldn't stop shaking. I lowered my arms as the tears started flowing. Then the woman drew me into a hug and I wept and wept on her shoulder.

I must've wailed, full on, for about a minute. It was a relief to get it all out. When I looked up, the scene around me had changed dramatically. Someone had set up a cordon several metres away. People were crowding against it, more flooding towards us all the time. Two ambulances were parked nearby. The whole area was crowded with police officers. Someone had lain a sheet over Mel's body. I glanced over at Lewis. He was being carried onto a stretcher. His eyes were open.

I sat up. 'Lewis?' It came out all croaky.

He tried to look round at me, but his head was in some kind of neck brace. The paramedic bending over him looked up at me. 'He's alive. The bullet lodged in his flak jacket. He was knocked out by the fall against the tree. We'll run some tests at the hospital.'

I stared, my heart pounding as the paramedics loaded

Lewis into the nearest ambulance. He was alive. A huge grin spread across my face. Where the hell had Lewis got a flak jacket?

Of course. From the RAGE guys he and Mel had brought down. But then why hadn't Mel . . .? My mind flashed back to how Elijah had shot her – in the throat.

She'd had no chance.

The grin fell from my face. I suddenly, desperately, wanted to be with Theo.

'Where's Theo?' I grabbed the woman police officer's rough jacket. My eyes darted round the clearing. There was no sign of him.

'The boy?' she said. 'Already gone in the first ambulance.' She put her arm round my shoulders and guided me to the remaining vehicle. 'We'll get you checked over too, then after your interview I expect you'll be able to see him.'

I stumbled into the back of the ambulance. As I sat down on the narrow bed, tiredness consumed me. I laid my head on the pillow and slid my legs along the mattress. I wanted to ask how long the interview would take, but before I could even open my mouth, I was asleep.

81

Theo

I told them everything.

The nurse cleaned up my arm and the doctor sutured it.

Then the police came in and I told them everything. At first I could see they didn't believe me. I don't know what they thought. Maybe that I was some weirded-out kid into cutting himself with bits of blunt wood for kicks.

Then the results of my DNA test came back, and they went to their records and realised Elijah and I were this perfect match.

After that they talked to me again – this time with open mouths and wide eyes. Then the FBI turned up and I had to go over it all again.

It was dark before they left me in peace. I was tired but, even though my arm didn't hurt any more, I couldn't sleep. Elijah was still out there somewhere with Daniel. The doctors confirmed that Daniel was too small for Elijah to be able to use his heart, so at least he was safe for the time being. But then there was RAGE. It was a big organisation. Simpson and his outfit might be gone, but there would still be people who would make it their life's work to hunt me down. Me and Daniel and Rachel.

I had no idea how much of what I'd said the FBI believed.

Despite what Elijah had told me about the government paying for the compound, no one was prepared to come right out and admit it existed.

Elijah *had* told the truth about that. The government didn't know about his cloning work. Or at least that was what the FBI said to me. I explained what little I knew about the Hermes Project – the comparisons between Daniel and the other kids. The men I was speaking to looked as if they didn't believe a word I was saying. I couldn't blame them. I could barely believe it myself. And so the questions went on and on. Who I'd seen. What I'd done. Anything and everything Elijah had ever said to me.

I noticed nobody asked me what I wanted. I mean, they kept saying stuff like: *Rest. Tomorrow we'll have you speak to our psychiatrist. Tomorrow we'll start planning what happens next.*

But no one said, 'Hey, Theo. Ready to go home?'

The truth was, of course, that I wasn't ready to go home, even if it had been an option. I was pretty sure the FBI was going to relocate me. That meant a new home, a new name. A whole new life with Mum.

I still wasn't sure I ever wanted to see her again. They told me she was on her way – that I could speak to her if I liked. But I said no. Not now. Not yet.

417

They told me Lewis was okay, but I kept seeing Simpson falling to the ground. And Mel, bleeding from her throat.

Nightmares when I closed my eyes.

It hurt me more than I would have believed possible that she was dead.

I wondered how Rachel was coping with it all. I'd asked to see her but they said she was sleeping.

It was now ten o'clock. The city lights outside my tenth-floor hospital room window shone like tiny candles. I wanted to be out there, lost in the sprawl of the city, somewhere where no one knew who I was, where no one cared about me and I cared about no one.

Except that I wanted to see Rachel more. I couldn't stop thinking about her. How she looked. How she'd felt when I held her. How much I wanted to be with her. Talk to her. How much I wanted to do all sorts of stuff.

I don't let people in.

That was a lie. *Face it.* I had let Rachel in. She was under my skin and inside my head. Not like other girls who were just smiles and bodies. Not like girls in magazines or on the internet. Not like Jake's girls – the friends of the ones he was constantly chatting up, who'd look at me shyly but who never seemed real.

You can snog girls like that, then walk away from them, no problem. But with Rachel it was different.

I hoped she'd wake up soon.

Morning. So early it was still dark outside.

A soft rap on the door, then a nurse ushered Mum into my

room. I was standing by the window, staring out. I could see her reflection in the glass – her long hair and her dangly earrings.

'Theodore?' Her voice was fearful and hesitant.

I didn't turn round.

She took a step closer. Her face was a pink smudge in the glass. I couldn't make out her expression. 'They said . . . they said you didn't want to see me, but . . .' I could hear the tears bubbling up in her voice. 'I came as soon as they called, sweetheart. I've been so worried about you. Since Elijah rang and told me about RAGE coming after you and that I had to get out of the house straight away. I mean, I thought . . . I hoped he'd keep you safe, but . . .'

Her voice tailed off.

I said nothing.

'You're angry with me,' she said.

No shit, Mum.

'I didn't know Elijah had got like he is. I never dreamed he would hurt you. He wasn't like that when I met him. He was young. Idealistic. He wanted to help people. He—'

'It's not that,' I said.

Mum moved closer. In the window's reflection I could see her hand reaching out to my shoulder, then dropping away.

'Oh, Theodore,' she whispered. 'Is it because I didn't tell you the truth about . . . about your father?'

'Theo,' I snapped. 'And yes.'

There was a long pause. 'I only made up things because I was trying to protect you, Theo.' She sighed.

419

I remembered the photograph of the man I'd thought for years was my dad. Nothing would ever stop that lie hurting.

Nothing. Ever.

'If you'd told me more of the truth from the beginning then none of this would have happened.' My voice shook with anger. 'I wouldn't have tried to find out about Elijah. I wouldn't have gone blundering into RAGE . . .'

I wouldn't have met Rachel.

'I know it seems hard now,' Mum sniffed, 'but when we're settled and all this is behind us maybe you'll be able to see how I was only trying to protect you. They're going to give us new identities, Theo. The Foreign Office at home and the people here, I've been talking with them. They want to monitor you, but also to keep you secret. We'll be able to leave all this behind, make a fresh start, just you and me.'

I nodded. I knew this was good news. It meant I would be as safe as I could from RAGE and Elijah. Still . . .

I turned round at last. Mum tried to smile at me, but her lips were trembling. I felt a pang of guilt at the look of utter misery on her face. I looked away.

'What about my friends?' I said. 'What about Jake? And Max?'

What about Rachel?

Mum shook her head. 'Maybe you could talk to them on the phone. I think there's a safe line.'

We talked for a little longer. Mum told me how Roy had been discovered bound and gagged but unhurt in the toilets at Rachel's school disco. Unsurprisingly, he'd resigned on the spot. Then she told me things she'd never told me before. How in love she'd been with Elijah when she'd agreed to carry me. How young she was then. How she'd have done anything for him.

After a bit, we were okay with each other. Sort of.

She was still my mum. And I knew I'd been selfish, the way I'd behaved, running off before. And she'd always done what she thought was best for me.

Anyway, pretty soon she'd be all I had.

She started asking questions about Rachel. How I felt. Stupid stuff like that. She told me she had no idea there was another clone. That Elijah had kept Rachel a total secret. I guess I believed her. To be honest I didn't really care any more.

I pretended I was tired after about half an hour. So she left. Then I just lay there, thinking about Rachel again. The next time the nurse came in I asked her if Rachel was awake.

'I'll find out,' she smiled. 'Is there a message?'

I shook my head. 'Just . . . just if it's okay for me to visit her.'

82

Rachel

I swam up from a deep, deep sleep.

I was so warm and comfortable I couldn't tell where I ended and the bed began. I lay there listening to the low murmur of voices around me.

Mum? Dad?

I forced my eyes open. They were standing beside the bed, talking to a guy in a suit. I tried to hear what they were saying, but the whispers were too hissy and soft.

Then Mum glanced across and saw I was awake.

'Oh sweetie.' She bent down and clawed at my hand. 'You've been asleep for *hours*.'

Dad leaned over me. His eyes were full of tears. 'Hey, Ro,' he said. 'We were starting to think you had some kind of sleeping sickness.'

I blinked blearily at him. 'What time is it?'

'Ten o'clock,' Mum said briskly. 'Tuesday morning.'

I frowned. Everything that had happened at the memorial and in the park had been in the morning too. Had I lost a whole day?

I struggled onto my elbows. 'Is Lewis all right? Where's Theo? Have they found Daniel?'

Mum and Dad exchanged glances. The man in the suit cleared his throat.

'Lewis and Theo are both fine,' he said. 'We have an APB out on Elijah Lazio and the little boy. They won't get far.'

He turned to Mum. 'We can continue with this later.'

She nodded. The man left the room.

'Continue with what?' I said. My heart thudded.

'The relocation plans, sweetie,' Mum said. 'But we can go over it later. Right now I think—'

'I want to know now.' My voice rose angrily.

Mum's eyes widened.

Dad patted my arm. 'There's nothing definite to know yet,' he said. 'Just that the US and UK governments are going to resettle us. They'll want to keep an eye on you and you'll have to go in for tests and research every few months, but they'll help set us up in a new life where you'll be safe.'

'Where?'

Will Theo be there?

Dad shrugged. 'Somewhere far away, where no one knows us. Where there'll be no connection with Elijah or anyone from the past. They'll move us to a safe house tomorrow.'

I stared at him.

No Theo. No Theo. Forever.

'Oh, Ro, what possessed you to go to Elijah's compound? We've talked to Lewis. He should never have—'

'It wasn't Lewis's fault.' I sat back. 'It was *my* idea.'

'We know.' Mum shook her head. 'How could you, Rachel? Going behind our backs like that? Provoking Elijah. Don't you realise how powerful he—'

'How *could* I know about him, Mum?' My heart pounded. 'You never told me anything about him. Remember?'

Stony silence.

Dad cleared his throat. 'I know it'll be hard to leave school and all your friends, but we don't have a choice, Ro.'

'I don't want you to call me that.' I glared at him. 'I'm not her. I'm not Rebecca.'

Dad looked startled. 'What d'you mean?'

'Well that's why you call me "Ro", isn't it?' I snapped. 'It's what you called Rebecca.'

'No.' Dad frowned. 'It's because you were such a fat, roly-poly little baby.' He glanced at Mum, then back at me.

I stared at them.

'Not that you're fat *now*, Rachel,' Mum said smoothly. 'Not if you go easy on the ice cream and biscuits, anyway.'

A nurse poked her head round the door. 'Theo was wondering if he could visit,' she said.

Dad shook his head. 'I don't think . . .'

I sat upright, my heart beating fast. 'Tell him ten minutes. Mum, where are my clothes?'

83

Theo

She was sitting at the end of her hospital bed. Alone, thankfully.

My heart pounded.

Oh, man.

Now I was here I didn't know what to say. At least, I knew there was a word for how I was feeling – a short word beginning with L. But I had no idea how to say it.

I shut the door and leaned against it.

'Hi.'

'Hi.' Her eyes shone as she smiled at me.

I smiled back. 'You okay?'

She nodded. 'You?'

'Yeah.' I ran my hand through my hair. 'I'm just a few doors down,' I said. 'There are security guards at the end of our corridor.'

'Oh?' Rachel said. 'Is your mum here?'

'Yep.'

'How's your arm?'

'Fine.' I showed her the bandage. 'I have to keep it dry for a few days.'

'A few days.' Rachel's voice shook slightly. 'I guess we'll both be gone by then.'

'I guess.'

There was a pause. Then Rachel looked down at her T-shirt.

'These are gross clothes,' she said. 'Mum brought all the wrong things with her.'

I nodded, not really paying attention. The clothes looked okay to me – a pair of jeans and a blue T-shirt.

I didn't want to talk about clothes.

I took a deep breath. 'Rachel?'

A knock on the door. Lewis poked his head round.

Rachel squealed and ran over to him.

He hugged her and waved at me across the room.

'You guys hungry?' he grinned.

We ate lunch with Lewis. Which was fine, except when Rachel said she was really sorry about Mel, and Lewis looked as if he was about to cry.

Then all the parents turned up and wanted to see us. It was weird meeting Rachel's dad again. He told me he'd known I existed and about my code name, Apollo, but no details about my life. He said how scared he'd been when I'd turned up at his house with Rachel. How I'd seemed weirdly familiar. How he'd realised who I must be when I ran my hand through my hair – just like Elijah does, apparently.

After a few hours I was interviewed again – this time by the FBI in a little room at the end of the corridor. I asked them about Daniel and Elijah, who still hadn't been found. I hoped Daniel was all right. It was weird – I hardly knew him, yet he was my younger brother. Sort of.

Mum and I talked for a bit about what was going to happen next. She'd got permission for me to call Jake and Max on some safe line. So I did, even though it was really late at home.

Jake was all overexcited about everything that had happened.

'So there were guns and a shoot-out, dude?' he said breathlessly. 'That is way cool.'

It was impossible to explain to him how totally not cool everything that had happened yesterday had been. So I changed the subject.

'Seen anything of Max?' I asked innocently.

Jake snorted. 'Some. Between you and me I don't think she's into boys.'

I laughed. 'You mean she's not into you.'

Jake sighed. 'Maybe I should try Rachel again.'

'She's not coming back,' I said quickly.

I explained about the relocation stuff. That I didn't know yet where I was going, but it wouldn't be back to London. Jake fell silent. Then we talked a bit more about school and football and stuff. Then we said goodbye.

It was weird thinking I might never see him again. Or at least, not for a long time.

I suddenly realised what it was going to be like, going to a new town and a new school. Starting all over again making friends. Never being able to really say who I was.

Never letting people in.

I called Max.

Perl and Java were barking in the background. She asked a few questions about what had happened, then launched into a long and complicated explanation of how she had hacked into some bunch of government records to create the new identities which Lewis and Mel had given up to RAGE.

'The police were here all yesterday afternoon. I was nearly arrested,' she said.

Yeah? I was nearly killed.

I thanked her for everything she'd tried to do.

'How's Rachel?' she said.

'Good,' I said.

I checked my watch. Nine-thirty p.m. At this rate Rachel would be asleep again before I could see her. I started trying to say goodbye, but for some reason Max didn't want to end the call.

'Jake keeps coming round,' she said eventually.

'And?' I said, checking my watch again. 9:38.

'He's a jerk,' she said flatly.

'Mmmn.'

'Still,' she said. 'I guess he's quite a cute jerk.'

I grinned. 'You should tell him,' I said.

'Mmmn,' she said.

We said goodbye.

I put down the phone and stood up.

No more delays. I was going to see Rachel. Now.

I cleaned my teeth and strode to the door.

As I reached for the handle, it opened.

She was there. In front of me.

With Lewis.

'I've come to say goodbye,' Lewis said.

'Right now?' I said. But one look at Rachel's face told me it was right now. She was miserable about Lewis going. My stomach twisted into a knot.

Lewis nodded. 'Tomorrow I have to talk to the FBI. Tell them about Elijah's work. What I know of it. And about RAGE. If I cooperate fully they're going to relocate me under their witness protection programme too.'

He shook my hand and kissed Rachel on the cheek. I couldn't bear watching how fiercely she hugged him.

I walked over to the window.

The door shut with a click.

'I have to go too,' Rachel said.

I turned round. Her eyes glistened with tears.

'Tonight?' My voice sounded hoarse, like there was no breath holding it up. Like all the life was being sucked out of my body.

She nodded.

We stared at each other. 'You saved my life yesterday,' she said softly.

'You saved mine by coming to the compound,' I said. 'You and Lewis.'

Rachel sighed. 'I'm going to miss him *so* much.' She walked towards me. She stood beside me at the window. Right beside me.

'I love how much he loved Mel. Did she ever mention him?'

'Er . . . no. Not that I remember.' My mind raced.

If she loves him loving someone else, then surely she can't . . .

Rachel looked up at me. 'I don't want to go tonight.'

My heart hammered. My mind was flailing around for something to say.

'I just spoke to Jake,' I said.

'Yeah?'

'He asked how you were,' I said. 'I think he and Max might hook up, actually.'

Why are you talking to her about Jake, you moron?

'Oh,' Rachel said.

She half turned and looked out of the window. She was standing so close to me now we were almost touching.

Say something. Say something.

And then she glanced sideways up at me. Gave me this totally beautiful, sexy look.

And I realised I didn't need to say anything at all.

84

Rachel

The door shut behind Lewis. I took a deep breath.

'I have to go too,' I said.

Theo turned round from where he was standing at the window. His eyes were so sad and serious. 'Tonight?'

'You saved my life yesterday.' I could feel my cheeks reddening. What was I trying to say: *thank you*?

'You saved mine by coming to the compound.' He made this little face. 'You and Lewis.'

I didn't want to think about Lewis going away. It just reminded me that in a minute I would have to say goodbye to Theo. My insides crumpled up.

'I'm going to miss him *so* much.'

Theo looked at the floor.

I stared at him, wondering what he was thinking.

I walked over to stand beside him at the window.

'I love how much he loved Mel. Did she ever mention him?'

'Er . . . no. Not that I remember.' Theo was looking

awkward. I suddenly felt embarrassed, but I made myself look right up into his eyes.

'I don't want to go tonight,' I said.

I want to be here with you.

Now Theo looked panic-stricken. 'I just spoke to Jake,' he said quickly.

'Yeah?'

Why are you changing the subject?

'He asked how you were. I think he and Max might hook up, actually.'

Why are you talking to me about Jake?

'Oh,' I said. I turned away.

Maybe he isn't interested. Maybe I'm being too obvious.

I looked out of the window. The stars were out high in a clear sky and the city was a million lights. It was beautiful. And it suddenly struck me. Even if Theo didn't feel like I did, the important thing was that I loved him. And loving him was the most amazing feeling I'd ever had in my whole life.

We might never see each other again. But nobody could ever take that feeling away from me.

I glanced sideways up at him.

God, your face is beautiful.

He stared at me for a second. Then this slow grin spread across his face and he bent his head and kissed me.

85

Theo

It felt like we'd only been kissing for a few minutes. But it was almost midnight when Rachel's parents came looking for her.

Her dad gave me a massively dirty look. Like he knew exactly what we'd been doing. Rachel didn't help the situation by blushing the deepest shade of red I'd ever seen in my life.

She walked over to her mum and dad at the door.

This was it. I couldn't believe it. She was going away to a new life and I was never going to see her again.

She looked back at me. Then she turned away. She put her hand on the door handle.

I was never going to see her face again.

'Can't we even email each other?' I said.

Her dad folded his arms. 'It's not advisable,' he said. 'The less contact between you, the less opportunity for RAGE to track either of you down.'

He turned and put his hand over Rachel's, pressing down on the handle. The door opened.

'Just two more minutes,' I said. 'There's something I forgot to tell Rachel.'

She looked up at her dad. He glanced at her mum, who pursed her lips.

'Well,' she said. 'I guess two minutes won't make any difference.'

'Please, Dad?' Rachel pleaded.

Her dad sighed. 'All right, but the car's waiting.'

I waited until they'd shut the door behind them.

'Listen,' I said. Then I put my arms around her and I told her.

86

Rachel

It was the end of my first day at my new school. A week since I'd seen Theo.

I went everywhere in a daze. I had barely registered our new town, our new house, our new car. I lived in my memories, dreaming of seeing him again. Going over what he'd told me.

Today was when he'd said I should do it.

Five p.m. GMT. That's when he'd said.

I walked down the corridor to the main school exit. It was a more modern school than my old one. Smaller but less crowded and cramped. The teachers seemed nice and some of the other kids had been friendly. At least there were boys here. Not that I was interested in any of them.

Out onto the tarmac. A light drizzle had just started falling. It was the very last week of term. I was only in for an orientation day. I'd start properly in January.

I lifted my face to the rain. It was getting stronger, the raindrops like tiny needles in my face.

'Hey, rain-girl.' The sneering voice stopped me in my tracks. I looked round. A girl – bigger than me – was standing right next to me with her hands on her hips. She had long, dark hair and a hard, thin face. Two mousier-looking girls stood on either side of her.

I stared at her face. She didn't look much like Jemima from my old school. But she had the same sneering, triumphant look in her eye.

'Where are you from, then?' she said.

'Out of town,' I said. I'd been primed with various ways of heading off intrusive questions about my past. My heart thumped. This girl didn't look like she was going to let me head her off all that easily.

'Oh yeah?' The girl glanced at her friends. 'That a nice place, Outuvtahn?'

She was taking the piss out of my accent. My face burned.

'It was okay,' I said levelly. 'Maybe not quite so rainy.'

'Oo-ooh,' the girl said sarcastically. 'So you're too good for round here then?'

My mind raced. What was the right reply? And then I realised. There wasn't one. I didn't even have to be having this conversation.

'I didn't say that,' I said sharply. I stared at the girl. On the surface she was all bluster and threat. But underneath, behind her eyes, I could see she wasn't as sure of herself as she was making out.

I kept my gaze rock-steady on her eyes. 'Actually I like it here.' I smiled. A quick, easy smile. 'See you later.'

I walked away.

Nothing followed me. No objects. No people. No swear-words.

Nothing.

The new house was only a few minutes away. Dad was still at work – he'd got a new job at some film processing shop. Mum was unloading her latest shopping – a new tennis outfit. She wanted to buy one for me, get me started at the local club, but I told her I wanted to learn karate instead. They teach it at the new school.

I pretended to be interested in Mum's new clothes, then I rushed out, saying I had to get something from the high street. The rain had stopped and the sun had come out. Everywhere smelled fresh. I went straight to the internet café I'd spotted earlier in the week and went online. I found the chat room easily enough. Theo had been very clear about the address.

I registered and logged on. My mouth was dry. Was he going to be here? Would he have remembered?

I scanned the screen for Theo's username.

There.

Message posted by ItsObvious at 5:01:

Funny what u miss when u move. Sights, sounds. People.

I smiled. Then put my hands over the keyboard. I'd picked my own username earlier in the week. Theo had told me to make it something he would be sure to identify as me.

I typed quickly.

Message posted by ClØn* H*@rt at 5:03:

Yeah, missing people is definitely the worst. Still. So long as u have a way of keeping in touch, I guess u can survive.

Message posted by ItsObvious at 5:04:

Survive. As in better than nothing. Just. Anyway, it's been raining for days here. Is it raining where u r?

Message posted by ClØn* H*@rt at 5:05:

No. Was b4 but sun shining now. It sucks not knowing anyone.

– I know. My school's rubbish

– Mine's okay, I think. At least this one has boys.

– Boys?

– You know. Boys. Not fit ones though.

– Good. Because I don't suppose ur boyfriend would want u hanging out with fit boys.

– I guess not. I hope I c him again soon.

– Me 2. I hope that a whole lot.

– Yeah. Soon. One day, soon.

Are you who you *think* you are?

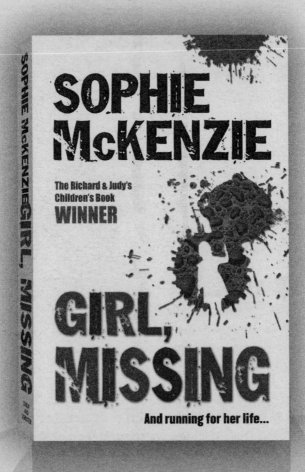

SOPHIE McKENZIE

The Richard & Judy's
Children's Book
WINNER

GIRL,
MISSING

And running for her life...

Lauren is adopted and eager to know about her
mysterious past. But when she discovers she may
have been snatched from another family as a baby,
her whole life is turned upside down...

"BRILLIANT ...YOU CAN'T STOP READING" – ROBERT MUCHAMORE

SOPHIE McKENZIE

THE MEDUSA PROJECT
THE SET UP

AUTHOR OF AWARD-WINNING BESTSELLER *GIRL, MISSING*

Fourteen years ago, scientist William Fox implanted
four babies with the Medusa gene – a gene for psychic
abilities. Now those babies are teenagers – and unaware
that their psychic powers are about to kick in ...

READ THE FIRST EXCITING BOOK
IN THIS BRAND NEW
SOPHIE MCKENZIE SERIES!

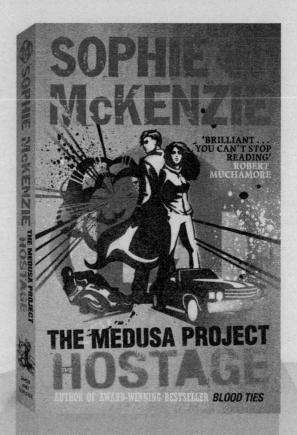

Teenagers Nico, Ketty, Ed and Dylan have been brought together by government agents to create a secret crime-fighting force - The Medusa Project. But can they save Ketty's brother and prevent their cover – and themselves – being blown sky high?

READ THE SECOND EXCITING BOOK IN THIS BRAND NEW SOPHIE MCKENZIE SERIES!